I0611139

The Life

—

Kimberly Morgan

Dedication

This book is dedicated to my mother, Marilyn, who always

encouraged me,

my children for believing in me, and my friends and family who stood

by me.

I thank the Lord for my talent. I love you all.

— Kimberly

PART 1

Chapter One

Saturday May 6, 1989 3:00 p.m.

It had to be at least one hundred degrees out here. It was the nasty, humid heat where you could see the steam vapors rising from the black asphalt of the streets. Combined with the heat of the grill, it was enough to kill somebody. Everybody was complaining, but nobody was leaving. Instead they endured just like I was.

My brother, Chiloe, stepped onto the wooden homemade deck and closed the sliding glass door behind him. In one hand he held a cigarette; in the

other was a Schlitz Malt Liquor Bull. He stood by the grill and took a long drag on the cigarette. He wore a not so white wife beater that showed off all six of his tattoos. At least the ones that were located on his arms. Four on one arm, two on the other.

"Dade is bringing his daughter," he announced to no one in particular.

My twin sister, New-New, lay across the wooden bench with her head in my lap. Her knees were propped up and she held her well-jeweled left hand over her eyes to shield out the sun. She didn't make a sound and I figured she was asleep. So I nudged her in the side of her head.

"What girl?"

"Chiloe's talking to you," I said.

"No he ain't, neither," she said and turned over to face the back of the bench.

We weren't too thrilled about meeting this new girl. She wasn't even really our cousin. Her father dated our mother off and on, so we called him Uncle. Uncle Dade. Since this was my sister Rosie's seventeenth birthday party, I guess he figured this was a good time for us to meet his daughter. We didn't want to meet her. From the bits and pieces we gathered from our mother, she was some stuck up little brat from a well to do neighborhood in a part of the city that we didn't know anything about. We didn't have a thing in common except for the fact that she, New-New, and I were all twelve years old. I mean, shit, I had four sisters and four brothers. What did I need with a play cousin?

Someone playing dominoes at a folding table down in the yard lost and the table and dominoes went flying over. Chiloe put his cigarette out on the banister and headed down the steps of the deck. I watched him walk over to chubby dude with the dirty black t-shirt and dirty hat to match, the culprit who turned over the table, and whisper something in his ear. Afterward the guy politely nodded and picked up the table. Then he picked up every single domino, apologizing all the while, and placed them back on the table. He left our back yard in a hurry after that. Chiloe sat down at the table in the chair of our departed visitor.

New-New sat up and looked around. "You smell that?" she asked.

Before I could answer she was yelling, "Rajul! The food is burning!"

My oldest sibling and largest brother came bellowing out of the sliding glass door. I don't even remember him opening it. It was like he just came through it. He opened the lid of the grill and waved the smoke away.

"Why ain't you tell me this shit was burning?" He asked.

"I just did, stupid."

"Now you walk your butt to the store and get some more hamburgers."

New-New lay back down on the bench and turned her back to him.

"I ain't walkin' nowhere. You walk, you need the exercise."

I saw his fist coming before he even balled it up. He planted it deep in the back of New-New's bare thigh. Even I flinched at that one.

"Owww!" New-New yelled and jumped up off the bench.

"Now since you up, take your ass to the store."

I could tell New-New wanted to cry, but she wasn't about to. She rubbed the back of her leg. "Where the money at, Nigga'?"

Rajul dug down in his pocket and pulled out a wad of bills. He counted out two twenty dollar bills and threw them at New-New. Then he went back to taking the burned food off of the grill.

"I'mma tell Momma," New-New said as she walked towards the sliding glass door.

Rajul turned around and gave her a smirk. That was the least of his worries.

"Come on Lonna."

I got up off the bench and followed my limping sister through the house.

"I hate him. I'll be glad when he moves."

We both knew she hardly meant that as she opened the big wooden front door to our dilapidated two floor house. At the same time Uncle Dade's car was pulling up in the front of our yard. He drove a red Camaro that enhanced his persona of being God's gift to women. One of them was my own mother.

New-New and I stood silently as he parked halfway on the yard and halfway in the street and got out of the car. The passenger side door opened. Our mouths fell to the floor as we watched this overly developed girl with long black hair pulled into a tight ponytail in the back of her head, come towards us. She wore a red jean skirt that stretched across her thick thighs and hips, a white and red t-shirt that fit snuggly on her surprisingly mature breast and some red Keds. I had to admit she was pretty. Damn pretty.

"Hey," New-New and I said in unison. We didn't realize that we were blocking the doorway.

"Hey," Uncle Dade replied looking down at us. He was at least six foot five. "Where your momma at?"

New-New walked over to the stairs and yelled, "Momma!" She was good at the yelling thing.

I moved out of the way also and Dade and his daughter walked into the house. I could see the resemblance. They both had very light complexions and puffy cheeks. Uncle Dade had wavy hair that I knew he wasn't born with. The girl and I were the same height and, upon closer inspection, we were probably the same size. Her body just seemed to have a lot more curves.

"Hey," I said not knowing whether to talk to her or not.

"Hi," she said and her face lit up. She had the funniest colored brown eyes I had ever seen. Tinged with a little gray and almost transparent looking.

"I'm Lonna," I continued mostly because I liked to see her face light up.

"I'm Karla."

"You wanna go to the store with me and New-New? It's right at the corner."

She looked up at her father who just shook his head and shrugged. He was more concerned with my mother at that moment than he was with Karla.

"Okay," she said pretty happy that he wasn't concerned with her.

I heard Momma plummeting down the stairs before I saw her. She had been dipping into the liquor a little bit much already. Her shorts were way to short and her shirt was too. We could see all kinds of stretch marks on her stomach from nine kids.

New-New, Karla, and I headed back towards the door, leaving the arguing that Dade and my mother were about to do behind us.

"This is New-New," I said as we walked closely together. She and I always traveled together in this neighborhood. Not that we really needed to. Everyone knew us and the rest of our family, so no one really messed with us. We just felt better being close together at all times.

"Are y'all twins?" Karla asked and I was surprised. Not just at her country accent, but that she had noticed. Usually nobody saw it because I was a lot heavier than New-New and her hair was bleached blond.

"Yeah, we're twins," I said.

"Why are you limping?" Karla looked very concerned about New-New's leg.

"My stupid brother hit me in it."

Karla shook her head and continued to look worried. She didn't know that we got beat up by our brothers on a regular. It was their way of showing love. It was nothing to us.

Instinct made us move to the sidewalk when we heard the loud engine. Uncle Dade was slowing down a few feet behind us. He roared up beside us and slowed down again. The driver's side window came down.

"Call me when you ready to go home."

Then he was gone before poor Karla could even get her mouth open, leaving a cloud of smoke behind. I couldn't believe that somebody would just drop their kid off in a place they had never been before.

"Come on," I said patting her on her back. I liked her and I didn't know why. There was something so innocent and sweet about her. I wanted to be her best friend.

I hated this store. There were always drunks trying to pick up women, drug dealers making deals and even some prostitutes hanging around. We passed four of them as we walked though the automatic doors.

"You know what?" New-New said, "We should take this money and go to the mall and not come back until later on tonight."

"Yeah right. Not for Rajul to do to me what he did to you."

We crossed the store to the frozen meat section. New-New handed Karla and I each a box of prepackaged frozen hamburgers. As we turned to leave I heard her gasp as she almost dropped the box she was holding. I followed her gaze to the end of the aisle, standing by the bakery counter. Andrew McCarthy, his brother Ray and their friend Jason were buying cookies.

New-New nudged me hard in my left side. "Go talk to him for me."

"And say what?"

"Tell him to come to the party."

"You go talk to him."

'Him' was Andrew. He was tall with light brown skin and wavy reddish hair cut into a box with a part shaved into it, and slightly slanted gray eyes. New-New had been in love with this boy every since he moved into the neighborhood five months ago. I couldn't deny the fact that he was cute, but he was nothing to be swooning over the way that she did.

"Come on, let's go this way. I don't want him to see me."

The three of us turned to walk in the opposite direction towards the dairy products. Until we heard, "Hey, New-New!"

I don't know where she thought she was sneaking off to anyway with that bright blond hair. Like she didn't stand out in a crowd.

"Yeah," she said turning around coolly.

"Y'all having a party?" Andrew asked walking towards us with his boys in tow.

"Yeah." She shrugged as if she didn't care at all that he was standing only inches away from her. Like she didn't have his name written in cursive on every daggon' notebook that she owned and had now moved on to our bedroom walls.

"Who's this?" He asked looking at Karla whose face turned the color of her shoes.

"This is our cousin Karla."

Andrew's eyes went back to New-New but Karla had undoubtedly caught Ray's full, undivided attention.

"What's up Karla?" he asked grinning from head to toe. Ray was the color of deep rich chocolate with big brown eyes. He and Andrew looked nothing alike. They had the same father but different mothers. They both lived with their father who was in the military. Andrew's mom lived in DC. Ray's mother died five years ago when he was eight.

"Hey."

"You so rude," Ray said talking to me but still ogling Karla. "You ain't gon' introduce us?"

I just shrugged and turned my head. She didn't need to know him. He wasn't anybody special.

"I'm Ray. This is my brother Andrew. And my boy Jason."

Karla said hi to all of them. Then I said, "We better get these hamburgers back to Rajul."

New-New turned to walk away and Karla and I followed.

"You comin' to the basketball court tonight, New-New?" Andrew yelled behind us.

"I don't know," New-New said without turning around and she kept on walking.

"Why don't you like them, Lonna?" Karla asked me on the way back to the house. I liked her and all, but she did ask a hell of a lot of questions.

"She only talk to older boys," New-New said. "She likes Kelly."

I stopped dead in my tracks. How did she know about that? And if she knew, who else knew? I'd never told anyone about Kelly and me.

"Who is Kelly?" Karla asked.

"Rosie's boyfriend's twin brother. He's seventeen years old."

Karla's eyes got bigger than they already were.

"Don't tell anybody, Karla."

She shook her head and said that she wouldn't. For some reason, I knew that she would not.

When we got back to the house, my mother had disappeared back into her room, and Rosie had already cut her birthday cake. She sat down in the yard on her boyfriend Kerry's lap. Kelly sat on the deck drinking a beer with Chiloe, Rajul and two of Chiloe's friends; Bobby and Mike. My sister GG who was a year younger than New-New and I was eating cake with my older brother Marco, (who was four years older than New-New and I) and my little sister Bree (she was nine). Jay, the baby of the family, was out in the yard playing with some other kids his age. He was seven.

When Chiloe saw Karla, his bottom lip dropped down to the stained wooden floor of that deck. I wasn't the only person who noticed because Rajul cleared his throat and asked, "Who's your friend, Lonna?"

"Uncle Dade's daughter, Karla," I said sitting down on the floor of the deck in front of the dirty glass door.

Rajul just nodded and turned back to the grill to finish cooking. New-New helped him unpack the hamburgers from the box then she went to sit on the steps of the deck. But Chiloe, could not take his green eyes off of Karla. He started making room for her to sit between him and Kelly. And when she sat down you would've thought the boy was in a trance. He looked her up from head to toe then back up again.

"So you're only twelve?" He asked.

"Yeah," she said nodding.

"You look a lot older."

Karla just shrugged. "I know."

"Oh damn," Chiloe said putting his hand that didn't have a beer in it on top of his head. "I didn't even introduce myself. I'm Chiloe."

"Are you the one who punched New-New in her leg?"

New-New smirked and I looked down at the ground, busying myself with a string on my shorts.

"Naw. That wasn't me. Not today anyway."

Karla shook her head and looked at New-New. "Who hit you?" She asked very defiantly.

New-New pointed to Rajul who looked the other way.

"You know you put a bruise on her leg, right?" Karla asked.

Chiloe just sat there smiling.

"I ain't put no bruise on her," Rajul said as if he were offended.

"Yes you did."

It was clear Karla wasn't going to back down.

"Did I put a bruise on you, girl?" He asked New-New.

New-New stood up slowly and sure enough there was a big purple and blue spot the size of a fist on the back of her right thigh.

"Damn," Chiloe, Marco, and Kelly said at the same time.

"Why did you do that?" Karla asked. "As big as you are and as little as she is you should know better."

I could tell Rajul was thoroughly embarrassed now. "She know I just be playin'. She know I ain't mean to hurt her all like that."

We all knew that was his way of apologizing. And we were all surprised to hear that much.

New-New nodded and said, "I know."

Rajul looked over at Karla and she smiled at him. He shook his head and in spite of himself smiled back.

"Where you from, girl?" He asked.

"Engle Park."

"Off the strip?"

She nodded.

"That ain't no rich neighborhood," Chiloe said.

"Who said it was?"

Everyone turned to look at me. Any neighborhood outside of this one was rich to me. And besides, I thought that everybody who was an only child and had fathers were rich. Even if they didn't live with them, at least they knew who they were.

"I'm sayin', it don't look like this neighborhood."

Yeah our neighborhood was pretty run down. It sat off of one of the busiest streets in the city and stretched from one side of the road to the other. It was filled with all the elements of a bad neighborhood and most of them stayed in my own house. The house that we lived in was the biggest in the neighborhood. And it was probably pretty spectacular, twenty years ago. But now it was run down and old. The white paint on the outside was peeling badly. The stairs and the floors were hard wood and creaked. The bedrooms needed a paint job years ago. The kitchen was small with old timey appliances. All three of the bathrooms had floors that were dry-rotted and the ceiling had water damage. It seemed like with all the money that my mother received from social services, not to mention what she got from disability because of her 'bad back', and the social security from Rajul, Chiloe, Rosie, Marco, G.G, Bree and Jay's father, she would take some money and fix up the house. It wasn't like she was using all that money on the bills and us.

Chiloe and Rajul were the biggest drug dealers on our side of town at the time, so they paid most of the bills and supplied clothes for New-New and I because we were their favorites. Marco had a legitimate job at the grocery store we ventured to earlier (on top of going to school full time), GG, Bree, and Jay were mama's babies so she didn't mind providing whatever they needed. That left Rosie who was pretty good at fending for herself. Not only did she have a boyfriend who gave her whatever she wanted, she dabbled in a little bit of everything. Some drug dealing, but mostly prostitution. Of course, Kerry didn't know about any of that. Or maybe he just didn't want to know. Everybody else knew though.

"You gonna be spending a lot time over here with us?" Chiloe asked Karla. He was breathing down her daggon neck.

"I don't know."

"Whatcha' mean you don't know? We good peoples."

A shadow appeared at the end of the balcony steps and every one immediately grew quiet. Her name was Marjorie and she was a hoochie to her heart. She was dark like midnight and wore a lime green shirt and lime green shorts so short, I could see the powder on her coochie hairs. She stomped past New-New and on up the stairs until she stood in front of Chiloe. She gave Karla a dirty look, rolled her eyes and put her hands on her hips and waited. For what, nobody knew.

Finally Chiloe got tired. After first pretending like she wasn't there, and then staring her down, it just didn't look like she was going anywhere.

"What girl?" He barked and Karla jumped looking at Chiloe like he was crazy.

"We need to talk," she said.

"Well, I'm talkin' right now. I'll be wit' you when I'm done here." He turned his attention back to Karla and Marjorie's hands fell off her hips. She just stared at his face, truly hurt.

"You been saying that for an hour."

Chiloe shook his head and spoke calmly. I could tell he was trying very hard to control himself, probably for Karla's sake. "And I'mma say it for another hour. Now leave me alone, girl."

Marjorie turned and walked back down the stairs. Her footsteps were considerably lighter than they had been on her way up.

"Man, you need to get your girl," Rajul said laughing so hard his belly was shaking. Marjorie was still within earshot and I knew she could hear the laughter.

"Man, that ain't my damn girl. Crazy bitch. She think just because I broke her off some, we a couple and shit."

"Chiloe, don't talk that way around her," Marco said directing his head in Karla's direction.

"You know the game, don't you girl?" He asked.

"No, not really," Karla spoke matter-of-factly, shaking her head and giving Chiloe a look like he had her mistaken with someone else.

Chiloe almost dropped his beer and I could tell some went down the wrong way. He managed to talk through his choking though. "You a virgin, Karla?"

Her face turned beet red again. That was my cue. "Come on New-New, come on Karla. Let's go."

Karla wasted no time getting up off that bench and walking into the house in front of me. Next came New-New. I watched Chiloe as his eyes just followed Karla until he couldn't see her anymore.

Chapter Two

Saturday, May 27, 1989 1:57 p.m.

I met Kelly at the corner around two. As much as I wanted to see him,
I had to hurry and get back home. Karla was due over at any minute.

Kelly was holding a basketball and wearing white mesh shorts and a white jersey. He wore sweatbands around his head and his right wrist. He looked so good. My stomach felt as if it were tied in a knot as we got closer and closer. I knew I could smell him.

"What's up?" he asked me putting his forehead to mine. We were only a few inches apart in height even though he was five years older than me.

"Nothing. What's up with you?"

He sighed heavily and we began to walk down the street opposite my house and the basketball court. The sun was so bright that I could hardly see in front of me. I could feel the beads of sweat forming on my forehead and around my neck.

"Last night, this kid got shot in my neighborhood, man," he said quietly. I just nodded. He continued, "He was only like sixteen. We went to junior high school together."

"What was his name?" I asked as if I knew the kid.

"Lance Brown. He quit after ninth grade, 'bout the same time I did. I hadn't seen him though in a couple of years until about a month ago. Then all of a sudden somebody shot him."

"Why?" I asked, but I knew the answer. The reason why people got shot in my neighborhood was the same reason why most people got shot all over this city. It was more prevalent in my hood though. I never would have reacted the way Kelly did. He took death so seriously, especially when the victim was young and black. He hated black on black violent crimes.

"You know why," he said finally.

We sat down on the curve of the dead end street. I had never ventured beyond this dead end; it was nothing but woods and maybe a dirty pond. But there were plenty of neighborhood legends about people getting killed and raped back up in there.

"If I didn't need the money," he said dribbling the basketball on the ground, "I would stop, Lonna. I really would."

I had no idea what he needed the money for, but I knew better than to ask. Even though Kelly and I had been together for so long, he was still a private person. His business was his business.

22

"I wish all the killing would stop, though." He shook his head. "That could've been me out there last night."

"No, it couldn't have." I put my arms around him. I hated when he talked like this. I couldn't digest the idea of losing him in gun smoke.

He looked at me and smiled. Then he touched my hair that was carried back from my face with a red headband. "You look so pretty. What you doing today?" He asked.

"Karla's coming over."

"Dang, she spend more time at your house than she do at home, don't she?"

I smiled because it was close to the truth. She had been to my house every weekend for the past month. But tonight she was spending the night. She had never spent the night before and it took two weeks of begging to get her mother to let her come this one time. Maybe if we got her back home safely, it wouldn't be so hard the next time.

I stood up, remembering that I needed to get back home. Kelly stood up with me. "I guess I'll see you later," he said.

"I'll be at the basketball court."

He nodded and I knew what was coming next as he leaned in for a kiss that seemed to last forever. Then we parted ways at the intersection where we'd met.

I cleaned the house from top to bottom, cooked some spaghetti, and washed some clean sheets and towels. Everybody thought I was crazy as I hustled around making sure everything was perfect.

"Lonna, it ain't like Karla's never been here before," Rajul said as I pushed his feet off of the coffee table to dust.

"I know that. But she's spending the night. She never spent the night before. We could at least try to clean up."

Out of the corner of my eye I saw Marco head for the kitchen. "Don't you even touch that spaghetti. I will break your fingers."

He went back and sat down on the couch with Rajul.

"You mean we can't eat any food?" Bree asked. She was lying on the floor in front of the couch watching television.

"Yeah, we can eat as soon as she gets here."

"As soon as who gets here?" Chiloe said coming through the basement door dressed like he was going to play ball. But I seriously doubted it.

"Karla," I said.

"Karla's coming over?" He asked like he hadn't heard me.

"Yeah. She's spending the night," Bree chirped in. "And we're gonna eat spaghetti."

Rajul smacked his teeth. "Lonna cooked it, so I ain't eating it."

I poked him in his stomach. He reached out to grab me, but I ducked. Chiloe grabbed me by my arms as soon as I was out of Rajul's reach. He pulled me into the kitchen.

"Why didn't you tell me Karla was spending the night?" He asked.

"Why? You don't want her over here?"

"Naw, it ain't that. I just wasn't prepared,"

"What do you have to prepare for? She's not coming to see you."

He seemed to ignore that comment. "How long she staying?"

"I want her to stay until Monday. But I don't know. Why are you asking all these questions about her? It's not like she's never been over here."

I knew exactly why he was asking so many questions. I left him in the kitchen when the doorbell rang so that I could be the one to answer it.

Karla held her pink suitcase like she was staying for a week. Uncle Dade stood behind her with his large hands on her shoulders.

"Hey Uncle Dade. Hey Karla."

I took her hand and dragged her into the house. I was eager for our weekend to get started.

"You wanna see Momma?" I asked Dade.

He shook his head and told Karla to call him when she was ready to come home. Then he headed back to his car. He and my mom had not been seeing a lot of each other lately and I was thinking they probably weren't together anymore. It was not a surprise to me, as much arguing as they did. And I really didn't care as long as they didn't try to separate Karla and me.

I closed the door.

"Come on," I said already half way up the stairs.

She started the creaky stairway with me and down the long hallway. The first door on the right was my mom's and it was closed. I could hear the television loud and clear behind it. She had been doing nothing but sleeping all day, which was not unusual. All the pain medication that she took for her 'bad back' made it hard for her to stay awake, not including the alcohol. I rarely saw my mother.

There were a total of four rooms up here. Bree, New-New and I shared one. Rosie and G.G. shared another at the end of the hall. Marco and Little Jay slept in the one across the hall from ours. Chiloe had made his own little room down in the basement and Rajul usually slept down there on the couch when he was home.

I opened the door to our room where New-New lay across her bed talking on the phone. Bree and I shared a bunk bed while New-New got the single twin size bed. I don't know how or why it had worked out like that. Karla put her suitcase down in front of the dresser and sat down on the bed beside New-New.

"Get off the phone," I said to New-New, knowing she was talking to Andrew.

She waved me away and I heard an, "I love you." Then she hung up.

"I love you, Andrew," I mocked her. "I'll see you at the basketball court tonight so we can freak behind the bleachers."

She threw a notebook from off of the nightstand at my head and sat up. Her blond hair was beginning to grow its black roots again and I could see them clearly since she had braids. If it wasn't for the roots, her skin color, hair, and gold jewelry would have run all together. I could barely tell where one ended and the others began.

"What's up, Karla?"

"Nothing much. I bought all my tapes for us to listen to tonight."

"Okay, but we can listen to 'em when we get home because tonight, we're going to the basketball court."

Karla shook her head. "Oh lord."

"What?" I asked sitting down beside her.

"I don't feel like seeing Ray. Every since we broke up, he been calling me like three and four times a day. I have to tell my mom to say I'm not home."

I laughed because she never should have talked to him in the first place. She knew she didn't like him. "I've never seen a relationship that only lasted a week!" I said.

"He's worrisome, that's why. Calling me all the time. Coming over my house. All in one week! My whole family knows him. He walked all the way from here to my house!"

"Did you give him some?" New-New asked whispering as if we weren't alone in the room.

"Hell no!" Karla said whispering back.

"She saving it for Chiloe," I said.

"What?" They asked me at the same time. I wished I had kept my big mouth shut.

"Look, y'all don't tell anybody this," I said getting down on my knees in front of Karla and New-New. I leaned close to them. "But Chiloe likes you, Karla."

Karla's eyes grew wide. And she gasped. But New-New just shook her head coolly. "No he don't. Chiloe's eighteen years old. He got enough ho's around this neighborhood. What would he want with a twelve year old girl?"

I had no idea what he wanted with a twelve year old girl. But I knew what was true. I just didn't have proof. Karla's eyes went back to their normal size and she sat back on the bed satisfied that New-New's explanation was feasible.

"Come on, let's go eat."

A Saturday night in my neighborhood was all about going to the basketball court right up the street from our house. Brightly lit by dozens of streetlights, it was the center point of the neighborhood. Every teenager in the vicinity would crowd it, either playing basketball, dealing, fronting on the hoods of their newly washed rides, or just hanging in the bleachers. And usually my sister and I were the youngest females there. It was an unspoken rule around these parts that age didn't matter as long as it was kept on the low and wasn't too ridiculous. And now that rule applied to Karla too who, seemed to have caught the eye of Mike. As we both sat on the cool metal bleachers, watching him play basketball with Kelly and six other boys, it was obvious that the game was the last thing on his mind. After every shot, throw, and pass Mike would turn to look at Karla just to see if she were watching. If she was, he played it off like he was looking for someone else.

Then there was my Kelly. Every now and then he would steal a glance at me. He played it off cooler than Mike though. He was smooth like that. We had made an agreement a long time ago that no one would know about us not only because I was so young, but he was just a private person. And besides New-New and Karla, no one knew. He tossed the ball to Mike who was so busy looking at Karla that it hit him in the head. Everybody cracked up.

New-New stood behind the gate that surrounded the court close to Andrew. She'd planned that spot perfectly because it was the only inch of ground on the court not lit by a street lamp. It was dark and shaded by trees. No one would even think to look over there. No one except for me. She and Andrew stood so close that I couldn't tell where he ended and she began. There was no doubt in my mind that they were doing 'it'. How often and when, I didn't know. My sister and

I were close, but we didn't discuss those kinds of things. Now Karla and I, we were a different story.

And speaking of Karla, I noticed every now and then she would look over at Chiloe leaning on the hood of someone's car. He wore a blue hooded sweatshirt with the pockets in the front that both of his hands were stuffed into. And every now and then he would look over at her. And then he would smile that crooked smile of his that females seemed to love.

Behind that pretty smile and those green eyes though, was nothing nice. Chiloe had a history around this neighborhood. Nobody messed with Chiloe. Too many dudes had been hospitalized from crossing him. And as for females, not one that came across him could honestly say that she didn't want him. And a lot of them had actually had him. Then there were the pitiful few who had lost their hearts to him. I never remembered Chiloe ever claiming any girl as his own. So these ladies were left with broken hearts and ruined reps. I mean there were dozens of them, but I had never seen him look at any one the way he looked at Karla.

The basketball game was finally over and another one was getting ready to begin. Mike and a few other dudes headed towards Chiloe but Kelly was coming my way. His shirt was off and anyone could see he was a little on the skinny side. But the two home done tattoos on his chest and left arm seemed to take away from all that to me. I could see the green band of his boxers under the shorts that he wore. He stopped beside the bleachers but continued to look straight ahead.

"Meet me tonight," he said only loud enough for me to hear.

"Where? What time?" I whispered back so low I could barely hear myself.

"In your backyard. One."

I nodded and he walked away to join another group of boys.

"Are y'all doing 'it'?" Karla turned to me and asked. She was so earnest and sincere about it.

"No," I shook my head. It surely wasn't because I didn't want to. But Kelly was taking his sweet time and I knew it was because of my age.

"When are y'all gonna do 'it'?"

Karla had no experience with sex. Although the girl could get as many dudes as she wanted, and she could hug and kiss on one until she had him about to die from the ache of blue balls. She tried to live vicariously through New-New and ,I but I knew just as much as she did.

"I don't know. Probably when I'm older."

"That's nice of him to wait like that."

I shrugged my shoulders. "He just don't wanna go to jail for messing with a JB."

She looked confused so I clarified. "Jail bait."

"Oh."

Sometimes I got the feeling that I wanted someone I could flaunt in public. Like New-New and Andrew. Or Rosie and Kerry. Even Karla and Ray, the short week that they were together. But there were no guys my age that interested me. There never had been. Not the ones at school and not the ones in the neighborhood. They were all interested in playing basketball and other sports or walking around the hood looking goofy. They were immature. Besides, I was actually stuck on Kelly.

I remembered when I first saw him. He came to the house with Kerry to see Rosie. I was just eleven, but I knew he was the one for me. I wasn't even all that much into light complexioned boys. But there was just something about him. The way he hardly said a word. He just sat and observed, his eyes slightly closed and penetrating. And even though we were different ages and came from two totally different places, his mother was a teacher and he lived in a nice well to do area, I felt we had so much in common, besides the fact that we were both twins. I admired him from a distance though, making sure not to hang around him or to put myself in his path all the time. From being around Chiloe, I knew what guys his age thought about girls my age. I didn't want him to feel that way about me. It was hard avoiding him all the time, knowing that the only thing I wanted to do was plop myself on his lap and bury my face into his sweet sweaty neck. I remained strong though.

Until the day I just happened to be down in Chiloe's room listening to the radio and watching television at the same time. All of my siblings, except for Rosie, had gone to the park. I was home with cramps from a period that had just started for the first time three months ago.

I lay bundled in Chiloe's comforter on his comfortable pleather couch. Chiloe put all kinds of things down there to make it seem more like an apartment rather than a room in the basement. He had his bed, which were just some rails and a mattress; the couch where I lay, a floor model television, and a stereo system. There were posters of half naked girls on the walls along with some album covers. He even had a knock off Persian rug on the floor that he purchased at the flea market.

I heard the door of the basement open, and thought maybe it was Chiloe coming back home. He'd only been gone for about ten minutes. Maybe he forgot something.

"Can I get some heat down here please?" I asked without turning around to look behind me.

There was no answer and I hadn't really expected one. It was the middle of July and I knew he wasn't going to cut any heat on. The basement was just going to have to stay cold as usual.

The person behind me though was getting closer and closer until they were standing right in front of me. I removed the covers from over my head and looked up into Kelly's hazel eyes. He wore a white t-shirt and black shorts. His black baseball cap was turned to the back.

"Hi," I said wondering what he wanted. Then it dawned on me that I was in Chiloe's room. He was probably looking for him. I knew that Kelly did some 'deals' for Chiloe every now and then.

"Chiloe went to the park. He probably won't be back until later."

"I know," was all he said as he sat down on the couch where my feet stopped.

Ok, so then what did he want?

I sat up and looked at him. Suddenly I was aware of how I probably looked. Hair undone, raggedy white and yellow shorts with a white batman t-shirt, and all.

"What'cha watchin'?" He asked looking at the television.

I shook my head. "Some Eddie Murphy movie. I think. I wasn't really watching it."

Then a slow song came on the radio. He looked at me and I stared back at him. I knew I probably looked like a deer caught in some headlights. But I was maintaining. I was constantly imagining the day when I would finally get a chance to be alone with Kelly. In my mind it was always in my room. Never this basement. And he brought me a dozen red roses. Slow soft music would be playing. I would be wearing a light blue negligee. Light blue was my favorite color. My hair would hang past my shoulders. Nice and neatly curled, not all over my head like it was now. I would be lying across my bed that wasn't a bunk bed anymore. In fact it would be the only bed in the room. And he would come over and kiss me. Gently at first and then harder and harder.

My imagination never dared to venture past the kiss.

"Do you have a boyfriend?" Kelly asked me.

It took me a minute to realize what he'd said. I was stuck on that kiss.

"No." I shook my head slightly.

"Why not?"

I hated that question. Why did I need a reason to not want any of the boys in my classes, on my school bus, or in my neighborhood? Why did I need a reason to only want him?

"I don't know."

My voice was a lot calmer than I expected it to be. In my daydreams we never said a word. But here he was, wanting to talk.

"What grade are you in, sixth?"

I nodded my head.

"Is there anybody you like?"

I rolled my eyes back in my head. "Why you ask so many questions?"

He smiled and shifted positions so that he was facing me. "You're pretty, you know that."

I know I was blushing, but I kept cool. I shrugged my shoulders and said thank you like it was something I was use to hearing.

"Do you want a boyfriend?" He asked.

"Maybe. Depends on who it is."

He smiled that cocky crooked smile that a lot of guys I knew had. But when he did it, I felt my breath catch in my throat.

"What would you say if I asked you to go with me?"

My heart stopped right then. In my dreams he never asked. But right now in reality, knowing that he wanted to know what I would say if he did ask, it was no longer cold in here.

"I'd probably say yes."

That's when he leaned over to me. Messed up hair and all, and his lips touched mine. Next thing I knew, we were doing a tongue dance. It felt awkward to me. I'd never French kissed a boy before. And to be doing it with someone five years older than me was scary. I wanted to do a good job. I didn't want him to think I was a baby that didn't know anything. So I closed my eyes and just let him lead. He was slow and very gentle.

"You can't tell anybody about us," he said releasing my lips. His hand stayed put on the back of my neck. Gentle but strong. "You know I'm too old for you, right?"

I nodded because I couldn't speak. This was my boyfriend now.

That was a whole year ago. My feelings had not changed for this boy and even though we never told anyone about us, I felt that we'd grown closer.

The thought gave me chills as I descended the steps of the deck. Out of the darkness I felt the thin strong arms grip my waist tightly and pull me close. The sweet smell of sweat and musk filled my nose, relaxing me. Even though I couldn't flaunt him, times like these made our relationship worthwhile.

"Hey girl," he whispered in my ear as he kissed my neck.

"Hey," was all I could say between the giggles and the breathlessness.

"You miss me today?"

I nodded enjoying the way his grip on my waist tightened and we seemed to be swaying back and forth with the wind. Through his mesh shorts, he was starting to harden. So I took his hand and led him over to the steps of the deck where we sat down. There he wrapped his arms around me again. He put his lips close to my ear.

"I've been thinking."

"About what?" I said hoping that it was something good and related to us. Last time he said that he had been thinking, I had to hear about poverty and the plight of the black man for an hour and a half.

"Me and you."

I sighed totally relieved.

"What about me and you?"

"We been together for a year, right?"

I nodded.

"Well in six more years you'll be eighteen, right?"

I nodded again wondering why he was asking me questions that he already knew the answers to. I heard the wind blow softly through a nearby bush and I yawned in spite of myself.

"Let's get married when you turn eighteen."

I turned all the way around and looked him directly in his beautiful eyes just like I had before our first kiss. He seemed serious enough to me, but I still could not believe what I was hearing.

"Look," he continued mainly because of the way I looked at him. "I've been saving my money. I'll probably run with Chiloe for about another year or two. Then we'll be able to afford a nice crib. I'll get a real job. You can go to college, and we won't make no babies until after you finish college. 'Cause that shit's important. You're too smart not to take your ass to college. Maybe I'll go back to school when I make sure everything's straight with you."

I was still speechless or maybe just scared to open my mouth. I didn't want this moment to magically disappear. What was the question again?

"You wanna marry me, Lonna?"

I nodded not even realizing that I was nodding. I heard a cricket nearby. A car sped off from somewhere and somebody around the corner was having a very late night gathering.

Kelly reached into the pocket of his gym shorts and came back out with a ring. I was pretty sure he purchased it from a pawn shop. I didn't care as he slipped it onto my finger. It was a tad too big, but I'd be damned if I wasn't going to wear it anyway.

I had never really thought about marriage. I wasn't like New-New who substituted her last name for Andrew's constantly just to see how it would sound. I liked things the way they were for the moment. I hadn't thought about a future with Kelly.

"Alright then," he said looking down at the ring dangling from my finger. "If anybody asks where you got the ring from, you found it. Alright?"

The only thing I could do was nod my head again.

"What's all this mess?" G.G. screamed, coming into the kitchen. Chiloe followed close behind her as she looked from me, to New-New, to Karla.

It was nine in the morning and the three of us were attempting to make pancakes. It hadn't turned out so well though. The kitchen was smoky and there was pancake batter over the floor, stove, and somehow on the refrigerator. We took turns cooking while one of us would go shower and dress, so no one really knew who the real blame was.

G.G. angrily grabbed the dishcloth off of the sink and began to clean. She shook her head that was wrapped in a blue bandanna back and forth. We excused ourselves from the small kitchen, which was too tight to begin with and walked quickly into the living room trying to decide what to eat as we listened to G.G. bang dishes around. We knew we couldn't go back in there.

"Come on let's go eat some breakfast," Chiloe said more to Karla than anyone else.

I imagined that New-New and I looked as if we'd seen a ghost. Chiloe had never taken us to eat anywhere except the McDonald's drive through. Then I gave her a knowing look because it wasn't about us. It was Karla.

All the same though, we all agreed and five minutes later we were climbing into his black Chevrolet Berretta. Chiloe made New-New and I sit in the back while Karla sat up front with him. We were glad we had gotten away before anyone else woke up. We'd offered to take G.G. but she declined with just a roll of her eyes. We weren't too upset about it though.

In the last few months, it had become obvious to the whole family that G.G. just didn't want to be here anymore. She would complain and mumble around the house. She never wanted to spend time with any of us. She spent most of her time on the phone with our Aunt Mila who lived in the country off of Interstate 95. She was considered our rich aunt who was the sister of Rajul, Rosie, Chiloe, Marco, G.G., Bree and Jay's father. She was also married to my mom's brother. And it wasn't that they were rich or anything, they just had more money than us or any of our other relatives. G.G. was crazy about her, but the rest of us could have easily done without her.

"Where are we going?" Karla asked Chiloe over the thumping bass of Chiloe's music.

"Where you wanna go?" Chiloe asked back.

I looked at New-New hoping she had caught his tone. It was flirty and implied more than what he said. She just shook her head.

"Pancake House."

Good choice. Now to see if he actually took us there or told her no. If he agreed to take us, that definitely meant he liked Karla.

"Okay."

I knew it. I celebrated a personal triumph in my head. I turned to look at New-New and mouthed, "I told you so."

She rolled her eyes at me and sat back in the seat. I strained my ears to hear the rest of the conversation going on in the front. The loud bass in my ears wasn't helping that much.

"What school do you go too?" Chiloe asked Karla with one hand on the wheel and the other on his gear shift. He usually leaned all the way over to the driver side window when he drove to make himself look cool. But I noticed, this morning, his body shifted closer to Karla.

"I go to Christian School," she replied. It wasn't something that she was embarrassed about neither. It just was. That was the way things were with her. I didn't think I could have handled it so well. Having to wear dresses all the time and read the Bible was not for me.

44

"Christian School?"

She nodded.

"Why you go to Christian School?"

"Because there are a lot of girls in public school that want to fight me."

"Why?"

She shrugged. "I don't know."

I didn't know either. Karla was cool with me. Yeah she didn't know a lot about living in a neighborhood like mine, but that wasn't important to me. And she was cool with New-New. There weren't a lot of girls that were cool with New-New.

"I saw you talking to that little boy, what's his name? That boy that New-New supposed to be goin' wit', his brother."

"Ray?"

"Yeah. I saw you talking to him last night. Y'all supposed to be goin' together?"

Karla shook her head and I looked over at New-New again as I poked her leg and motioned for her to lean in closer. With much reluctance, she leaned forward in her seat to hear the conversation better.

"We just broke up."

Chiloe nodded. "That's what he was beggin' and cryin' about. Why y'all break up?"

Karla shrugged. "He just got on my nerves."

"Stop messin' around with them little punks, man."

New-New rolled her eyes back in her head once again as Chiloe swung the car wildly in to the parking lot of the pancake house. It was crowded which was to be expected on a Sunday morning. We sat parked between an empty Maxima and an old white couple getting out of a Lincoln, Town Car. They looked nervously at the little black car filled with black people that seemed to travel in a cloud of loud music coming from all directions. The little old man grabbed his wife's arm and checked the locks on his car twice before finally going into the restaurant.

Chiloe held the door open for Karla and then let it swing back in the faces of New-New and me. We waited only a minute for a table, listening to the other customers who were also waiting complain over the sound of dishes banging against each other, then we were seated in the back of the smoking section.

Chiloe made sure he was seated beside Karla in the little booth while New-New and I sat directly across from them. Karla squinted her eyes and wrinkled her brow at me in confusion. I pretended not to see her as I flipped half heartedly through the menu. She should have listened to me when I told her the first time.

"Do you wear contacts?" Chiloe asked studying her face from the roots of her hair to her chin. I wondered how she could breathe with him taking up most of her oxygen.

She looked up from her menu and at him. "No. Do you?"

He shook his head and I watched his face turn a soft pink. I poked New-New in her thigh, yet again, to get her attention away from our menu. We both giggled under our breath as we watched our truly gangsta' brother blush.

Karla convinced her mother to let her stay until Monday. It was Memorial Day and school was closed. At ten o'clock Sunday night we lay on the ragged cream colored rug in the middle of the hardwood floor, listening to the radio.

Breakfast turned into shopping at the mall, where Chiloe bought each of us an outfit and Karla shoes to match hers. Then there was a movie and lunch at a sandwich shop. For dinner, he cooked on the grill for us out on the deck.

"Now do you believe me about Chiloe?" I asked nobody in particular as the three of us lay in the dark.

47

I heard New-New laugh. Then she said, "I don't know but you need to come over here all the time, Karla."

Karla smacked her teeth. "I don't have anything against your brother, but he's way too old for me. My momma would kill me."

"Girl," New-New said propping her head up on her elbow. I could see her bright skin and blond hair clearly now by the grace of the streetlights outside. "Age ain't nothing but a number. Just ask Lonna and Kelly."

They both looked over at me. I hadn't told anybody about the night before and under their intense gazes I couldn't hold back any longer. I sat up.

"Kelly asked me to marry him."

"What?" I couldn't tell which one of them asked that, but they were both sitting up with me.

"You can't get married. You're only twelve years old," now that was Karla.

"Not right now. When I turn eighteen."

"How you know y'all still gonna be together when you turn eighteen?" New-New asked.

"The same way you know your name is gonna be Leonay McCarthy."

I heard a big gasp from where Karla sat, like she had choked on something. "Your name's Leonay!" She yelled and toppled over laughing.

"Shut up!" New-New said popping Karla's thick bare thigh.

She grabbed it and said, "Ouch," but she just couldn't stop laughing.

There was a knock at the door.

"Who is it?" New-New yelled rather harshly.

The door opened slightly and Bree's little round head peeped in. "Can I come in?"

The three of us thought about it. She slept in Rosie's room whenever Karla stayed over. We needed her bed, plus we figured she was too young to be hanging around us. But she was cool though. So we let her in.

"What y'all doing?" she asked laying across my outstretched legs after stumbling over a few objects in the dark.

"Talking."

"What'cha talking about?"

"Boys."

"I like boys," she said matter-of-factly.

"Who do you like?" Karla asked egging her on.

"I like Andrew."

We laughed. "That's my man, punk," New-New said throwing a piece of paper at her. Bree laughed so hard, she rolled off of my leg.

"So who do you like, Karla?" I asked her seriously. We all knew who liked her. But no one knew who she was interested in. It hadn't been Ray, that was for sure.

She just sighed and looked down at the rug where she found a string to play with.

"I don't really know. There's a dude around here that I think is cute. But besides that, I don't know."

"Who?" New-New demanded.

"Mike."

I was about to comment on the way he'd ogled her at the basketball court just the day before and all the other days since Karla started going to the court, but at that moment we heard a car pull up outside and the four of us rushed to the one open window that over looked the street in front of our house. We watched Rosie get out of a van that looked green, but it was hard to tell. She pulled her short white skirt down, which didn't really do any good, and headed towards the house.

"That ain't Kerry." I said even though we could all see that. Kerry drove a red MR2.

"Where's she been?" Bree asked. We all knew, but none of us were about to tell her. Instead we just shook our heads and said we didn't know.

Chapter Three

Every since I could remember, Chiloe was my mother's favorite. She bent over backwards for him and I couldn't remember him ever getting fussed at by her for anything. He was the true apple of her.

But that didn't bother Rajul. What bothered Rajul was how she was always on his back about something. Even though he paid most of the bills and took care of every need of almost everyone in the house, he could never get any appreciation from her. The day Rajul left was a day I would never forget. It seemed like every bad thing that ever happened to my family and me, started that day.

It was four-thirty in the afternoon and I sat in my favorite leather recliner next to the window. It had been around a few years and you could tell by the slits in the leather where parts of the cushion were coming out. New-New sat on the tattered beige couch that was just as old as the recliner writing a note to Andrew. It always baffled me why they even bothered to write each other notes when they went to the same school, rode the same bus, and our neighborhood's were a hop skip and jump away from each other. Yet, they still found it necessary to write each other notes.

We both heard her way before we saw her. Her steps were heavy and awkward. Our separate activities came to a halt and we looked at each other, because we knew she had been drinking.

She stumbled down the stairs struggling to stand still with every step. Her jean skirt was tight and barely covered her panties. Maybe she looked okay in it before nine kids. But afterwards, she forgot to throw it away. The thick curly black hair that had once hung to the middle of her back, due to her Indian ancestry, was now super short and gelled back into a thumb long ponytail. Her skin had once been a deep golden-brown with red undertones. But because of the alcohol's affect on her liver and whatever drugs she was on, her skin was now dark and blotchy in more than a few places. Alcohol had also rotted away most of her teeth awhile ago.

"What'chall doin'?" My mother asked very sweetly. That drunken sweetness that made my skin crawl. Her speech was slurred to death.

"Homework," I answered for both New-New and I.

"Yeah, y'all make sure you do that homework, now."

She started patting her sides like her skirt had pockets, but it didn't. And even if it did, she wouldn't have been able to put anything in them because it was so tight.

"Have you seen Rajul?" she asked finally not able to locate what she had been looking for.

We both shook our heads. Neither he nor Chiloe were home when we got out of school at three thirty. Rosie was helping Bree with homework in her room. Marco was at work, and Little Jay was playing outside. G.G. was at a friend's house in another neighborhood.

Momma ventured into the kitchen, she was probably just as unsure as we were about what she was looking for. But we were glad she was in there when the door opened and Rajul stepped in. New-New turned around on the couch and tried to wave him back out without saying a word. He didn't understand what she meant and before he could comprehend, Momma was coming back around the corner. She looked at New-New waving at the door and then at the door. I put my books down, not knowing what to expect. New-New put her forehead in her hands and closed her eyes.

"You fa' muda'fucka'," my mom said slurring so badly we could hardly make out what she was saying at all. She was walking straight towards Rajul. "Where's my money you owe me?"

Rajul was used to this. He also knew she was drunk so he wasn't holding that against her either. "You ain't got no money," he said and simply headed towards the basement. But she was following him.

"Yes I do. You nothin' but a thief. You steal my money. You steal my food. You fa' muda'fucka."

Rajul took a deep breath, stopping in front of the single wooden door that lead to Chiloe's room. "I don't have your money."

She continued. "You ain't shit," she spat at him. "Just like your damn daddy. Fa' muda' fucka."

He turned around. He held his hands up as if he were going to try to talk her down from this outrageousness she was going through. But before he could, she slapped him. A hard stinging slap right across his cheek. So hard, that as big as he was, he stumbled backwards. He recovered soon though and when he did, his huge heavy fist came slamming down against Momma's left cheek. I had felt the playfulness of that fist and could only imagine how it felt when it meant business.

She fell to the floor, undeniably hurt and holding her cheek. Rajul stepped right over her and headed to the front door.

New-New jumped up off of the couch and ran after him. "Rajul, don't leave," she said grabbing his arm and clinging to him.

"Naw, New. I ain't puttin' up with this shit no more. Pack my stuff for me. I'll be back to get it later on."

"You better not come back here, you fat muda'fucka! I'll have yo' ass thrown in jail!" Momma was still holding her cheek and trying to talk through a mouth full of blood. Two of the few teeth she had left lay on the floor beside her.

Rajul just shook his head and walked out the door, New-New still clung to his arm.

When Chiloe walked in New-New and I were cleaning up blood from the carpet. Momma had gone back upstairs with the front of her shirt and her skirt covered in big blotches of red from her mouth and nose.

He stood over us looking at the blood stain that we were trying desperately to get up with a towel and Comet.

"Where's she at?" He asked.

"Upstairs?" New-New and I said in unison.

Neither one of us asked him how he knew. I folded the wet towel up until it sat in a neat little square and left it beside the now faint spot of blood as New-New and I followed Chiloe down to the basement. Rajul kept most of his stuff down here in Chiloe's room.

"Where's Rajul at?" New-New asked as Chiloe handed me a white plastic trash bag to put Rajul's stuff in.

"Erwin." He didn't offer us anymore info and we didn't press for any. I knew he was upset. Rajul was everything to Chiloe and when something upset him, it upset Chiloe.

Rajul's clothes were so big they filled up the trash bag quickly. Before I could squeeze anything else in, Chiloe handed me another one and I continued removing his clothes from the one closet in the room.

"What time is he coming to get his stuff?" New-New asked.

"He's not. We're taking it to him."

I was too scared to even ask questions as we pulled up in front of the shack like house at eight-thirty that night. The meager front yard was full of cars as if someone was having a party. The house was gray and sat up on cement blocks. We had to jump to get on the porch, there were no steps.

"Okay," Chiloe said holding his hand out to New and I. We took turns being hoisted onto the porch. Then Chiloe threw the bags up and jumped up after them.

He knocked on the old rickety door that looked like someone had, at one point, decided to rip it off the hinges. A guy that was not my brother answered. He looked from me to New-New and then at Chiloe.

"What's up man?" He asked questioning the presence of my twin and me.

"You better open this door," was all Chiloe had to say and the boy didn't need any more encouraging. I could tell, though, he had a big problem with us being there.

We followed Chiloe through the kitchen where three boys sat around a small round wooden table lit by one light bulb in a small lamp. One was counting out bills by hand. The other two were watching him intensely making sure he counted every single bill correctly. One of the dudes doing the watching had a toothpick in his mouth and when I looked back at him, he raised his head in a single nod. I quickly turned back around and continued walking, staying close to my sister who was right on Chiloe's heels.

This house smelled of dry rot and the floors creaked worse than the floors at home. We entered a smoke filled room with the stereo letting go of some 70's funkadelic song. It was so loud it seemed to be coming from all points of the house. Through the smoke I could make out a couch with three boys on it. One boy had a half naked female in his lap. Another one sat beside him. There was another one at the end of the couch. They were passing a blunt back and forth between the six of them.

Also in the small room, were three more chairs. In one sat another boy with a girl on his lap and in another chair sat my brother. He had his own blunt because he didn't like to share.

We each sat one of Rajul's bags by the chair that he occupied. The second hand smoke from the weed was making me slow because I hadn't even noticed until then that the room was blue. And everyone in it was blue. I hated those colored light bulbs, they gave me the creeps. Not that I didn't already have them out here.

Chiloe squatted down beside Rajul's chair and whispered something in his ear. Rajul looked at him and said, "You sure you can handle it?"

Chiloe nodded and they shook hands in that male bonding sort of way.

I breathed fresh clean air into my lungs once I got outside. It felt so good I had to lean over and rest my hands on my knees.

"Are you okay?" New-New asked.

I nodded, for fear of losing the fresh air through my mouth if I opened it.

"Come on," she said rubbing my back and we climbed into Chiloe's car.

New-New lay in the back seat on her way to being asleep with her left arm flung over her face. I sat beside Chiloe.

"Y'all are cool with me," he said out of the blue when we were so far away from that shack that I could no longer see it. "You know that right?"

I nodded my head then I realized he probably couldn't see me because it was too dark.

"Yeah I know."

"Y'all are the coolest sisters I have. I like y'all better than the rest of them."

I looked at him. "I'm talking about Rose and G.G."

I understood and lay my head back against the seat.

"Rosie, she a damn ho. I mean an actual prostitute. Hoppin' in and out of cars all night long. She take any kind of drug she can get her hands on. She got that stupid Kerry boy blind or pussy whipped, one. He need to be careful or he gon' catch something."

Then he startled me by grabbing my arm. "You better not ever do no shit like that. I'll kill you, girl. If you need somethin' you come to me!"

"Okay, Chiloe." I said snatching my arm away.

"Then G.G," he continued on as if in a trance, "I don't know where she get off thinkin' she better than everybody else. I don't know why Momma just won't send her to live with Mila. That's where she wanna go so bad. But Momma won't get no money for G.G. with her gone, huh?"

"I guess not."

I could see Chiloe shaking his head out of the corner of my eye. I was trying to keep my eyes on the road just in case he decided not to.

"Marco, he's trying to do right. I respect that. I ain't gon' fuck with that. He work to damn much for me though. And trying to go to school." He stopped to shake his head once again. "Bree'll be okay if she stick with you and New-New. I kind of worried about New-New when she dyed her hair blond and shit. But she gon' be alright as long as she stick with you."

Then he paused and I heard him take a deep breath.

"You and Karla."

I turned to face him now because he had my full attention.

"Yeah Karla."

I wished New-New was awake, but maybe it was for the best. I doubted Chiloe would tell me anything with an audience. We'd never really had a conversation like this before.

"You're thirteen going on fourteen. You got more sense than most girls your age and some my age. I know you not stupid. So I know you know I got feelings for Karla."

"I knew that when you first met her."

He nodded. "And I know she's young and that's what's killing me. But damn if I don't think about that girl all the damn time. It's just something about her." He sighed and shook his head. "I ain't talkin' about just fuckin' her. But I know she's too young for us to have a so-called relationship or whatever. I don't know what I wanna do with her."

"You wanna grab her and kiss and hug on her."

He laughed. "Well yeah, shit. But still what's supposed to happen after we finish kissing and hugging?"

"I don't know Chiloe."

"I'm just gonna leave that alone. She just gonna have to be somebody that I'm down with. Never thought I'd be down with a female like that. Especially one so young. But that's the way it's gonna have to be." He nodded as if he were truly convinced of that.

New-New and I took turns taking a shower to get the smell of marijuana and dry rot off of us. Bree was already snoring softly, as I climbed over her head to the top bunk. Rosie always made sure she and Jay got to bed on time. That was the only good thing about her that I could think of.

I snuggled into my nice warm sheets, with those smells still in my nostrils, but thanking the Lord that I was at home.

Chapter Four

Saturday, November 16, 1991 9:30 p.m.

It was fifty degrees outside, but it had to be a hundred in here. There were thirty people crowded into my living room. The couch, love seat and my favorite leather recliner were pushed against the sliding glass door to make room for everyone.

The Twin's (New and I) fourteenth birthday party was the big neighborhood bash that Chiloe planned it to be. He cooked the food outside on the grill, and made sure everything else was perfect. From the strobe light that was giving me a headache, to the local DJ who lived around the corner from us.

Karla was spending the night tonight. New-New and I were both hoping that she would find someone that she really liked here. Maybe having a bigger variety, since there were more than just neighborhood boys in my house, would help. Or maybe she and Mike would finally hook up. She dated a guy in her own neighborhood but that ended in a couple of weeks. I was beginning to think she had a problem with intimacy.

New-New and Andrew were all hugged up on the hardwood floor amidst a body of other people hugged up. Each of his hands was strategically placed in the middle of a butt cheek. They were so close; I figured they would probably topple over at any second.

I was waiting for Kelly. He told me he would be here, but as always, we weren't going to act like a couple. Maybe we would dance once or twice. I snuck a glance at the engagement ring that I purposely wore on the wrong hand on my middle finger instead of my ring finger. There was brown tape wrapped around the bottom of the ring to make it fit better. I smiled thinking of how our marriage was all he talked about lately. It made me excited to listen to him.

Karla was trying her best to make it over to me. She was blocked by arms, legs and torsos everywhere though. Then when she finally got around G.G. and her new boyfriend of about three weeks, she was grabbed around her waste by Chiloe. Those two were so cute.

"You wanna dance, Lonna?"

I looked to the left of me to see Byron, a boy from school. I could remember him and New-New talking for about a month, on one of the many times she and Andrew had broken up temporarily. But besides that, I didn't know him that well. So I shook my head no. The last thing that I wanted was for Kelly to come in and see me dancing with someone else.

That song ended and another one began quickly. Karla finally got away from Chiloe and continued over to me in my position against the wall by the food.

"Girl, if one more nigga' touches my butt, I'mma kill 'em."

I just smiled at her knowing full well that she loved the attention. She was even dressed for it in lightly faded jeans that she purchased, to her mother's dismay, with the three rips right under the crotch on her right leg and, three on the shin area of the left leg, and three in the back right under her butt. The white long sleeved shirt she wore stopped right at her belly button and was perfectly ripped three times in the front, but nothing showed thanks to a red halter top that she wore underneath. Her hair was pulled tightly up into a pony tail on the top of her head with a red Scrunchy.

"Why are you holding up the wall?" She asked with concern all over her face.

"I'm waiting for Kelly."

She nodded because she understood. Then she decided to help me hold up the wall. I was grateful for her company. Together we watched the crowd as they seemed to sway back and forth together to a song.

"I saw you and Chloe dancing," I said leaning closer to her so she could hear me over the music.

She smirked and shook her head, pony tail swaying back and forth. "Your brother is a trip."

I smiled and looked toward the stairs and noticed G.G sneaking Damon up. I hit Karla on her arm and pointed at the stairway. She shook her head again. It wasn't the first time he had been invited to that part of the house. In fact since Rosie moved in with Kerry, two weeks ago, I couldn't count on both hands how many times G.G. bought him home. Karla seemed to be reading my mind because she asked, "How's Rosie?"

Rosie was nine months pregnant and due any day. We couldn't be sure if it was Kerry's baby or not and I knew neither one of them knew. But still, Kerry didn't mind claiming the baby as his own. As a matter of fact, they were getting married next month.

"Fine I guess. She came over to check on Bree and Jay the day before yesterday."

Behind Karla's back I could see a tall dark skin cutie with a Reagan cut, died red at the ends, approaching her. He smiled at me briefly and tapped her on her shoulder.

"You wanna dance?" He asked. He'd probably been waiting all night to ask her that. Her dance ticket had been quite full.

Karla looked at him and then me. I could tell she was quite pleased with what she saw. I nodded so that she would go on. He looked extremely grateful as he took Karla's hand and led her to the dance floor, which was nothing but the middle of our large living room floor with the carpet rolled up.

I sighed heavily and leaned back against the wall, almost knocking over the bookshelf. I looked around to make sure no one saw me and noticed my brother sitting on the arm of the couch where three other wallflowers sat talking amongst themselves. His face was blank, like a white sheet of paper and his eyes seemed to be glued to Karla dancing with this guy from school. The guy was pretty nice. We weren't particularly close, but we shared a couple of classes together.

I left my position by the wall, where I had been standing so long the prints of my green Rebooks had become imbedded in the floor. Making my way through the crowd to Chiloe, I bumped into three couples freaking, a guy with a drink who lost it after I bumped him, and two girls.

"You wanna dance," I said standing a foot away from Chiloe's ear. I still got a good whiff of the Old E that he was sipping on though as he shook his head and smiled then slowly got up from the couch.

As we neared everyone else on the floor the doorbell rang. Chiloe looked down at me as if to say, "It's your party, you answer the door." So I did, but he followed close behind.

Mike's eyes seemed glazed as sweat poured from his chocolate brown face to his white t-shirt that was now clinging to him like a second skin. His breathing was hard as he tried desperately to catch his breath, but he couldn't seem to do it. He even tried bending over and putting his hands on his kneecaps. That didn't work to well neither.

"What's wrong with you, man?" Chiloe asked, gently pushing me aside so he could get a better view of Mike.

But still Mike couldn't seem to catch his breath. He stood up straight putting both hands on the top of his head that was covered by a black Raider's baseball cap.

"Man," he said with a struggle. "Man, they got Kelly man. Up the street."

I don't even remember what else was said. Did Chiloe even respond? Did Mike say anything else? I don't even know how I ended

70

up out of the house and running up the street in the direction that Mike pointed, in between all his huffing and puffing.

Bobby sat on the ground with something cradled in his arms. The street was dark that night because of two broken streetlights that had been that way for about a month. As dark as it was though, I could see the white tennis shoes and socks. Two legs just lay limply on the ground parted slightly. I knelt down in front of Bobby, and forced him away.

Gently taking Kelly's upper torso in my arms, nestling his head in the crook of my arm, and pressing him close to my chest, I rocked slowly. So much so that I didn't even realize I was rocking until I felt a hand on my left shoulder, and then my right. I watched the tears on my cheek mingle with the blood on the front of Kelly's green shirt while I stroked his hair. I leaned over as far as I could without crushing him and kissed him on the lips. I could feel a slight whistling of air coming from his nose and I realized he was still alive, but probably not for long.

My twin sister was beside me now. She was on my left and Karla was on my right. Both of them seemed to be holding me at the same time. Or maybe all three of us were holding Kelly. I couldn't tell.

In the distance I could hear the piercing sirens of an ambulance. I hated the sound of sirens. It always meant something. It never meant nothing. They were never just because. Or just for the heck of it. They always meant something.

Kelly made a gurgling sound from deep in his throat and a stream of blood flowed from his pink slightly parted lips. As many people as there were out on the street that night, everything was silent. No one said a word as Kelly took his last breath in my arms. It escaped his body like cigarette smoke. Then he relaxed against my chest. I tried to convince myself that if I could just get closer to his face, to share my breath with him, to somehow get part of my living spirit into him, I could bring him back. But I knew that was not the case. All I could do was cry and both New-New and Karla held me tighter because they knew he was gone without even asking me if he was gone.

"You ok?" Kerry asked me sitting down beside me.

I just nodded my head yes. I had been to his mother's house before when no one else was home and I hated being back under these circumstances. So I sat on the couch alone with a Styrofoam cup of cherry Kool-Aide in my hands.

"You know," Kerry began and I couldn't look at him because he looked so much like Kelly. "Momma asked who you were and why I wanted you to ride with us in the limo and sit with us on the front row at the funeral."

I sighed heavily, still not looking at him. I had forgotten that no one was supposed to know who I was. I had thought nothing of it when Kerry called me the night before to let me know I was supposed to ride in one of the baby blue limo's that the funeral home provided for the family. And as I sat on the front row right beside Rosie, Kerry's future wife, I didn't question why I was there. It had seemed natural to me.

"So I told her."

I looked at him then. What did he tell her? He wasn't even supposed to know anything so what could he possibly tell her?

"I knew about y'all," he said reading my thoughts.

"You did?" I asked looking at him now only because I felt foolish by not looking at him.

He nodded his head. And the more I thought about it, he didn't really look like Kelly anymore. His hair wasn't cut as low. He didn't have that significant part that Kelly wore always on the right side of his head. And his eyes. His eyes didn't touch me like Kelly's had.

73

"Yeah I did. How could I not? He talked about you all the time."

I smiled knowing that he loved me. I wished I could tell him that I knew.

"You meant the world to that boy," he said shaking his head like he couldn't believe it. But didn't he love Rosie just as much? "He talked about y'all getting married, you finishing school, all kinds of stuff."

My face was hot and I couldn't reason out why. I could feel it down to my neck though.

"I know me telling you this isn't gonna bring him back to you. But I want you to know, and he would want you to know, you weren't just some deep dark secret he kept hidden away. He just wanted to make sure nobody ruined it for y'all. That's the way Kelly is . . ." then he corrected himself, " . . . was. He always wanted stuff to go off smoothly. No trouble."

I knew that about him. I smiled as I remembered all the conversations we had on Black history and America. How he taught me so much. How he was the most nonviolent person I had ever met. How could he die so violently?

"He's got a whole bunch of pictures and other stuff up in his room. Would you like some of that stuff?"

I thought for a second. Then I nodded my head. Yes I wanted everything he was willing to give me. Dirty clothes, bed sheets, anything. Anything that would keep that boy in my life.

"Okay. I'm gonna go though his stuff sometime this week. I know Momma can't do it. I'll pack you a box and bring it on over."

I nodded my head again and managed a very small, "Thank you."

There was a soft knock on my bedroom door as I ventured through the medium sized box full of Kelly's things. There were t-shirts, pictures that the two of us took of our selves, love letters from me to him, and music tapes. Whoever it was didn't wait for me to respond. The old brass doorknob turned and Chiloe walked in.

"What's up?" He asked me. We hadn't spoken since the night of my birthday party. I couldn't tell if he was mad at me for not telling him about Kelly and me or if he was mad at me for dating one of his boys.

I shook my head though closing up the box. I didn't feel comfortable going through it with anyone else. I wanted to be alone, to savor Kelly's spirit that hung on to all of these items.

"Karla's downstairs. She didn't wanna just barge in. She said she's spending the night."

I felt relief that she was here.

Chiloe crossed the room in two long strides and sat down beside me on New-New's bed. I held my breath preparing to be dug into by his harsh words and yelling. But instead when he opened his mouth, it was quite gentle.

"I can't believe I didn't know about you and Kelly, man. How many years? Three? And nobody knew?" He shook his head and I didn't bother to give him the short list of people who did know. Kelly was five days in the grave and all that didn't matter anymore.

"I use to think he was just gay or something," he continued, "and that was why he didn't want to talk to no females. All he was concentrating on was gettin' money. It was like he couldn't even see anything else. I ain't have no idea that y'all . . ." His voice trailed off and he looked at me. I noticed the tears falling down my own cheeks right when he did.

"I'm sorry, Lonna. I don't know what else to say to you. I know I should've said something. But I don't know what to say. I ain't want you and New-New to have to go through this shit. Losin' somebody to the streets ain't no joke. That's another reason why I just can't mess with Karla. I never know when my time will be up."

I felt emotions rolling around in me that had been held back since my birthday night. I had the sudden urge to break something, anything. I wanted to scream and yell. Instead I began to cry. Loudly.

"It hurts so bad!" I moaned in total agony. "Like somebody just ripped my heart out."

Chiloe put his arms around my shoulders almost smothering me in his massive muscles. "It's gonna be alright. You're one of the strongest people I know. You gon' be alright."

PART 2

Chapter Five

Friday, February 7, 1992 5:30 p.m.

We could hear the loud feminine voices traveling from the front door all the way to the sidewalk. There was a light green Toyota Tercel parked in the driveway, still running with the driver side door open. Then we saw the object, a vase or something, hurl towards the front door as if on its own. There it shattered into a million pieces and Lonna and New-New broke into a sprint across the front yard, followed by me.

We were hit by fouler than foul words both in English and Spanish. Aunt Mila waved her hands in the air, very animatedly, in Lonna's mother's face. Her body was rigid and poised to pounce at any moment. Greta, who was just as much as animated as Mila only more violent, wasn't worried a bit though. Uncle Felix, Greta's brother, sat on the couch just watching the two women that he'd known most of his life go back and forth. G.G. stood halfway between him and the door holding a suitcase. Another suitcase and a duffel bag sat by Uncle Felix's legs.

"You don't take care of her!" Aunt Mila spat. "You don't take care of none of them! You don't deserve to be a mother!"

"You better get your burrito eatin' ass out of my house," Greta replied but, I knew she didn't mean it. She wanted to fight first. I could sense it in the air. I got assurance to that with her next words. "Don't you come in here tellin' me how to raise my kids! Bitch!"

Mila looked offended but we all knew she didn't want to go toe to toe with Greta. As many prescription drugs and alcohol that she took, I did believe Greta could whoop her ass. So instead she grabbed G.G. roughly by the arm and headed towards the door.

"You're a damn crack head! I don't even know why my brother had children by you!" she yelled over her shoulder. "That's all you are, a drunken crack head! That's why he would never marry your ass!"

Greta followed her to the door not even trying to avoid the broken glass on the floor even though she was bare foot. Uncle Felix rose from the couch then looking as if he just wanted to get this whole thing over with so that he could go home. He swung both the suitcase and the duffel bag into his arms as he tried to squeeze himself out of the front door without touching his sister.

"You bitch!" Greta yelled again as G.G. got into the backseat of the car and Mila sat behind the wheel of the car. "I'mma send the police looking for you and my kid. Your ass is going to jail! You bitch!"

Then Greta picked up a piece of the vase she had probably thrown, the biggest piece she could find and threw it at the car. It missed Felix's head as he was getting into the passenger side by seconds. Mila didn't stop though. She quickly backed the car out of the driveway, leaving skid marks and peeled off down the street.

Greta slammed the front door of the house and the whole foundation shook. "You kids clean up!" She yelled then headed upstairs where she would probably spend the rest of the week. That's when we noticed Marco sitting on the stairs.

"What happened?" New-New asked him as the three of us prepared to clean up the broken vase, first by taking off our jackets.

"G.G's been calling Mila, telling her a whole bunch of lies. Stuff like we don't have any food or clothes." Marco stopped and shook his head. "She called her yesterday and told her the lights were getting ready to be cut off. So that's when Mila drove down here and got her."

Lonna stopped picking up the vase and looked at New-New. She rolled her eyes back up in her head and said, "G.G. gets new clothes every week. And the lights look like they're still on to me."

Marco shook his head. "I told you she was lying."

"And even if all that was going on," I said not looking up from the broken vase. I was down on all fours picking up sections. "Why didn't she come get all of y'all?"

Marco shrugged this time. "She only wants G.G. New-New and Lonna are not her blood anyway, because they have a different father than the rest of us. Our father is her brother. But she don't like the rest of us."

"And G.G.'s the only one that likes her," Lonna said.

We spent the rest of the night cleaning up G.G.'s room for Bree. None of us could wear the few clothes G.G. left behind so we put them aside for Bree. At the rate she was going, she would probably be in them in a year or so. G.G. left nothing else behind though. She had to have been packing for a few days.

Bree used scotch tape to hang her posters up on the wall. Rainbows, Disney movies, crap that New-New and Lonna wouldn't let her hang up on their wall. They kept them stuffed in the back of the closet instead.

The problem was getting her to sleep in her bed that night. She wanted us to leave a lamp on and her new bedroom door open. We agreed and went to bed. Only ten minutes later as we prepared for bed ourselves, she knocked on our bedroom door.

"What do you want?" New-New asked as Bree peeped her little head in the door without waiting for one of us to open it.

"Can y'all leave y'all door open too?"

"No!"

"Come on y'all," I said sitting on the bottom bunk where I always slept. I was in the middle of cutting my toenails. "This is her first night by herself. We can sleep with the door open."

Lonna and New-New didn't say anything so both Bree and I took that as a yes. Bree opened the bedroom door up all the way then she went off to bed too.

About two hours later we lay awake listening to the radio. This was one of our rituals. The quiet storm on the radio and the lights completely off, each one of us lost in her own thoughts. Mine were on an idea for my novel I began to write just two days ago, and occasionally Mike would sneak himself somewhere in the middle of it all. That was until I felt someone other than the three of us in our room. My face was to the wall so I turned over to face the middle of the floor, the space between Lonna's bunk bed and New-New's bed.

"New-New, cut the lamp on," I said.

"Why, what's wrong?"

"I don't know. Just cut the lamp on."

Sure enough as soon as New-New reached over to the nightstand and cut the light on, we saw Bree lying fast asleep in the middle of the floor. There was no telling how long she'd been there, but she was quite comfortable with her own pillow and a sheet.

"What are we gonna do with her?" I asked no one in particular.

New-New got out of bed, and scooped Bree up off of the floor. Even though New-New was easily the skinniest one in the house, she was extremely strong. I grabbed Bree's pillow and sheet and we took her back into her room where we tucked her into her own bed.

"At least she's sleep now," New-New said as we slipped back into our own beds.

When I woke up around one that morning, Bree was in the bed next to New-New.

The thunderstorm outside is what woke me up. I looked over at New-New and Bree sleeping across from me. Then I stretched my neck to see Lonna on the bed above me. She was fast asleep too. None of them had heard a thing.

The radio was still playing as I quietly climbed out of the bed and crept out of the door. I tried my best to make it down the stairs, but they were old and creaked under every footstep no matter how softly I tried to walk. I figured if someone woke up, I could just say I was going to get water, if that someone wasn't Lonna because she would quickly see through that.

The clock on the VCR in the living room read one-thirty. I didn't know if Chiloe was still up or not. I knew he kept late hours sometimes, but maybe the storm put him to sleep. As I entered the basement, though, the smell of marijuana hit me right in the face. I debated going back up the stairs thinking maybe he wasn't alone. But for some reason I kept on down the carpeted steps.

It was dark and I could hear his radio going. I prayed that he wasn't with a girl. I did not want to cause anybody any embarrassment, including myself.

Chiloe was alone. He sat on the old pleather couch that smelled like it was made out of cigarette smoke, smoking a blunt. The only form of light in the room came from outside his sliding glass door along with the power button and digital display on the stereo.

He heard my footsteps and turned around.

"Oh, hey. What's up?"

"Nothin'. Can I come in?"

"Yeah come on."

I walked over to the couch. Chiloe put the blunt out and sat it in the little tin ashtray on his wooden coffee table in front of the couch. I knew he would never offer me any. Chiloe didn't want New-New, Lonna, and I doing any of that.

"Why you up so late?" He asked me.

I saw that before I interrupted him, he had been sketching in a notebook. It lay between us on the couch now with a pencil stuck in the spirals. I picked it up and looked at the picture of a Mercedes with rims, sitting low with a spoiler on the back.

"The thunder woke me up," I said. "This is good. Can I look at the rest of them?"

He shrugged his shoulders and nodded. Then he leaned back.

"Why are you up?" I asked flipping through the various cars and naked girls.

He shrugged again. "I couldn't sleep I guess."

I nodded, understanding completely until I came to a picture of a girl with long hair. Her hair covered half of her right eye and the right side of her face. She seemed to be looking down at something.

"Is this me?" I asked trying to keep a casual tone of voice.

Chiloe just nodded.

"I like it."

Then I closed the notebook. I didn't want to see another picture of me. I wasn't sure if I would wrap my arms around his neck and start to kiss him or if I would leave the room in total embarrassment. So I sat the notebook on his coffee table.

I could see the rain steadily pouring down through the sliding glass door across the room. For some reason, probably for the light, the blinds were pulled all the way back. The backyard was beginning to flood and it was cold down here in this basement. I shivered involuntarily.

"You cold?" Chiloe asked me sitting up.

I nodded and watched him get up off the couch. He took the brown and gold comforter with a leopard in the middle, off of his bed. Then he sat back down beside me, wrapping the comforter around me so tight I couldn't move my arms. He let his arms rest around me. I figured he was just high, but when I looked into his eyes, there was none of that high dazedness. He was not the kind to get high easily, he did it too much and too often. His tolerance for marijuana was very strong.

"Is that better?" He asked in my ear and I shivered. This time from his warm breath on my skin. We had never been this close before.

"Yeah."

"You know you can relax. I'm not gonna hurt you. You're too young for me."

Was that supposed to make me feel better? I knew him well enough to know he wasn't going to rape me. But there was still something about him that made me terribly nervous. I watched him do so many bad things to so many people and I wondered what the difference was between me and them. The same way he treated the various girls around this neighborhood, he could do to me in a heartbeat. For that very reason, I refused to let myself get caught up in him. Yes, I loved the looks he gave me and the attention he bestowed on me. But that was as far as I could let it go. I had been infatuated with older guys before and I knew Chiloe's track record was horrible. I refused to take his advances and the knowing looks Lonna gave me, seriously.

So I relaxed against his naked chest and let him play with my hair with one hand. The other hand held mine under the comforter. He said nothing as he breathed heavily on my neck. Goose pimples were beginning to form on my arms.

"Thought you said you weren't cold anymore," Chiloe whispered to me and the sweet smell of marijuana flowed into my nose and mouth.

"I'm not."

"What do you wanna do, Karla? With your life?"

I looked at him and wondered if he really wanted to know. Then I told him. "I want to be a writer."

"A writer? What do you write?"

"Poems, short stories, novels."

"How long you been writing?"

"Since I learned how to."

He looked at me and smiled. "Write me a poem."

"When, now?"

"Naw, whenever you get a chance."

I nodded, knowing full well that I would not. The last thing I wanted to do was start writing this man poetry. What would be the point?

"So what else?"

I shrugged. "I guess I want a family. I really don't know though."

"What's wrong with the one you have?"

I looked up at him. "Who? My mom and my grandma? It's just me my mom and my grandma. That's what's wrong. Why do you think I come over here all the time?"

"I thought it was fun being an only child."

I shook my head. "It's lonely. I mean I got a little cousin, but it's still lonely. If I do ever have kids, I won't have just one."

He laughed and I felt it in his chest. "Yeah, but don't have nine."

I smiled into his face. "What you wanna to do with your life, Chiloe?"

He just shrugged all the time looking out the window at the rain. "I don't know. I guess I wanna be able to have stuff and give my family stuff without having to hustle for it."

His hand began to get tighter around mine, but not enough to hurt. Just enough for me to feel the contours, scrapes and blemishes of it.

"I want a wife. A good wife. Not one of these hood rats running around here, neither."

I wondered if he would even recognize a good woman when he did find her. With the way he treated women I seriously doubted that he would. Then I wondered if a good woman would ever find him. I doubted that too.

He leaned over and kissed my cheek. The flirting was on as I ever so slightly moved my body against his. It was like dangling a piece of candy in front of his face. A piece that he couldn't have. But I liked the way his breathing became heavy whenever I moved closer to him. He let go of my hand and slid his arm around my waste.

"I know I can't have you, girl. But damn if I don't want you so bad."

He was squeezing me and running his lips along my neck and cheek. I turned my face slightly to his so he could stare into my beautiful brown eyes and his lips caught mine right between his. I had to admit his lips were soft and the kiss was so sweet. My heart and my mind were doing battle against each other. Even as he released my lips, without even trying to sneak his tongue in my mouth, my heart hurt from getting beat up.

I watched his green eyes travel all over my face as if making sure I was real before he kissed me again. "I love you," he whispered into my lips.

"No you don't," it was an automatic response. Something that I didn't even have to think about.

"Yes I do. I've loved you since the first day I saw you."

I was refusing to believe this. This twenty-year old man wanted me and was in love with me. Any other fourteen-year old girl would have been in heaven undoubtedly. And while in heaven, her panties would have come off with a quickness. But I was not that regular girl.

"How many other females have you said that to?"

He shook his head, licked his lips, and positioned his forehead right up against mine all at the same time. "None."

"You're lying," I said not really feeling that he was. There was something so sincere in the way he looked at me.

"No I'm not. You can ask any girl around here if I ever told them I loved them. If they say yeah, they liein'. Tell them to come say that shit to my face, and I bet they won't."

Then his lips were on my neck, ear and cheek again. My mind was starting to lose again. I watched through an aroused drunken haze as he stood up before me and pulled me up with him. The next thing I knew, we were standing at his bed. Then laying down on it. Kissing. His hands never moved below my waste, except to gently caress my legs. He pulled the sheet of his bed up to cover us and rested his muscular body on top of mine. I could hardly breathe but it was okay. I could feel the strong beat of his heart through my thin t-shirt as he began to kiss me again.

My senses were aware of everything going on around us. The hip hop music playing on his stereo, the slight smell of dry rot, the rain pouring down outside, the rattling of the heater, the creaking of the bed, the scent of marijuana. The feel of his hands on me.

"Wait," he said abruptly and got off of the bed. I watched him as he walked to the door of the basement and locked it. Then he walked back to the bed seemingly unaware of the huge bulge in the front of his shorts. He stared me down intensely as he approached the bed and lay down beside me. Then he wrapped his arms around me and pulled me close to him until we were sharing a pillow.

I tried to think of something to say, but my mind was pulling up blanks. It seemed that no words could fit this situation. Apparently he felt the same way. So he kissed me again.

The rain had stopped but I was freezing. I didn't know what time I fell asleep but I felt well rested. I needed to get back upstairs quickly.

The bed creaked under my weight, waking Chiloe as I tried to slide off.

"I guess you gotta go back upstairs before your girls start looking for you."

I nodded. Then I said, "Don't worry. I'm not gonna tell anybody."

He shrugged as if he didn't care and sat down beside me on the edge of the bed. "Didn't nothin' happen. It ain't like we had sex."

I moved away from the bed and Chiloe grabbed my arm.

"I meant everything I said last night."

He was pulling me closer to him until I sat on his lap. The smell of his breath was stale now because of the weed and it was turning my stomach. I didn't move, however. I stayed where I was.

"What are we gonna do now?" He asked me.

I knew there was no possibility of us having a relationship. I didn't trust him with my heart. I probably never would. "I don't think there's anything for us to do," I said plain and simple.

He just nodded. He didn't ask me why, but he couldn't look me in my eyes. It felt like the subject was dropped.

I got up off of his lap and headed back upstairs.

"So where were you at last night?" Lonna asked me on our way to the basketball court.

She hadn't said a word about me being missing all morning even though she was awake when I climbed back up the stairs to her room. New-New was still asleep. I thought maybe she figured I'd gone down to watch television. I should have known better. Nothing ever got past her.

Even though she was up later than us, New-New had already left to go to the basketball court to see Andrew. This was unusual because we always traveled together. Lonna and I figured something was going on so we stopped dragging our butts and got out of the house as quickly as we could.

"I think you already know," I replied. I wasn't going to look at her.

"So, did y'all do *it* ?"

She was always so blunt and forward with everything. I blushed.

"No. But it was still nice."

She sighed and out of the corner of my eyes I could see her shaking her head. "So what's gonna happen?"

I shook my head this time. "Nothing."

She didn't say a word. She didn't need to. She always understood me without saying a word.

95

"Oh shit," she mumbled as we neared the basketball court. Even though it was cold the sun was extra bright and I had to shield my eyes to see what she was talking about.

New-New was surrounded by four girls. She was face to face with one and from what I could tell, they were arguing back and forth. New-New didn't have on her gold jewelry (rings, earrings, bracelets, and necklaces), which she never left the house without. Her hair was back in a ponytail and she wore a purple sweat suit with snow white tennis shoes. Fighting clothes, why hadn't I noticed that when she left the house?

"Is there a problem here," I said pushing my way between New-New and the other girl. She was a whole foot taller than me. Her skin was light brown and her eyes were so slanted I didn't think she could see out of them. I had seen her around the neighborhood before. She had beef with us for no reason at all. The other girls around her followed her lead in not liking us.

Lonna was already taking off her earrings and slipping them into a pocket on her jeans, but fighting was the last thing I wanted to do this afternoon.

"This bitch better learn to stay out my man's face!" New-New yelled, mainly in my ear.

I was never much of a fighter. Truth be told, I'd only been in one fight in my whole life and I lost. That was way back in the fifth grade.

"Who you callin' a bitch," the girl said stepping closer to New-New and I. At the same time her girls moved closer too.

Lonna pushed me out of the way and stood with both of her arms stretched out. "Fuck all this talkin'. If you wanna go, let's go. If not, get the hell on."

New-New wasn't about to wait for the girl to decide if she wanted to fight or not. Once again, I was pushed out of the way and New-New swung at the girl with the slanted eyes over Lonna's head. The girl swung back but caught Lonna in the cheek. And the fight was on because Lonna was pissed. We fought and fought, outnumbered four to three, with everybody pounding on somebody.

Then I felt someone pulling on the collar of my windbreaker. I watched through blurry eyes as Rosie pulled New-New and Lonna, one by one, from the circle of violence that had erupted on the damp cold ground of the basketball court. I wondered where she came from as she told the other girls to take their beat up behinds home. And beat up they were. Even though there had been three against four, we'd done a pretty good job. New-New's hair had come out of her pony tail. There was a ball of black hair on the ground that I guessed was Lonna's.

"What are y'all doing?" Rose asked.

"What are *you* doing?" Lonna asked. "Ain't you supposed to be home with your husband and kid?"

Rosie ignored the question. "Who's boyfriend y'all out here fighting over?"

We inadvertently looked at New-New, who lay back on the ground propped up on her elbows. She stared straight ahead as if this whole scene had been perfectly normal.

"How many times have I told y'all there's only one thing on this earth worth fightin' over? And that's money."

We all sighed heavily and rolled our eyes.

"Now if this nigga' ain't payin' your way, ain't no point in fightin' over him. Y'all better learn." She pointed one long fake red fingernail at us.

A red Cadillac Seville pulled up to the corner of the basketball court and stopped.

"Y'all go on home. I gotta go. Don't tell nobody y'all saw me."

'Nobody' was basically her husband. Even though Rosie was married to one of the nicest men I had ever met, and had a three

98

month old son, she was still hustling. But just to buy the drugs that she was now taking on a regular basis. Even though Kerry would have given her anything under the sun, he would never fund her drug habit, if he even knew about it.

We watched her in her tight black leather skirt and leather jacket, walk towards the car. First she leaned in the driver side window. Then she walked around to the passenger side and got in. The car drove off quickly.

I put some ice in a zip lock bag for New-New's eye after I combed out Lonna's hair. A few strands were still shedding, but there was no huge bald spot like she was afraid there would be. After I combed it, I brushed it and braided it into one long braid down her back. None of us were putting much account into what Rosie said. But I still had quite a few questions of my own.

"Can anybody tell me why we just got in a fight?" I asked handing New-New the ice. The skin around her eye was steadily growing darker and darker.

"Damned if I know?" Lonna said fiddling with her pony tail.

"Because every time I turn around that ho is up in my man's face. I had to let her know." New –New took the ice away from her eye. "Thank y'all for having my back though."

"You knew better than going up there by yourself," Lonna said.

The front door swung open and banged against the wall like it always did when Chiloe opened it. Our eyes locked for a brief second as he was followed into the house by Bree and Little Jay. Then he looked at Lonna and New-New.

"What happened to y'all?"

"We got in a fight," Lonna said.

"Fight!" Bree seemed very excited. "With who?"

"Some girls."

Chiloe took New-New's hand away from her eye to look at it. Then he examined Lonna's puffy cheek. Next he looked at me. "Where are your injuries?" He asked holding my chin and moving my face from side to side. Then he looked straight into my eyes.

"I don't have any."

"Why not?"

"'Cause she's a better fighter than we are," Lonna said laughing. She knew how funny that was.

"No, I just know how to duck and move."

Chiloe let go of my face and smiled. I glanced quickly at Lonna who just looked up at the ceiling.

"Let me guess, you were fighting over a boy." He was addressing me and I was compelled to make it clear that it wasn't *my* boy. Lonna did it for me though.

"Talk to New-New."

"Man, you fightin' over that boy again?" Bree said laughing and shaking her head.

"What'cha mean again?" I asked looking at New-New too.

"This is the third fight she done got in over that boy," Lonna said. "He keeps telling her to stop it, but she acts like she done lost her mind or something. And he's just as crazy as she is. He done been in four or five. He got suspended from school last week!"

I looked at New-New thoroughly confused. Was somebody that made you feel as if you had to fight over them constantly, really worth all the trouble? I didn't think so. And why didn't I know about these other fights? No wonder she'd gone to the basketball court by herself.

Chiloe always took the long way whenever he drove me home after a weekend with Lonna and New-New. Especially when it was just the two of us. Today, however, felt different. It was just three o'clock on Sunday afternoon. I fought hard to keep from going down to the basement the night before. All the tossing and turning that I did woke Lonna up.

"Why don't you just go on down there," she said leaning her head over the side of the bed and looking down at me.

"What are you talking about?" I was playing dumb but I didn't know why I even bothered.

"You know what I'm talking about."

"I can't make it a habit of going down there."

She smacked her teeth and lay back down. "I don't see why not."

Chiloe pulled into the parking lot of a park off of the boulevard. Despite the cool weather, there were quite a few cars around and the park was packed with children.

I looked around. Then over at him.

"I just wanna be alone with you for awhile." Then he grabbed my hand. "When are you coming back?"

"I don't know."

He never asked me that. Usually I just popped up when I popped up.

"Why?" I asked.

He shook his head as he caressed and kissed my hand. His cheeks were becoming pink. "I can't stop thinking about you."

He didn't know that I couldn't stop thinking about him either. But for different reasons. I felt fear around the center of my chest with just the mere thought of him. I was young, and I realized that. What I was doing here with him, I didn't know.

"I just wanna know one thing. Then I'll leave you alone."

I looked at him knowing pretty much what he was going to say before he even opened his mouth.

"Do you feel the same way about me?"

I wanted to run and hide or something. Anything to keep from answering that question. I couldn't even think of a remark to change the subject.

"I don't know," I said shrugging.

I hated the way he was looking into my eyes and the pressure he was putting on my hand. I looked over at the children on the swing to keep from looking at him any longer.

"Why not?" He asked me.

I had known Chiloe for two years. And I had never seen him act this way. All the girls who cried and swooned and pouted over him, I'd never seen him act this way over not one. But that still didn't excuse the fact that I knew what he was capable of.

"Chiloe, I know how you treat females your own age. So I can imagine what you would do to me."

He sat back and looked at me astonished. "You don't trust me?"

I shook my head slowly. Wasn't that what love was all about? Trust?

"I've never treated you like any of those chicks. You know that. What I said the other night don't mean nothin' I guess."

I hated the fact that he was angry with me. But my heart would not let me be untruthful to him. I had to admit I felt better, even if he didn't.

"I thought we agreed that we were going to let this go?" I asked trying my best to calm him down.

He looked at me and shook his head. "We ain't agree to nothin'. You said it shouldn't go any further, not me."

"What is it you want from me?" I asked quite frustrated by now. This was a situation that I did not want to be in. The last thing I wanted to do was hurt Chiloe, but I didn't want to be hurt neither.

That one question seemed to end all questions, at least for that moment. Chiloe just shook his head and started the car. The rest of the drive home was silent.

I sat down on New-New's bed and gazed around the room. The wooden beds, the old rickety dresser with traces of hair spray on the mirror, the creaky floor. How would I begin to heal, if there was even such a thing? Why did this have to happen to me, but I wouldn't have wished it on anyone else?

My mind was inflicted with the thought that I was almost Kelly Gordon's wife. How would our children have looked? Where would we have lived? How long would we have stayed married? Would I still have loved him like I did when he died?

I consoled myself a little by convincing my heart that we probably wouldn't have made it to marriage. By the time I reached high school, Kelly Gordon would have been forgotten anyway. Then I told myself, we didn't make a good couple. We were way too different. Him being so serious, always up on world issues and the problems of Black people around the world. We didn't have a thing in common. It was all puppy love for me. Being with an older man was exciting for me. I'm sure it would have worn off soon though.

I took my engagement ring, finally having the nerve to touch it after all these weeks, and put it in my underwear drawer. Maybe I would give it to my first born daughter.

There was a loud knock at my door.

"Come in," I said closing the drawer quickly. I had no idea why. There was no secret to keep anymore.

A face that I hadn't seen in a week peeped through the small opening he made with the door. Then he came in making sure to close the door behind him.

"Where have you been?" I asked Chiloe wanting to run and hug him. But I maintained.

He sat on New-New's bed in the same spot I sat in two seconds ago. "I was in Erwin, at Rajul's. His new house."

"You could've told somebody where you were going."

"I couldn't Lonna. I just had a lot of shit on my mind. I needed some time to think and recuperate."

I wondered what in the world he was talking about as I sat down beside him. I knew something happened between him and Karla. When he dropped her off at her house that Sunday, he came back a little disturbed. She wasn't saying much of anything about him.

"What's wrong?" I asked.

He shook his head dismissing that whole line of questioning. Then he said, "Them boys that got Kelly . . ."

I knew instantly what he was going to pronounce to me. I didn't want to hear anymore but I couldn't stop listening.

". . . they been took care of."

I knew he did it. And the realization of it was enough to knock my mind into a zone. I always figured my brother had murdered someone in the past, just judging by the type of person he was, New-New had even joked about it a few times. But now, without a doubt, I really knew. I also knew Kelly would not have wanted it this way. Kelly had never been violent, he hated violence. This would have made him sick.

"It's not going to solve anything," I said shaking my head slowly. "It's not gonna bring him back."

Then I sighed heavily. I was tired all of a sudden.

"If I could bring him back, I would." Chiloe stood up. "But I can't. This is the next best thing."

"For who?"

He turned around and looked at me, realizing the weight of my question and knowing he couldn't answer it.

Then he walked out.

Chapter Six

Saturday, April 11, 1992 2:00 p.m.

Why were we out here at the basketball court as cold as it was?

I was snuggled in Mike's Raider's Starter jacket, but it didn't seem to be doing any good. His scent was heavy on the coat and it felt good to be breathing it in. But it wasn't doing any good. Even the cap pulled halfway down over my face, wasn't doing any good.

"Girl," Lonna said lifting the edge of the cap up so that she could see my eyes. "It's not that cold out here. With Mike's jacket on, you bound to get jumped."

She motioned her head towards the group of girls standing by a gold Buick Skylark. There had to be about eight of them and I recognized three from the fight New-New, Lonna and I had been in two months earlier. I also saw Marjorie, the girl that tried her little heart out to get Chiloe's attention at Rosie's seventeenth birthday party. It wasn't until three weeks later that Lonna told me the girl had been pregnant by Chiloe. He'd given her money to have an abortion that she didn't want, and had hardly spoken to the girl since. They all seemed to be staring at me now flaunting Mike's jacket and hat.

Mike was back at the house with Chiloe and everyone else playing craps on the deck. Andrew was with them and as New-New kissed him goodbye, Mike noticed the thin jacket I wore. I had no idea it would be so cold in the middle of April.

"Here," he said standing up from his kneeling position on the deck floor and began taking his jacket off. Everyone on the deck watched as he wrapped it around me and zipped it up. Then he removed the hat that he was wearing and shoved it down, unnecessarily hard, on my head.

Stunned at the fact that this boy who had never said more than two words to me was now protecting me from the harsh wind, I still summoned up the nerve to complain. "You gonna mess my hair up."

"Shut up. Who you tryin' to look good for anyway?"

I smiled and he smiled back at me. I couldn't remember ever seeing him smile before. I guess I hadn't paid close attention. He had a beautiful smile that stretched from ear to ear with sweet deep dimples. He was only wearing a long sleeved thin shirt under the jacket and now he shivered from the cold.

"You gonna be okay?" I asked feeling everyone's eyes on us, but also feeling that they weren't even there.

"Yeah, I'll be alright."

Then he went back to playing craps like nothing had ever happened.

"I wish she would come over here," New-New said referring to Marjorie. "I can't stand that girl."

"You better not wish they'll come over here. There's a hundred of them and three of us." I was compelled to remind Lonna and New-New of this. They both loved to fight, New-New over Andrew and Lonna just for the hell of it. Since Kelly's passing, it was fast becoming one of Lonna's favorite past times. Sometimes they forgot we were vastly outnumbered.

"What's up with that anyway?" Lonna asked still watching the boys on the court but referring to the jacket I wore. The boys on the court today were mostly gang bangers that we didn't know. Or at least didn't associate with.

"I don't know," I said plainly just shrugging it off. I refused to get my hopes up concerning anyone, especially Chiloe's cohorts. I was more like a trophy than anything else.

"Let's go y'all," New-New said standing up from her spot on the bleachers. We had already been out here for thirty minutes.

"Hey yo!" We heard behind us as we headed away from the court and down the street. The three of us turned around at the same time.

One of the gang bangers from the basketball court was limping up behind us. I couldn't tell if there was something wrong with his leg or if he thought that it was just something that was cute. Either way, it wasn't cute and I didn't like him being so close to us.

"Oh lord," New-New said grabbing my arm. "Come on let's go."

I knew something wasn't right about him if New-New didn't even want to deal with him. She was the most fearless person I knew, besides Lonna. So I turned back around preparing to head back to the safety of the house.

But I felt the grip on the hood of Mike's jacket and a tight ball of panic formed in my stomach. I was suddenly paralyzed from the waist down. My girls must have heard the horrifying gasp that caught loudly in my throat because they turned around. I could see the fright on their faces.

Scared to death, but still, Lonna was Lonna. "You better let her go, Naheem."

"Naw," he said calmly and the grip on the jacket tightened. The smell of liquor was engulfing me and I just knew I was going to throw up. Out of the corner of my eye, I could see New-New sprinting up the street.

"You think you cute don't you?" He asked me. There was crust in his eyes that looked to be about two days old and his lips were disgustingly chapped as if they would split at any moment. In the corner of his mouth were dry white spots that stood out in great contrast to his coal black but ashy skin. His nasty, ugly face was an inch away from mine and I was an inch away from hurling right on him.

I swallowed hard and didn't say a word. I felt Lonna close to me, trying to pull me away. But his grip was getting tighter and tighter.

"You think 'cause you got on your little boyfriend's jacket, I'm supposed to be scared. Man, fuck that nigga' Chiloe."

He thought this was Chiloe's jacket. He had one just like it. And apparently he thought I was Chiloe's girl. My arm was starting to hurt and I could feel the tears starting to wail up in my eyes. I could've kicked myself for showing even the slightest hint of being afraid, and for wearing Mike's jacket that day, and for even going to the basketball court.

Naheem's dirty hands were clutching my chin tightly. "Give me a kiss, girl," he spat at me.

I closed my lips so tightly they were becoming numb as I felt a cold tear slide down my cheek. Lonna was still holding on to the sleeve of the jacket trying her best to free me.

But before he could put his pasty cracked lips on me, before the most grotesque thing that I could ever imagine happened to me, it stopped. His hands were off of my face and he'd let go of the jacket. I opened my closed eyes and saw him heading back to his friends who had stopped playing ball and were watching us.

As Lonna wrapped her arms around me, I looked up the street and could see Chiloe and every boy that had been on the deck with him in tow. New-New was leading the way. Before I knew it, she had her arms around me too.

"What happened?" Chiloe asked wiping away the tears from my face.

As I opened my mouth to say something, New-New answered for me.

"Naheem grabbed her and wouldn't let her go," she said.

"He tried to make her kiss him," Lonna chimed in.

"He touched my butt last week," New-New told Andrew.

Andrew's grey eyes turned green, I was amazed. I didn't know that was possible. "He touched your butt?" He asked her.

New-New nodded. "It won't no big deal. But he grabbed Karla and he wouldn't let her go."

Andrew looked at Chiloe and they both started to walk over to the basketball court. I was grabbed gently from behind by Mike who pulled me into his arms.

The boys had gone back to their game like nothing had happened. But Chiloe and Andrew weren't concerned with the other boys. They just bypassed them. One of them had just passed the ball to Naheem. It bounced right out of his hands as Chiloe hit him. One hit with his right fist and the boy fell to the ground with a loud and sickening thump.

Andrew and Chiloe were on top of him then, stomping him into the hard asphalt like he was nothing more than a roach. His fellow gang members stood nervously by just watching. None of them made a move to help him and I didn't know if it was because of Mike and the other five boys that stood surrounding us.

Whatever the reason, their boy didn't seem to be doing much fighting back at all. Andrew was on one knee pounding into the boy's head with a tightly closed fist. Chiloe was still kicking the life out of him and stepping on him with his hard Timberland boots, wherever he could.

Then I heard the police siren. I didn't know if it was near or far, if it was headed here or somewhere else, but I felt the panic rise up in me like vomit. Before my mind caught up with the rest of me, I broke away from Mike's tight embrace and headed towards Chiloe. I grabbed him by the waste of his jeans and tried my best to pull him off of Naheem. He felt my tugging and turned to look at me, foot still poised to land another kick to the side of the boy's body.

"Come on, Chiloe," I pleaded with him. "That's enough."

He put his foot down, looked at me, and nodded. Andrew got up slowly and I could finally see Naheem's face. What was left of it, anyway. His blood covered the blacktop like graffiti and his right eye seemed to hang from the socket.

I broke back through the crowd that had formed around us, still feeling queasy, but I could breathe easily because it was over. Until I turned around to see Chiloe wasn't behind me like I thought he would be. Instead I saw him take Naheem's left leg into both of his massive hands and twist it. The sound of bone was almost deafening to me as I heard the pop and crunch.

Naheem couldn't even let out a moan because of the blood that filled his mouth. And now his right leg wasn't even attached to his body.

I watched Chiloe carefully and almost lovingly clean the blood from his Tim's as he sat on a stool in front of me on his bed.

After Andrew's public display of affection, he and New-New retired to her room. Lonna lay on Chiloe's couch watching television like nothing happened.

"Why you pull me off of him?" Chiloe asked not even looking at me. Tim in one hand, white washcloth in the other.

"I heard the police coming." I shrugged it off already regretting my decision. Would he think we were more than what we were, or that I cared more than I did?

"You didn't want me to go to jail?" He asked grinning.

"Why would I?"

"Well, you don't trust me. Maybe that's the best place for me."

"Oh lord," Lonna said getting up from the couch and heading towards the basement door.

"Where you going?" I asked not making a move to follow her, even though I knew I should.

"Upstairs to eat."

She closed the door behind her and Chiloe and I looked at each other.

117

"Are you okay?" He asked me.

"Yeah."

He went back to cleaning his shoes. "Well my boots not. I'm never gonna be able to get this shit out."

"Why didn't his boys help him?"

Chiloe wiped his forehead with the back of his hand. "Them little wanna be gang bangers, they know me. They know if they don't mess with me and what's mine, I don't mess with them. That little punk Naheem, he just moved here about three months ago. Apparently they hadn't taught him the rules. So I had to teach him."

He stopped then and put the shoe down. "What was up with you and Mike?"

"Nothing." That was the truth even though it was none of his business. Nobody told him to go after Naheem like a Rottweiler.

He eyed me suspiciously and I could tell he didn't really believe me. I didn't really believe me. But that was the only answer I could give right now.

PART 3

Chapter Seven

Friday, November 19, 1993 5:55 p.m.

I could not believe how dreary my world looked from this one little window. I hated winter rains. It just meant colder and drearier weather in a land where the sun was barely shining anyway.

"You ok?" My mom asked me, stepping into the living room. She looked out of the window where I sat in my favorite gold chair with my legs curled up under me.

"Yeah, I guess so."

"Have you prayed?" She asked me.

"All the time."

"Well then everything will be ok."

I wasn't really concerned about everything. Just my Grandmother. What would happen to my family if she passed? Then it hit me that I hadn't really been spending much time with my family at all. Four years to be exact. I had just seemed to adopt a new family and this one seemed sort of obsolete. Of course I really didn't feel that way. It probably looked that way though.

"I'm sorry Momma," I said not even having the courage to look her in the eyes.

"Sorry for what?"

I shrugged and looked down at my home done acrylic nails. They were a soft pink color, so no one could tell they were not professional. Just one of the things Lonna taught me.

"For not being around when y'all needed me. For always being . . ." I stopped not wanting to drag Lonna into it. This was not her fault. "For always being gone."

My mom placed the palm of her left hand on the top of my head. The fact that I was two whole feet taller than her didn't matter now since I sat so low. "Momma's cancer would have come back if you had been around or not. You didn't make her sick."

"I know. But still." I sighed loudly enough to fill my own ears even though the voices of so many other people filled the house. I could see my younger cousin Veronica and her mother standing at the edge of the carport looking out at the rain.

"I just feel like I should have been there more."

My mother shook her head. "You're young. You do what young people do. None of us knew the cancer would come back."

She also caught sight of Veronica. She was raised, almost single handedly by our grandmother. At least I did have my mom and my father's parents not to mention Lonna and her family. But Veronica had no one else besides her mother, my mom's younger sister.

"Everything will be ok," was all she could say.

It was hard to hear the doorbell over the slew of church people and relatives that seemed to crowd my house. This had been going on for two weeks now, every since my grandmother had taken ill with the reoccurrence of her breast cancer that first surfaced ten years ago. Only this time, it all seemed more serious to me. After spending Thanksgiving holiday in the hospital, she was now home but receiving chemotherapy on the regular. The curly black hair that once hung well past her shoulders was now dispelled to patches. Her once husky frame with the straight posture was now frail, weak, and hunched over. She wasn't the grandmother I had known all my life that practically raised me.

I made my way from my room, where I sat by yet another window listening to the radio and jotting down words in no particular form and calling it a poem, through the crowd of people in the kitchen and onto the back door. I always wondered why people came to the back door instead of the front. Why they never took the time to climb the stairs to the wide porch surrounded by a bed of flowers of all different types. Why they never bothered to knock on the synthetic wood of the huge, ancient maroon door that had been there since I was a baby. I wondered all of these things as I opened the back door to see Mike standing under the carport. His eyes watched the door expectantly from under his baseball cap that I was beginning to think was attached to his head. It matched the black t-shirt under his leather bomber and black jeans that he wore loosely around his waist but seemed to fit his hips perfectly.

"Hey," I said stepping outside of the door and closing it before I could get any questions from my mom or other family members. It wasn't that my mom was strict about things like this, boys visiting and so on. In fact she was very lenient when it came to my male visitors. She knew me and knew that boys liked me. But I couldn't begin to explain what Mike was doing on my porch because I didn't know myself.

"What's up?" He asked smiling at me showing all dimples. He was much too cute and I felt my body involuntarily give way to shivers.

"Nothing much. What's up with you?" I pulled my white bandana that was tied neatly around my head down further on my forehead so that he couldn't see my eyes, knowing that this line of conversation was just so I could get to why he was really here. Had Chiloe sent him?

"I just came by to see how you were doing. I haven't seen you around lately. And I was hoping you were ok."

I smiled flattered but leery. Why all of a sudden was he concerned about me? I didn't understand. True, I hadn't been to Lonna's house in three weeks. I felt an obligation to be at home with my grandmother being sick. Mainly because of all the time I had already spent away from home. But I talked to Lonna every day.

A gust of wind rolled by blowing in some cold rain. I shivered, but this time just from the weather. "Well my grandmother's been sick, so I haven't really felt like hanging out."

"Oh, I'm sorry to hear that. For real. Is there anything I can do?"

I didn't mean to make the facial expression I know I made. The wrinkling of my eyebrows, and the squinting of my eyes. I didn't really mean to do that. But why all of a sudden did he want to do things for me? Once again my thoughts ran back to Chiloe.

"No, I'm cool."

He looked at me through his dark eyes, that were partially shaded by his cap, like he could read my mind and he knew better. Like I needed him, I just didn't know it yet. At that moment I felt a cold rush shoot through my arms giving me major goose pimples up and down my body, perking my nipples, along with the undeniable urge to kiss his well rounded lips.

"Well, I guess I'll let you get back to your family. I just wanted to make sure you were ok."

"Alright then. I'll see you later."

I didn't stick around in the cold wet air to watch him walk back to his car. But I did peep out of the small window of the door, from behind the lime green curtains to watch him drive away.

"He didn't say what he wanted?" Lonna asked me.

I sighed and turned over on the familiar bunk bed. It seemed like I had been sleeping here all my life, but in reality it had only been four years. Maybe Mike's coming over had been a good thing, it had finally gotten me over to Lonna's. My home away from home.

"Do you really think Chiloe would put him up to that? I mean with him liking you as much as he does, I doubt he would send one of his boys over to see you. And I think Mike has probably liked you forever anyway."

"I don't know. I just felt like the whole thing was a set up."

"Why didn't you ask him?"

"Ask him what? How?"

She sighed like I was taxing her brain. "Ask him who sent his ass over your house and why."

I shook my head even though I knew she couldn't see me in the pitch blackness of the bedroom. She was almost completely submerged in the cover on New-New's bed that had been unoccupied for quite some time. Now that she was pregnant with Andrew's baby, there was no need in New-New staying home and pretending that they weren't doing the damn thing every chance they could. Bree lay on the bunk above me, fast asleep.

"So . . ." she said. I could see her shadow sitting up. I knew I was getting ready to be asked a ridiculous question that I wouldn't know the answer to. "Do you like him?"

See.

"I don't know. I never really thought about him like that. I mean I have but I didn't entertain it for long."

"Uh huh."

"But I'm not thinking about him like that now. I've got too much going on for real. My grandmother is sick and I don't know what's going on with her."

"Yeah I understand."

I sighed and turned over on my back now, just staring off into the thick darkness. Soft music continued to play. That seemed to be the only constant in our lives. Slow jams on the radio Monday through Friday, ten o'clock till two.

"When did shit get so complicated Lonna? When did we start worrying about people's motives, when did it become unsafe for us to go to the basketball court unless we had a group of boys with us to stomp somebody's brains out? When did we have to start worrying about one of us getting pregnant? When did we have to start worrying about our boyfriends . . ." I stopped and caught myself.

"Dying?" She asked. Her voice seemed small all of a sudden in this huge room.

"Yeah."

"I don't know Karla."

All that I could say was, "I want things back the way they were."

Chapter Eight

Thursday, June 3, 1993 10:03 p.m.

The bones in my right hand were being crushed together as New-New squeezed them, slowly draining the blood out of my finger tips, turning them white. I was pretty sure I wasn't feeling as much as she was, but I was damn near close.

"I can see something," Andrew said peering over the shoulder of the doctor, between her legs, like he was reading the newspaper.

"That's the head," the doctor informed him. "Now give me three big pushes."

And big they were. I grimaced, pretty sure I could feel that big ol' head coming out of me. And then Lenora Alise McCarthy entered the world. Seven pounds, ten ounces, with a head full of sandy red hair. The doctor placed her on New-New's stomach which was now fully exposed due to her thrashing around like a mad woman. Lenora let out a wail like a dying monkey and then began to cry normally. I swore at that moment that I would never have a child, as I walked out of the room leaving the new mother and father with their baby and the hospital staff.

My mother sat in the waiting room on the edge of her seat. Hands folded in her lap trying her best to concentrate on whatever was on television. Around her sat Bree, Jay and Marco. Chiloe had gone to the parking lot to smoke a cigarette or something even stronger.

"It's a girl," I announced to everyone what we had already known. My mother stood up and put her hands together. Sort of like she was clapping. Bree was just happy to be an aunt. Jay continued playing with his Game boy after acknowledging me with one look and a nod of his head. Marco clapped his hands and thanked God.

"What did she name her?" Bree asked grabbing me around my waist. She was the touchiest, feeliest thirteen-year old in the world.

"Lenora, and get off of me." I pushed her away playfully.

"What does she look like?" My mom asked.

"Go see." I was not about to try and explain the look of that baby. Her hair was red and her eyes were green. Her skin was a very tan, almost orange color. She looked like both her mother and father, who favored each other anyway.

My mother excitedly bumbled out of the room and I sat down beside Marco. I felt my whole body collapse into the worn plastic seat, piece by piece. I had been in the delivery room with my twin sister since ten o'clock that morning. The true thug in her refused any kind of pain medication so I had to suffer along with her as she screamed in agony and bounced from one side of the bed to the other. Finally, the doctor told her she had to lie down and open her legs. My eardrums burned from her blood curdling howls of pain and my arms hurt from supporting her weight, holding her legs open, and letting her crush my bones. All I wanted to do now was close my eyes, listen to the soft hum of the television until I became unconscious.

But then Chiloe burst into the room. "What happened? Did she have it?"

"Yeah," Marco informed him before I could summon up the energy to open my eyes.

"For real?" He asked as much as excited as my mom had been. "Where are they? Are they still in the room?"

"Yeah they're still in there. Mom just went down there to see them."

"Anybody call Karla."

Damn I had forgotten all about Karla. She was dealing with her grandmother's illness though and I hated to bother her. The chemotherapy had failed and because her grandmother had suffered a mild heart attack, radiation was now out of the question. She knew it wouldn't be long before she passed away so I hadn't seen her in two weeks. I understood though, and I called her every day. But today, for the first time in four years, she had totally slipped my mind.

"No I haven't called her."

"Well call her and ask her if she wants me to come get her."

I looked at him now out of one eye, suspiciously. Karla had her own car; she'd had it for four months. A black Nissan Sentra. If she needed anything, it wasn't a ride. Before I could peel myself out of the soft cushion of the waiting room chair, my mom burst back into the room. A pillar of joy, no doubt.

Every since the news of New-New's pregnancy hit home with us, my mother seemed to have made a full turn around. There were no more days and even weeks spent in her room. She was up cleaning and shopping for the baby, making sure New-New had everything that she needed. She even cooked dinner twice. She was beginning to put on weight again and looked much better even though her teeth were still missing and her hair was still patchy.

"Oh she's so beautiful. Come look at her y'all."

"I'll be there in a minute, I'm gonna go call Karla."

She nodded as Bree, Marco, Jay and Chiloe headed out of the waiting room door behind her. I looked down at my watch to see what time it was and hoped that I didn't disturb anyone because it was after ten o'clock. I couldn't believe I had been at this hospital a full twelve hours.

"Hello," Karla answered with sleep heavy in her voice.

"Hey girl, did I wake you?"

"I must have drifted to sleep reading this book. What's up, everything ok?"

"Yeah, New-New had the baby."

"What!" I could picture her sitting up in her bed.

"Yep. She named her just what she said she would."

"Lenora."

I smiled at the way she said it. But New-New picked that name when she started planning to have Andrew's baby. We were twelve years old. "Yep. Lenora."

I could see her smile over the phone and was glad. I knew things had been so rough on her lately.

"Chiloe wants to come get you."

"Uh," she said and I knew it was involuntary. She never did mention the Mike incident that took place a little less than half a year ago. But I knew she still wondered and thought about it often. Mike never said anything about it either, sort of like it never happened. "I'll just drive. How about I just come over to the house when y'all get home? I know New needs her rest and I'll see the baby in the morning."

"That's cool. You can just spend the night. We'll probably be leaving here in another hour, but I'll call you when we get to the crib."

"Ok, I'll see you then."

I hung up the phone and joined the rest of my family in ogling Lenora. Rajul was now with us and even though he and Momma hadn't said more than three words to each other, there didn't seem to be any friction between them anymore.

Lenora looked a lot better now that she was all cleaned up with her striped hat and blanket wrapped around her to match.

"She looks just like Andrew," Bree said in amazement as we peered at her through the big glass window of the nursery.

"How can you tell, him and New-New look just alike," Marco said shaking his head.

"She sure is a funny color," Jay said.

"That's cause she's mixed with everything under the sun," Chiloe laughed.

"She sure is beautiful, I tell you that," my mom said but what did she expect? Two beautiful people could not make an ugly baby. That was impossible.

Karla's brown eyes were bathed in red and I could tell she had been crying. In fact she'd probably cried on the way here. She was never the one to wear makeup, but I could see where the salt from her tears left a stain rolling down her right cheek. Her hair, which she had chopped all off not too long ago, lay uncurled but brushed to the sides so that her tresses didn't lay straight down.

We didn't say a word to each other as she walked into the house and I took her duffel bag. I remembered the big pink suitcase that she used for years, but broke it finally on one of our many trips her mother took us on. She tried to stuff two weeks' worth of clothes in that suitcase for a weekend trip and ended up having to carry them around in big trash bags. I smiled thinking about that and she smiled back at me.

"You ok?" I asked already knowing the answer.

"Yeah, I'm fine," she said. She had too much pride for me to see her cry. And she would never admit that she was in need of comfort. Her pride was bigger and brighter than any peacock.

"Well, you wanna go upstairs or you wanna go chill at the basketball court?"

She shrugged, knowing full well she wanted to go to the basketball court. Yeah the prognosis of her grandmother was bothering her terribly, and yeah the last time we had gone to the basketball court she had almost been kissed by a nasty behind wanna-be gansta', still the thought of going to the basketball court was enough to perk anyone up.

It was now twelve o'clock. But that hadn't stopped any of the people out tonight. It was unusually warm for the beginning of June. The end of the school year was right around the corner for most of us, but Karla's private school let out a week ago. I studied her with her tear stained face and her new hair cut. All the way down to her nails that she'd done herself. I taught her how to do the acrylics so she wouldn't have to pay a Korean woman twenty five dollars to get them done. She looked as if she'd lost weight and I wondered if she was eating ok. I doubted it.

We took a seat on the bleachers and watched the boys play basketball. Mike turned around as soon as he spotted Karla out of the corner of his eye. He dropped the ball he was holding and stood for a good five minutes before the game could resume. Karla's cheeks were flushed and I could tell she was embarrassed. Especially since she didn't really know where Mike's head was at.

"Why all of a sudden is he sweating me like this?" She asked me like I could just pull the answer out of the sky and give it to her.

"I don't know girl. Don't even worry about it. If he's for real, you'll find out soon enough. If he's not, you'll find that out too."

Bobby left his spot from in front of a car that sat parked by the gate of the basketball court. He had been standing with three other dudes.

"Hey, I heard New-New had her baby. Congratulations."

"Thanks," Karla and I spoke in unison.

"A little girl right?"

Again we both nodded.

"Who she look like, cause I know New-New and Andrew look just alike."

"She looks like them," I said smiling. That had to be the hundredth time I'd heard that tonight.

"Oh, that's good. I'm glad she's ok. When do you think she'll be home?"

"Probably a day or two. That's what they were saying when I left. Chiloe said we're gonna have a cookout when they come home."

"That's cool, that's cool. I'll get wit'cha then."

Then he walked away. I noticed his girlfriend, LaShae, had joined the crew of boys. She was our age and very quiet. I hardly ever saw her hang out. Her mother was strict and had been from day one. At twelve o'clock in the morning, she must have snuck out.

"How long he been with her?" Karla asked. I knew she felt like she missed a lot, including most of New-New's pregnancy.

"About two months now."

"Oh."

"He don't hang with Chiloe that much anymore. In fact, Mike don't even hang around that much anymore. I mean, they still come over and stuff but not as much."

"What do you think?"

"As far as Chiloe and Mike, I think that hat and coat incident probably caused a little friction. But who knows."

She shook her head and we continued to watch the boys play. I was loving just being here with her because we had not spent any time together since her grandmother took ill back around the beginning of our tenth grade school year. For her birthday, in March, we ventured to the teen club by the county auditorium. But other than that and the night Mike came to see her; there had been no quality time.

"So your mom's ok with the baby?" She asked finally as Mike tried to shoot a free throw and made it by a hair.

"Yeah, she's excited. She spent the night at the hospital in the waiting room. We couldn't get her home if we called and said the house was on fire. I think she feels like this is a second chance or something. I'm just happy she's happy."

"Are you happy?" She asked looking me dead in my eyes. She was always trying to get into somebody's head.

It had been over two years since Kelly's death. I still kept a picture of him under my pillow, in my locker at school, and on my dresser mirror. I wore my engagement ring on a gold chain around my neck. And the clothes that Kerry gave me that once belonged to Kelly; I wore every chance I got. Not only that, but there had been no one else besides him.

The stresses of my everyday life had brought about habits in me that I knew I never would have otherwise acquired, like smoking weed and drinking. It wasn't an everyday thing and it wasn't abundantly. It was just here and there, socially I guessed. Like when we went to the club for Karla's birthday. I spent the night with her because I was way too drunk to go home. Then there was the dance at school where I took some swigs in the bathroom with some girls from the Court. That wasn't the only practice I had obtained from somewhere. There was the weed too. The weed was much less frequent than the alcohol though. There were fewer people willing to share weed than there were people willing to share alcohol. I had to face it, if I wanted a good high, weed cost money. There was the issue of the smell, also. I didn't even want to imagine what Chiloe would do to me if he smelled it on me.

No I was not happy in the least. I looked over at Karla wanting to tell her everything I was thinking, but not knowing how. So I just shrugged and said, "I'm ok."

She looked at me for a second, not knowing whether to believe me or not. Mike left the other guys on the court and was heading in our direction. I was thankful for the distraction as he stood in front of us, pulling his baggy dark denim shorts up. They were decorated with a woven belt, but that's all it was, decoration.

"What's up?" He asked mainly to Karla.

"Hey," she said looking off in the direction of the basketball court. Her cheeks were flushed again. I didn't know if Mike noticed, but under the light of the basketball court, I sure did.

"What's up Mike?" I asked taking the pressure off of her. "You know New-New had the baby."

"For real?" He finally managed to take his eyes off of her and took his baseball cap off to wipe the sweat from his forehead. Out of the corner of my eye, I could see Karla watching him, almost admiring him. But when he looked back at her, she quickly averted her eyes.

"Yeah, she had a girl. Chiloe's having a cookout when they come home."

I don't know if he heard me or not. It was like he couldn't take his attention away from Karla. Her cheeks were still red. "I see you cut your hair," he said finally.

She looked up at him, as if she hadn't noticed that he was still standing right before her. And without a smile or anything she said, "Yeah."

"It looks nice."

"Thank you."

Then she went back to watching the basketball, which was being tossed up by some kid that was new to the neighborhood. I knew she wasn't just being cold to get rid of him. She really thought Chiloe had put him up to this. I still didn't believe that was the case. He was really digging on her from what I could tell.

"Well tell New-New I said congratulations." He replaced his cap, adjusted his shorts, and went back over the game that was still in progress.

Karla just shook her head. "I can't believe . . ." She trailed off but I knew where she was going with it.

"You ready to go back home?"

She nodded and got up off of the bleachers. I followed her and watched Mike at the same time. He was watching her and his eyes were not letting up, even though a game was going on around him. I knew that boy had it bad.

"That's my mom's car," Karla said stopping in the middle of the road. We were at least five feet away from my house. In my drive way sat a gold four door Volvo. It just sat there, gloomy looking itself. And I knew something was up.

Karla continued her walk at a faster pace. She didn't want to know, for sure, what she already knew and I did too. My heart was in my throat and my stomach was beginning to do flips. I didn't want this to be happening to my best friend.

We opened the front door. I didn't remember the house being this bright when we left to go to the basketball court. Marco, Chiloe and Karla's mother stood there. I had no idea that they would be home. No one was saying a word. I could see the tears on Karla's mother's face, just like the streaks on Karla's. She just looked at Karla and everything was confirmed.

To my surprise Karla immediately burst into tears. I didn't think that she would do it. Not with everyone standing there watching her. That was just the way she was. "No, no," she whined shaking her head over and over again until finally she fell to her knees on the floor.

I was too much in shock to move. I never thought she would break like this. Before I could reach her to comfort her, Chiloe was down on the floor beside her, holding her close. Her mother was still crying not knowing what to do either.

He finally lifted her up and continued to hold her close. She was crying loudly as if in pain. I felt my eyes starting to burn and I knew it wouldn't be long before I would be crying too. I couldn't stand to see her this way.

"Are you going to come back to the house?" Her mother asked, wiping tears off of her freshly done makeup. She was never one to be caught slipping without makeup, no matter who died.

Karla just nodded, head still buried deep in Chiloe's blue t-shirt. She was trying to calm herself. But she just couldn't seem to pull it totally together. Chiloe wasn't rushing her off of him though.

"You want me to drive you home?" He asked stroking her short hair like a baby. The first and only time I'd seen my brother so loving and gentle with anyone was when Kelly died.

"No," she said lifting her head up. She wiped her eyes and nose with her hand. Then she grabbed her bag that still sat by the door, all this without saying a word to anyone.

"You gonna leave your car here?" Her mother asked, not quite understanding Karla's next move.

"No. I can drive, I'm fine."

The old Karla was back, just that fast.

"You sure?" Chiloe and her mother asked at the same time.

"I'm sure."

I finally found my voice under all the tears and stepped toward her to hug her. When I did, I could feel the wetness of her cheeks up against mine. My heart was broken terribly and I remembered Kelly.

"I'll go home with you," I said letting her go. "Give me a second."

She didn't object and I was glad. I wanted to be there for her and comfort her and I was willing to stay however long she needed me. School was basically over anyway. There was only one week left; it was going to be ok.

The smell of bacon and eggs seeping through Karla's bedroom door woke me up. I wasn't accustomed to smelling anything like this in the morning. But I knew I couldn't be dreaming. I sat up on the portion of Karla's daybed that rolled out from underneath. She called it a cot, but I considered it a bed. And speaking of beds, she wasn't even in hers.

"I'm over here," a voice said from across the room. I looked over at the closet and could see her sitting in the red velvet chaise lounge that she begged her mother for. She finally got it on her fifteenth birthday. She was wrapped in her favorite purple blanket.

"You sleep over there?"

"Yeah."

I threw the rest of my covers off of me and sat completely up. "You ok?"

"I don't know."

"I understand."

I couldn't remember the last time I had death in my family. But I remembered Kelly. I could feel her pain.

"You wanna come get some breakfast?"

I nodded and stood up. For some reason, as long as Karla and I had been friends, I never really spent that much time at her house. Her neighborhood was quiet and boring. She always wanted to be where the action and the boys were and that meant my house.

I followed her out of the room into the hallway. We could hear voices coming from the living room already. I felt nervousness creaking up on me. I knew she had a big family by the snatches of conversation I would hear whenever I did come over. Her grandmother had been the oldest and most interesting person I knew. She never talked that much, but when she did, it was worth listening to. I could never get enough of her stories about growing up in the country and being the youngest of nine children. Her brothers and sisters kind of reminded me of my own.

"Good morning ma," Karla said to her mother as she sat down at the big wooden kitchen table. They didn't have what anyone would consider a dining room. It was just a big kitchen and then a living room off from that. Her mother stood at the stove cooking up breakfast.

"Good morning y'all." She seemed weary, which was understandable. Her hair was combed neatly though and once again she wore her makeup. "How'd ya'll sleep?"

I said fine, but Karla just shrugged.

That's when I took a second to look around her house. I could tell it was old, probably about as old as mine. But the condition was a lot better. The kitchen walls were a bright orange with kitchen things hung everywhere. Wooden spoons, kitchen sayings, stuff like that. Right across from the table, pushed up against the wall was a huge china cabinet that actually had china in it. Plates, wine glasses, everything you wouldn't use on a normal basis. Everything had an old look to it, but it was all beautiful. Too beautiful to touch.

"Lonna, do you like eggs?" Karla's mother was asking me breaking my concentration from the different artifacts in the china closet.

"Yes Mam."

She smiled and sat a plate of them in front of me. As she did so, I could see two more people emerging from the living room. One of them was Veronica with a purple bandana tied around her head that made her look even more like Karla. If it were not for the slanted eyes anyway. The lady with her looked like a shorter, larger, older version of Karla's mother. Except for the bad hair weave. She waved hello to all of us and whispered something in Karla's mother's ear. Karla's mother just nodded and continued fixing breakfast plates.

I had to have met at least twenty different people in the course of an hour. All types of people were in and out of the house, some were church members, some were neighbors, but most were family. All questioned me on who I was and where my family was from. I was just glad to be locked in the solitude of Karla's room reading her book of poetry. I loved reading her work. It was the only time I did some actual reading. And it relaxed me too. It made me forget that I really needed a drink.

The door opened and Karla walked in. She sat down in her chaise lounge again without a word and tried her best to curl herself up into a little ball.

"What's wrong?" I asked fearing that maybe it was a stupid question. I just wasn't used to seeing her so upset. She had always been the sunshine of my life.

"They can't find the money my Grandma left for us to buy clothes for the funeral with."

I put her book of poems down, got up off the floor and sat down on the chaise beside her.

"How much was it?"

"About three hundred."

"Damn. Where did she have it last?"

"Nobody knows. And now everybody is blaming each other. My mom is blaming her sister, her sister is blaming her. I knew this was gonna happen."

"I'm sure they'll find it," I said for lack of anything else to say. I couldn't remember ever seeing her so stressed.

She was about to reply, but before she could, there was a knock at the door. "Come in," she said.

Veronica slowly opened the door, holding an envelope in her hand. She closed the door directly behind her and sat down on the chaise, between Karla and me.

"Some boy bought you this," she said handing it to her.

Karla took it slowly like it was a bomb or something. We both had a feeling of whom it was from. "Thank you," she said finally deciding to open it.

I stared at the light blue card with doves on the front as she seemed to read every word.

"Who is it?"

"Mike," she mumbled so low that I could barely hear her.

"A sympathy card?"

She nodded. Then she looked up at her cousin. "Did he bring this here?"

Veronica nodded. "He said not to disturb you. He just wanted you to have this."

Karla handed the card to me. I didn't bother to read the mushy poem mess. The only poems I read were Karla's. But I did read the signature. "If you need anything call me. Love, Mike." And then his phone number.

Part of me wanted to ask if she was going to call him. But the other part stopped me. I was pretty sure she didn't want to think about calling Mike. Not with her grandmother dying and the lost money.

"Should I call him?" She asked me, looking at me over Veronica's head.

"Yeah," I didn't even have to think about that one. I was glad she asked me.

"I'll call later."

There was another knock at the door.

"Yes."

This time Karla's mom opened the door just a little, and stuck her head in the crack.

"We're getting ready to go get Momma's dress and stuff. Are you going?"

Both Karla and Veronica shook their heads. I just shrugged.

"May I speak to Mike," I heard in the darkness of the room. Karla still wasn't sleeping in her bed so instead of pulling the cot like bed out for me, I slept in her spot.

I turned over to look at the clock radio beside the bed. It was only eleven. I couldn't remember the last time I had gone to sleep so early. But Karla and I had been watching a movie on HBO and the next thing I knew I was out like a light.

"Thank you for the card," she said looking at me as I sat up.

"Yeah I'm ok."

She shook her head. I could tell by the smirk on her face, she wanted to smile. But something deep down wouldn't let her. Instead she folded her arms defensively in front of her as she sat on the same chaise with her heavy blanket wrapped around her.

"The wake is tomorrow. The funeral is Thursday."

There was a long pause. Then she said, "Alright then. Take care."

And that was it.

"What did he say?" I asked eagerly.

"Just for me to let him know if I need him." She shrugged like it was no big deal at all. But I knew better.

Chapter Nine

Sunday, July 4, 1993 5:45 p.m.

I couldn't tear myself away from this baby if I wanted to. She was the most gorgeous thing I had ever seen with her sandy hair and green eyes. But I was getting thirsty and she was starting to smell funny. So I reluctantly handed her back to Andrew.

I couldn't even count the *"Are you ok's?"* and *"How are you doing's?"* that I had been receiving throughout this whole cookout. I was glad Chiloe had decided to postpone the baby's coming home cookout, due to my Grandmother's death, and just make it a Fourth of July/baby coming home cookout. But I didn't like being the center of attention like this.

And speaking of attention, eighty percent of it was coming from Mike. But Chiloe was doing a very good job of cock blocking. Whenever he would see Mike standing near me, or even looking like he wanted to stand near me, he would rush to my side. He even stopped in the middle of a game of dominoes just to block Mike's access.

"Can you believe them two?" Lonna asked me.

But I was too irritated with her to even answer. I hoped she didn't think I didn't know what was really in that Styrofoam cup she had been carrying around all afternoon. And I hoped she didn't think I didn't see the way she purposely avoided Chiloe and Rajul, just so they wouldn't smell the alcohol on her breath or the weed that had soaked itself into the material of her clothes. I was familiar with all of her little tricks by now.

"What'cha drinking?" I asked not cracking a smile. She looked at me dumbfounded but for only a second. Then she regained herself and shrugged.

I needed a soda. Someone decided they wanted to drink the last can of Sprite that had been chilling in the cooler beside fifty bottles of Old E. I heard the screen door open and close behind me as I headed for the kitchen. I turned around quickly expecting to see Chiloe, but it was Mike instead.

"What you want boy?" I asked playfully.

"Nothing. I just thought maybe I could get you away from Chiloe for a second or two so we could talk."

"Oh, ok."

We walked into the kitchen together and I flipped on the light switch, determined to find some soda.

"You got a boyfriend, Karla?" He asked me bluntly as he leaned against the entry way of the kitchen.

"No," I replied hunting through the refrigerator. I wasn't about to ride all the way to the store for a soda.

"Anybody you like?"

I closed the refrigerator and looked at him. "Why?"

"I was just wondering if me and you could go out sometime."

"Why? So you can brag to Chiloe and your boys about how you went out with me?"

He looked surprised and I didn't know if he was faking or not. "Why would I do that? We ain't even gotta tell nobody if that makes you feel better."

I shook my head at him. It seemed we had been playing this game since before my Grandmother died. I didn't like the idea of being some kind of prize in this competition between him and Chiloe.

"Why are you so angry?" Mike asked me.

"I'm angry because the only reason you're even talking to me is because you know Chiloe wants me. And you know it!"

I tried to storm past him. Like I was more pissed than I really was. Maybe I would take that ride to the store after all. But he was blocking my way. I was eye to eye with his broad chest in a blue jersey.

"What?" I asked looking into his face with the tight jawbones and slight facial hair. I got chills for some unknown reason.

"I wouldn't do that to you," he said plain and simple. "I've liked you for a long time. I was just scared to talk to you. I tried though."

I rolled my eyes to the back of my head. How many times had I heard that one before?

"Look," he continued, "I'mma be goin' to boot camp in '95. I just wanted to get to know you before I leave. I wanted to see if something could develop between me and you."

"Boot camp?" I asked taking my hands off of my hips. "You're joining the army?"

He shook his head, "Air force."

"Why are you just now telling me this?" I asked still suspicious, even though his large eyes seemed so sincere.

"Well since I'm leaving, I figured I might as well try. Shit, if you say no, I don't ever have to see you again really. But if you said yes, maybe I would have something to look forward to when I come home."

I stopped to think. Not wanting to make a stupid mistake. For years, I had been so careful. But now? What if he wasn't kidding and I missed spending time with him? What if he was just doing this to prove a point to Chiloe, and I ended up getting hurt in the process of him proving his point? Then what?

"When you wanna go out?" I asked finally.

"Shit, right now," he said laughing.

I looked at him like he couldn't be serious. But he was.

"Okay."

"Where you wanna go?" He asked.

I shrugged. "I know I want a soda."

We headed towards the door. "Should we tell everybody else we're leaving?" I asked turning back around. I knew Lonna and New-New would both be worried about me if I didn't tell them I was leaving. Not to mention Chiloe.

"No. We'll call them from wherever we end up at. I don't want anybody to know we went out somewhere. I don't want you thinking I'm just doing this for Chiloe's benefit."

I smirked knowing he was being sarcastic. All the same, we left the house together and no one knew.

The mariachi band played loudly moving from one table to the next. Someone was having a birthday party, wearing a big sombrero as the wait staff sang a Mexican version of "Happy Birthday."

Mike and I sat at a table almost in the middle of the restaurant just staring at each other. I didn't know about him, but I was trying to figure out what was on his mind. Like why all of a sudden were we sitting here, in a restaurant together?

"For awhile, I thought maybe you and Chiloe would be together. I gave y'all until the beginning of the summer."

I nodded digging into my cheese enchilada. "Okay."

"I've been wanting to tell you how I felt every since that night Chiloe and Andrew beat that boy down on the basketball court."

I shuddered at the thought of that. That guy still walked with a cane and wore an eye patch over the eye that he lost that night. His blood stains still covered the dark pavement right beneath the basketball hoop.

"I know you ain't never thought about me like that," he continued looking straight into my eyes like he was searching for something.

I wasn't about to tell him that I really had, but I had always considered Chiloe's friends off limits. As I sat across from Mike, staring into his face at the smooth dark complexion and the big dark eyes, I realized that he had definite potential.

I loved having him talk directly to me and having his eyes on me. I realized that I liked being in his presence and having people look at us as a couple. He was nice to look at with long muscular legs and huge muscular arms decorated with tattoos. Not only that, but his demeanor was calm and relaxing. Nothing like Chiloe or any other guy that I had come in contact with. He was mature, yet he still had a great sense of humor and I liked that.

"So what do you and your friends say about me?" I asked.

He swallowed his soda hard, about to choke, and then he shook his head. "Naw, to tell you the truth Chiloe don't even talk about you."

I was stunned. I had heard their crew talk about all kinds of girls. Why was I the exception?

"I mean you can tell he likes you. He just don't talk about you like that. I think he just don't wanna be disrespectful because he do like you. I know you're special to him and everything."

"Is that why I'm out with you?" I asked him again hoping that maybe this time he would slip up and tell me the truth if it were any different from the first truth he told me.

"I told you no. I told you why you're out with me. I really like you. I see why you're special to him though."

The mariachi band was now working its way around the room. "This is nice," I said as they stopped at our table before traveling on.

"I'm glad you like it."

"So what made you decide to go in the military all of a sudden?"

He cleared his throat and took a bite of his chicken enchilada in between sips of his drink. Then he swallowed and sat the soda down. I waited patiently for his answer, taking a bite of the bland appetizer tortilla chips that sat in the middle of the table.

"Family tradition," he said finally shrugging his shoulders. "I tried my best to run from it for as long as I could. But I finally had to take a look around me and I decided this is the best thing for me. I don't wanna end up in jail or worse. I don't wanna do the street thing all my life. I don't wanna do it anymore. I decided that back when Kelly got shot."

"I understand," I said nodding my head, mouth full of chips. I was already full from two hamburgers and a hot dog from the cookout. I hated not to eat all of the enchilada he paid for, but he didn't seem to notice as he finished up his own plate and continued to talk.

"So what are you gonna do after you graduate?"

I hadn't told anyone my plans as of yet, not wanting to hear any suggestions or ideas. But he was different. "Well, my mom is moving to Louisiana and I'm gonna try to get my book published. My agent is in the process now of finding me a publisher."

"You write?" He asked very interested and sat his glass down.

"Yeah, very much so."

"I never knew that."

"Well you wouldn't have since y'all never talk about me."

He flashed me a delightful crooked smile and I playfully rolled my eyes at him.

"Why you not going to Louisiana?"

"There's no reason for me to go. Everything I know is here. So this is where I'm staying."

He nodded his head as if he understood.

"I'm sorry I didn't eat anything, but we did just leave a cookout."

"Yeah, I know it's cool. You wanna catch a movie?"

I looked at my watch. It was already eight o'clock. We had been missing for about two hours now. Two more wouldn't hurt.

"Ok."

Two movies later we were on the way back to Mike's house. He'd left his car at Chiloe's so that I could go straight home from our outing. I had no intentions of hearing Lonna's mouth tonight.

We pulled up into the driveway and I cut the car off, leaving the radio on. I stared at the back of his father's burgundy Cadillac as I waited for him to make the first move to exit the car. I, for some reason, didn't want him to go. But it was time for me to get home and we both knew it.

"When can I see you again?" He asked and instead of leaning towards the door, he moved in closer to me.

"When do you wanna see me again?"

"Tomorrow."

"Ok, just call me."

"I don't have your number."

That was right. I scribbled my number down quickly on an old receipt on the floor of my car and handed it to him. I expected for that to be it. But he had other plans in mind as he gently reached for me and pulled me closer to him. Without any warning at all his lips were on mine and I could taste the soda and popcorn on his lips and tongue. His fingers were burning holes in my neck and shoulder and I couldn't remember ever being kissed like this and it was wonderful. Much too wonderful.

"Goodnight Karly," he breathed into my mouth and opened the door.

It took me a minute to realize he was even gone as my head stayed turned to the position he left it in. I slowly cranked the car back up and pulled out of his driveway as he entered his house.

I wanted to be mad at myself. I really did. This time yesterday, I was doing just fine without anyone in my life. Not having to answer to a soul. Doing things the way I felt they needed to be done. Like for example, the book, which was closer to being published than I had let on to Mike. I was already done with the follow up, determined not to miss out on the publicity or the money. I wanted to do everything and that was the good part of not having a significant other.

But now?

I closed my journal where I had been writing poems about Mike all morning. Starting with his eyes and working my way across his wonderful muscular frame and the gazillion tattoos. I even wrote about the dizzy feeling I still had from the kiss the feeling of him next to me in my car.

The phone rang, a loud irritating ring, pushing me out of the sweetest day dreams even I could imagine. I was more than prepared to disguise my voice and pretend it wasn't me, unless the person on the other end was Mike of course.

"Hello," I said deeply.

There was a loud sigh on the other end. Kind of like one of relief. "Where the hell have you been? And why are you trying to disguise your voice?"

Lonna spoke in an almost calm voice, as if to let me know she was at the end of her rope with me. I smiled because she cared.

"Me and Mike went to go get something to eat," I said softly.

"How you gonna go get something to eat when you were at a cookout to begin with?"

She had me on that one. It seemed so logical the day before. But now, it made no sense at all.

"I'm sorry," she said apologizing before I could answer her question. Not that I really had an answer anyway. "I was just worried about you, that's all. You left and didn't tell anybody . . ." then she paused and I knew it had hit her. "You were with Mike, huh?"

I nodded on my end of the phone, but I knew she couldn't see me.

"Hello?"

"Yeah, I'm here. I was with Mike."

"Still feel like it was a set up?"

"No."

I could hear the, 'I told you so' in her voice even though she wasn't saying a word. I lay back on the rumpled bed and closed my eyes.

"So, where did you go?"

"To eat and to the movies."

"You give him some?"

I laughed almost rolling myself off of the bed. I could remember when we were younger, always asking each other if we had done *it* with this boy or the other. The answer was always no. And this time, nothing had changed.

"You like him?" She asked and I could detect just a hint of sadness in her voice. She would never admit to it, but I knew her like the back of both of my hands. She hadn't had anything serious with anyone since Kelly died and that worried me.

"Yeah I like him."

"Chiloe?"

"What about him?"

"He's not gonna be happy."

I hadn't thought anything about Chiloe since the Kiss the night before. I realized he wouldn't be happy without Lonna pointing it out to me. But there was nothing I could do about that. I had already fallen quite hard, and I wasn't about to try to get up.

I wanted to be there about as much as I wanted a root canal. My mother was getting married. And unfortunately I was her maid of honor. It was no honor. Not really. I didn't like the guy. He had never done anything to me, not really. It was just the fact that it had always been my mother and I. Not to mention my grandmother.

But now there was an intruder.

The wedding was small. Just some members of our family, some people of Darwin's family, and all of their coworkers were in attendance. Those coworkers had witnessed the beginning of this union because both worked for the same law firm. My mother as a legal secretary and Darwin as an actual lawyer. They were planning to move to New Orleans in a year.

I fixed myself a plate that consisted of baked beans, sweet and sour meatballs, and barbeque. Then I headed back to my room, away from the noise of every one that congregated in our living room after the small ceremony. I was followed by Lonna, Bree, New-New and Veronica.

I shut the door behind us.

"Man, K, your family is off the hook," New-New said sitting down on the edge of the bed with Lenora in her arms. I couldn't remember the last time I had seen her without Andrew. But he was at home today while she attended my mom's wedding.

"You should have been here during her grandmother's funeral. They were really off the hook," Lonna said picking a meatball off of my plate because she had forgotten to get her own.

"Well, while I have all my girls here, I have an announcement to make." She propped Lenora up on my two down pillows and looked from Lonna to me. Then she said, "Me and Andrew are moving to DC after graduation."

"What!" Lonna and I said in stereo. Then Lonna added, "What the hell is in DC?"

"You know Andrew's mother lives up there. And her brother has a car dealership. He said he would give Andrew a job. And since he graduated, he can at least go ahead and get two years of college in while I finish these next two school years. Then we're leaving."

"Is this what you really wanna do?" I asked.

New-New nodded then she looked down at Lenora who was playing with one of my stuffed animals. "I just want me and him to have a new start. I wanna get out of this city. I mean, I can't go nowhere without seeing some chick I don' fought or some dude Andrew don' fought. I wanna go somewhere where we don't know anybody and we can just start over. We don't have to worry about somebody causing drama between us 'cause we went to school together. We don't have to worry about none of that."

"So you wanna go?" Lonna asked.

"Yeah I wanna go."

I nodded. What could I say or do? Even though Lonna and I spent the most time together, it still wouldn't be the same without New-New. But she had a family to think about now. She had been forced to grow up faster than Lonna and I. And now we had to deal with it.

"I wish you luck then."

Out of the corner of my eye I could see Lonna looking at me like I was crazy, but I ignored her.

Chapter Ten

Saturday, March 15, 1995 2:30 p.m.

I looked like someone had just poured a whole bucket of water over me by the time we made it back to Mike's house. I didn't know why I was exercising anyway; he was the one going into the military. I never had a problem with my thick butt and hips and I still didn't. But Mike needed his training, so in order to spend time with him; this is what I had to do.

"You hungry?" Mike asked as we entered the deserted house.

"I guess. Where's your dad?"

"In the field until Tuesday."

"Oh."

"Look, you can go take a shower, I'll get you a t-shirt and some shorts. I'll wash your clothes for you and make something to eat."

I was uneasy with the idea of him washing my clothes. I mean after all that exercising, they couldn't have smelled too fresh. What would he think? The thought of catching pneumonia from walking around soaked like I was, was even less appealing to me though.

"Ok."

Mike gathered up a towel, wash cloth, t-shirt and a pair of his gym shorts for me. He stood outside of the bathroom door while I undressed so that he could reach in to get them through the small opening I created.

"You alright?"

"Yeah, I'm fine."

I had a thing about taking showers in strange houses. I didn't even like to use the toilet in strange places. It had even taken me a while to get used to Lonna's house. But this house was pretty clean for it just to be inhabited by men.

Mike was rattling around in the kitchen when I finally limped back into the living room. Even with the fierce sting of the warm water beads hitting my muscles, my legs were still terribly sore from all the running. I never ran unless I had to and I was horribly out of shape. I was not going to squeeze a life time of physical fitness into one day.

I grunted loudly as I sat down on the beige carpeted floor of Mike's living room, in front of the stereo. I found some Phyllis Hyman and a Howard Hewett CD to play back to back on the compact disc player.

Mike peeped his head around the corner when Phyllis started to croon about her old friend. "You ok?" He asked smiling deep.

"I hurt, but other than that, I'm alright."

He shook his head, still smiling. "Well, just relax. The food will be ready in a second."

I didn't ask him what he was cooking. I didn't really care. I was almost too tired to eat anyway. Instead I grabbed his cordless phone off of the end table and dialed my mother's pager number. She promptly called me back.

"Hello."

"Hey ma?"

"Hey, where are you? This isn't the house number."

"I know. I just wanted to let you know that I'm at Mike's if you try to call the house and nobody answers."

"Uh huh. Mike's huh?"

"Yes Mam."

I could tell she wanted to say something. Maybe to remind me of why I was actually put on this earth. She hadn't even met Mike in the whole time that we had been together, mostly due to her traveling back and forth to New Orleans, helping her husband start his new practice and setting up her own job as his secretary. But she decided not to say anything. She always put faith in me like I knew what I was doing.

"How's the office coming?" I asked to fill the silence.

"It's ok. We've got three interviews for staff tomorrow and then I think I'm gonna call it a trip."

"Darwin getting on your nerves already, huh?"

She laughed instead of answering me.

"Well I'll see you when you get back, mom. Be careful."

"I will."

I hadn't noticed Mike setting up the plates of food on the living room coffee table. Fried chicken, rice, and corn.

"It's kind of left over from last night," he explained as I looked at him wondering if he had cooked all of this.

I wasn't that big on leftovers, but I said, "That's fine."

"I got water, Kool-aide, some flat Pepsi."

I smiled. "Water's fine."

He went back into the kitchen and came back not a minute later with two glasses of ice water. Then he sat down on the floor beside me. After watching me say grace, we began to eat as the soft music played in the background.

"You sure you gonna be ok once your mom leaves?"

I nodded my head. "I don't see why I wouldn't be. I'm trying to get this book deal. That should pay my bills for awhile."

"I'm talking about being alone."

I shook my head this time. "I'll be alright. I'm use to being alone. I'm an only child remember."

He just looked at me for a minute. Then he continued to eat.

"This is good did you make it?"

"Naw, Dad made it yesterday after noon. He left around eight."

I nodded as I finished up half. I could only take so much of leftover chicken. I tried to stand up and take my plate back into the kitchen, but my legs refused to move.

Mike jumped up seeing that I was in pure agony. "Let me do it, I got it."

He took my hand easing me back onto the floor and took both of our plates into the kitchen. All I could do was look straight up into the white ceiling chiding myself for being such a bum.

When he came back he sat on the floor with his legs stretched out in front of him.

"You want me to hook you up?"

I looked over at him. "How?"

"Come here."

It took all of my strength to crawl over to him but I finally made it, and lay across his legs. Then I felt his warm hands on my calves, kneading and rubbing with amazing strength and tenderness. I heard moaning and didn't even realize it was coming from me until one got caught in my throat. I was in pure heaven. Until Mike said, "Get up."

I looked up at him. What did he mean get up. Was I hurting his leg? Instead of asking though, I slowly got up, still very much in pain.

"Lay down," he said getting up on his knees and patting the carpet in front of him.

I was happy again and couldn't keep the wide smile that I felt on my face away. I lay down just as I was told, on my stomach, as he straddled me from behind. I felt the t-shirt being lifted up to my neck and then his warm hands on the small of my back. My moans were unmistakable this time and I knew he could feel the goose pimples covering my skin.

Without warning, there were the sweetest wettest kisses on the small of my back. Right where his hands had once been. No tongue, no teeth, just lips tracing a line from the small of my back to my hair line at that base of my neck. I was in pure heaven as I hoisted myself up on my elbows to better meet his eager lips. He lay flat on me with his entire weight pressing into the small of my back, putting his arms out to the sides of my body. I wanted to scream, dance, cry and run some more all at the same time, everything was becoming a blur.

Finally his lips let go of my skin and he leaned up, whispering, "You ok?" in my ear.

The only thing I could do was nod my head. I couldn't speak. I opened my mouth but nothing would come out except for a moan.

"You are so special to me, you know that?" He continued to breathe in my ear. "You're everything I've ever wanted."

I wanted so badly to believe him that I was quivering. But I could feel anxiety starting to swell around my lungs like a gas bubble. He was talking some serious stuff and I had never experienced anything serious before. Even though we had been together for close to two years, the idea of him and I sometimes scared me. Our relationship seemed so perfect, was that even possible?

His lips were back on my neck, gently sucking the skin in and licking and I forgot what I was thinking about. There I was squirming under the weight of his body but I could hardly move. I could feel the strong bulge in his sweat shorts pressing against my bare thigh. I closed my eyes and the let the music and the feel of so much warmth take me away.

I felt wet coolness on my thighs. Sort of like mandarin oranges being placed on me and quickly taken away. I opened my eyes slowly to see Mike lying between my legs kissing the inside of my left one. A quick glance at his clock radio told me it was 2 am.

"What are you doing?" I asked in between moans.

I could see the smile on his face but he wouldn't lift his head up. Instead, he continued kissing. I lay back on my pillow wondering how in the world I was going to get relief from the rhythmic pounding that could have easily been mistaken for a heart beat going on between my legs.

Mike seemed to read my mind because his hands traveled underneath the shorts of his that I wore. He relieved me of them in a second and lay back in what seemed to be his favorite spot for right now. Nervousness shot through every corner of my being as I lay in front of him fully exposed from the waist down. I never told him I was a virgin. We had never talked about sex at all; he was always the perfect gentleman only showering me with hugs and kisses. I was scared and my body tensed up instantly.

Mike wasn't moved by my tenseness even though I knew he could feel it. He simply said, "Relax Karly," as he played me like a guitar with two fingers. I prayed he wouldn't decide to get adventurous and stick those fingers deep inside of me. I wasn't ready for all of this yet.

But he didn't. He just continued to rub my clit sideways, back and forth with his thumb. Then he slightly pinched it between his thumb and his pointer finger. I moaned and stretched my pelvis up more for his access. Instead of pinching it again though, with both of his hands he gently parted my lips. With graceful ease he took me into his mouth. I squealed, feeling a pleasure shock run through me that I'd never experienced before in my whole seventeen years of living!

He sucked softly and gently on my clit, not coming up for air except to lick. I could hear soft moans of appreciation coming from his throat, almost drowned out by my loud ones, but still audible. I sat up on my elbows, watching him work his magic with his full face buried into my pubic area where hair should have been but I kept shaved.

Then the ball of fire started in my toes. Slowly, much too slowly, it spread up my legs, both of them, and into the pit of my stomach. I could feel it in the tips of my fingers, but I didn't know when or how it had gotten there. It was just there like a tree that had grown over night. I dug them into the waves of Mike's freshly cut hair and urged his face deeper into my wetness. His mouth made slurping noises as his tongue tried desperately to lick up everything.

And there it was. It was somewhere around the center of me, but it erupted through my mouth in a loud grunt that was anything but lady like. I didn't care. I just thanked God for this man, that we were home alone, and that he didn't live in an apartment.

Mike sat up on his knees and looked down at me. Wiping his lips with the back of his hands he gave me the sexiest crooked smile I had ever seen in my whole life. I felt something deep within me that was totally new to me. I couldn't put a name to it or even describe it, but it was there. Without another word, he climbed back up to his pillow where my head now rested, and lay his head inches away from mine.

"You okay, baby?" He asked me for the umpteenth time that day.

And for the umpteenth time that day, I could only nod my head knowing full well that I was not okay. My body was still having spasms and my clit was twitching uncontrollably.

He put one arm under my head and the other on my face. I could smell myself on his long muscular fingers. I kissed the tips of them before he wrapped me into his arms and we both fell asleep.

I looked in the mirror at myself for the fiftieth time. I was never one to think of myself as beautiful. There were even some days when I didn't consider myself cute. But tonight, in this black satin evening gown that was made especially for me by the lady in the sewing shop up the street from my neighborhood, I was gorgeous. For a second I wondered about my breast that seemed to poke out more than slightly from the top of my dress. But it added to the appeal of my dress, so I didn't complain.

Momma made such a big fuss over me. Making sure my make up was right, complaining that I should have grown my hair out for the prom, everything. I wasn't sure on how to tell her I was not planning on coming back home that night. However, I was sure the packed duffel bag on the bed gave me away.

And Mike looked extraordinary in his black tux. I knew it wouldn't look right on everybody, but at 6'2 he pulled it off very well. His eyes were bright and smiling as I came down the hall, purse and shawl in one hand, duffel bag in the other. He looked me up and down appreciatively and then slipped the corsage made of red roses and baby breath onto my right wrist.

After my mom used a whole role of film on us, we said our goodbyes and slipped into the warm leather seats of his black Mazda

929. He knew I was nervous by the shaking of my leg under the soft material of my gown. He placed one hand on my knee to steady the shaking.

"Why so nervous?" He asked.

"I don't know."

"Are we gonna eat first?"

I nodded yes, but knowing I was way too nervous to even swallow my own spit, much less some food.

We drove in silence, listening to the soft hum of his motor and the music on the radio. At some point my hand ended up on top of his that still rested on my knee, giving him encouragement to keep it there. He rubbed it so lightly I could barely feel it. But I knew it was there all the same.

After a heated debate the night before, we settled on going to an Italian restaurant instead of getting seafood. His argument that it was much better to smell like spaghetti instead of fish was pretty convincing. The restaurant was crowded with other people going to the prom. We greeted others from my school, I was more than proud to be on Mike's arm, as we made our way to a table near the window. We ordered soda and appetizers.

"You look beautiful," Mike said shaking his head at the same time.

"Thank you. You look nice too."

"I better, you picked this tuxedo out."

I smiled as I watched his loving fingers caress my hand from across the table.

"I wanted to let you know how happy I am to be with you tonight." He spoke seriously looking me straight in my eyes. He always looked me straight in my eyes.

"There's no one else I would rather be with. *Noone.*"

I took his hand into my own and kissed the palm of it. At that very moment I felt something pass between us that felt undeniably more than puppy love. It was something that shook my soul and caused me to shutter. I just hoped that he felt it too.

I didn't want to seem like a starry eyed kid, but I couldn't help it. I looked around the hall in total awe at the balloons and the decorations our prom committee spent Friday night and Saturday afternoon putting up. Our theme was 'A Night to Remember' and the colors were red and white in the balloons, streamers and the silk makeshift curtains that hung from the windows.

Mike took my hand and we headed to the dance floor that was already crowded with people who had decided to get their party started early. I had a hard time really throwing down in my black stilettos, so like almost every other girl, I removed them. Shoes in one hand, purse in the other, Mike and I partied until twelve thirty.

"Man, I can't remember having so much fun," he said exasperated as we sped down the boulevard on the way to the hotel that he booked for us.

"You didn't go to your prom?" I asked.

"Hell no! What I look like going to a prom. Especially with them ho's that I went to school with."

I shook my head and rolled my eyes up into my head. "That's too bad."

"Naw, not really."

Once again we were surrounded by others from my school. This was the hotel to be at tonight I could see. It was an old brick structure with twelve floors and I could only remember being in it one time before. My grandmother had a friend who lived down the street from us. Her kitchen caught on fire and her insurance company put her up in the hotel for a week. My family brought her and her husband food and other necessities.

Mike and I debated for a minute on whether we would hit the after prom or not as we settled into our room on the fourth floor. Then we both determined that maybe we had done enough partying for one night and opted to stay in. I watched him cut on the television as I wished the ice cream parlor across the street stayed open all night.

"I'm gonna go take a shower," I said finally breaking the silence that seemed heavy in the room. We had been talking and laughing all night and now all of a sudden, in the room alone, we had nothing to say. Or better yet we had plenty to say but didn't know how to say it.

"Alright then. You want me to go the store over there and get anything?"

I thought for a moment. "A chocolate bar and a soda would be nice."

"That's cool."

He stood up and I closed the bathroom door relieved that he wouldn't be there when I got out of the shower. I would have time to make sure I was absolutely perfect before he returned.

When he did finally make it back, fifteen minutes later, I was laying across the king sized bed watching Saturday Night Live. I hated the bedspreads on hotel room beds because the material always made me itch. So I took it off and threw it on the floor in front of the bed before I lay down in just my spaghetti strapped t-shirt and bikini panties to match. It had taken Lonna and me only five minutes to match the set, even though she wanted me to wear a skimpy lingerie set that I had no clue as to how to even put on.

"I had to go back in the store three times. The first time I forgot your soda, the second time I forgot mine."

I smiled because, if I wasn't mistaken, he looked a little nervous. Maybe it was all in my head though. I watched him gather his things to take his shower as I opened my soda. I didn't have a long time to wait though, because he was in and out in five minutes looking eager as if he thought I was going to disappear.

"How is the candy?" He asked eyeing me more than the chocolate.

"Fine. You want some."

I held the pack out for him, but instead he took it out of my hand and sat it on top of the comforter that still lay on the floor. I was surprised as what started off as a sweet kiss on the lips ended in a deep passionate lip lock with his tongue half way down my throat.

Neither one of us had ever discussed sex, even though it was one of my favorite subjects. To talk about anyway. I had gone for eighteen years without doing something I liked to think about so much. We both knew when he made the reservations for the hotel room what would happen. Unfortunately I still didn't know if I was ready for this or not.

He finally let me go and looked into my eyes. "I hope you don't feel like I'm rushing you."

I shook my head not knowing how I felt. He wasn't putting pressure on me. I was putting pressure on me.

Saturday Night Live's credits were rolling on the screen and they were doing that familiar wave they always did at the end of the show. Mike turned the television off and cut the clock radio on beside the bed. He fiddled with it until he got the local college radio station to come in nice and clear.

I sat up on my knees as I watched him turn the lights above the nightstand down to dim. Then he opened his soda and took a quick swig. He took his sweet time placing the soda back on the night stand and turning around to me. Then he grabbed me, pulled me close to him, and put his cold lips on mine again. I could still taste the sweet stickiness of the soda on his lips as he played with my tongue and my teeth. A gentle subtle force pushed me slowly down on the bed. And then he was on top of me. His body was all muscle and it pressed heavily into mine so that I could hardly breathe. The scent of the soap from both of us filled my nose and I could feel myself becoming weak.

Then he stopped abruptly and looked at me. I wondered if I had said or done something wrong. But I couldn't remember saying or doing a thing but kissing him back. Maybe he didn't like the way I moaned.

"I know this is probably the wrong damn time to be asking you this. But I need to know. How many men have you been with?"

I sat up on my elbows and looked at him, feeling sorry that he even had to ask me that.

"None."

By the look on his face I could tell that he didn't know whether to believe me or not to believe me. "You mean you've never had sex?"

I shook my head and said, "No."

"You're a virgin?"

"Yes."

He was shocked and I couldn't for the life of me understand why. I knew God still made virgins, so what was the big deal?

"Why?" He asked.

"Why?"

"Why? Why are you still a virgin?"

I shrugged. "I don't know. I guess I've never found the right person."

"Oh."

He lay down beside me and we looked at each other for a second. Then he worked up the nerve to let his fingers travel through my hair.

"I just never thought . . . I guess I always thought you and Chiloe . . ."

He didn't finish that sentence but I knew what he meant. I just shook my head in reply to that.

"Okay."

"What about you, how many people have you been with?"

He chuckled, covering his mouth with a closed fist. "You actually want me to count?"

"Oh goodness."

I turned my back to him and faced the wall.

"Naw! Wait!" He said playfully and gently tugging on my arm. "It's not like that. But you know everybody makes mistakes."

"Mistakes?"

"Mistakes. I guess if I had taken the time to think about what I was doing, a lot of stuff wouldn't have happened."

"Stuff like what?"

"Hurt feelings, misunderstandings, all of that. I'm not even going to lie to you, a lot of times I was dishonest. I was either trying to feel something that wasn't there or I was just out to get what I wanted and willing to say anything to get it. Now I do admit, the ones who knew what was up and didn't expect anything else from me, we were cool, it was all good. But the ones I hurt, I regret hurting them. A lot of it was just trying to keep up with my boys, seeing who I could get. But a while ago I realized that all of it was just bull shit. You know?"

I lay on my back looking up into his face watching the strong muscles in his chin as he talked. His left hand held my waist tight, insuring I would not be going anywhere. I could feel the very faint flutter of his eye lashes against my forehead as he kissed my nose.

"What happened?"

"Well," he began settling in closer to me so that his head rested on the pillow beside mine. "I just took a look around me. That's probably when I decided that going in the military was the best thing for me. Bobby and Shae got serious and that made me think. And I started noticing you more." Then he said, "Baby I'm cold, let's get under the cover."

I agreed only because I wanted to see what came after snuggling under the covers. But nothing did. We were back in the same position, just surrounded by the cold hotel sheets. I found myself growing sleepy lying there in his arms but nervousness was doing quite a job of keeping my eyes opened. At least for the time being.

"So anyway," he continued and I could hear the drowsiness in his voice also, "I just want a change. Just fucking isn't getting it anymore for me. I want something I can hold on to."

"I hear what you're saying, but how do we know that I'm what you need to hold on to. How do I know I'm not another one of your mistakes?"

"*I* know you're what I need."

He kissed my nose again and lay his head back down on the pillow. I could hear the people upstairs banging against the floor like they were about to come through the ceiling. The last thought I had, before I drifted to sleep, was wishing they had left that noise at the after prom.

It was unclear who fell asleep first. But in the middle of a dream I felt heaviness on top of me and breathing wasn't coming as easily as it had. My eyes flew open to see Mike hovering over me. Seeing my discomfort he put all his weight on his elbows taking it off of me. Then he smiled.

"What are you doing?" I asked.

"Nothing."

"What time is it?" I asked.

He shrugged as he said, "Three something."

We had only been asleep for an hour or so. It seemed eternity. I closed my eyes thinking maybe I could go back to sleep or fake sleep even. But Mike was not having that. When I turned my head to the side he began kissing my neck. I moaned and squirmed under him.

"Look at you just going wild up under me," he said smiling. I loved that cocky smile of his. The one that was actually a half grin with a twinkle in his brown eyes.

"Whatever," I said managing to turn over on my side under him. But I realized that was a bad idea when he started to lift my t-shirt and kiss my back. It was worse than his lips on my neck and I was starting to have bad muscle contractions in my stomach.

"Mike, stop," I moaned knowing good and well I didn't mean it.

But he stopped anyway. I turned my head and watched him sit back on his knees. "You want me to stop?" He asked.

I was so impressed that he actually stopped and asked me what I wanted. My heart melted completely from the warm look in his eyes.

"No, I don't want you to stop."

His hands took the place of where his lips had been on my back and he began to rub me gently. "You sure?"

"I'm positive."

"How positive?"

"Very positive."

He lay back down on top of me so that his lips could touch my ear lobe. With amazing gentleness he began to kiss it like a pair of lips. Taking his time to explore every crevice of my outer ear like it was the only thing in the world that held his attention right then. I was in Heaven.

"You want me to be your first?" He asked breathing deeply into my ear canal, sending shivers down my spine.

"Yes," I moaned, my voice shaky and crackly from the pleasure I was receiving.

"You sure?"

I just nodded this time. Hoping he didn't take this as a sign to lose all control and go at me like a wild animal. I had gone to school with so many girls who had been literally torn in half their first time that they cried and could hardly walk the next day. The thought of my body being ripped apart gave me the heebie geebies.

"You need to relax if you want me," he whispered.

I turned over and looked into his eyes. The people upstairs had stopped most of the noise but I could still hear someone walking around.

"Be gentle," was the best way to describe my feelings right then.

"You know that I will."

Then we kissed. For what seemed to be hours. Just tasting and exploring each other's lips like food. Neither one of us seemed to be getting our fill of the soft sweetness of each other's mouths and neither one of us could bring ourselves to stop. So at the same time, he removed my t-shirt completely. It landed somewhere on the floor. His boxer shorts joined them soon after and we lay totally naked, flesh to sweet flesh. I could feel my heart coming through my chest like a car crash trying to happen. His body was so warm and smelled so good I couldn't help but ravish his neck and chest with my mouth. Listening to his sighs and moans as he stroked my hair was causing the insistent pounding between my legs to become more and more unrelenting with every second. And then I could feel him struggle with me to let him kiss me on my cheeks and neck while his hands traveled the length of my body. I never would have been able to express how much I loved to feel his fingers dancing between my legs no matter how good of a writer I was. It gave me the most wonderful feeling when he touched me there.

"You are so wet," he whispered in my ear as fingers pushed inside of me. My breath caught in the back of my throat as he began to work it in and out. As he went in, he would go deeper each time. Through passion blurred eyes I could see him biting his bottom lips and studying me intently, trying to understand what made me moan the most, what made me quiver the most. And once it was learned, he continued to do it. Until suddenly my body exploded and went limp against him.

I closed my eyes for a second as he slid his fingers out of me. Just to hold on to the feeling he gave me a little while longer. But before I could reopen them, I felt both of his hands on my thighs, holding them apart. I sat up, steady on my elbows and looked down at him between my legs. His mouth wrapped firmly around me like I were a straw stuck in a cup of milkshake. My moans came out uncontrollably loud. The people upstairs were probably listening to me now. But I didn't really care, so I wrapped my legs around his shoulders and continued to moan simply because I couldn't help it. He held my midsection down with both of his strong hands so that I couldn't squirm away as I continued to thrash against his mouth. He wasn't doing this sweet and gently like the very first time. No, he was on a mission and I was his destination.

"Mike!" I yelled, body sore from the force of that orgasm. I shook uncontrollably like I was having convulsions. This wouldn't leave. It lingered on and on. Suddenly I felt Mike gently pushing to break down my walls. Somewhere between the moment he woke me and now, he managed to discreetly slip a condom on. He braced the bed sheets with both of his hands as he put all of his concentration into entering me without doing me any major harm.

I gripped his shoulders with both hands trying hard not to scream. I was a big girl, I could handle this. There was no doubt about that. So I opened my legs wider, just to give him better access. He looked at me thankfully and continued on his mission even more slowly.

"Damn girl, you are so tight?"

"What did you expect?"

He shook his head that was starting to break out in little beads of sweat. He wanted this badly I could tell. And it was fine because I wanted it just as much.

"I didn't expect this, I know that."

One more push and he entered me. But just a little. With a little more conviction he was in me halfway.

"Mmm," I moaned from both pain and pleasure. I was so full; I couldn't see any way to move around him like I knew I was supposed to.

"Karly, you feel so good."

"Do you like it?" I asked unsure if I was doing the right thing.

"Baby, you know I do. I ain't never felt nothing like this."

The fact that he liked this was enough for me. I wanted to please him so badly as I desperately rotated my hips around him. He was totally engulfing me and hindering my movement.

"Are you ok baby? Tell me if it hurts," he requested between moans and sighs.

"It's ok."

"Does it feel good to you baby?"

I had to think about that for second. And when I concentrated on the feeling of fullness down there I realized that it wasn't uncomfortable. It was more like a perfect fit.

"Yeah it feels really good."

"Put your arms around me baby."

I took my hands that were still gripping his shoulders and wrapped them gently around his neck. Then I raised my legs even more. "Damn," he groaned, hitting it just a little bit harder. Still keeping it at a steady pace and still being just as gentle as he could. He was deeper inside of me now and I was trying hard to keep up with his rhythm.

"Are you gonna cum?" He asked after what seemed like hours of us floating together. The word *cum* and the sound of his voice, gave me a sudden urge to do just that.

"Yes."

My arms got tighter around his neck and I held onto him for dear life as the wave of my third orgasm hit me. I didn't think my body could take anymore. But when he continued to ride me, I was in the loop for another one. They started to run so close together, that I couldn't even tell how many there were. But I knew without a doubt that they were there.

"I love you girl," he whispered in my ear as his body went rigid. I was still in the midst of a wave myself.

"I love you too," I whispered back unable to catch my breath. He was twitching inside of me, hitting something that was making me yelp like a hurt puppy.

"That's your spot," he explained trying to hold back long enough for me to get another one and another one just by him playing with that button. I knew he could feel the shocks of pleasure running through me to him and he was enjoying that.

"I love you so much," he said squeezing me tighter.

"I love you too," I said again.

"Don't ever, ever leave me. Understand?"

I nodded. That was all I could do because right then and there I was cuming again. But this would be the last time because he was cuming now too. He clutched my body in a death grip and groaned loudly in my ear. I didn't know if he was hurt or what as his body trembled as if he were ill.

Then he was still. Just like that. My body seemed to release him and he gently slid out of me. But my arms wouldn't let him go. And neither would his of me. We held each other close, sharing buckets of sweat from one another's bodies. Both of our breathing became labored. His from pleasure, mine from his body crushing me. Still holding on to him with both legs and arms, I gently pushed him to the side. He lay on the pillow beside me and looked at me. Eyes half closed like he was high on the best drug around.

"Are you ok?" I asked smiling at him.

He smiled back, even wider. "Yeah. Everything is perfect."

There were five messages from Chiloe on my phone Sunday afternoon. The first came about twelve in the morning. The second was at three, the third was at five in the morning. The last two were consecutive at twelve that afternoon, two hours before I got home. I was glad I cut the ringer off of my phone so that my mother couldn't hear the early morning phone calls.

I debated on calling him back or not. Then I picked up the phone and called Lonna instead.

"Hey girl. I looked for you at the after prom, but I didn't see you."

"What were you doing at my after prom?"

"Well, you went to mine, so I figured I'd crash yours. Me, New-New and some chicks from school. I ain't even gonna ask where you were."

"Don't."

"Where were you?"

I sighed heavily. "Mike got us a room at the Heart."

I heard her almost choke on whatever it was she was eating. Then she coughed, "The Heart? You fucked him didn't you?"

"Lonna, why do you have to turn every beautiful thing into a nasty thing?"

"It was beautiful girl?"

"Yes, very much so."

I could just see her shaking her head on the other end of the phone. "Get your ass over here and tell me what happened."

She was out on the front porch waiting when I pulled up. She could be so comical sometimes. I stepped out of the car and was about to yell to her but she covered her lips with her pointer finger.

"What?" I asked her stepping onto the porch and sitting down beside her.

"Chiloe is back there. If he hear you, he's gonna come around here."

I sat back in the whicker porch chair beside hers and looked at her, resting my chin in my hands.

"Well?" She asked impatiently.

"Well what?"

"Well what happened, girl?"

I smacked my teeth. "He picked me up, we went to Elizabeth's. We went to the prom. We went to the hotel. He bought me a candy bar. We watched Saturday Night Live. We listened to some music." I shrugged my shoulders.

"So how was it?"

"What do you mean how was it? It was alright I guess. I mean I don't really have anything or anyone to compare it to."

"Did you cum?"

I nodded because I specifically remembered that.

"How many times?"

"Lonna!"

"Well this is how you tell if it was good or not."

"I lost count."

"You lost count? Damn! Did he go down?"

I nodded again.

"Did you go down?"

"Lonna!"

"Oh come on. That's a valid question."

"No."

She nodded this time. "Ok, that's good. So was it more like making love or was it just fucking?"

"What?"

"Did y'all make love or did you fuck?"

"What's the difference?" I knew, but I wanted to hear her version. She was so funny.

"Making love is slow and passionate and sweet and he's telling you he loves you and you're telling him you love him and y'all are kissing and stuff. Fucking is when you just fuck and just go at it. No, 'I love you's' no nothing. Just a lot of moaning and cussing." Her hands beat against each other to emulate bodies smacking against each other, the back of one hand hitting the palm of the other.

"You're a damn nut!"

"You're a writer, you should know this shit. So which one was it?"

"It was definitely making love."

She covered her mouth with her hand, "Oh how sweet! And Mike be trying to act like he's so rough and tough and all that stuff."

I smiled thinking about the night we shared. Not just the sex but everything. His laugh, his smile, his stupid jokes. Our talk.

199

"I'm gonna miss him when he leaves."

"What to go in the military?"

I nodded.

"Karla, are you falling in love?"

"What? Who me?"

"Yes you!"

I shrugged for an answer, because I didn't really have a real answer. Even though I moaned it at least a thousand times that morning, I didn't know if I loved Mike or not. Wasn't that just something you said when you were in the heat of the moment? Did it really mean anything? When he said it to me did it mean anything?

"So, Karla's not a virgin anymore," Lonna said mainly to herself. "Hmmm, I always thought it would be Chiloe."

"Oh Lord." I knew we would get around to talking about him sooner or later. "You know that boy's called me five times this morning."

Lonna laughed and shook her head. "He probably was worried you were doing just what you were doing."

"So how was after prom?"

"It was okay. I didn't know you had so many fine nigga's at your school. I didn't come home until ten this morning because one of 'em had a room at the Heart too."

"Please tell me you won't up in the Heart."

"Yeah girl. Damn, what was his name? Jeff, Gerald, something. I can't remember. Girl, I got tore down."

"And where was New-New?"

"Oh she came back home after I left with ol' dude. Anyway he was short, dark, and had dreads. He had some good ass weed and it was all you can drink night up in his room."

I didn't want to think about the things that could have happened to her in some guy's hotel room that she didn't even know. Just for some weed and alcohol. That seemed to be all that mattered to her lately. And it worried me. I could remember a time when she wouldn't drink or smoke for anything. But now, it seemed to be all she wanted to do whenever she went out. In fact, it was the only reason she went out sometimes.

"Did you sleep with him?" I asked already knowing the answer.

She seemed to be thinking for a moment. Then she said, "Yeah I guess I did."

"You guess? Girl, did you use protection?"

"Karla, don't worry. I always carry condoms with me. No matter what."

"But if you can't remember if you had sex with him, how do you know you even used them?"

"Trust me. If the conversation turned to sex, then believe me, I whipped out a Trojan on him!"

"You need to promise me that you won't be doing that anymore."

"Doing what? Drinking? I can't promise you that. Smoking? I can't promise you that."

"Going to some strange dude's hotel room and having sex with him!"

She shushed me. Then she said, "Yeah girl, I promise you that one."

I didn't believe her.

I couldn't believe Mike actually wanted to meet my mother. I had never been with a dude that specifically asked to meet my mother. Usually it just happened eventually. We sat across from each other at the kitchen table eating dinner that consisted of cubed steak, rice and gravy, cabbage and dinner rolls.

"So you're going in the military, Mike," my mother said looking Mike flatly in his eyes. He looked back at her without blinking and it was like a showdown at the O.K. corral.

"Yes Mam. I leave in three months."

My mom nodded her head as if he'd passed that little test.

"So you did graduate from high school then?"

I dropped my fork in my plate and tried to hold in a laugh.

Mike looked at me and smiled and then back at my mother. "Yes, Mam, I did. I'm not as smart as Karly, but I did make it through high school."

He was so polite and I knew he was winning her over. Until she asked, "What's with all the tattoos?"

I couldn't hold it anymore and I laughed. Mike laughed too but he managed to do his quietly. Then he nodded. "I see where Karly get's her straight forwardness from."

My mom just smiled but still expected for him to answer the question.

"Well, I just like tattoos. I have some friends that have died so I have their names on me and I have my mom's name because she passed. Most of the other ones are just for decoration. I guess you can say, it's a hobby of mine, because I designed all of them."

I didn't know about my mom but I liked his answer. It was mature and concise.

"Okay," was all my mother said. I looked at her to try to see disapproval or something else on her face, but she wouldn't look at me.

"And how old are you?"

"Twenty-one."

"And you've known Karla how long?"

"Six years Mam. Lonna's brother and I are good friends."

That's when my mom stopped and looked at me finally. She remembered our conversations about Lonna's brother. She had to. There had been so many that she couldn't have possibly forgotten. I could tell she was confused by the look on her face, but it was just like my mom not to say a word because she figured I knew what I was doing.

"Have you ever been arrested?" Mom turned back to Mike for the next and final question.

He just smiled that cute half smile of his that showed the dimple in his right cheek and said, "No."

"Okay."

I could see that she was done. At least for now until she thought of something else.

"You like him, Mom?" I asked knowing that she did because if she didn't he would have been gone a long time ago.

"He's alright."

"You and your mom are a lot alike."

I just looked at Mike knowing exactly what he meant as we sat in his car outside of Baskin Robbins. I was convinced he was trying to make me fatter with all the food he'd fed me in the past twenty four hours. We were eating again.

"If you say so."

"Can you cook like her?"

I shook my head smiling. "Naw. Karly don't cook."

Mike smiled and started the car up. As we drove silently down the almost deserted streets of our small city listening to his CD player, I thought back to earlier this morning in the hotel room. And the conversation I had with Lonna.

"Did you mean what you said last night?" I asked out of the clear blue knowing that I startled him.

But he refused to be caught slipping. "I don't know which part you're talking about. But the answer has got to be yes because I meant everything I said last night. I meant everything I have ever told you."

He was so slick with it that I had to believe him. But I still just wanted to be sure. "When you said you love me, did you mean it?"

"I've loved you for a long time. I fell in love with you when you almost got jacked up by that dude on the basketball court. I mean your ass didn't even scream. You just held your own. Everybody else was gonna let Chiloe and Andrew stomp his ass in the pavement but when you heard the police sirens you went and got Chiloe up off him. I respected you that day. Even though you were crying, you were holding your own."

I had been trying, every since that day, to block it out of my memory. That boy still walked with a limp and wore an eye patch over his right eye. He'd also been messed up mentally from the complete kicking in of his brain.

"But, to answer your question," Mike continued, "yes I love you. I love you very much."

We stopped at a stoplight. My leg was shaking horribly. He couldn't steady it with his hand this time because there was an ice cream cone full of ice cream in it. So instead he asked me, "You nervous?"

"No," I lied.

"Did you mean what you said?"

"Huh?"

"You heard me, Karly."

"Would you be mad if I told you I don't know?"

He looked at me confused for a moment but then the light turned green.

"I mean, I've never felt the way I feel about you for anyone else. And last night was wonderful and special to me. But I don't know if it's love or not. I just don't know. I know I wanna be with you though. And I know I don't want you to leave me and go in the Air force but it's something you gotta do." I paused hoping he understood me and that he wasn't mad at me.

"Okay." He nodded. "That sounds like love to me, but I'll leave it at that."

"Will you please hold still," My mom said trying her best to hem the dress I was wearing.

"I am Ma."

"No, you're not. You're just itching to get up there with that boy, he ain't going nowhere!"

I looked over at Lonna who just laughed. It was ok, because she would be going through this same thing tomorrow.

By the time my mother finished sticking and sewing, the white dress was well above my knees. "I think it's too short," she said standing back and shaking her head.

"Momma, my gown will cover it. Nobody will know."

She still wasn't satisfied, I could tell. But she just shrugged and started to pack up her sewing kit. At the same time, I began putting my super sheer stockings on, careful not to wrinkle my dress or tear the stockings.

"I'mma go slip my dress on," she said finally after she made sure I didn't run my stockings.

"Ok."

Then she turned to Lonna. "Make sure she looks decent before she leaves out of here. You know she's trying to rush."

Lonna nodded and smiled. Yes it was true. The only thing separating me from the perfect man was my closet and a wall. He'd been at my house since eight that morning, as much excited about me graduating as I was. It took my mom telling me to go get dressed for us to separate ourselves from each other and even then, I was still itching to get back to him.

"You look so beautiful," Lonna said as she curled the back of my hair. It was cut really short back there and she wanted to make sure it was done perfectly.

"Thank you."

"Are you nervous?"

"You know I am. You know I don't like to be in front of a crowd."

"You'll do fine. You always do."

I looked at her sensing there was more to that remark than what met the eye. She must have forgotten how well I knew her. "What's that supposed to mean?"

She sat down on the chaise and looked at me. "I mean just what I said. You always do fine. Everything you touch turns to gold. You haven't even walked across the stage and you already got a book getting published."

She stopped and looked over at the acceptance letter from my publisher that lay on my night stand. Still neatly folded and in the envelope, it arrived yesterday. She was the only person who'd seen it besides my mother.

"Yet," she continued, "you always doubting yourself. At least you're not a total fuck up."

"I don't know any total fuck ups."

"You're looking at one."

I took her hand gently in my own. "No, I'm looking at my best friend in the whole world. And she ain't no fuck up. Why do you even think of yourself like that?"

She looked at me like I was just too blind or too stupid to see the obvious. "Come on, Karla. You see what's happening."

That was all she needed to say and I knew what she meant. I was at a total loss for words. And she knew it. She got back up and finished curling my hair like the conversation never took place. "Come on," she said after spraying me with enough oil sheen to suffocate me. "Let's go graduate."

I wasn't joking when I said I hated crowds. Crowds of any kind. Even if they were cheering me on during this graduation and I never had to worry about seeing any of these people again. My legs were shaking terribly as my principal's secretary called out my name. I came walking across the stage like I really knew what the hell I was doing, shook my principal's hand, who was mad at the crowd for not holding their applause like he asked them three times, and headed back off the stage to my seat. The girl who happened to be the same height as me and that's why we were seated next to each other, grabbed my hand in encouragement but I was just grateful I had not tripped over my white size nine patent leather pumps that Mike bought for me as part of my graduation gift.

"You looked so cute up there," he said to me as we sat on my living room floor eating pizza and watching a movie. New-New was back at home with Andrew and Lenora. Lonna was God knows where. But Mike was right here with me, I was a high school graduate and everything was all good.

"Yeah right. Did I walk to slow? I thought for sure I was gonna fall."

"You know you weren't gonna fall," he said shaking his head and laughing.

"I really thought I was. If I had I would've laid right there like I was dead until the ambulance came and got me."

He laughed so hard he almost choked and I rubbed his back laughing with him.

"I've got something to show you," I said when he calmed down. His cheeks were still puffy with food.

"Oh yeah?" He said grabbing me around my waste, but first checking the hallway to make sure my mother was nowhere in sight.

"Stay right here," I said getting up. He held his hands out and looked at me like I was crazy still on the verge of laughter. "Karly, where am I going?"

I ran to my room and grabbed the envelope off of my night stand. Then I headed back up front.

"Here," I said handing him the letter. He read the outside and then looked up at me. I watched as he opened the envelope and his eyes traveled over the letter.

"For real, Karla? They're gonna publish you?"

I nodded.

"Why didn't you tell me this sooner?"

"I don't know," I shrugged. "I guess it just really didn't seem real to me. It still don't."

He shook his head and continued to look at me. "This is a three book deal. That's a lot of money."

"Can you imagine?"

"What are you gonna do with it?"

Then I shrugged again. "I just feel so overwhelmed right now. It's kind of like I don't know what to do. Everything's happening to me all at once. It's crazy."

He put his arm around me and pulled me close to him on the floor. I let him wrap his arms around me because it felt so good. And I placed my head on his shoulder. "Everything is gonna be ok. Just roll with it."

That sounded like something Lonna would say. And my mind drifted back to her again. I had never loved another female, outside of my family, the way I loved her. And it didn't seem the least bit strange to me, she was my best friend and I couldn't imagine being without her. That was why the world wind path she was on was killing me slowly.

And I knew most of it was because of Kelly. His death hurt her more than she would ever be willing to let on. All of these changes in her and between us started when he died. When he took his last breath in her arms it was like the old Lonna took her last breath too. And she was replaced with this self destructive one. But I loved her the same if not more.

I sat beside Mike in the balcony of the auditorium. I feared not being able to sit through all of this. Especially, if it was as boring as mine. But Lonna and New-New, were like sisters to me. I would not have missed their graduation for the world.

"Leonay?" Mike asked as New-New's name was called to walk across the stage and receive her diploma. He had a look on his face as if he would break out in uncontrollable laughter at any moment. I smiled back because I felt the same way just six years ago when I first heard her real name.

Lonna was directly behind New-New. Her long black hair hung under her cap, touching the middle of her back and slightly curled at the ends. She was so pretty. I felt my eyes begin to ache and blur over.

"You're not gonna cry, are you?" Mike whispered to me and I smiled at him again. He squeezed my hand, and pecked my cheek. Directly behind me in the auditorium stands, Chiloe cleared his throat harshly. I looked at Mike who just shook his head and shrugged.

Of all the graduates, Lonna and New-New had the biggest family. Greta, Rajul, Chiloe, Bree, Jay, Marco, Kerry, Rosie, Gerald, Mike, Andrew, and me. Marco looked so handsome in his police uniform. He had to go back on duty directly after the graduation.

Rosie looked half dead to say the least. She had emerged from county rehab just two weeks ago like someone waking from the dead. She hardly spoke a word now and her whole bony body seemed to tremble. Her eyes darted suspiciously back and forth, constantly paranoid about something. She was a shadow of her former self, having lost so much weight. I could remember when her butt was so big you could sit a drink on it. But now, she looked barely able to hold herself up. I wondered how she even managed to get dressed for this occasion. Her soft curly hair was pinned up while she wore a modest beige flowered dress. It was a long way from the red leather miniskirts she used to rock. Then it hit me that Kerry, being the loving husband that he was, probably dressed her just as he did himself and Gerald.

Chiloe stood far off to the side with Rajul while we took pictures of the two graduates. I could feel his eyes on me, but I refused to give him the satisfaction of even the slightest glance as Mike and I posed for a number of pictures. I was able to snap one of him and his older brother though. And then one with his whole family. On the second family photo, I was included as Mike took the picture three or four times.

No one was surprised that Lonna graduated. She'd always been smart. But New-New's pregnancy put her future up in the air. Andrew made damn sure that his girl finished school though, no matter what. I gave him major props for that.

Rajul stood on the deck, one arm around the waist of his flavor of the month, the other holding a beer can. "So what's next Karla?" He asked me.

I sat on the wooden rail of the deck, waiting for another hamburger to cook. Mike stood right in front of me wrapping himself up in my arms. He turned around to look at me as I shook my head just thinking about all of the things I would be facing after tomorrow. My mother was leaving for New Orleans in another week.

"You gonna tell them?" Mike said nudging me gently in my thigh.

"Tell them what?" Lonna asked slowly climbing the stairs. I noticed the Styrofoam cup in her hand and I knew she wasn't drinking soda, water, Kool-aide, or iced tea.

"About the book," I replied disgusted with her.

"Tell 'em baby," Mike said putting his arm around me. He was clearly more excited than I was.

"I found a publishing company to publish my book."

The statement was directed at Rajul, but everyone else down in the yard seemed to have heard me over the music and they stopped. I was uncomfortable and it reminded me of the first day I sat on this deck. My face burned.

"You're kidding," Rajul said. "Congratulations." He punched my arm in his brotherly love sort of way. It hurt like hell.

"Did y'all hear that?" Lonna shouted above the music and the happy chatter coming from down in the yard. Chiloe sat at a folding table playing cards with another group of guys. New-New, Andrew, and Greta sat under the cheap canopy Rajul bought the day before, holding their daughter for other relatives to admire. Jay was in the yard playing, or at least trying to play, Frisbee with Gerald and a group of children of all different ages, including Bree. "Karla's book is getting published!"

Some people clapped, some people yelled, 'Congratulations!' I looked at Mike to see if he was happy about the little chain reaction he had caused. He smiled back at me. But I was still so unsure.

I walked into the club that night, holding tightly to Mike's arm. All the festivities of graduation made me tired, but it wasn't about to end before we did our club thing. I wasn't even a club person, but I wasn't going to give up the chance to show Mike off a little more before he got out of town. He only had a little over two more months.

Unlike prom, there were people from all the surrounding high schools and some people who hadn't seen the likes of any kind of school in years. There were girls that I never would have guessed would come out of the house looking like they were. If they could fit their big behinds into it, they had it on. I felt over dressed in my daisy dukes and yellow top. Lonna and I were dressed alike, something we never did. Her outfit was blue though.

Mike and I squeezed our bodies onto the dimly lit dance floor amidst a hundred other bodies. He grabbed me by my waste and pulled me closer to him where he began a slow and sensuous grind into my hips. Another boy tried to sneak up from behind with the hopes of having the pleasure of doing the same thing that Mike was doing to me. But Mike quickly pushed him away, letting him know I was strictly off limits. There was no way he was going to share what he was rubbing on through my thin shorts as he bathed my neck in breath tinged slightly with alcohol.

I turned around slowly to the beat of the music so he could get full access to my butt bumping and rubbing against his groin as he pulled me even closer to him. I was so close, not only could I feel the throbbing in his pants but also every muscle in his upper thighs.

"Damn girl," he whispered in my ear.

"Damn, boy," I thought back.

One song led straight into another one and we were still on the dance floor going at it. Neither one of us were tired of the feel of body against body. He was fully erect now and even though his jeans were baggy, I knew he didn't want me to move for fear of everyone being able to see how much he enjoyed dancing with me. The "Damn girls" turned into low moans and gentle bites to my ear and neck. I had a feeling he couldn't wait to get me to his house where I would be spending the night. I couldn't wait to be there.

A brief glance around the club as I continued to pop my thang against him, and I spotted Lonna with some girls from her own school. They looked raunchy in short and tight wear and the fake hair pilled high on top of their heads. I recognized the leader of the hoochie pack as Jackie, one of Lonna's friends who dropped out of school after ninth grade and made a career of being a hoochie. And it wasn't that I was jealous. Even though Jackie was a beautiful golden brown complexion with large brown eyes, it was the way she carried herself that made her unbearable to me. Seeing them together was like watching my friend being flushed down a toilet stool. And the toilet was much too dirty to reach my hand in and pull her out. She was too far down the chute to reach her anyway.

I shook my head and turned back around to face Mike. Watching his eyes move from mine to my breast, that were bursting pleasantly from the tight shirt I wore, was a far more relaxing scene to me.

"I'mma hate to leave you, girl. You know that?" He asked breathing hard on me the way he did when he wanted some so badly.

"Not as much as I'm gonna hate for you to leave."

"You gonna miss me?" And with that he squeezed my ass just hard enough for me to moan a little too loudly because the people dancing next to us looked over.

"Yes."

"I love you," he said laughing.

"I love you too, baby," I said back deciding to leave all the pretense of me not really knowing. I knew exactly what I felt in my heart and I knew exactly what this was.

Neither one of us heard him the first time; we were so lost in each other. But then he cleared his throat again. Mike looked up and I followed his eyes. I knew who it was already.

I turned around to see Chiloe standing behind us.

"What's up man?" Chiloe asked us like we had been caught stealing.

"Hey," I said turning back around to Mike but I could still feel Chiloe's eyes burning holes through my back.

"What's up, Chiloe?" Mike asked his voice strong and steady. I smiled at the way he stood up to him without even realizing he was doing so. His arms even became tighter, protective around me.

"Y'all look like y'all having a good time."

I looked up at Mike who just nodded and said, "Yeah, it's live up in here."

"Where y'all goin' when you leave here?"

"My crib."

If I wasn't mistaken I heard crickets chirping. But then Chiloe said, "Oh. Alright then. I'll get wit' y'all."

Then he disappeared somewhere in the crowd.

Lonna didn't come home with us that night. In fact I wasn't even able to find her when it was time to leave. I had her paged, but the girl was nowhere in sight. I was worried but Mike and I left the club at one in the morning anyway. After a night of dancing, my body was sore. But not too sore for what I knew lay ahead.

It started to rain as soon as we pulled up in Mike's driveway. We made a mad dash to the front porch as he fumbled with the keys for a quick second under the porch light by the door. He let me in first when he finally got the door opened.

The house was dark and quiet. His father was in the field and had been for two weeks now. He had another two weeks to go. Mike cut on every light in the house before we finally made our way to his room.

"Are you hungry?" He asked me.

I thought for a second and realized I had not eaten since the cookout and that was around twelve that afternoon. I worked the two hamburgers, baked beans and one hotdog off at the club.

"Yeah I guess so. What you got?"

"Bologna, ham, roast beef."

"Oh my goodness! I thought you meant real food!"

"What?" He raised his hands up like he didn't know what I was talking about. "That is real food, girl!"

I shook my head as I sat down on his bed, ready to cut the television on. I didn't know what I was going to find at one o'clock on a Sunday morning. "Roast beef is fine."

I could hear him laughing all the way into the kitchen while I began flipping channels. I finally found a decent movie on HBO. I thought briefly about calling Lonna even though I knew she wasn't home yet. I shrugged off the idea finally and began to get undressed so I could go to bed.

Just as I came out of my shorts and shirt, Mike appeared at the door with two paper plates, one in each hand. Between his teeth was a Styrofoam cup.

"You don't know how to knock?" I asked standing in the middle of the floor with my red lacy bra and matching panties. He sat the plates down beside the television set on his dresser and said, "No."

"What are you staring at me for?" I asked getting ready to cover myself with one of my favorite t-shirts, it actually belonged to him, that lay across his bed still waiting to be put on.

But he grabbed my arms, both of them, forcing them down to the sides of my body. "Don't you dare cover yourself like that."

Then he let go and stood back, never taking his eyes off of me. "Finish undressing."

223

I looked around making sure he was talking to me. Not only was the television bright but the one light bulb that hung over his bed from the ceiling was enough to make one go blind. Usually when I undressed, or he undressed me, we were under the covers in the dark.

"Can you hit the light?" I asked.

But he shook his head. "No."

And not only were the lights getting to me, but he was staring at me. Straight at me like this was some kind of show. Even though his warm gaze on me was making me unbearably hot, I was so uncomfortable. My underwear started to feel damp between my legs as I shifted my weight from one leg to the other.

"Today, Karly," he said as he seated himself comfortably on his bed and leaned back on one elbow. "Start with the bra. And then the panties."

The way he said *panties,* made me feel as if I were gushing. But it couldn't have been that much. Wouldn't it be dripping down my legs by now? And the look in his eyes said he wasn't playing with me. This was not a game and my stomach muscles began to tighten involuntarily while I slowly began to unfasten my bra. I couldn't even look him in the eyes instead I opted for the beige carpet. I flung the bra on the bed just as Mike stood up in front of me. I just knew he could smell and feel the heat coming from my underwear. I could not remember ever being so embarrassed.

He put his hands on my sides, under my breast and slid them down to the elastic band in my panties. Rubbing me with his whole entire hand, he removed my underwear down to my ankles and held them as I stepped out of them. On his way back up, his hands traveled the length of my body, front and back, until we stood face to face.

"You are so beautiful," he whispered.

"Thank you," I said back still not wanting to look him in the eyes. But his hand held my chin firmly so that our eyes interlocked in a tight knot. His other hand stroked my back.

"Remember the first time we made love?"

I nodded.

"Can we make love like that tonight?"

I was sure in a second there was going to be a huge puddle on the carpet. Why did he have to keep looking at me like this? Why did he have to keep talking to me like this?"

"Yes," I barely squeezed from my throat.

"Can we do it with the lights on?"

My body began to shake uncontrollably. I felt dizzy. The tightening of my stomach muscles was making me want to throw up.

"Why?"

"I wanna see you. I wanna see the faces you make. I wanna see you arch your back."

I couldn't take it anymore. My hands were on him, pulling his t-shirt off of his body and tossing it to the floor. A look of complete satisfaction came over his face as I undid his belt, sliding boxers and jeans to the floor at the same time. He was totally erect and waiting for me as I pulled him down on the bed on top of me. His words and stares had been more than enough foreplay for me. But he was determined to bring me to the point of begging.

He flipped me over on my stomach so that his hands could travel my back and my behind. Tender strokes turned into firm massages. My skin broke into a million goose pimples when I felt his warm lips on me. I couldn't contain the moans and groans that were anything but lady like. He knew what lips on the spot under my hairline did to me as he kissed and licked it while pulling my short hair at the same time. My body was going limp and I feared I would explode before he could even enjoy it.

"Mike," I said turning myself over but staying under him all the while.

I didn't have to say anything because he knew. He smiled that cocky smile, knowing he was in full control of the situation.

"You sure?"

"Yes."

"Hold on."

He sat up, off of me and slid to the edge of his bed. I watched him grab a condom and struggle to get the wrapper open. His hands were shaking.

"Give it here," I said taking the fresh condom from him. I sat up as he turned to face me and watched the expression on his face as I slid the condom down on him. He moaned again.

"Come sit on it."

"What?"

"Come sit on it."

"I don't know if I can do that." I wasn't experienced like the girls I was sure he'd been with before me. I didn't know a damn thing about sitting on it or anything else. I would never want to do anything to make him feel that I weren't good enough.

"You won't have to do anything baby. I'll do everything. Just come here."

I hesitated, for a moment, but I finally crawled over to him. Gently I placed one leg on each side of his body and I guided him into me. He gripped my hips, I lowered myself down on him, he propped himself up on both pillows.

"Ride with me, baby, not against me," he said as his body began to move slowly. With his hands still on my hips, he controlled every movement I made by swaying me here and there. I never would have thought it would feel so good. It was kind of like riding a wave and I loved it.

"You like it don't you?" He asked almost breathlessly.

"Yes."

He was burning a hole into my face watching my facial expressions at the same time biting his lower lip in total concentration. I continued to ride as he continued to drive me. I could feel him coming dangerously close to what he lovingly referred to as 'my spot' and I moaned. He knew exactly what it was for and pushed me down a little bit harder on him. I grabbed his shoulders and called out his name.

"Mmm mmm mmm," he said pulling me down on top of him. "Just ride with me baby," he reminded me as he stroked my hair and face like a baby. With his other hand, he pressed deep into the small of my back and continued to guide me with his hips. He seemed to be even further inside me now that our bodies were closer with our chest touching.

"You gonna cum for me baby?" He whispered in my ear. I nodded too enthralled to even speak. I was being overcome by involuntary tremors. He went even further inside and I screamed out his name again. There was no pain, he was a perfect fit for me. But the agony of pleasure I was feeling seemed to be far worse than it ever had before.

"You gripping me so tight down there, baby," Mike said as he continued to steadily move me. Just because I was at the tip of an earth shattering orgasm meant nothing to him. He wasn't about to speed up or slow down and disturb the groove we had going on. My heart felt as if it would come through my chest at any moment. I knew I was soaking him and I wondered how he could possibly maintain. Didn't he feel what I was feeling?

"Are you gonna cum?" I asked, regaining my composure for a second. I wiped the sweat from the top of my hairline. I couldn't remember sweating like this before.

"You know I am."

"When?"

"Sit up."

So I did. He buried his fingers into the thick flesh of my hips once again and began to move me up and down on him, almost violently but not quite. He groaned with every long thrust and I realized I was zoning again. Not too long after, his plunges became faster and I heard him call my name. He arched his back to get even further into me. I could feel the twitching of him inside of me and I knew he had reached his goal. And mine too. He pulled me back down on top of him.

The sound of thunder crashing outside of Mike's bedroom window woke me with a start. I could feel my heart pounding wildly against my chest and I fought to control my breathing as I looked down at Mike snoring softly beside me. I was braced with an unshakable fear for Lonna. The clock on the VCR read 4 am.

I turned away from Mike, ready to climb out of the bed, but there was a firm grip on my left thigh.

"Where you going girl?" Mike asked, his voice full of sleep and I wondered if he was even awake.

"I'm going to call Lonna and make sure she got home okay."

Mike turned over and reached under his side of the bed. He pulled out a cordless phone but the battery light was blinking on and off.

"Mike this phone is dead."

He sat up and looked down at the phone in disbelief. Then he said, "Okay. Let's go in the kitchen."

"I think I can find the kitchen."

"I'm going with you."

I gave up trying to argue with him. It was obvious he wasn't letting me out of his sight. I slipped on his t-shirt that I never got a chance to wear that night. He got out of bed just as naked as you please and followed me down the brightly lit hallway and into the kitchen.

I tried to dial Lonna's number on the white telephone mounted on the kitchen wall but Mike was breathing down my back. Morning breath and all.

"Mike, come on now."

"What?"

"Can you let me use the phone please?"

"Alright, alright."

So he sat down in a chair at the kitchen table, watching me the whole while. First I tried to page her. Without even giving her time to call me back, I dialed her home number.

"Hello?" I couldn't tell if this was New-New, Bree, or even her mother.

"Is Lonna there?" I asked feeling guilty for calling so early in the morning. But my worry had gotten the best of me.

"Is this Karla?"

"Yeah. Who is this?"

"This is Bree. Lonna's not in her bed. Hold on I'll go check downstairs."

"Okay."

I heard her lay the phone down hard on what was probably the nightstand. I waited for her to return, listening closely for any beeps of another call coming in all the while playing with Mike's leg with my right foot.

"She ain't here, Karla" Bree said out of breath. And I felt even guiltier. She probably ran up and down the stairs looking for Lonna.

"Do you know if she even came in at all last night?"

"Uh uh, I don't know. I went to bed at twelve."

"Damn," I mumbled and shook my head. "Alright then. I'll see you later on. I'm sorry for waking you up."

"It's ok. You know we're having another cookout for New-New tomorrow since she's leaving Monday. You gonna be here right?"

"Yeah, I'll be there. Now go back to sleep. I'm sorry."

I hung up the phone and looked at Mike. "She didn't come home last night."

"So what'cha wanna do?"

"I don't know. What can I do?"

"Come back to bed and go back to sleep and then we'll think of something when we wake up again. But by then, she'll be home so there won't be nothing to think about."

He stood up from his chair at the kitchen table and pulled me close by my waste. "Come on back to bed, Karly. I'm sure if something was wrong we would know by now. She probably went with them ho's she was with at the club. She'll be home in the afternoon."

I did what he said. Knowing that he was probably right, especially about going with them *ho's* from the club. I didn't want to think about my friend out there with them doing God knows what. As I snuggled close into his underarm pit, I couldn't seem to keep my eyes closed. Every bout of thunder, or police siren seemed to wake me. I spent thirty minutes tossing and turning beside Mike until finally he sat up in the bed and cut the television on.

"Karla baby, you gotta get some sleep."

"I can't."

"Well watch TV. You'll drift off soon."

For the next two hours, with my head on Mike's stomach, I watched for any news breaks about Lonna. Until finally I did fall asleep.

Chiloe eyed us suspiciously as we climbed the wooden steps of the deck. I guessed he knew where I'd spent the night. He probably called my house a couple of times to no avail.

"What's up man?" Mike said greeting everyone on the porch with a handshake and a nod of his head.

"Yo man, you call here this morning?" Chiloe asked from his position beside Rajul at the grill.

"It was me," I said placing myself strategically in Mike's lap. I felt the familiar throbbing as I made myself comfortable.

"The caller ID had Mike's number."

"I know. It was me. I was looking for Lonna."

"Oh," Rajul said flipping a steak that had to be as big as my head. I knew he was going to devour that one himself. "She passed out on the couch."

"On the couch?" I tried to ignore Chiloe's penetrating stare as I feigned surprise that Lonna was passed out. "What time did she get home?"

"Shit," Rajul looked at his watch like that was really gonna help him to tell me when she came through the door. "Probably 'bout two hours ago."

I looked back at Mike who just shook his head. "I'll be back."

I passed Chiloe on the way to the sliding glass door, holding a beer in his hand trying to sneak looks at me. He didn't want Mike to see the pain in his face but I did.

Lonna lay across the couch like someone who had just fainted. Her left arm was strewn across her head while her right arm hung limply from the couch down onto the carpet. She wore the same cloths she had on the night before.

"Lonna!" I yelled in her ear hoping that she had a head ache.

"What?" She jumped a bit startled but not too much. She didn't even bother to open her eyes.

"Where have you been, girl?"

"Right here."

"No you have not. I called you at four in the morning and you weren't even home. Where were you?"

She breathed deeply and loudly. "I went with Jackie and 'dem. I spent the night with them because it started raining."

There was more to it than that and we both knew it. Instead of pushing the issue, I sat down on the other end of the couch and looked at her. She finally removed her hand from over her eyes and looked at me.

"What?"

"I was worried about you last night, that's what."

"I'm sorry, K."

I shook my head. "You know Momma's leaving in three weeks."

"Yeah, I know. Have you decided what you're gonna do?"

"I'm staying here."

"You gonna stay in that house by yourself?"

"Yep."

I spoke what I had been thinking for a few months now, slowly because I didn't know how she would take it. You never knew with her anymore. "You can always come stay with me."

She sat up then. "For real? You mean it?"

It was the perfect way to keep an eye on her and to do my best to keep her out of trouble. All she would have to do is get a job and we could work on her problems together.

"Yeah I mean it."

She nodded her head, but then she remembered her hang over. "Cool." She grabbed her head and tried to smile but it was much too painful.

I watched my mother leave the week after I graduated. The next Saturday morning I lay in my own bed snuggled close to Mike, watching him sleep. For an hour or so I studied the pattern of his breathing and the rise and fall of his muscular chest wondering how in the world I was going to do without this man that had become so imperative in my life.

Then I looked over at his duffle bag laying lonely on my chaise lounge, just waiting for tomorrow when his father would pick him up from my house and drive him to the military base. From there he would be transported to Georgia for basic training. I actually contemplated stuffing myself into that bag, but I knew it wasn't going to work. So instead I turned over to face the wall. And cried.

I was on my second Kleenex when I felt his arm go around my waist and pull me closer until my body was facing him again.

"Why are you crying?"

"I don't know." I wiped the tears away quickly. "I'll be ok."

"You know I'm coming back to you, right?"

I nodded. Knowing that wasn't enough to appease me but it would have to do. I couldn't ask for any more.

"I've got all these plans for us when I come back, Karla. But I can't do what I'm supposed to do knowing that you're back here crying. I need you to be strong for both of us."

"I will. I promise." I sucked back some snot into my nose and wiped my eyes.

"You gonna be a soldier?"

I nodded again. Then he kissed me searchingly like our mouths held every answer to every question and could mend every piece of our broken hearts right then.

Even though my body was worn out and sore from all of the lovemaking sessions that had taken place over the weekend, I never wanted it to end. As I watched him throw his duffel bag into the trunk of his father's Cadillac, the only thing I could think of was that I never wanted this to end.

He walked slowly back to the carport where I stood. I wanted to beg and plead with him not to go. But that was selfish and I wasn't a selfish person. So I stood quietly just waiting for him to speak.

"I love you Karly," he said. And that was all he needed to say.

"I love you too."

Then he grabbed my arm and pulled me close to him. "I'll call you as soon as I can. I promise."

"Okay." I nodded. Trying to act like that was enough.

He kissed my neck, then my cheeks, my forehead, and finally my lips. Already swollen, he kissed them until they burned. His embrace was tight, and I felt myself melting deeper into him. I couldn't move and didn't want to.

"Come on son," his father said from the driver side of the maroon Cadillac. But I didn't let go. He would have to let go if he wanted to go anywhere. And finally he did.

"I love you," he said again.

"I love you too."

"Be good. Be careful."

"You too baby."

Slowly I could feel each part of his body as it moved away from mine until the only thing still touching were our fingertips. Soon, though, even they grew apart and I watched the boy I loved so much walk to his father's Cadillac and get in. Then I watched him wave and blow me a kiss as the car disappeared up the hill that was my street.

PART 4

Chapter Eleven

Friday, August 18, 1995 3:12 p.m.

I didn't realize how small Karla's house was, until I moved in. I was used to being in a three floor house with a huge backyard and a deck. Even though that house seemed centered in the middle of the ghetto, that made no difference to me. It was big. But Karla's house was tiny. Granted it had three big bedrooms and three bathrooms, that was all there was to it though. The kitchen took up most of the house because the table fit into it. Off from the kitchen was the living room where the front door was located. I didn't understand that concept because everyone always used the back.

My bedroom was all the way at the end of the hall. Not that the hallway was very long. I could stand at the bedroom door and see all the way into the kitchen. The fact that this was where Karla's grandmother died was what bothered me the most. In this exact room. Karla replaced the bedroom set, sending the old one to Good Will, but still. I didn't know how I was going to sleep at night.

Bree's room was the first in the hallway, Karla's old bed room, right beside Karla's new room. Bree was the only one that didn't have a bathroom in her bedroom; instead it was across the hall. But she wasn't complaining. Just happy we elected to take her so she would not be stuck at home with a house full of men. Greta would miss her, I was sure, but she was better off with us.

"Where you want this?" Karla asked carrying a crate of tapes albums, and CD's.

"Just sit it there in the closet for now," I said gesturing towards the closet with the broken door not bothering to turn around. I was too busy looking through the window directly above the bed. I had a good view of the back yard and into the yards of the people behind and beside us. There was nothing but a bunch of trees and an old clothes line that hadn't been used in years. The grass was green and fresh with dandelions sprinkled here and there. I could just imagine Karla as a little child running through all this, bright clean white dress, those white socks with the lace around them and white leather shoes. Oh and let's not forget the long pigtails on both sides of her big head.

"You ok?" Karla said standing behind me, her hands were on her hips and she looked like someone's mother.

"I don't know," I said shrugging my shoulders. I should have been more than overjoyed to be moving into a nice house in a nice neighborhood, rent free except for some utilities, with my best friend in the whole world. Karla was going to be doing her thing on the writing circuit. Marco lined up a real job for me through a friend of his who worked at the technical college, my cash flow would be looking steadily right. But there was something wrong and I couldn't put my finger on it.

"Can I have this," a voice said in the corner. I looked past Karla and into the doorway of the bedroom. There was Bree with her little hands on one of my posters of my favorite rap artist. A big, "NO!" was about to form on my lips but I stopped myself. I was an adult now; it was time for me to start playing grown up. I would get some of those African American prints like Karla had on her wall. No more posters.

"Yeah you can have them," I said finally.

She smiled gratefully and bounced off to her own room. I shook my head and sat down on the bed ready to unpack one of my many boxes. Karla still watched me closely. She had her eye on me every since graduation and it was starting to unnerve me.

"What's wrong?" She asked me again.

"I told you I don't know."

"That's all you can say today? You should be happy."

"I know, I know."

She sat down beside me on the bed. I got a good whiff of her vanilla body spray. Lately she always smelled like chocolate, vanilla, or coconuts.

I looked back out the window through the blinds that I left open. Everyone seemed to have a purpose these days. New-New and Andrew had a baby now and were living in DC doing the family thing. More than likely they would have another baby on the way soon. Karla had Mike, even though he was gone to basic training in Georgia, and her writing career. Where did that leave me? Staying in a house that wasn't even mine. Working a job I really didn't want but the pay was good. And drowning all of these feelings in as much alcohol and drugs as I possibly could without killing myself.

"Don't worry," Karla said putting her arm around my shoulder squeezing me close to her like she was reading my mind. "Things will come together for you girl. You're young. We're all young. And the stuff that's going on now, may not last. But you gotta remember that we are young."

I looked at her, wondering if she thought that was supposed to make me feel better. Life was supposed to begin after you graduated, not five years down the road.

I was about to tell her all of this, but we were interrupted.

"Hey, Karla. The door was open, so I came on in."

I looked up into the face of this girl, ready to pounce on her. Who the hell was she walking up into *my* house like she lived here herself?

"Hey, Phoeny, its fine."

Karla looked at me and back at the girl she had referred to as *Phoeny*.

"Lonna, this is Phoenell, Phoenell this is Lonna."

The chick held her hand out like she wanted to shake. I looked at it, then at Karla wondering who the hell this girl was and why I hadn't heard of her before.

"I've heard a lot about you," Phoenell said putting her hand back down.

"I ain't heard nothing about you."

Maybe I was tripping, but damn. She just waltzed up in here like she owned the place and I was supposed to throw her a damn party? I didn't think so. And why hadn't I heard about her before?

Karla and I were supposed to be best friends; we were supposed to tell each other everything. I guess I had been wrong.

"Phoenell lives up the street. We've been in school together since ninth grade."

I wanted to scream a big fat, "SO!" But I didn't. I just began to busy myself unpacking one of my boxes.

"Look," Phoenell said shaking her damn head because I could see her out of the corner of my eye. She was lucky I didn't punch her in her throat right then. "I just wanted to make sure you were still coming over tonight. You know Flip wanna meet you."

"Phoenell, I told you I don't want no parts of him. I have a man."

"Who's gonna be gone for a whole year."

"That does not matter Phoenell."

"Alright, alright. But just take a look."

"I'll come, but when he gets there, I'm leaving. I mean it."

"Okay. I hear you." The girl turned back to me and said, "It was nice meeting you Lonna."

I stopped what I was doing and turned around. "Humph," was the only thing I could muster. Once again I knew I was tripping. But that was the only thing I could say.

Karla activated her car alarm as we walked through the dirt filled yard up to the front door of the house. The small dingy yellow house for some reason gave me the creeps. It was situated in the very back of Karla's neighborhood, away from civilization and away from all of the other houses that seemed to look alike with well manicured lawns. This one had dirt for grass. The shudders were hanging on for dear life. The mailbox had no door on it. And the screen door looked as if it had been banged around too many times. Forgotten, was the word that came to mind.

This didn't look like much of a party to me. There were about seven people in the small living room that smelled of cheap liquor and marijuana. I felt my stomach tighten like I was going to throw up all over the dirty beige carpet. Karla grabbed my arm for me to walk up and stay close to her because I was still standing by the wooden front door, afraid to come in.

I couldn't believe she had talked me into coming here. What was this, a get together maybe? I tried to think of a good word to call this, when I realized there wasn't one. Why was it so stifling in here to me?

Karla exchanged greetings with three girls standing by the stereo where Snoop Dogg was steadily pumping. Each girl had a can of beer in their hand but they weren't drinking. It was for the effect I was sure. They thought they were cute. I chuckled at the thought as one adjusted her glasses. I could show them what real drinking was.

"Where's Phoenell?" Karla asked the one with what had to be home done box braids. They were a dirty blond color and her roots were black. Each one seemed to be doing its own thing with all different lengths.

She pointed down a short hallway where I saw two different doors. "She in there with Ron."

Karla shook her head disapprovingly at the thought of Phoenell being in there with *Ron*. Karla briefed me on Phoenell during the short ride to this place, I guess to make me feel a little sympathy for her. Phoenell was the product of an interracial relationship, like my brothers and sisters, and had been in an abusive relationship for five years. Not only did her boyfriend beat her on a regular basis, he was a well known drug pusher that lived right there in the house with her under her momma's nose. Her mother was one of his faithful customers.

I looked over at the two boys sitting on the dingy plaid couch, not feeling nearly half of the compassion that Karla did for Phoenell. The two boys were passing a joint back and forth and bobbing hard to the music. I wanted some of that blunt but I had no idea who they were or where their mouths had been. My eyes drifted above their heads to a cheap flea market picture of three black girls with different skin tones. Beside that was its counter part of men. I felt the need to throw up again.

"He hit her again," the girl with the uneven braids said almost whispering.

Karla just shook her head again.

"He gave her a black eye."

"Why did he hit her this time?" Karla asked.

"She tried to break up with him."

She just shrugged and looked at me. I was at a loss for words. I heard about boys hitting their women. It happened a lot in my neighborhood and I was sure my two oldest brothers had probably done it a time or two. But I had never met anyone that it actually happened to. What kind of girl was she to continue to get her ass beat by some dude?

I was about to ask Karla that very question when I was interrupted by a loud, "I'm gonna throw all y'all mudafuckas out of my house!"

A short lady with hair the length of my pinky finger sticking up all over her head stumbled from the kitchen into the living room. The way she carried a pessimistic half empty 40 ounce bottle of Old E in one hand and held a cigarette in the other brought my mother to mind with a quickness. I wondered if maybe they'd been separated at birth as my eyes traveled down to her red and black checker workman jacket and black jeans that over the years had turned grey. She swaggered over to us.

"Where that bitch at?" She asked struggling to stand upstraight.

Apparently the girl with the braids knew exactly who the *bitch* was because she answered quickly. "She's in the room."

The woman left us and half walked, half crawled to the hallway. "Phoenell! Get your ass out here with your damn company! I'mma send all these mudafuckas home! Get your ass out here now!"

One of the three doors opened and out walked a tall almost handsome brother. He was dark and a little too skinny for my taste, but cute all the same. His skin was a deep rich cocoa color and he wore a goatee like he invented them. Behind him, with thick wavy black hair pulled so tightly back into a pony tail that her eyes were slanted was Phoenell. She tried to look confident as she stood cowering behind that boy. Her eyes tried to meet those of the other people in the room, but they soon found their way back to the ground. Probably because of the huge shiner she had on the left one.

"I gotta go," the boy said. He could barely look at her for being so busy looking around at everybody else. His eyes briefly landed on me, but I looked away in disgust. I wanted him to know he didn't impress me not in the least bit when actually he had.

He left quickly, with two other boys who stood by the front door. That was when Phoenell spotted Karla and me standing beside the girl with the uneven braids and her face lit up. She walked quickly over to us and hugged Karla tightly like she hadn't seen her just that morning.

"What's up girl? I didn't think you would make it," she said letting Karla go finally.

"I told you I would be here."

I didn't like this girl. It wasn't just the fact that she let herself get beat down by a dude. There was something else about her that I wasn't too crazy about. Maybe it was jealousy of the relationship she and Karla had formed in a period of four school years. I didn't know, but no I didn't like her.

"Where'd you get that?" Karla asked pointing to the blue/black bruises around her eye with the finger nail of her pinky finger, careful not to touch it.

She just looked at Karla and shrugged her shoulders. Then she looked down at the floor almost in defeat.

"Why don't you end this now before that boy kills you?"

"He didn't mean to hit me so hard, for real. He was just mad because I said I didn't want him no more."

"She need to stop playing like that! Provoking that damn boy!" That was the highly intoxicated woman who had seated herself on a stool between the television and the front door. "She play to damn much! He should've beat her ass!"

Phoenell shook her head and looked up at the ceiling. I couldn't believe what the hell I was hearing. If this woman was her mother, how in the world could she condone her child getting the shit beat out of her for any reason? No matter how stupid she was.

"It smells like ass in that room, Phoenell!"

If I met one more drunk person I was going to scream, but as we turned to look back down the hall where that voice came from I realized she wasn't drunk. She was too young to be drunk. But then again, I did seem to be in the twilight zone, so maybe it wasn't too implausible.

"Hey Dakota," Karla said and the girl smiled. She looked to be about the same age as Bree. She was short and pudgy. She and Karla could have been sisters; except her hair was red, thick and wavy. Her eyes were grey.

"Hey Karla." Then she turned back to Phoenell. "That room stinks. How am I supposed to sleep in there and it smells like that?"

"Well, what do you expect? Sex don't smell like roses!"

I looked back at the drunk woman sitting by the door, but she just shook her head. I wanted to go home badly.

"Well can you do something about it?" Dakota said becoming quite indignant.

"What you want me to do?" Phoenell asked back.

"Spray something, wash the sheets."

"I'm not doing it right now. You'll just have to wait."

Dakota turned with an exasperated sigh to the drunk woman who was now arguing with an older man who seemed just as drunk as she was. He seemed to have materialized out of nowhere looking very unkempt with a hardly combed air fro and a shirt that looked as if it had not been washed in two years. I felt the need to throw up return.

Somebody changed the tape in the tape deck and Dr. Dre started playing. The girl with the uneven braids began moving her nonexistent hips to what she thought was the beat of the music. I snickered because she was way off. Everyone turned to look at me and Karla gave me one of her looks to hush.

"Y'all want something to drink?"

I did but not one everybody and their drunken ass momma had their mouths on. Karla had a soda while I had a fresh can of Schlitz Malt Liquor. Phoenell's mother had apparently stepped outside with the dirty man and they were talking loudly in the front yard. It sounded as if they were arguing, but no one else seemed to be paying them any attention.

Fifteen minutes later I was starting to catch a buzz, but still felt like going home, when the door swung open and in walked Phoenell's boyfriend with five other dudes. I was in Heaven as we seemed to be invaded by them. Or maybe it was just the beer as I quickly guzzled down the remainder and looked for something stronger to pour into the can. I knew Phoenell's momma had to have something somewhere. I found it when I slipped into the kitchen and spotted the bottle of banana flavored MD 20/20 on the cluttered table. The bottle had already been opened by someone, who I didn't know. I quickly poured what I could into my can, tipped the bottle up carefully making sure it didn't touch my lips and drank what could not fit into the can. Then I hurried back to Karla's side before she realized I was missing. Ron made his way across the room with one hand in the pocket of his sagging jeans. Behind him was a shorter dude with a stocky build and a beer belly. He tried to let his jeans sag, but they didn't make it. He was dark and older. Very older.

Karla squinted her eyes as she watched him approach her. Apparently this was Flip. The person that Phoenell was so eager to hook her up with. He spotted Karla from a distance standing in her front yard a few weeks back and had been bugging Phoenell about meeting her up close and personal. I wanted to laugh but the look on my best friend's face said I better not say a word or she would probably leave me in this place.

"What's up?" He asked Karla, all the while looking down at her breast.

Karla opened her mouth to speak but I don't think anything came out as I moved away and over to the couch. That's when I noticed Ron staring me down out of the corner of his eye. Those damn drinks were really kicking in because I found myself staring back right in his girlfriend's house. I mean he was fine, so a little flirting wouldn't hurt. Not a bit.

I sat down beside one of the boys on the couch, making sure to keep one eye on him and one eye on Ron. He offered me a hit off of his blunt and I was drunk by now so I took it without a second thought as to where his lips had been. I would probably regret it when little black headed bumps started to form around my own mouth.

I heard the short dude ask Karla if she wanted to go outside and talk. She looked over at me and then shook her head.

"No, I gotta keep an eye on her," she said pointing to me.

"What'cha think, we gon' do to her?" Ron asked. All sorts of possibilities of what he could do to me ran through my head at that very moment.

Karla didn't even acknowledge him though. He might as well have been invisible.

"Well, can I have your phone number or something?"

I watched Karla hesitate, taking the time to roll her light brown eyes back into her head, while I took another hit off of the fat roll of marijuana. Then I realized I had never given it back to the boy after the first one. I started to giggle. Everyone turned to look at me.

"You know what, I have a boyfriend. So I'm not going to give you my number and I don't think we should see each other."

There was Karla. Always so straight forward. The dude looked hurt almost. I gave the boy back his blunt and stood up ready to make my way to the door where I knew Karla was headed.

"Y'all leaving?" Phoenell asked. What did she think this was? Karla wasn't here to save her from getting her ass kicked.

"Yeah. I think I better get her home." She gestured towards me again. I walked on out the door.

The drunk lady and the dirty man were gone. I sobered up a little as the cool air hit me in the face, a pleasant change from the stifling air of that house. My walk was still uneasy as I made my way slowly to Karla's car.

"Hey," I heard a male voice behind me and turned to see Ron and the dude I was sharing the blunt with.

"Hey," I said back. My voice was shaky I knew, but I was attempting to sound sexy.

"Yo," he said coming closer to me and making sure the dude with the blunt was with him. "What's your name, yo?"

"Lonna."

"Well, Lonna, can I get your number. Call you sometimes?"

I knew that was what he wanted all along. "What about Phoenell? Ain't that your girl?"

He swung his arm at the house like it and everything in it was the last thing on his mind. Then he pulled a piece of paper from his pocket and a pen that I guessed he carried for moments like this.

I scribbled my phone number down quickly and to the best of my abilities at that particular time and handed it back to him.

"This is *your* number, right? You ain't givin' me a fake one, right?"

"No," I said my eyelids starting to feel like they weighed fifty pounds on my face.

"A'right then, I'll call you."

As he headed back to the house, Karla stepped out of the screen door. She didn't pay either one of them any attention as she approached the car quickly with concern written all over her face.

"Are you okay?" She asked me.

Actually I didn't think I was because I was nauseous. But I just nodded my head. She opened the door for me first and then went around to her side and got in.

I wanted badly to tell her what had happened, but I wouldn't. I knew how she would disapprove and probably be mad at me because Phoenell was her so-called friend.

So I sat quietly in my seat all the way back to her house, resisting the urge to throw up.

I heard the doorbell ring. Like in the middle of a dream or something. But I knew it was real when it rang a second time and the house seemed to vibrate along with it.

I turned over on my back and debated whether or not I wanted to answer it. But I wasn't the lady of the house. Karla was, so she could answer the door. It was probably her punching bag friend anyway.

So I turned back over.

As soon as my sleep became a reality to me though, I could feel tugging on my arm. Like something in this house was just refusing to let me sleep. Then I remembered this was the room Karla's grandmother died in, less than three years ago.

I squeezed my eyes even tighter hoping that who or whatever it was would think I was already dead.

"Lonna."

Oh God. Whatever it was already had Bree and it was using her as bait to get at me. I wondered if Karla had been gotten too.

"Lonna wake up."

"Go away. I'm not coming with you."

"Lonna, it's me, Bree."

"I know who you are. Leave me alone."

"Lonna, Chiloe's here. I think something's wrong."

I opened one eye and looked at my sister in the darkness. If it had not have been for her bright skin I probably wouldn't have been able to see her.

"Cut the lamp on."

She reached over to wooden night stand beside the bed and did just that. I squinted, trying to let my eyes focus on the pink hair rollers in her head. Karla parted, combed, and rolled Bree's hair every night so that she could let her long curls fall to her shoulders in the morning, just like mine did. I sat up and threw the cover away from my body. The clock on my night stand said three-twenty three. My head hurt horribly as I remembered the MD 20/20.

"Damn," I said hoarsely and dug my fingers into my eyes to relieve them of the matter that was clouding my vision. Then I started to make my way to the bedroom door. Bree followed close behind almost on the heels of my bare feet. I should have worn socks, because the floor was freezing.

Bree was right. Chiloe stood in the kitchen, right in front of the door, looking frantic. I could never remember him looking that way before. So out of control and . . . terrified?

"What's going on?" I asked looking from him to Karla. Karla just looked back at me as bewildered as I was. She knew just about as much as I did as she stood dressed in her night clothes. There were even lines on her face from whatever her head had rested on during the night.

Chiloe began shaking his head almost hysterically. "There was beef tonight, up at Dapper Dan's. Bobby called me and told me what was happening. By the time I got up there, Rajul was gone. I been calling the house but nobody answered."

"Well he's not here, Chiloe," I said.

"I know he ain't here. I just . . ." he stopped. "I ain't know where else to go. I can't get up with none of my boys. Not one. Not even Bobby ass."

He looked at Karla. I realized he was scared. And all of a sudden I was too.

We hardly saw the black car with its head lights off whiz past us in the pouring rain. But we heard it and felt the wind knock us as it passed. For some reason at the same time, Chiloe decided to pick up the speed. I could see Karla in the darkness, gripping her seat belt in the front seat beside him while Bree and I sat in the back. She was starting to sniffle and I knew she was upset. The fast driving, at night, in the storm was scaring her half to death. I wanted to ask Chiloe to slow down, but my mouth would not open. So I sat back quietly and took her hand in mine. I squeezed gently.

Chiloe made a sharp right onto the dirt road after thirty minutes of driving without speaking. I thanked the Lord that we were closer to our destination with all body parts intact. We weren't out of the clear yet though, as we traveled through the endless maze of trees that seemed to want to block our path. The path to Rajul's front door had never seemed so long. Maybe the rain and the darkness of the night had something to do with it. With the erratic way Chiloe was driving, we could crash into one of these Weeping Willows or pine trees at any second. I wished I hadn't even thought of that as I prayed for the sight of Rajul's front door.

Karla reached over and cut the blaring music down; giving our ear drums a rest from the bass that had been pounding in them. She thought that would calm Chiloe down some. Maybe he would drive a lot safer. But it didn't work. He didn't even seem to notice what she had done. Something more than a mere beef at Dapper Dan's was up and I wished Karla, Bree, and I had stayed home. We could have just let Chiloe and his boys deal with this craziness. We had no business in this car.

Just as Bree squeezed my hand with her eyes shut tightly, the car came to a screeching stop, lurching us all forward. Karla grabbed the dash board with both hands and I grabbed the back of Chiloe's seat. Bree still held onto me. Chiloe already had his door open and was on his way out of the car, it seemed, before it even stopped.

We followed suit, running to get out of the rain. Chiloe was already in the house by the time we made it onto the front porch. I didn't know if he left the door wide open or if it was already like that when we pulled up. We could see only his tall shadow as he moved about the dark house, not knowing where to go first.

"Rajul!" he barked loudly.

There was no answer.

"Rajul!"

Karla left us and went to the left towards the dining room and kitchen. Chiloe watched her for a second as she disappeared around the corner. Then he shot up the stairs. My first instinct was to get some light in the house and then follow Karla to wherever she had gone. But I couldn't see to find a light switch. I didn't know Rajul's house like I knew my own. And with the way Bree was hanging on to me, I couldn't make it very far anyway. So we went to the right, through the foyer down three steps into the den. The light down here was a little better because the television was on. There was no one here though. I walked Bree over to the couch so that she could sit down. She was shaking as she placed her wet hands neatly and tightly into her lap.

I found the light switch for the den by the book case to the right of the couch beside a window and turned it on. That's when I screamed.

Bree didn't know what the hell I was screaming at and I didn't want her to know. I ran to her before she could get to me. My intention was to grab her and take her into the living room, but when we turned to head out of the den, Karla ran straight into me.

"Was that you screaming?" She asked looking from me to Bree.

All I could do was nod my head because what I wanted to say would not come out of my mouth.

"What's wrong?" She grabbed me by the shoulders and tried to stop me from shaking. It wasn't helping.

I looked at Bree wanting desperately to get her out of this room before I told Karla what was wrong.

"Behind the couch," I said as we headed toward the foyer, leaving Karla wondering what the hell I was talking about.

The light in the den helped me to find the light in the foyer right above the ugly white couch with the multicolored flowers that sat under the window by the front door. I sat Bree down again, but in that ugly chair this time.

"Stay right here."

"Lonna, what's wrong?" she asked grabbing my elbow.

I just shook my head. I didn't know what was wrong and I wasn't gonna sit here and try to explain it to her like I did. "Just stay here."

Karla was standing behind the couch looking down. I walked over to her so that I could get a closer look at what she was looking at, what I had discovered. There we both stood, my arm intertwined in hers, looking down at the girl with her black mini skirt hiked up to just below her white panties, because that was the way she fell. One hand was halfheartedly placed over her stomach, the other stretched out above her head. The front of her shirt was soaked in blood like she had bled for hours. Her eyes were open and that was the part that was creeping me out.

I looked at Karla for answers, knowing good and well she didn't have any. All she did was shake her head.

"Where's Chiloe?" I asked realizing that we hadn't heard from him in a while. And the even bigger question, "Where is Rajul?"

Karla shook her head again if she ever stopped the first time. "I don't even wanna know."

She headed towards the stairs, leaving me in the den with the dead girl. I looked back down at her and realized that she wasn't even half bad looking. And she was probably younger than Karla and I. Native American, I thought from the long brown hair that fanned out around her head and rich cocoa skin, just because it reminded me of my mother's so long ago. Suddenly I felt sorry for her parents, who more than likely did not know where the fuck she was. Out here in the middle of nowhere.

I could hear Karla going up the stairs right over my head. I walked slowly back into the foyer, finding Bree right where I left her. I sat down on the arm of the ugly chair, determined to wait for Karla, Rajul, and Chiloe. Wherever they were.

The sound of the police siren and the flashing blue lights coming in through the curtain woke me. I looked around for a second unsure of my surroundings. Everything came back to me when I looked down at Bree asleep beside me, her head resting on the arm rest at the other end of the couch.

I got up and walked towards the front door. An ambulance was parked in front of the police cars and a second one was pulling up behind it. Ambulance number one was unloading a gurney and two police officers were headed towards the door. I let them in as they lead the way for the paramedics.

They stared at me and I stared back at them not really knowing what to say. I didn't even know who called them because I hadn't thought to do that.

Out of the corner of my eye, I could see Karla coming down the stairs.

"Upstairs?" The first officer asked her because she looked more like she knew what was going on than I did.

She nodded. "And the den behind the couch."

I wondered what the hell was upstairs as I watched the first set of paramedics take the gurney up the steps. The second went down into the den.

I looked at Karla questioningly. She sighed heavily as she took my hand and lead me into the dining room. All of a sudden I switched places with her on the night of her grandmother's death. I sat down in a chair at the wooden kitchen table and she sat down beside me.

"What's going on Karla?" I asked already knowing. I felt my heart sinking down into my feet and I was taken back to five years ago when Kelly died. I had the same damn feeling.

"Lonna," she began. I knew she didn't know how to tell me my brother was dead. I could have saved her the pain of telling me. But for what? If I had to hear it from anyone's mouth I would rather it have been hers any day than anyone else's.

"Lonna," she tried again. She dropped her head and looked down at my hands which were placed strategically inside of hers. The thumbs of each of her slightly larger hands caressed the palms of mine while her fingers gripped them tightly.

"What?" I asked wanting her to just say it so we could get this over with.

"Rajul . . ." But she trailed off again. My heart was in my throat again and I found it hard to swallow anything. Not even my own spit.

"Rajul," she tried for the final time. "Rajul is dead."

I had wanted her to just say those words so maybe I would know for sure. Now that I knew, I didn't know what my reaction should be. I wanted to cry, but for some reason no tears would come.

She let me go and I stood up. I could see the forensic techs coming in to do their investigation.

"I called Marco. He should be here in a little while. I'm gonna drive Chiloe's car back to the city and take Bree home. Do you wanna go?"

I didn't know what I wanted to do. I didn't even know if I wanted to go upstairs and check on my brother or not for fear of what I would see. I knew he was in pain and it was a good thing Marco was coming. He was the level headed one; the one that always knew what to do. A lot like Karla.

"How is Chiloe?" I asked finally tired from watching people come in and out of my brother's house. The sound of the metal screen door banging open and shut was beginning to irritate me and I found myself becoming angry for no reason. I could feel blood rushing to my head and my cheeks growing flushed and I desperately needed a hit of something.

Karla still sat in the metal dining room chair, shaking her head. Her large silver hoop earrings swung from side to side with every movement. "He's not good at all. I've never seen him like this."

She got up from the chair and walked to the screen door as Rajul's massive body was loaded into the back of one of the ambulances covered by what looked like a black tarp. I wanted to yell at him to get his ass up off of the stretcher and come back in the house. He needed to explain to us what happened. But I didn't say a word. I just stood and watched the back of Karla's head as she watched the ambulances.

It was six in the morning when Marco pulled the car up in front of our house. I was hoping just maybe Karla changed her mind and decided to stay at our house, but Chiloe's car was not there. I knew she had gone on home and taken Bree with her. I should have gone with her when I had the chance.

There was the feeling of dread again as my two brothers and I walked towards the front door of the house. My stomach began to hurt terribly and I had the urgent need to take a shit. I hated the early morning noises of barking dogs, early birds, and our feet against the grass wet from morning dew. I also hated the sound the door made when Marco opened it. I wanted my world completely silent, but nothing would let me have it that way. Everything insisted on pounding my eardrums causing my head to hurt along with my lower abdomen. The need to throw up hit me suddenly as the smell of the house glided through my nasal passages. Was it the stench of death?

Chiloe flopped down hard on the couch in total darkness. He just sat there staring at the blank television. I went to him, without thinking, to comfort him like he had me when Kelly died. I wrapped my arms around his t-shirt covered shoulders. He was perfectly still like a mannequin. I lay my head on his arm, as it was silently decided that Marco would be the one to tell our mother that her oldest child was dead.

I watched as he ascended the stairs, his long, muscular legs moving at a steady pace. He walked with an air of aloofness as if this was an everyday thing for him. Being a cop had made him somewhat cold to things like this. Even if it were his own family.

I heard him politely knock on my mom's door and then open it. The voices were muffled and incoherent until I heard the scream of "No!" and a loud thump hit the floor above my head. I looked at Chiloe who was still quiet and his eyes never left the television. It didn't even seem like he was breathing. Between him sitting motionless like a dead man and my mother upstairs doing what sounded like convulsions on her bedroom floor, I felt the need to run out of the house screaming for something.

"I'm going to bed," I said to no one in particular because Chiloe obviously wasn't listening. I unwrapped myself from around him, with a kiss on his shoulder, and headed for the stairs. The thought of having to sleep in this house tonight, depressed me even more. Why hadn't I gone home with Karla? It never occurred to me to call her. I felt stuck.

There were footsteps coming down the stairs as soon as I made it to the first one. I prayed it wasn't my mother. I was relieved to see it was Jay. The noise must have woken him up.

"What's up?" He asked me holding his hands out in front of his well built but tall body.

I took him by the hand helped him down the rest of the stairs. Then I pulled him close to me so I could tell him what was going on without Chiloe having to relive everything. I put my arms around him.

"Rajul is dead, Jay. He got shot at his house." I was so quiet I could barely hear myself talk.

He pushed away from me and looked into my eyes, clearly not sure if I was for real or not. But then he noticed Chiloe sitting alone in the early morning light and he realized that this was not a joke.

"Why?"

Tears came to both of our eyes. I shrugged, I still didn't know why. All I knew was that I needed to get away from him and what was left of Chiloe. I needed to be alone. I left him standing there and climbed the familiar stairs to my old deserted bedroom.

Stopping in front of my mother's door I pressed my ear to it and could hear her painful wails. I wondered if she were sitting on the floor. I could picture Marco with his arms wrapped around her trying his best to soothe her. I hoped that he would stay the night so I wouldn't have to deal with any of this in the morning, as I opened the door to my bedroom that was just the way I left it six months ago.

I stripped down to my underwear and climbed into New-New's old bed.

My butt seemed pasted to the seat with sweat as another rush of hot air seemed to hit me straight in my face. Even under the green canopy of the funeral home, I was still burning up.

I undid the top two buttons on my black dress and looked at Karla who sat right beside me. I could see that she was as hot as I was, because she was sweating. That was something that she never did. I fought the urge to wipe the side of her face like a doting mother and turned back around in my seat to look straight ahead at Rajul's casket.

The night before I dreamed of him and that was something new to me. I never dreamed about anyone in my family. But last night I could see him so clear. He was sitting on Momma's bed but she was nowhere in the room. I sat on the ugly blue shabby throw rug that I really never would have been caught dead on. But in my dream there I was in the same dress that I wore to Kelly's funeral. And there were flowers. Not roses or carnations. But a weird green flower that I had never seen before. It had four green pedals and a red center. Something that looked like a cross between a clover and a sun flower. These weird little mutant flowers seemed to be all around me. Sort of like I was sitting in grass. Rajul's lips were moving, but I couldn't hear a word coming out of his mouth. It was like he was on MUTE.

I snapped out of the terrible memories of that dream and looked past Karla over at Chiloe, sitting on the other side of her. He had not said a word since Rajul died. Not a word to anyone. Not even

Karla and that surprised me. Even though she had spent a great amount of time with him, mostly at our house, they apparently sat in silence.

My mother sat beside Jay, who sat in between her and New-New. New-New's face and makeup were streaked with tears as she held on tightly to Andrew's free hand. His other hand held Lenora. I thought about taking the baby for him so that he could just concentrate on New-New, but a bigger part of me said to leave it alone. So I did. Nor did I want to adjust myself in my folding chair to look at Marco and Bree who sat directly behind me. And I definitely didn't want to look at Rosie.

I sat there staring at Rajul's coffin with the spread of red roses on top; just because it seemed to be the only thing I was halfway comfortable looking at for the moment. I wondered if the girl's funeral had been this sad. Her name was Pasha and she was two years younger than Karla and I. A baby to me. But she had been the flavor of the week right then and was in the wrong damn place at the wrong damn time.

I fought back the urge to scream and disrupt this whole façade. I looked at the dudes standing around, in their baggy jeans, t-shirts and bandanas that hung from their pants pockets, like they were actually listening to what the preacher was saying. Like the next night they wouldn't be back on the streets playing cops and robbers in the hood. Like they wouldn't shoot somebody else's brother in the blink of an eye. Like they wouldn't seek retribution for what had happened to Rajul.

Then my mind flashed back to Chiloe, and I knew he would seek revenge. He'd done it for Kelly, he would without a doubt do it for his own brother. Only uglier. Much uglier.

I shook my head at all this shit and Karla's motherly instinct made her rub my shoulder making sure to catch me if I fell into a crying tizzy. I reveled in the feel of her hot sweaty hand against my bare back.

After the releasing of the three doves that stood for Rajul, peace, and love, I sat in just one of the two family limos the funeral home provided. My mother stared blankly out of the window, not looking at anything in particular. Jay and Marco hadn't left her side all day. They both sat on either side of her, Marco holding one of her hands in his own. She seemed to sigh heavily as if on the verge of major tears at every stop light. I couldn't remember seeing her cry that day. How upset could someone be that they couldn't cry?

I shook my head again and there was Karla. Crammed in between Chiloe and I like sandwich meat between two pieces of bread. It was amazing to me how close she had stood to all of us and my sister GG hadn't even found it important enough to attend the funeral. As far as I knew she had not called either. I knew she never really felt kinship towards any of us, but the girl really had no sense of decency either.

Chapter Twelve

Sunday, September 17, 1995 3:27 p.m.

Karla was steadily taking clothes out of Rajul's drawer, folding them and dropping them into the cardboard box. I believed she had her own little system going, but I was about to interrupt her.

"Has Chiloe said what he's gonna do with the house?" I asked her without turning to see her facial expression. I continued to empty Rajul's closet with my back to her.

"No. He still hasn't said *anything*."

"How long can he go without talking?"

"I guess longer than we thought he could."

I put all the hangers into a neat pile on the floor and walked over to Karla so that we didn't have to speak so loudly across the room. I didn't want anyone else to overhear where the conversation was about to go.

"Did he find out who killed Rajul?" I asked only inches away from her ear.

She looked at me sadly and I knew the answer. I knew before the question even left my lips. It had been almost a month since she and Chiloe found Rajul dead in this very room. Chiloe would never let someone who had done this awful thing live any longer than that. He didn't work that way.

I knelt down to the carpet. There was still a blood stain even though it had been washed with carpet cleaner and everything else we could find. It would always be there I guessed, until someone decided to change the whole carpet. I ran my fingers over it.

"Don't worry," Karla said kneeling down with me.

She didn't give me a reason not to.

New-New and Bree were taking their sweet time in the kitchen, loading boxes with the few dishes that Rajul had and cleaning out the refrigerator. There was steak and pork for days, dozens of half empty cereal boxes in the cabinets and loads of beer bottles under the sink.

"How was it up there?" New-New asked with her back to us. She was dumping items from the freezer into a large black trash bag, but not before she took the time to inspect everything making sure no one else would want it.

"Okay," I said knowing she meant if it was a mess from Rajul's murder. Whoever had done it, made it seem so effortless. The police said themselves that there was no sign of a struggle and no sign of forced entry. The killers walked right in, caught Rajul coming out of the shower, and that was that.

I wished my mother had come with us. She had never seen Rajul's home and didn't even know where he stayed. She would have been impressed with the beautiful antique furniture in the living room and the dining room, the techno look of the den, and the country look of the kitchen. She would have loved the three spacious bathrooms that all boasted garden tubs and floral decorations. I wished our house in the hood could've looked like this. However, my mother had not been out of her room since his funeral and I doubted that she would be coming back out any time soon. It hurt me to see her regressing so badly. I did not know if it bothered her more that Rajul was gone, or the way she treated him when he was here.

Marco had successfully managed to handle most of Rajul's assets, both legal and illegal. The illegal funds, that were suspicious to anyone who did not know what he had been up to since the age of twelve were divided among us, except for G.G. He'd also handled the one insurance policy, that once the funeral was paid for and divided between everyone (except for G.G.), gave us each about two thousand dollars. On the whole we were all about ten thousand dollars richer, including Karla who had been a part of the family more so than some of the family members. Chiloe had made sure that she received proper compensation. Wordlessly of course.

I walked over to the one kitchen door, that lead to the vast back yard. There was a huge red dog house where Rajul's Rottweiler lived for three days after his death, until Marco took him home with him. Everyone else had forgotten about the dog. Maybe Rajul should have kept him in the house with him that fateful night. Maybe Rajul would still be here. That thought brought tears to my eyes unwillingly.

No one even heard the front door open because of the music coming from the stereo in the den. Karla cut it on so that we wouldn't have to work in the death filled silence of the huge house. But we all heard Marco call, "Hello!" I was relieved to hear his booming voice. He had been such a comfort to the rest of us that I hardly wanted to leave his sight, even to go home at night.

"We're in here!" Bree yelled with her head in the cabinet under the sink. She was cleaning what was left of the unopened beer cans and cleaning products.

Marco wasn't alone as he entered the kitchen. He was followed closely by Jay, and to all of our surprise, Chiloe. I didn't know if he had been back to the house since Rajul's death or not. Karla probably knew but I didn't ask her. Here he was now, though, with eyes set on

Karla. She smiled, not just at him though, but at all of them. I watched him sit down at the other end of the table as Jay gave Karla a tight hug.

"How is everything?" Marco asked walking around inspecting the kitchen. I didn't know what he expected to find, but I knew what the question meant. The same thing that New-New meant when she asked, 'How was it up there?'

"Okay," I replied again.

"Are y'all almost done?"

"Yeah, almost."

"We're not doing the basement though," Karla informed him being that everyone was scared to go down there.

"Ain't nothin' in the basement," Chiloe said and we all turned to look at him in bewilderment. Even Bree's head came from under the cabinet. New-New's head came out of the freezer. These were the first words he had spoken to anyone in four weeks. "I cleaned everything out down there last week."

I looked at Karla and she just shrugged, looking as surprised as everyone else. Obviously she had not known anything about it.

"What was down there?" I asked.

He looked from me, to Marco, and then to me again. There was my answer right there. Drugs, guns, or maybe both.

"Wath'cha gonna do with the house?" New-New asked the question that had been on all of our minds.

But he just shrugged and sat back in the seat, stretching his long legs in front of him. "I don't know."

We knew that would be all anyone would get out of him concerning this house. He would probably never sell it or rent it out for that matter. It was going to sit right here just like this because it meant so much to him. Just like Rajul meant so much to him.

"Well, we're done," New-New said closing the freezer and stepping down from the folding chair. I held my breath as she did because she was by now seven months pregnant with her second baby. She touched the floor safely and I exhaled.

"Ya'll come on home. We know you're tired." Marco rubbed New-New's shoulders as she sat down in the folding chair she had just finished standing on.

"We gotta do the den," I said from my position at the kitchen door. I just couldn't tear myself away from the sight of the sunshine bathing the fresh green grass. Rajul had taken perfect care of the yard just like he had the house.

"Don't worry about the den."

Once again, everyone looked at Chiloe. I wondered why we didn't have to worry about the den. Was he going to live here? Finally I just shook my head and turned back towards the door. It was no telling what was going through his mind and I wasn't about to debate it.

Then Karla's pager went off and everyone's attention was taken from Chiloe. She unhooked it from her baggy khaki pants and looked down at the number. The smile that covered her face was as bright as the sunshine outside of the window and she immediately headed for the beige phone that hung on the kitchen wall beside the refrigerator.

I knew for a fact the cord only stretched but so far into the dining room which sat beside the kitchen. So we could all hear her enthusiastic, "Hey Boo." I snuck a quick glance at Chiloe and I could see his jaw muscles working furiously and his face turning red as he watched the phone cord as Karla said, "I miss you too."

Then she went into an explanation of where she was and how she would be home tonight. Her voice dimmed but only slightly as she whispered, "I love you too, Mike." Karla could only be but so quiet.

My sisters and I had food on our mind. By the time Karla's car, followed by Marco's pulled up at my old address, it had pretty much been decided that we would talk Marco into cooking out. The taste of charcoal cooked burgers and hotdogs was strong in my throat and there was no doubt that even if he refused, Karla and I would do our best not to burn down the house with the grill.

I watched all three of my brothers remove themselves from Marco's tiny Civic. Although he made a fare amount of money for a single man, he was such a cheap skate that he would never think about getting a newer or bigger car. Not unless the one he had just all of a sudden died. He even lived in a one bedroom house that cost him little to nothing every month.

"So you've adopted a son, huh?" I asked Karla nudging her in the rib as we walked toward the front door. She knew I was talking about Jay and how close they had become. He spent almost as much time as Chiloe did at our house. Sometimes it was just to play video games with Bree, or follow Karla around like a lost puppy dog.

She shrugged her shoulder for what had to be the millionth time that day and said, "I guess." Then she looked behind us and yelled, "Marc you gonna cook on the grill for us?"

Marco shook his head, "I have to work tonight. Ask Chiloe."

She turned all the way around to look at Chiloe who couldn't even seem to look her in her eyes. I knew it was the conversation between her and Mike from earlier that had him still seething on the inside. I wondered exactly how long he was going to keep this fire for Karla flaming. It had already been six whole years now.

"I guess we're on our own, "I said putting my key into the front door. Everyone piled in behind me almost knocking me over.

The house was still and quiet. I hadn't expected anything else. I figured Greta would still be in her room where she had been since Rajul's death. Everyone else that would have been up and about was with me, even though we had hopes that Rosie would appear soon. Her husband and son hadn't seen her since Rajul's funeral.

The first thing Jay did was cut the television on. Bree flopped down on the couch with him. New-New planted herself in the old recliner that had been in the same spot for years. Karla and I headed towards the deck to get our little barbeque started.

I'll never forget how the heat just seemed to hit us in the face when we slid the aged glass door back. Even though we'd only been outside seconds earlier, anyone would have sworn that within that short time the temperature had gone up ten more degrees.

"I'll start it up for y'all," we heard behind us. I put the charcoal down and handed the lighter fluid to Chiloe. "Go get the food," he said not looking at either one of us as he began to prepare the grill. I didn't know if he meant just for me to go so that he could be alone with Karla, but she followed me off of the deck anyway.

The television was loud, but I still heard the creaking of the stairs. Everyone around me was quiet, not saying a word and that was odd. Karla passed me in the living room where I stopped. She seemed to be moving in slow motion to the kitchen, though, as the lighting seemed to get brighter and brighter. I felt like I was going to pass out, and I didn't even know what passing out felt like. I knew my heart rate had gone up a couple of notches and I was sweating around my brow.

When I blinked, Marco was standing at the end of the stair way. His face was red, almost as if he had been running, but not quite the same. I couldn't tell if he was breathing hard or not, but I saw his chest pumping up and down through his thin brown tee shirt with the Mexican flag on the front. Why hadn't I noticed that tee shirt before? He looked back at me and his mouth began to move. But I couldn't hear a word. They were getting lost somewhere, not reaching my ears.

I saw Bree and Jay jump up and run to Marco. He grabbed them both, one in each of his muscular arms. I couldn't hear either one of them, but I could see Bree clawing desperately to get to the stairs, but Marco was holding her back. I blinked again and both New-New and Karla were at my side. One of them was shaking me.

"What's going on?" I heard myself ask, but then I wondered if it were actually me asking that. New-New grabbed my chin, rather harshly and I knew it would leave a bruise, and made me look at her.

"Momma is dead," she said shaking her head like she couldn't believe I could be so dumb.

I watched, desperately trying to hide the fact that I was disappointed in this whole situation. There was none of the fan fare like Rajul's funeral where people were in line, crowding over other people's graves trying to see what they could. This was small and not half as sad.

Bree was crying of course, and I had to practically hold her up to keep her from falling face first into the grass. Chiloe shed a tear or two but it was none of the sulking he had done for Rajul. The rest of us looked on at the lavender casket in blank bewilderment not believing our family had taken such a turn of events.

There were no white doves for Greta. Mainly because none of us felt that strongly about her. I didn't want the funeral home director and the graveyard owner to look at us as a bunch of cold hearted, unfeeling brats. But the truth was the truth and not even G.G, the best damn actress in the family could fake the funk this time. She stood still as a statue beside Chiloe's folding chair just staring. I wished that one of us would stand up and explain our indifference. That our mother wasn't actually a mother until it was too late. That even though we loved her, we didn't know her. That we were basically footing the bill for a stranger who committed suicide by overdosing on pain medication out of guilt more than sorrow.

People from the neighborhood church came to visit and bring food after the funeral. We didn't really go to church enough to know any of these ladies in their wide brim hats, carrying big plates of chicken, fried fish, collard greens, and ham. Easter and maybe one Sunday every three years did not constitute as even attending church, but the word around the living room was that my grandmother, Greta's mother, had been a member at that very church.

I sat on the couch, thinking that if I saw another piece of chicken I would scream. Was that the official food of funerals or what? Karla was making conversation with the ladies, easily blending in with them. She loved church and church people so it was easy for her. I wanted them to leave so I could plunder my mother's room.

"So where's Rosie?" G. G. asked sitting down beside me on the couch. I just shrugged not wanting to be totally rude, but not being able to control myself. "I haven't seen her since Rajul's funeral."

"Well Kerry was there," she said continuing to push me for answers that I didn't have. I wasn't even sure I knew what the question was.

"Yeah. He comes over all the time, him and Gerald."

I wanted to ask her why her ass had not even showed up for Rajul's funeral. She could have had her good for nothing boyfriend bring her. What was her excuse? Where were all the questions that we should have been asking her?

"I'm leaving at about four. I gotta get home."

"For what?" I mean she didn't have a job, she had nine months to go before her high school graduation, and she didn't have kids. What in the world would make her rush from here in such a hurry? Not that any of us would be heartbroken over her decision to leave, but damn, it was her mother.

"Well, I didn't wanna tell anybody this yet," she paused like someone was actually listening to her and started to speak softer, "But Damon and I are getting married."

"Oh yeah?"

She nodded. "See, he's going in the military next year so I have to rush and do this. I gotta get back home for our appointment with the pastor."

I just looked at her, anger welling up in me like a gas bubble. I could not believe that she was thinking of seeing a pastor and her mother had just died. And even more than that, when was she planning on telling us about the wedding? Were any of us even invited to the wedding? Then I decided that I did not even want to go to her wedding. I didn't like Damon, and come to think of it, I didn't too much care for her either.

"Well congratulations", I managed to choke up, disgusted by each and every syllable as it came out of my dry mouth. I knew right then and there that I desperately needed a drink or something.

I got up from the couch and headed towards the front door, but Karla caught me by the sleeve of my dress. "Where you going Lonna?"

I loved her to death. I really truly did. But this having to watch my every step was beginning to bug the hell out of me. Especially at this particular moment. "I'm going to get some fresh air."

"You want me to come with you?"

I took a deep breath, doing my best to fight an urge that was becoming more and more uncontrollable by the second. "No. I'm fine. I'll be back in a little while."

I left her standing at the door. She probably knew exactly where I was headed. But there was nothing I could do about it. She would never understand the pressure I felt at that moment.

Somehow, in the course of a month, I had lost two family members. Granted my mother and I never really even spoke more than two sentences to each other at one time, it was hard because she was my mother.

The words *orphan* played in my mind over and over again. My mother was dead and I had no idea who my father was. At least my other brothers and sisters could attest that their father was dead. A Mexican man who was off and on with Greta for years. He'd been around to spend time with all of us even though somewhere in the middle New-New and I popped up, and as luck would have it, we had a different father. A missing name on a birth certificate was all I knew about him.

I thought about Karla and her father, Dade. At least she knew him even though they didn't have the best of relationships. They hardly even spoke to each other at all. Her mother was more than three hundred miles away now. None of this really seemed to bother her all that much. Every day I wished for her strength.

My weaknesses really hit me as I walked through the automatic doors of the corner grocery store and the cool air rushed me right in the eyes. I remembered the first day I met Karla. She, New-New and I walked to this store. That had seemed like ages ago. We were twelve years old.

I grabbed a bottle of orange looking MD 20/20 and proceeded to register number five. Register number five knew me, and had known me since junior high. He was dark and chubby with glasses that never seemed to come clean. But he was good for something, that was for sure.

He looked up from the little old lady he was ringing up, taking her time writing a check, and immediately began shaking his head, just like he always did when he saw me. I just smiled and placed my pointer finger over my mouth, shushing him in case he decided to open his big one. He gave an exasperated sigh as he rang up the next customer in line.

"Look, Lonna, I can't be doing this all the time. I'm gonna get fired," he whispered angrily at me.

"No you won't. You only do it for me and you know I ain't no undercover cop or nothing. You know me. And I ain't gonna tell nobody."

"Yeah, but they got video cameras in here watching us. If they don't see me checking your ID then I could get fired!"

"Fine," I said pulling my wallet out of my black purse, that matched my black shoes, and holding my driver's license in front of his face. "Here, here is my ID."

"You still not old enough to buy this stuff, Lonna."

"Harold, will you just ring the shit up, please. We go through this every time I come in this store. And you not gonna tell me those damn cameras that you claim are everywhere can read the birth date on my license. Now please ring this shit up so I can go home!"

We were still whispering but people were starting to stare at the pretty girl in the knee length black dress and the wide brim black hat, holding her wallet in the face of the chubby cashier who looked scared enough to jump out of his skin.

"This is the last time I'mma do this."

He said that every time I came in here. I just took my drink in the brown paper bag and walked out of the store.

I didn't know where to go now. I had my drink but there was still something missing. I passed the guys hanging around the front of the store with their newly shined cars and booming systems. I didn't know any of them and I was to sober to ask for any kind of illegal substances. I wondered what had happened to all of the drug dealers we had grown up with, the ones my brothers use to beef with all the time. I would buy from them back in the day so I wouldn't have to mess with Chiloe's people. But now there didn't seem to be anywhere I could get a hit anymore.

I hurried myself to the pay phone slightly behind the store. I dug deep into my patent leather purse for a quarter and a nickel. I found the change Harold gave me from the liquor and dialed Ron's pager number.

I hadn't spoken to him since right after Rajul's funeral. Rebuilding my family had been first and foremost on my mind. But now, the more I thought about doing that, I wondered if it were really worth it.

I entered the payphone number at the prompt and hung up. The guys standing in the front of the store were starting to stare at me as I waited and prayed for the phone to ring soon. After ten minutes of watching them, watching me, I was about to give up and head to the basketball court. Maybe I could just sit on the bleachers and drink. That was better than nothing at this point. But then the phone rang.

"Hello," I answered quickly praying it was Ron.

"Yeah did somebody page Ron?"

"Yeah I did. Do you know who this is?"

He thought for a moment. Then he said, "Lonna?"

"Yeah, what you doing?"

"Nothing much. What's up with you?"

"I want some things."

He giggled like a little girl. Then he asked. "Oh yeah? What you gonna give me?"

"Some things."

He giggled again. It was an irritating sound to me. "Alright then. Where you at?"

"I'm in the Doone. At the grocery store on the corner."

"A'right. I'll be up there in five minutes."

And true to his word, in five minutes he pulled his shiny Legend, that I had a feeling was brand new, right up in front of me. It put all the other boys on that block to shame with its glossy white paint and blinding rims. I slid onto the leather passenger seat, feeling myself become one with it, almost proud to be getting into his car. Almost.

"Why you so dressed up?" He asked as I fastened my seat belt.

"My mom's funeral was today."

He looked at me confused for a moment, wrinkling his eyebrows. "Your mom died? Oh man, I'm sorry."

I shrugged already putting that behind me. I knew he really didn't care anyway.

"How's Phoenell?" I asked just to get off of the subject of my mother.

"She's around."

"Hmmm."

He looked over at me to see what I knew that he didn't want me to know. But I didn't let anything on. Instead I looked back at him, making sure to keep steady eye contact. I had no intentions of making him think I was weak.

"Where we going?" I asked finally. Maybe I should have inquired about this when I first got into the car. I had a feeling it would not have made me any difference at all though.

"Me and some of my boys got some rooms at the Creek Inn. You don't mind do you?"

I shook my head. As long as I could get something stronger than weed, it was cool with me.

By the time Ron dropped me off in front of my mother's house, it was four in the morning. Karla's car was gone. She had probably taken Bree and gone home a long time ago.

"Hey, can you just take me to my crib? My ride ain't here."

Ron looked at me like I had just flown in from another planet. "What so your girl can see me droppin' your ass off and go back and tell Phoenell? Hell no."

So I got out of the car and stood on the lawn while he drove off with a quickness. As the early morning breeze hit me I noticed that my dress was torn from under my right arm on down to my hip. But that didn't bother me as much as spending the night once again in this house. It seemed lately that no matter what I did, I always ended up back here.

Chapter Thirteen

Sunday November 12, 1995 10:07 p.m.

The rain was coming down heavier, the further I got into the country. I could barely see even though my windshield wipers were on full blast. I briefly considered pulling over and waiting for the rain to let up, but I had a feeling it wasn't going to die down any time soon. And I wanted to get where I was going quickly.

There was always the possibility that Chiloe wasn't even here. That he'd picked another spot to do his mourning. I would have driven all the way out here for basically nothing. There was also the possibility that he didn't want to see me. That I would be disturbing him and maybe he wouldn't even open the door to let me in. I was worried about him. All of my pages to him had gone unanswered in over three days. That wasn't like him. I knew that their family couldn't take another tragedy, especially one as brutal as loosing Chiloe. So I had to know for myself what was going on.

I could see my turn coming up only because of the passing headlights of another car. I turned slowly down the gravel road praying that I would not get caught in a deep mud puddle. Or even worse, run into a ditch because of my lack of visibility. I was doing less than ten miles per hour down the road until I could see the beautiful wooden white house with the porch that stretched from the front yard to the back.

I remembered when Rajul bought this house four years ago, putting it in Chiloe's name because of his credit. There had been so many cookouts that Lonnie, New-New, and I attended, but Chiloe and Rajul adamantly forbade us from going to any of the numerous parties Rajul threw.

I parked beside Chiloe's Range Rover in the front yard and breathed a sigh of relief that he was here after all. In the short amount of time that it took me to run swiftly but carefully to the front door, my heavy jacket became soaked all the way through to my arms from the rain.

I knocked three times, but there was no answer. I wasn't surprised as I turned the door knob and the door swung open. Even though, he should have known better from what happened to Rajul. I stepped into the house slowly not knowing what I would find. Maybe this had all been a mistake and I should have stayed my behind at home. He might not have been alone and maybe that was why he didn't answer any of my pages.

But there were no sounds in the house at all. Not the sounds of love making, talking, breathing, nothing. And it was completely dark except for the light from the porch outside.

"Chiloe," I called not knowing if it was safe to say his name or not.

I took a left at the entry of the living room and headed through the kitchen and into the dining room. I passed the huge beautiful oak table with the matching chairs all sitting under the crystal chandelier. Suddenly, I could hear music coming from another part of the house. I followed the soft bass into the den where I could see the faint light coming from the immense stereo against the left wall of the room. Chiloe sat on the floor with his back up against the couch, a beer in one hand.

"What are you doing here?" He asked me. He wasn't looking at me. His eyes were covered by his right hand that was propped up on his right knee.

"I was worried about you."

"You shouldn't have come here."

I walked over to him and took my jacket off. Then I sat down on the floor in front of him just waiting for him to look at me.

"I should not do a lot of things, but I do."

I looked at the floor surrounding him, down at the five beer cans thrown here and there. I wondered if that was all he had been living off of.

"Have you eaten?" I asked him.

He shook his head quietly and put the beer bottle down. He knew what I was thinking.

Thunder rolled through the sky and shook the foundation of the house. Lightening hit somewhere off in the distance. I worried about all the trees that surrounded the house.

"There's some food in the refrigerator if you want some," Chiloe said looking at me now. He reached over and grabbed my hand that held my car keys ready for me to make a quick exit. But I could feel him pulling me closer to him. He reeked like he hadn't taken a bath in a couple of days. But still I didn't move away from him.

"How a nigga gon' lose their momma and their brother in the same damn month?" He asked me.

I shook my head in reply not really wanting to open my mouth and let the foul scent in.

"I ain't got no damn body now. Nobody."

I looked at him not believing what he was saying. "You have a big family that loves you to death," I said without thinking about the stink entering my throat. "Everything in that family revolves around you. And you gonna sit here and tell me you don't have nobody? I know you loved Rajul and I know you're mom was crazy about you. And I also know that there is nobody else in your family that can take their places. But you're not alone and you know that."

He gripped me tightly as he stroked my hair. The smell of all the alcohol he drank seemed to be coming out of his pores and was beginning to make me sick. Maybe I did need to move.

So I got up and headed for the kitchen.

"You want anything?" I asked over my shoulder.

"No."

There was bread, bologna, old chicken salad, mayo and a pack of ham. I took the mayo and bologna and made me a quick sandwich. There was nothing to drink but beer and water so I chose the water.

Chiloe was lying across the floor on his back. His arms were folded under his head.

"I guess I better take a shower huh?" He asked a little sheepishly. He knew I didn't want to get to close to him.

"Yeah that would probably be nice. How long has it been?"

He shrugged and smiled. "I don't know. A couple of days I guess."

I shook my head because that was disgusting. Then I turned the television on. "Go take your bath. I'll be here when you get back."

He nodded and headed towards the stairs. The sound of the wind was banging against the shudders of the old house, giving my heart a run for its money. Two people died in this house and here I was sitting in the very room where one of them was found behind the couch. Watching television. In the dark.

I moved from the floor up to the soft sofa to soothe my butt and also get a better view of anything that could be beside or behind me. I thought about going home since I knew that Chiloe was ok. A little smelly, but he was ok. But I had told him that I would be here when he got out of his much needed shower. I didn't want him to worry about me if he came back and found me gone. I figured I would leave once he finished his bath.

"Okay, I'm better now," Chiloe said entering the den. But when I looked up, I was speechless. He was almost totally naked.

I caught myself. I didn't want him to know that I was surprised. As long as we had known each other, I had never once seen him naked. In fact the only man that I *had* seen naked was Mike. I was hoping to keep it that way.

"That was fast," I said like I wasn't the least bit impressed. I mean Chiloe had always been one of God's most beautiful specimens. His olive skin and green eyes were nothing short of magnificent. Yet and still, after seeing Mike, it was like he couldn't compare. Mike was like a sculpted piece of smooth brown wood, cut to perfection. And I could just imagine what his body looked like now after all of the training he was getting from boot camp. I fantasized about that body every chance I got.

"Is it cold in here to you?" He asked sitting down on the floor right in front of the couch. He was making no moves to put clothes on, although he did have a green towel wrapped around his waist.

"Maybe you need to put some clothes on," I said looking at him like he was crazy.

"Am I making you uncomfortable?"

"No, but you're the one complaining that you're cold."

He smiled. I hadn't seen him smile in a few weeks.

"You and Mike still together?" He asked.

"You know the answer to that."

I felt the time for me to go drawing closer and closer. I didn't think staying here discussing my boyfriend with a naked man looked to good right now.

"I gotta go back home, Chiloe. I just came out here to make sure you were ok."

"Karla, you not gonna stay here?"

I didn't know if he was really hurt or if he was just faking it. I never knew with him.

"I've gotta go home."

"Karla," he said sitting up on his knees in front of me, "how long have we known each other?"

"Years."

"I thought we were friends."

Oh lord. Was this his version of a guilt trip? "You know that we are."

"Ok, you tell me then, if I was Lonna or New-New, wouldn't you stay?"

I shook my head trying to get out of answering this line of questioning. But I

knew that he wouldn't let me.

"Go 'head. Look me in the eyes and tell me you wouldn't stay if I was Lonna or New-New."

I looked down at the carpet, at the television, out of the window. Everywhere but at him.

"Okay, Chiloe, damn. I'll stay."

He sat back down on his butt. "I don't want you to do anything you don't wanna do."

This is what I hated about him. The things that made me so mad about him to begin with. Every single time he opened his mouth I remembered why we weren't together.

Chiloe smiled again because he knew exactly what I was thinking. He took me by my arm and pulled me down on the floor with him.

"I just don't wanna be alone. That's all. If you really have to go then you can go. But if you don't have to go, then please stay."

I was reminded of a few years back in a cold dark basement and the rain pouring down outside of a sliding glass door and I remembered how my curiosity had taken over the best part of me, which was my mind.

"I'm not gonna have sex with you or anything like that so don't even ask, don't try anything, just remove the thought from your mind."

Chiloe placed his pointer finger in the middle of his chest and looked at me as if he was insulted that I would ever think that he was thinking such a thing.

"Now you know better than that. Have I ever in all the years we've known each other, asked you for sex?"

I really had to think about it, but then it dawned on me, Chiloe did not need to ask *anybody* for sex. Females just threw themselves at him for free and with no strings attached. On a daily basis.

"No, you haven't."

"Alright, then. What makes you think I would ask now? Especially since you with my boy and everything."

He didn't mean that last part. And we both knew he didn't.

Instead of asking me to excuse the fact that he said something so totally ridiculous, he pulled me down on the floor with him and into his arms. His bath had been quick but he did smell a heck of a lot better. So I innocently lay my head on his chest and closed my eyes. I pictured him being Mike. That Mike was holding me instead of him, because that was where I really wanted to be. With Mike.

Lonna sat behind her desk staring blankly at her computer screen. I could tell she had a rough night. Her hair was pulled back into a tight ponytail stretching her eyes so that she almost could not see. It was an attempt to make the dark circles under her eyes go away, but it didn't work. Not only had she done the pony tail trick, but she had tried the vanishing act with a bottle of concealer too. That hadn't worked either.

I sat down in the chair opposite her desk.

"What's up?" I asked.

She just shook her head.

"Are you busy today?"

She shook her head again.

"What's wrong?"

Lately this was just the way she was. Of course I knew about the drugs. Everyone knew about the drugs. From New-New down to Jay. But recently, things just seemed to fall further downhill and I didn't know how to stop any of it.

"Where were you last night?" She asked.

I fought back the urge to tell a lie. She was my best friend in the whole world and I could not remember the last time I lied to her. There was never any need to. We had total trust for each other.

"I was at Rajul's with Chiloe."

She seemed to come alive then as she sat up in her chair and leaned closer to me.

"Oh yeah?"

"Don't even think it 'cause we didn't do a thing."

She sat back again, but still staring at me like she expected for me to recant my version of events.

"So what did you do last night?"

Her facial expression did a three sixty. She was back to that blank look when she shrugged her shoulders. That was the answer I got whenever I asked her where she had been. I could count on one hand the times we had gone out since we moved in together.

I shook my head because I was beginning to think like someone's wife.

"Never mind," I said standing up from my chair and heading to the door of her office. "Give me a call if you wanna go to lunch or something."

I got no oral reply. Just another shrug of the shoulders.

"Hello?" I answered the phone. I had been furiously writing all morning and hadn't even realized it was lunch time.

"Hey baby."

Mike's voice sent instant shivers up and down my arms. I was speechless for a second. He always did that to me. I could think of a million things to say when we weren't on the phone, but the second he called me, my mind just went blank and I became mesmerized by him. I usually expressed myself a lot better in the letters that we sent back and forth though.

"Hey baby," I choked back at him.

"What'cha doing?"

"Just some writing. How are you, when you coming home?"

He laughed that beautiful deep laugh of his that I loved and said, "You know I got a couple more months. But I'm alright though. Training is kicking my ass."

"Oh come on, you can take it, you grew up on the streets, remember?"

He laughed again. "So how is everybody?"

"Well, Lonna is the same. But everybody is ok."

I didn't want to mention Chiloe. For some reason, even though I knew nothing at all had gone on, I just felt too guilty to even mention him.

"Everybody's gonna be ok, don't worry."

"Ok."

"You miss me?"

I smiled. "Yes I do. Very much so."

"I miss you too. Write me one of them sexy letters, ok?"

"I will baby. I'll do it on my way to Ohio tomorrow night."

"Ohio?"

"Book signing."

"Damn, my baby doing the damn thing all over the country, huh?"

I laughed and he laughed too.

"Just don't forget about me while you out there."

"You know that's never gonna happen, Mike."

He sighed then said, "I got six people trying to bum rush me for the phone."

Needless to say, I was disappointed but I understood. All of our phone conversations went this way. "Okay baby. Be careful. Take care."

"I will love. I love you baby girl."

"I love you too."

And with that he was gone. I sat back in my chair, heart so full of love that I thought I was going to burst wide open at any second, staring at the 8x10 picture of Mike and I at that prom that I kept on my desk. My mother refused to give me the picture of me by myself but she had no problems parting with the picture of Mike and me. Not that she had anything against Mike. Out of all the boyfriends that I had in my life, I knew she liked him the best. And I did too.

My phone rang again. I checked the caller ID but I knew it wouldn't be Mike.   One call once a week was his limit.

It was my father.

"What's up, Dad?" It was easy enough to answer even though we hadn't spoken a word to each other since Greta's funeral. One glance to the back row and I noticed him standing there, dark shades and Kangol hat on like he was a bonafide mobster. I hadn't expected to see him there but he and Greta had dated for so long that I should have known he would come.

"What's up Karla? How you doing?"

"I'm fine. How are you?"

"I'm doing good. I wanted to know if you wanted to have dinner tonight."

I was stunned to say the least. I checked my desk calendar to make sure it was not his birthday or a holiday I had forgotten. It was neither.

"Why what's going on?"

He laughed so hard he choked. He had breathing problems from thirty years of smoking. I guess I wasn't helping the situation very much.

"Nothing, nothing," he said trying to recapture his breath.

"Oh, ok. Alright then. Is five ok?"

I could visualize him looking at his Rolex to see or running through his head to make sure he hadn't made any other appointments for that time. Like some club or some woman he may accidentally have double booked with. I chided myself for thinking that way and made up in my mind to give him the benefit of the doubt.

"Okay," he said finally.

"You want me to pick you up?" I asked.

"Okay. Is your car clean?"

I shook my head because he just couldn't resist no matter what. "Yes," I said through clenched teeth trying my best not to hit the RELEASE button on my phone.

"Okay then."

My father and I sat across from each other at the round table near the window of the slightly crowded restaurant. Neither one of us spoke a word as he chewed his catfish silently. My cheese burger was under cooked so I waited patiently for it to get done right, every now and then taking a bite of my fries and a sip of my Coke.

"How's everything going?" He asked finally after the waitress sat my newly cooked food down in front of me.

"Everything's good. I have a book signing in Ohio, I'm leaving tomorrow."

He nodded and took another bite of his food. Then without looking at me he said, "I've been meaning to tell you how proud I am of you with that."

"Proud of me?" I had to repeat him because I was more than sure I had not heard him correctly.

"Yeah, proud of you."

"Thanks." I cleared my throat and thought about how much of an awkward moment this was for me. I hardly remembered my father telling me he loved me, much less that he was proud of me about something.

"So how is New-New and Lonna doing?"

"They're fine. New-New's due next month. Lonna is working and everything. She's Lonna."

He smirked and shook his head. Then he cleared his throat. There was a lot of that going on between the two of us.

"You do know me and their mom use to date back in the day. Right?"

"Yeah, I know."

The thought of the first time I met Greta came to mind. The sight of her tumbling down the stairs in her short shorts and halter top with stretch marks that did just that for miles and miles flashed before me. She was something else, that was for sure.

"Well we dated for a long time, you know. Longer than what you may think."

"Ok," I said for lack of anything better to say.

He put his fork down then and cleared his throat again. "I know you're wondering why I'm telling you this."

"Yeah pretty much. You know what you do in your rec time is your business."

I expected that to provoke a smile, but it didn't. Not even half of one. Instead he shook his head and looked at me seriously. "It was more than rec time. Much more."

All of a sudden, I wasn't very hungry anymore, in fact I was downright queasy. Then I thought better of it and took a bite of my almost ten dollar cheeseburger anyway. "Much more like what?" I said with a mouth full of food, but not really caring about manners anymore.

"We have two kids together."

Maybe I had the wrong Greta. Maybe we were talking about someone else. But I was for sure we started this conversation off talking about Lonna and New-New. Maybe I had missed a big chunk of something somewhere. I began to replay it in my mind, word for word.

"I should have told y'all this a long time ago. I meant to tell y'all when you graduated. I guess I just chickened out. Then I was going to tell y'all when Greta died, but I just couldn't."

"Okay, okay. Who is *y'all*?"

My father shook his head. I hated these long dramatic pauses. We weren't on television. This was not a soap opera.

"You and New-New and Lonna."

This time, I shook my head. He couldn't possibly be telling me what I thought he was telling me. So I asked him, "What are you telling me?"

"Y'all are sisters."

There was no dramatic music, because like I said, this was not a soap opera. There were no flashes of light, no rumbles of thunder. It was just me, my father, and other restaurant patrons who were involved in their own lives and own conversations. Nobody else cared that the two girls, I had grown up with, lived with, shared everything with were my true to life sisters.

"Boy you were busy weren't you?" I asked, still for a lack of anything else to say.

"I guess you can say that."

"Any reason why you never claimed them but you claimed me?"

"Greta wouldn't let me," my dad said as if pleading his case to a jury. "We were always arguing about that. Greta hated me. I mean she had a good reason to hate me. I was a player and I was married to your momma. She didn't find that out until after the fact. But she was back and forth with that Mexican guy . . ."

"Everybody else's father," I interjected.

"Yeah, but then he died in a construction accident not to long after the last child was born."

"Jay."

"Yeah. I tried to claim them then, but she still wouldn't let me. It's not like I never wanted to though. Why do you think I made it point of introducing you to them? I was hoping you would hit it off, but I never thought it would turn out like it did."

I still didn't know whether to be pissed at him or happy. I had two wonderful sisters, sure. But they didn't know it. I wondered about my father's timing. Lonna was well on her way to having a full blown drug habit. This wouldn't help it any, not by a long shot. I wanted to be mad about the position he was putting me in, but I couldn't even bring myself to do that.

"So why tell me now?" I asked.

He shrugged. "I'm sick Karla. You know that. I got a lot of secrets to take to my grave, but this is not one of them. I wanted you to know, before it was too late."

"Did you know Momma?" I asked as I lay across my bed, phone pressed hard to my ear.

"No I didn't know for sure. I had an idea though."

My mom sighed heavily into the phone and I looked searchingly around the room. For what I didn't know.

"Especially when I saw them. But I couldn't prove it. I asked him one day when he came to pick you up to take you over there. But he just walked away."

321

I turned over on my right side, just letting the phone rest on my head. "I can't tell them. Lonna's not gonna take this well."

I did not want to tell my mom about Lonna's drug habit. I didn't want to taint her opinion of Lonna. And I did not want her to worry about her only child living under the same roof with a drug addict. Even though I knew Lonna well enough to not be worried about my own safety, I was sure my mother would be skeptical.

"Well let your Daddy tell them. That's his responsibility, not yours."

It was easier said than done. I wasn't used to keeping secrets from Lonna or New-New. But I knew my mother was right.

Chapter Fourteen

Thursday, November 19, 1995 6:20 p.m.

Marco sat on the couch with his girlfriend Renda, while Lonna sat on the love seat with me perched on the arm of the chair beside her. Bree sat on the floor in front of us and Jay sat in a chair at the dining room table. We were all looking at Chiloe and this beautiful dark skin girl who strangely looked out of place to me. Her eyes were wide and bright and her face was full with dimples on both sides. Her hair hung well past her chin in a straight bob. She was full figured like me, quite adorable and humble. I wondered what the hell she was doing with Chiloe.

"So y'all got married?" Marco asked like he hadn't heard him clearly the first time.

I on the other hand, I had heard him loud and clear and still couldn't believe it. He had just met this girl a month ago and now they were husband and wife. She was Mrs. Chiloe Garcia. I was confusedly hurt and I could feel it welling up in me like a gas bubble, but I suppressed it. I knew I didn't love Chiloe so what was the problem?

I let it go, but Marco didn't.

"And y'all known each other for how long?"

"A month," Misha said. Her voice was so even toned and pleasant. I bet she had never raised her voice for anything. "Look, I know this is all of a sudden and a shock to y'all. I really am sorry it was done this way. Chiloe was in a hurry to get married though, and well you know how that goes."

"Yeah we know how that goes," Lonna mumbled. Then she asked out loud, "Are you pregnant?"

We all looked at her because she had just said what we all had been thinking every since we got to this urgent family meeting called by Marco. Why would two people that obviously had nothing in common and who had only known each other for one full month, all of a sudden go down to the county court house and get married? Why? And Chiloe of all people?"

"No, I'm not pregnant. We just wanted to get married."

Chiloe was not saying a word. His eyes just kept darting back and forth between Misha and me. What did he expect for me to say? I wasn't even part of his family, I didn't even know why I was here to begin with.

"Congratulations," I said hoping that would make the disappointment I felt in my heart go away. Maybe if I could somehow turn this into a celebration instead of what it was, I could take away the feeling that he married this girl just to spite me.

"Thank you," Misha said and she smiled at me. Her eyes showed a glimmer of recognition and I wondered if Chiloe had told her about me. Had he told her how much he professed to love me?

"Are y'all gonna stay here?" Jay asked. Up until now it had only been Jay and Chiloe in the house. I was sure Jay was not to big on living with some strange woman.

"No," Chiloe said finally opening his mouth. "We gonna stay in Rajul's house." Lonna just shook her head and rolled her eyes up into her head.

"I know how this may look," Misha said shaking her own head. "And I'm sorry about it, I really am."

Bree cut in this time before Lonna could say another word. "It's okay, Misha. We don't have anything against you. It's just that we didn't know anything about you and this is all a big surprise for us. That's all."

Bree had expressed the sentiments of the house better than any of us had.

"Who's gonna stay in the house then?" Jay asked.

"Well, you can stay with me until you turn eighteen." Marco quickly volunteered. "But I guess the house will just sit here because there's no way we're selling it."

"Naw, we can't sell it," Lonna agreed.

I stood up then and headed for the door. I would just wait out in Lonna's car for her. I'm sure once I left she wouldn't be that far behind me.

"Karla," Chiloe called after me and I turned back around to look at him, wondering what in the world he could possibly have to say to me. Nothing right now, not in front of his new wife. I cringed at the thought.

He opened his mouth to speak, but nothing came out.

"What?" I asked. I wanted out of this house quickly. Just looking at him gave me bad vibes right now.

"Thanks for coming."

I meant to say, "You're welcome," or even "Okay." But instead I turned back around and walked out of the door. I didn't mean to make a scene like that and leave Misha wondering what the hell my problem was. I didn't mean it but I did it anyway.

"Thanks for coming, what the hell is that supposed to mean! He's not even the one who invited us! What the hell!"

Lonna rubbed my back with her right hand as her left hand gripped the steering wheel. "Girl, Chiloe done lost his mind, that's all. I guarantee you that marriage won't last."

"She seems nice though," Bree said with her head in between the two front seats of Lonna's Camaro that once belonged to Rajul.

I looked back at her and rolled my eyes.

Lonna smacked her teeth, in that Lonna sort of way and said, "The only reason Chiloe married that girl is to get back at you for dating Mike."

I looked over at her amazed that she'd read my mind so accurately. I thought about that poor girl who probably thought Chiloe loved her. She had probably gone against her parent's wishes to marry that good for nothing bastard. And to think he was only with her to make me feel bad.

"How could he do her like that?" I asked no one in particular.

"Because he's Chiloe."

The door bell rang at nine o'clock that night. I had only been back from Ohio for one day and with all of the drama from the day, I hadn't had a chance to unpack. My clothes were still in their suitcases as I sat in front of the blank screen of my computer.

The wind was blowing fiercely, almost knocking me backwards when I opened my front door to let Chiloe in.

"What's up?" I asked trying to keep my voice even. He hadn't called or anything, but just decided to show up at my door.

"What's up?" He asked back digging his hands deep into his pockets. "You busy?"

I shook my head knowing I should have been telling him yes I was very busy and I needed to be alone. Where was his wife anyway that he wasn't at home with her?

"Can we talk for a second?"

I nodded my head and cut one of the antique lamps that decorated the end tables on. He sat down on the couch while I sat in my favorite chair, legs drawn tightly underneath me.

"I know what you're feeling right now." Chiloe placed his elbows on his knees and leaned forward, pressing his fingertips together.

"What are you talking about?"

"I'm talking about me and Misha."

I took a deep breath about to go into my heavy speech that I had already gone over fifty times in my head. Just for this special occasion. But instead I just sat in the chair, leaning my head against the edge of it so that I was looking at him over my nose. If he was expecting a reply, he was going to be disappointed.

"I know I probably have a lot of explaining to do."

Still no reply from me.

He sat back this time and looked at me, clearly not knowing what to expect from me now. This was going to be one of the worse conversations he had ever had or the worse conversation he never had. I could see his Adam's apple working up and down with anticipation.

"You expect for me to just be by myself and wait for you forever while you and Mike have a ball, huh?"

I knew he would get to that sooner or later. At the mention of his name I felt defensive. "Mike don't have a thing to do with you marrying this girl. Unless, of course that's the only reason why you married her."

The look on his face was priceless. It was a look of hurt, shame, and surprise all at the same time. His cheeks were instantly flushed and his lips seemed to hang open in a severe case of CatGotYourTongitist. I leaned back again in the chair just like the words had never once escaped my lips, giving him time to recover and resume the conversation that he was supposed to be having by himself anyway.

"She's the only one that's been there for me . . ."

"That's a damn lie. First of all you've only known her for a month, so when and for what was she there for you? Second, everybody's been there for you. All this has been all about you, Chiloe. Everything's always about you. But you're so all about you that you can't even see that."

He was shaking his head like he hadn't even heard a word I had said. "You only know one half of the story. You don't know how it feels when I see you and Mike together. Or when I hear you telling him how much you love him on the phone. I'm supposed to be cool with all that. Why can't you be cool with this?"

"Chiloe, I love anybody you love. That's the point, though. You don't love Misha. You're just doing this for spite and it's wrong."

He continued shaking his head and looking at me almost in disbelief. "So what was I supposed to do? Just sit around waiting on you right?"

"Of course not. But why pull an innocent person into this shit?"

If Chiloe was feigning hurt, he was the best damn actor in the world. His face seemed to fall completely into his lap. I wanted to go to him and hug him, tell him I didn't mean to be so cruel. But something in me would not let me do it. He needed this. For once in his life, he needed for someone to be cruel to him.

"You just don't know how I feel about you Karla. I've always loved you."

He was getting up now and coming towards me. I didn't know whether to run, scream, or just sit there. It was too late anyway. Before I could even catch my breath to get out of the chair he was in front of me, on his knees, arms wrapped tightly around me so I couldn't move at all.

"Karla, please . . ." He was begging me for something but neither of us knew exactly what it was he wanted from me. He had a wife. And I had Mike.

"What Chiloe?"

"Just let me stay with you tonight."

"What!?" I tried to pull back and push him away but he wouldn't let me go. He looked as dumbfounded as I felt. "You have a wife. Go home to her."

"I know that I have a wife . . . but Karla . . . ." He broke off and looked down at the multicolored carpet, his grip on my waste so tight I could hardly breathe. It was almost desperate. Then it hit me like never before that this was what he truly was, desperate. "I need you Karla. I need to be with you right now. Please. I won't even touch you. I promise. Please."

I hated myself for even feeling the least bit of sympathy for him. For even feeling his pain or whatever it was that was reeking from him. But I did none the less. I felt every ounce of everything that I didn't want to feel.

"Get up, Chiloe," I said. He looked at me for a second. And then he backed up, still on his knees. I stood up and pulled him up with me. Without a word, because I was too ashamed to say anything, I cut the lamp off on my way out of the living room followed by Chiloe.

Jay sat down on the couch more humble than I had ever seen him. His baseball hat sat low and snugly on his forehead, covering up his light eyes. His long legs were bent at the knees and spaced far apart while his fingers of each hand intertwined with each other and rested on his stomach. I sat down in the gold chair across from him and we both pretended to watch television.

I was lost in my thoughts of the night before. Even though nothing had happened between Chiloe and I, we had hardly even touched as we slept side by side facing each other, in the same bed, I was still riddled with guilt. Just knowing that I had done something that would cause Mike, and now even Misha, pain was killing me.

The aroma of my Macaroni Supreme continued to steadily drift from the oven all the way into the living room making me hungry along with guilty.

"You hungry, are you eating with me?"

Jay had to hold his head all the way up in the air just so that we could make eye contact. I wished he would take that crazy hat off. But instead he just nodded and went back to watching television.

"Five more minutes and I'm taking it out," I said to no one in particular. It was a good thing because he didn't answer me anyway.

I knew the problem wasn't me. He never would have gotten on his bike and drove all the way over here from downtown just to sit on my couch if he were mad at me. And I hadn't done anything to him that I could remember anyway. But this silence was driving me insane.

"What's up, Jay?" I asked finally. "What's going on?"

He looked at me again, holding his head all the way up to the sky. And again I wished he would take off that hat. But he didn't and I didn't ask, fearing he would lose his train of thought and we would go back to sitting in silence.

At first he shook his head. But then he thought about it and decided to answer me instead.

"Can I tell you something?" He asked. At first I had to make sure he was serious. He should have known by now he could talk to me about anything. Living with Marco and his girlfriend, there really was no one there he could really talk to. But I kept reminding him that he only had one more year to go.

"Yes, you can tell me anything. What's up?"

He leaned forward on the couch. Now I couldn't see his face at all. Just a dark shadow. That was when I realized how dreary it had become outside. The living room was on its way to being totally dark.

"Some stuff is going on, Karla. And I don't know what to think anymore." Oh God, I thought. What had he gotten himself into? Drugs, a gang, some girl was pregnant? Oh Lord. Where was Lonna when I needed her?

"I don't know what to do Karla."

Beyond my own better judgment, and reluctantly, I asked, "What's going on?"

I don't even think he heard me. At least I couldn't see his face to tell, and he kept on talking as if he didn't hear me.

"I mean at first it started off as just fun and games, you know what I mean? It was fun, so I did it. But now it's like . . ." he stopped and shook his head. "I don't know, Karla."

"What is it?" I asked raising my voice just a tad. I didn't want to scare him into not telling me anything, but this being coy about whatever it was, was getting on my nerves. He never had a problem expressing himself before.

To my relief he finally removed the baseball cap and wiped his forehead with the back of his hand. I could still see little beads of sweat forming on his brow. Something was troubling him bad. Part of me didn't even want to know. If it was eating him up like this, what in the world was it going to do to me? His eyes wouldn't meet mine. Instead he just stared straight ahead out of the window. That made me get up and cross the room to him. Something in his eyes looked crazed almost. I wondered how much more I could take from this family before I cracked up my damn self.

Jay swallowed hard. Hard enough for me to hear it. Then he looked down at me sitting on the couch beside him now. Well not exactly at me, but somewhere in my vicinity. His eyes still wouldn't meet mine.

"I fucked a dude," he said looking back down at the carpet.

I wouldn't dare ask him to repeat it. I heard what he said just as sure as my food was burning and the rain was beginning to pour down outside. I got up slowly and walked into the kitchen. As if in a daze, I slipped my oven mitt onto my right hand and removed my casserole dish that held my mom's favorite recipe from the oven. I was wrong, it was slightly brown on top. I loved crispy cheese anyway.

I sat the casserole dish down on the stove top so that it could cool. Then I shut the oven off. I made sure to place the oven mitt back on the counter top far away from the oven or the hot dish and walked back into the living room. Jay was still staring down at the floor, his right leg shaking hard and I had visions of it flying across the room.

I sank deep into the couch beside him. Just trying to get a good grip on the situation, but I didn't think that was possible. Not right now, with the rain coming down so hard and Jay's leg seeming to shake the whole house.

"It was two weeks ago," he continued without me having to edge him on. "I mean we've known each other forever and shit. I didn't know he was like that, I swear to God I didn't. I mean he's just like me, he had girlfriends and everything." He stopped and shook his head. "We just started hanging out more and more since him and his girl broke up. I mean I knew something was there, you know what I mean?" He looked at me then, right into my eyes, to make sure I did know what he meant. I just nodded because I didn't think my voice would work at that particular moment. No, I was quite sure it wouldn't. He continued, "And then I was at his house, and I don't know what happened, K. We started kissing. I ain't never kissed no dude before, but we just started kissing. The next thing I knew . . ."

He stopped there because he knew I knew the rest. He had told me already. I wished I knew what to say. Anything to say. But I was speechless this time. We sat in silence for what seemed hours. The rain calmed down to a light drizzle but that did nothing for the sun. It wasn't going to make its way from behind the clouds today. I could tell.

"I haven't told anybody else," he said as if I asked.

"What is there to tell?"

"Don't you get it?" He looked at me like I was the stupidest person in the world. Maybe I was.

"Why would you go around broadcasting that you slept with another male?"

He shook his head this time and sat back on the couch. "That's not all though. I've been having these feelings a long time."

It was confusing for me. He was masculine to no end, just like a younger version of Chiloe. He had girls in every project around the city, not to mention the ones in the well to do neighborhoods. Girls from different schools were constantly fighting each other like cats and dogs because of him. I could go anywhere with him and he could come out with fifty different phone numbers of fifty different females who just threw themselves at him with no shame and no dignity. And he never missed an opportunity to take advantage of their offers. Never. Even though, he was only a teenager.

"You can't possibly be gay, Jay," I blurted out before I could catch myself.

But he shook his head like he agreed with me. "I like both."

That was hardly any better or possible. "So what are you gonna do?" I asked only wanting the best for him. I could imagine how his family was going to take this and I did not come up with a pretty picture at all.

He shrugged. "I mean, I like him a lot Karly. A lot."

This had obviously been wearing him down for the past couple of weeks. I hoped he would feel better now that he had gotten it off of his chest.

"Don't worry. You don't have to make any major announcements and I won't either. We'll just take this thing one day at a time."

Jay nodded seemingly satisfied with the answer I provided and put his hat back on as I left him to go fix plates.

Chapter Fifteen

Thursday, March 21, 1996 7:41 p.m.

I still couldn't figure out what it was about this girl that I just did not like. If it was her neediness towards Karla, the way she let a man beat her ass on a constant basis, I just could not figure out what it was. Even as I sat there looking at her from across the living room, her on the couch and me in both Karla's and my favorite chair, I wanted nothing more than to bust her in her forehead.

The bad part about it was the girl was totally harmless. She was quiet like Karla. Even though I was sure she could have beat somebody down to a bloody pulp if necessary, she never said anything out of the way to anybody. On top of that she was very pretty. Flawless peach skin, slanted dark eyes, long wavy black hair. There was nothing unlikable about her at all. It was me. I just didn't like her.

Karla bumbled into the living room holding a wicker tray with three ice cream bowls on it. She sat it down on the coffee table and passed out the ice cream like we were in kindergarten. And just like a kindergartner, I didn't want Phoenell to have any. That was terrible, but it was the truth.

"Damn," Phoenell said shaking her head. "It must be nice having your own place and stuff."

Karla nodded and sat down on the other end of the couch. She put her sock covered feet up on the coffee table and sat back with the bowl of chocolate chip ice cream in her hand.

"It's ok. I told you, you can move in if you want to."

I almost choked on a chip. She had been offering away space in the house without even asking anybody if it was okay. There was no room for her anyway. Karla had a room, Bree had a room, and I had a room. But knowing Karla she would have taken her king size bed out and replaced it with a bunk bed just to let Phoenell stay.

Luckily, though, Phoenell shook her head. "No, I can't leave Dakota over there by herself."

Karla nodded like she understood but I just rolled my eyes and continued eating my ice cream.

Phoenell continued because she had not noticed my eye movement. "I probably won't move until she graduate."

"What about you?" Karla asked.

Phoenell sighed and shook her head again. "I don't know, Karla."

Phoenell was part of Karla's plan to save the world. At first I thought it just included me. But since I met this chick it was clear to see that wasn't the case. That sparked some jealousy in me like I had never experienced before. I was dumbfounded.

"So what should we do tonight?" Karla asked.

There she went again trying to make me choke. *We* were not doing anything tonight. Not with Punching Bag's boyfriend hunting her down like a deer in the woods. There was no way I was going to be seen with them. The last thing I needed was some drama like that. And anyways, Jackie and I had plans.

"Me and Jackie gonna hit the clubs tonight."

Karla looked at me like I was from another planet. I knew what she thought of Jackie and the rest of the girls from that side of town. We got into it every single time I even mentioned her name. But instead of her saying anything out of the way like she usually did, this time she just turned her attention to Phoenell. I caught a cramp in the back of my head from gritting my teeth so hard.

"I can't go to no club," Phoenell said shaking her head like someone had invited her.

"We'll go to Dapper Dan's and play some pool."

They both seemed pretty satisfied by this decision and let it go. For some reason I just was not. Karla could have at least tried to convince me to go. But she said nothing and I was hurt.

I was about to throw a tantrum and stomp out of the living room. I needed to get dressed in a little bit anyway. But there was a persistent knock at the door. Karla sat her ice cream on the coffee table and got up to answer it.

The heavy black screen door swung open Marco walked in hurriedly, still wearing his police uniform. There was a look in his eyes that scared me. The sight of Marco, the strongest person in our family agitated worried me. If he was upset, how were the rest of us going to handle whatever was going on?

Karla didn't sit back down. Instead she stood by Marco waiting for him to let us know what was going on.

"Have you seen Chiloe?" He asked Karla more than anyone else.

She looked at me and then back at him. A look came over her that I wasn't used to seeing on her. Something similar to guilt.

"No. Why?"

Marco sighed deeply and the lines in his forehead deepened. "Him and Jay got in a fight. With each other."

"What?" I asked and I was up off of the couch immediately. "Why?"

"I bet I know why," Karla said. She sat down then and put her forehead in her hands. Now she was looking distressed also. I just wanted to know what in the world was going on.

"What happened?" I asked either one of them. But Marco was the one that answered. "He caught him with another dude. In the house."

"What do you mean *'caught him with another dude'*?"

"Let's just put it this way, they won't playing spades."

I sat back down beside Karla, hoping that maybe she could give me a clearer picture. I knew I wasn't hearing what I thought I was hearing. I knew my baby brother wasn't gay. He was a rough neck, in the lines of Chiloe and Rajul. If he was gay, anyone could be gay.

"Karla?" I asked. But she just continued to hold her forehead.

"Where is Jay?" She asked, ignoring me.

"At my house. He said he's okay. It's not like he didn't fight back, so wherever Chiloe is, he's feeling as much of it as Jay is."

Karla seemed to breathe then and sat back on the couch. I was relieved to hear that Jay could hold his own as much as she was, but I still didn't understand what was going on.

"Are you saying Jay is gay?"

She looked at me finally and nodded. "Yeah."

"How long have you known?" Marco asked, still standing. His muscular frame leaned against the front door.

"He told me a while ago." She shook her head. "He didn't want to tell anybody and I told him he didn't have to."

"When were *you* going to tell somebody?" I asked not believing that she had kept this secret from me. If she was hiding this, what else had she not been telling me? I never thought we would get to the point of keeping secrets from each other.

"I wasn't. It wasn't my secret to tell. And you see what happened? I was just trying to protect Jay."

We were supposed to be so much deeper than this. When did Jay's feelings start taking precedence over mine? I got up off of the couch and left Marco, Phoenell, and most of all Karla.

Even after dwelling on the situation at the club the night before and the rest of that morning, the fact that Jay had gone to Karla with his little secret did not sit well with me. I couldn't figure out if it was the fact that he was *my* brother after all, why did he have to tell Karla instead of one of us; or was it that Karla kept a secret from *me?* Or maybe I just wanted to be angry about something.

"Why didn't you tell me?" I asked Karla who was pretty much ignoring me by watching television instead of me. One hand held a remote, the other rested on her thigh. Lady like as she was at that very moment, I wanted to bust her head open for some reason that I could not even explain.

"Because he felt like no one else would understand. I guess he figured everybody would react like Chiloe."

"I'm not Chiloe."

"We know you're not Chiloe. But he didn't want to take any chances. You can't blame him for that."

I just shook my head. I didn't know if it was the coke I tooted for snack early this morning before the light of day or the toilet water blue MD I drank for breakfast. But I felt myself playing tug of war with Reasonable and Unreasonable. Unreasonable had a big kid in the loop of the rope and he was winning for the whole team. Reasonable was still hanging in there though and I was rooting for them.

So I just sat down in the gold armchair by the window and waited for whatever my problem was to subside. Karla seemed to be waiting with me because she didn't say a word.

When she finally did speak, what was close to fifteen minutes later, the only thing that came out of her mouth was, "You high?"

Unreasonable wanted to jump out of that chair and start ranting and raving about why I hated staying here with her. And more. But by now Reasonable had put down the damn rope, walked over to Unreasonable and was choking the hell out of the fat kid in the loop.

"Yes."

"On what?"

On what? What exactly did she mean on what? Was there a difference?

"Not crack," was the only answer I could give her that was truthful. But she still looked at me like I had lost my damn mind.

"Not crack?" She asked still not moving from her position on the couch and still holding the remote in her right hand. "You know how many other drugs that leaves? Are you on all those other drugs?"

I smiled in spite of myself. "No." But I wished I was.

That's when she finally brought her long thick legs from tucked underneath her and leaned forward on the couch. "We need to talk."

Did Mike feel the way I did when she said that to him? Like he just wanted to run out of here and not talk? Never talk. Not even listen.

"About what?" I choked up.

"About you and the drugs and the alcohol."

 "What about it?"

"It's gotta stop." Her big brown eyes were wide like they always were in the face of conflict.

I just looked at her once again, this time really not knowing what she meant. When did it have to stop? Was she giving me some kind of deadline? Was this an ultimatum? Did I have a choice in the matter?

"You're killing yourself. Can't you see that?"

I smacked my teeth, planning to say something sarcastic, funny, and witty. But the only thing I could do was the teeth smack. Nothing else would come out.

"Bree is worried about you all the time. I'm worried about you all the time. New-New calls down here every other day checking on you."

"New-New? She's not even here!"

"That don't mean a thing. She could see something was wrong with you at your momma's funeral. You not fooling nobody but yourself."

I smacked my teeth again. Wanting to say something witty again. Damn, I could have kicked myself.

"So," she continued like she knew I didn't have anything to say, "I called this place out near Eastover and they will take you. I'm using part of my royalties from the second book."

Okay, now I could not sit still and take this. "What do you mean a place out near Eastover?"

"A rehab place. It's really nice, Lonna. You know I wouldn't send you just anywhere."

"Rehab?"

"Yes, rehab."

I stood up from the chair then. She didn't flinch as I fought for control of my mind. There was a voice screaming inside my head and I didn't know if it was me or someone else.

"I don't need fuckin' rehab, Karla!"

"Oh, you don't? You went out after your momma's funeral and got high, didn't you? But you don't need help? Every week, it's the same thing you getting high and getting drunk. It's getting worse and worse, but you don't need help? You're using drugs, hard core drugs, but you don't need help?"

"Hard core drugs." I was mocking her, but she was not affected by it. She just went back to watching television. While I stood there looking stupid.

"Either you go, or you gotta get out of here."

I just looked at her, mouth wide open, but nothing coming out. My arms were flailing in the air, but it wasn't helping my mouth any. She wasn't even looking anyway. I could not believe that we had been friends for so long, and she was doing this to me! She was actually willing to put me out. Miss Big Time Writer! I wondered who put her up to this. Was it because Mike was coming back home in five months? Was she planning on moving Phoenell into my place?

Tears were streaming down my face. I couldn't see through them as they covered my burning eyes like a white sheet. And she wasn't doing anything but watching the damn television like I was nothing to her. Like I didn't even matter anymore.

"We're leaving in the morning," she said, eyes still glued to the TV. But then she looked at me suddenly, her eyes were cold like I'd never seen them before. I felt goose pimples travel up and down my arms. "If you plan on living here."

I had never hated anyone in my life, the way I hated her right then. I had to sit down to keep from running across the room and breaking her face. I wondered how long she had been planning this against me. Was I supposed to feel bad because she was using her damn book royalties to do this? That was her decision, not mine and I didn't feel sorry for her one bit. I read the book and it wasn't all that great anyway.

I thought about all this as I finally got up and headed to the front door, not knowing where I was going because I didn't have my car keys. They were on the kitchen table where everyone kept their keys. I wasn't about to walk back inside and across the living room to get them, though. I didn't want to risk making a detour to the couch and knocking Karla in her head. So wherever I was going, I was walking.

I entered the Blue Club eagerly, not knowing exactly who or what I was looking for. I felt my heart pounding to the beat of the bass coming from all points of the crowded space. Jackie was on my right, looking like she had just stepped out of a Blackploitation flick, hoochie skirt and all. Her hair was cut short bringing attention to her bad skin and the yellow whites of her eyes. Her hair had been wearing thin for a few months now. This was a chick that needed rehab, not me. She dropped out after ninth grade to become a full time crack head. I on the other hand graduated from high school twenty-fifth in my class of three hundred. I never went anywhere near crack. But my so-called best friend was throwing me in a rehabilitation center somewhere in the middle of farmland. I smirked and shook my head. If she had been anywhere near me, I would have given her the finger, really hard.

"Come on girl," Jackie said pulling me towards the small, winding stairway that lead upstairs to what was considered the VIP section of the club. There were no real VIP's though, so these seats were occupied by drug dealers. The cream of the crop, so they thought. But I knew none of them would have been able to hold a candle to Rajul and Chiloe back in the day. Those were real boys who weren't afraid to get down and dirty for theirs. Being up in the club surrounded by females was not their thing. They would have been out there on the floor counting their money and roughing nigga's up for it.

A medium sized man, short with a large afro stood blocking us at the top of the stairs. He gave me a quick once over and then shook his head. But as he did so, he moved out of the way. I could feel my cheeks burning with the heat of embarrassment. Jackie on the other hand didn't seem to mind the fact that we were up in this club to buy drugs as she took my arm and pulled me towards a very dark, very handsome dude with long dreds who sat regally in the third table from the stairway, surrounded by females. No matter how many times I saw him, I was amazed at how good he looked every time.

We couldn't sit down. There were already six girls squeezed into that booth, all just wanting to get a feel of Lou. So we stood at the end of the table watching him talk on his cell phone without moving his mouth. Jackie was antsy, practically jumping from foot to foot. And her hands were shaking. I was sure mine weren't shaking. I was not addicted to anything. Not the way she was.

"What's up Jackie," Lou said finally closing his flip phone with one hand and slipping the other around the darkest girl I had ever seen. He looked at me and winked his eye, showing straight white teeth. He knew what was up. He had known Jackie since elementary school; his mother lived in the same low income housing development, right behind her mother. He took better care of himself though. Nails neatly manicured, clothes pressed, dreadlocks clean.

"What's up, Lonna?" He said flashing all this at me.

"Nothing much," I said trying to steady myself. Hoping I wouldn't fall over and that I wasn't shaking.

"We want some stuff," Jackie said looking from me to him in disbelief. She was straight to business when it came to her illegal substances.

Lou motioned to a young boy with a baseball cap and a tan Gucci warm up outfit that looked two sizes too big, sitting as if ready to pounce at any second at the table across the walkway. He looked barely old enough to drive, much less to be up in a place like this. But he came eagerly when called.

"Hook these ladies up," Lou said.

I had to tear myself away from Lou and follow Jackie who was already on the little boy's heels. We were lead through the cloud of hot bodies, to a side door close to the bar and then down a long well lit hallway. I wanted to ask him if he was new, but for some reason, this just didn't seem like the appropriate time. Jackie was walking much too fast and I could barely keep up.

The boy knocked on the third metal door on the right, at the very end of the hall. A much taller man answered and invited us in. He was lanky with a bald head and I could immediately picture him in a basketball jersey dribbling down the court.

This was a store room. Like a supply closet only slightly larger. The little dude left while Jackie and I fished out money for our stuff.

Between the two of us we had enough to keep us high until the next night. But the next night I would be in rehab. I shook that thought out of my head as Jackie and I got what we came for and began to dig in, right there in the store room closet.

There was a knock at the door. Jackie looked up at me and whispered, "Oh shit."

The lanky dude with the bald head yelled, "What!"

The door opened slowly and before I knew it, Lou had reached in and was gently pulling me out of the store room. I wasn't too thrilled because I knew half of the stuff that I paid for would end up in Jackie's nose. But how could I say no?

Without a word he was guiding me through another door in the long hallway. He didn't even bother to cut the lights on as he put me up against the wall and reached underneath my short jean skirt. Foreplay was irrelevant at times like this; I learned that a long time ago. My panties hung loosely from one leg, my skirt was around my stomach and the next thing I knew, my legs encircled his waist tightly and my back was pressed hard against the cold concrete of the wall as he entered me roughly.

"Shhh, girl," he said covering my mouth because the sounds that were coming from me were anything but human. The fact that he could actually hold me up and take it was enough to push me over the edge like I had never experienced before. I knew it wasn't the drugs. I had sex so many times with my mind blown off of some cocaine or even heroine that I couldn't even remember half of the men I was with. But this experience was nothing short of amazing. His body was hard and much larger than he looked sitting at the table. He was at least a foot taller than me and had to bend his knees to position himself just right.

He was moaning harshly in my ear too along with an explicative every now and then. He gripped me tighter as he ground me into the wall. I knew it would probably be over soon so I worked my hips around him furiously just for the purpose of me being able to get another one before he shot his load into the condom he was wearing.

"So where you be at?" He asked me as I bent to slip my panties around my other leg and pulled my skirt down to cover my hips. I noticed the smell of stale water along with the loud noise coming from the other side of the room. We were probably in the boiler room.

"After tonight, I'll be in rehab."

"Rehab?" He looked at me and rubbed his chin. "Well come holla' at me when you get out."

I nodded, actually believing that I would. Then he handed me a plastic baggy. I had no idea what drug of choice filled it and at the time, it didn't really matter to me.

"This is for your time. I know your friend probably done snorted yours by now."

Jackie was driving like a bat out of hell. But it was funny to me. Riding in the middle of the lanes, swerving in and out of traffic, even driving on the wrong side of the now deserted road. Everything was hilarious to me.

The Spotlight, I vaguely remembered from the weekend of graduation. The picture of Karla and Mike on the dance floor stood out in my mind though. She had no idea that I had watched them the whole time. Sexing each other up on the dance floor like two porno stars. How dare she try to act like her shit didn't stink now?

"How 'bout some weed?" Jackie asked me gesturing towards the bar of the club. This one was a lot tamer than the first. Weed was probably going to be the only thing the we could safely find.

We crossed the dance floor and headed towards the bar where I spotted Bobby and LaShae. Boy, they'd been together a long time. I hadn't seen either one of them since Greta's funeral.

For some reason I found myself pushing through the bodies of people and making my way over to them sitting side by side on the bar stools. I almost knocked LaShae off of hers as I squeezed in between them and turned my back to her. I began rubbing the tight muscles in Bobby's arms through his lime green t-shirt. I knew better. First of all, I always went out of my way to stay away from my brother's friends since Kelly's death. And even though Bobby and Chiloe had not hung out together in forever, I still considered him one of Chiloe's people. Second, his girl had never done a thing to me. She was nice and sort of reminded me of Chiloe's wife. Only she was much more street and ready to whoop my ass. I could see first the surprise in her face and then just pure rage.

"Girl," Bobby said trying his best to push me away while he shook his head that was covered in a Duke Baseball cap, and gave LaShae a look of utter confusion. But he just could not seem to shake me. "Are you drunk?"

"No, I ain't drunk." I said and it was the truth. Jackie was at the other end of the bar guzzling down something and striking up a deal for some weed with an older looking man, but I hadn't had one taste of alcohol since before we left her house for this excursion. But as I took off his hat and began to run my fingers over the cornrows that his girlfriend had done up so nice and neatly in his hair, I realized maybe I should have told him the whole truth. I should have told him I was high and I wasn't thinking straight. Then maybe his girlfriend would not have grabbed my arm so hard. This in turn, made me punch her dead in her face.

It was like listening through a paper towel tube as I heard other people around me yelling, "Fight, fight." I had no idea if that was what was egging me on or not, but I soon found myself on top of her, pounding into her head. People were crowding me and I could feel someone's arms around me, but they were not the least bit affectionate. Someone was trying to pull me off of her. Then someone grabbed my arm and I was being pulled to the front door.

"Girl, you gonna get us in trouble," Jackie said racing down the street in her car away from the club. It was now raining, but for some reason to me, it looked more like snow. I laughed at the thought of snow in North Carolina in the middle of March. I laughed at the specks of LaShae's blood that covered my knuckles and the front of my shirt.

"What are you laughing at? This shit ain't funny!"

I don't know why I didn't say anything, I just continued laughing. I saw us on the wrong side of the road. I saw the oncoming car. At least I think I saw the oncoming car. Either way . . .

Chapter Sixteen

Monday, March 25, 1996 11:45 a.m.

The left side of my face was burning from the heat of sun light shining directly on it. I turned over ready to reach up above my head and close the blinds, but I couldn't. I couldn't move my left arm.

I opened my eyes and tried to no avail to sit up in the bed. I could not do that either because of the sharp pain that shot through my body. The sun was streaming through the room window no more than three feet away from the bed. Karla sat beside the window; she sprang up when she heard the rustle of the bed sheets.

"You okay?" She asked but not in the loving manner that I was accustomed to hearing from her.

I nodded but as soon as I did, I realized my head was sore along with the rest of my body.

"What happened?" I asked through a dry clammy mouth.

Karla quickly recognized my discomfort and after she poured me a cup of water from the pink hospital pitcher she pushed a button on the side of the bed so that it automatically moved upward.

"Well, after you beat LaShae into a coma, you and your little friend got into an accident."

I shook my head feeling truly bad for LaShae.

"Don't worry," Karla said quickly reading my mind again. For some reason I couldn't say anything. "She's gonna be okay. She was only out for a couple of hours."

She sat down on the edge of the bed and placed her hands in her lap. I knew I was in for it and I was scared. I had never actually been lectured by my mother, but I knew what it felt like by the way Karla did it.

"You know you're in a lot of trouble, right?"

I didn't need to answer. We both knew the answer to that.

"You've been charged with assault and drug possession. I talked to a lawyer yesterday morning. He said he can probably get you some probation but now you're going to *have* to do rehab for at least a year."

I grimaced because there was that word again. *Rehab.* Just because one night of partying had lead to a girl being beaten unconscious, a car accident . . .

"What happened to the people in the other car?" I asked.

"They're ok. The reason why you're so hurt up is because you weren't wearing a seat belt."

"And Jackie?"

364

"She's in jail. Driving without a license, DUI, driving with no insurance, drug possession."

Damn. She counted off each charge on her finger. She never could just answer a question and leave it at that. I thought about the time Jackie would probably do because she couldn't afford a lawyer. And I was just getting off with rehab. A rehab I didn't even want to go to because I didn't have a problem to begin with.

I found myself becoming angry.

But Karla didn't notice. She was staring out of the window and into the sun, it seemed. And she continued talking.

"You have some broken ribs. Some fractures. A concussion. You've been out for a couple of days."

I just turned my head towards the hospital door because I was still angry. The sight of cards and flowers sitting beside my bed didn't help to ease it at all. It wasn't going away.

"How could you let this happen to yourself?"

I clenched and unclenched my fist so tight; my acrylic nails left scars in my hand. I wanted to jump up and smack her or attack her, or something harmful. But my pain restrained me, and it was a good thing.

"I love you, Lonna. You're my sister, and I can't stand to see this happening to you."

Her calling me her sister was not a big surprise to me. We were close like that; at least we used to be.

"Lonna, we have the same father." She looked down at me with a weariness in her eyes that was so unfamiliar to me.

I was trying my best to understand and digest what she was telling me. But the cloudiness of my brain would not let me. "The same father?" I asked.

"Yes, the same father Lonna." She was irritated and I could feel it. It could not compare to my irritation though, so I was determined not to let that stir me. If we were sisters, how was it that no one had bothered to tell me before? How had she found out? Was this another one of her little secrets like the Jay situation?

I closed my eyes and started singing a song in my head. To my surprise though, she didn't even say anything else. I felt her move off of the bed and I opened my eyes. She was standing by the window now just looking out over what I was sure was the parking lot. Part of me felt bad for all of this. Everything. But then there was that part of me that still didn't think I deserved what was happening.

I lay my suitcase on the bed and looked around the plain beige room. It was not so different from my room at my mother's house, just a pinch larger. There were two twin beds with an oval multicolored rug and a nightstand separating them. In front of the one window in the room sat an old wooden desk with a chair to match. Beside the window was an empty closet. The only form of entertainment in the room was a clock radio that sat on the nightstand with a lamp.

I was more depressed than I had been in months, trying to recall how I had gotten to this point. And Karla, I couldn't understand why or how she could do this to me. I thought we had been friends above anything else. Now, she was putting me in my place, which for now was a drug rehabilitation center. I wondered if the whole world knew by now that the locally famous author had used her royalties from her much publicized second book to stick her drug and alcohol addicted sister into a rehab. I wondered if she made it a point to tell everyone, do press conferences, tour schools telling little kids to stay away from drugs or you'll end up like my illegitimate sister, Lonna. Never mind that I had only been in here for two hours now.

There was a knock at the metal door, which was painted to resemble a wooden door.

"Yes," I answered non to enthusiastic like.

A short white lady with a full head of auburn hair walked into the room slowly and carefully like she was entering a lion's den. She tried to smile but everything about her told that she was uncomfortable. They did not get a lot of people of color here, especially the thick kind with cold eyes and tattoos to match. Most people like me couldn't afford a place like this. That made me even madder at Karla. "Are you all settled in?" The timid lady asked. Her name was Fidora and she was the house mother.

"No." How could I possibly be settled in? Didn't she see that the closet was still empty? Didn't she see that my suitcase was still on the bed, unopened?

"Well, we're going to do dinner in about fifteen minutes. Then maybe if you need any help I can get one of the other girls to come help you."

Other girls? I was sure she was talking about one of the other black girls in the facility. I just nodded. She walked out leaving the door cracked, meaning that I had no choice as to whether I was coming to dinner or not.

The cafeteria in the house was not a cafeteria at all, it was a kitchen. Just like the one back at Karla's house. There was a large maroon stove, a large refrigerator to match, and one bench like table in the middle of a simulated wooden floor. There were already four girls in the kitchen. Two were cooking, and the other two were setting the table. The white lady that told me to be here to begin with was standing at the little island in the middle of the kitchen preparing a huge salad. It hit me that I was stuck out here in the middle of the nowhere with no men!

"Hi," one of the girls standing at the stove turned to me way to cheery. She was mixed with something and had long black hair much like my own. Part of it was in a pony tail, the rest hung down in stray strands around her face. She was very tall and very thin.

"Hey."

"Lonna," Fidora said, "we take turns cooking and cleaning. Since you're new, we won't make you clean tonight, but tomorrow you'll have to do one or the other. We want you to jump right into things here so you can feel at home."

Or did she want me to jump right into things so I would not feel like a threat? I smirked because I would never feel at home in this God forsaken place.

The girl with the hair sat the pot of spaghetti in the middle of the table and then she sat down beside me. She was trying to be my friend. I wasn't with it.

Fidora sat across from me as everyone else tried to squeeze in.

"Everyone this is Lonna. She's from Fayetteville. She's gonna be staying with us for a while."

"Hello, Lonna," everyone said in unison like robots. It made my skin crawl and I desperately wanted to go home.

I couldn't believe Karla put me here.

"Lonna," Fidora continued. I guess she wasn't done with me and I was getting sick of hearing my name come out of her mouth. "This is Rachel," she pointed to the chipper ass girl with the hair sitting beside me. "This is Myra," she pointed to a white girl with short, shoe polish red hair. "This is Traci," she pointed to a jet black girl who was in desperate need of a hair do. "And this is Joi," she grabbed the shoulders of the slightly overweight Asian chick sitting beside her. She was cute though and looked healthy. I wondered how she had gotten here. But then again, I was cute and looked healthy also.

We ate with Myra babbling on about something that happened in group yoga therapy and why she felt men should not be allowed in.

It took away from the whole experience for the women because they were concentrating on the men. And shit like that.

"There's men here?" I asked.

"Yes," Fidora answered for her. "They live across the bridge, but you do use the same facilities."

"Unfortunately," Myra smirked. "The women are afraid to express themselves and open up to the healing powers of yoga with the men sitting there ogling and judging them."

Okay, now I got it, she was a lesbian for sure.

After dinner, I tried to retreat to my room, but Rachel followed me.

"I know you probably don't want my help," she said slipping in before I could close the door. "But I'm going to help you anyway."

She stood beside the bed where my suitcase sat. "You remind me of me when I first got here. Quiet and mad at the world. I didn't think I really needed to be here."

I just looked at her as I finally opened the suitcase up. She didn't know a thing about me, so what was she talking about?

"I realized though, that I needed to be here and my father put me here for a reason. Not because he hated me but because he loved me."

I stuffed some underwear into the top drawer of the dresser.

"Do you give this speech to everybody that comes in here?"

She shrugged and started hanging up my other clothes. "No."

We worked in silence, emptying out my suitcase, until she came across Karla's book.

"Hey I heard of this girl. She's the one who wrote that real violent book that everybody's talking about. Is this it?"

"Yeah, that's it."

"You don't sound too happy about it. It's not good?"

"No, she's the one who put me here, that's all!"

"This girl? That wrote this book? You know her?"

"Yeah, I know her. She's my sister."

"Wow," Rachel said as she sat down on the bed and flipped through the paperback like she was speed reading. "She must really love you."

"Yeah okay. If that's what you call it!"

"I mean really. This place isn't that bad. It's quiet and it helps, it really does. I've been here for four months and I feel better than I've felt in ten years! I mean they know you gotta have money to come here, so they're gonna do whatever they have to do to get you clean and keep you clean."

If she had only been here for four months that meant she had eight more to go. I thought about my long year and wondered if I would become as cheery as she was. I hoped not.

"So Fayetteville, you're really close to home. I'm from Virginia Beach. My dad heard about this place from one of his rich colleagues. He's a CEO at a tobacco plant in Richmond. And after I got high one night, tried to kill myself, and him, he decided it would probably be a good idea to send me here."

She looked at me, sitting on the desk with my arms crossed defensively over my chest.

"What about you? What made Karla decide to put you here?"

I shrugged. "I guess because her boyfriend is due back soon and she didn't want me around, or maybe she didn't want having a junkie sister to ruin her image."

She shook her head at me. "After writing this book, I don't think there's anything that's going to make her image worse. You know they've grouped her right along with gangsta' rappers. That's what they said on CNN anyway. You know that little talk show they do with Connie Chung at night? I hear she's thinking about making it a movie and a whole bunch of black groups are protesting it. I feel if she had been white with white characters, it wouldn't have been such a big deal. They don't expect for black females to come like this. Makes me proud, you know?"

"Whatever." I was sick of talking about Karla, that back stabbing bitch.

"You know you really shouldn't be mad at her. She's just trying to help you. In her interviews she seems like a very sweet person."

"Don't let her fool you."

She shook her head, exasperated with me, I could tell. "Well come on. Let me show you around."

This place was like a neighborhood all on its own. There were six brick houses, much like the one that I was staying in. All of these housed women just like mine. They tried to group people together by age starting with eighteen. As we crossed the long stretch of field, Rachel pointed to a larger brick building.

"That's what we call *the* Store. You can get what you need there. Cigarettes, pads, tampons, candy, soda. You can mail things and pick up your mail, after it's been closely inspected. It closes at eight."

We passed The Store and kept on walking.

"That's *the* Church," she said pointing to a shed like building with a cross on the front. "They hold services for Catholics, Christians, and Jehovah's Witnesses, so if you anything else, you're shit out of luck."

We kept walking and the place seemed to evolve into a college campus. There were three brick buildings that were all about three floors high. Each one lead to the other with a pretty brown brick pathway.

"Over here is where we do group and personal counseling," Rachel said pointing to one of the buildings. "Over here is the library and the gym. They do yoga therapy there, to strengthen your mind and stuff." We turned to face the other building. "And over there is the infirmary. When I first came here I spent a whole month in there, trying to adjust to the crap they give you to un-addict yourself from some other crap."

I didn't tell her that I had spent most of the morning having a physical and assessment done to determine what type of medication I would be given. I was also given an HIV test. I was sure she probably already knew because all of the house mothers were registered nurses who administered everyone's medication that lived in the house. I was told the medication would probably have a horrible effect on me, along with the symptoms of withdrawal, so for the first six months that would be the main focus. The other six months would be centered on physical and mental therapy.

Rachel pointed beyond the infirmary to the woods. I could barely see the small bridge, that only lead to some more woods.

"The men stay over that bridge. So, if you wanna get you some, you know where to go. Now I wouldn't think about starting no serious relationships with any of them, because . . ." she stopped and shrugged, " . . . I mean they're here, right?"

She was right.

"Okay. So now you have it. The library is open every day, except Sunday, until eight. The gym is open Monday through Friday, nine to eight, Saturday eight to eight and Sunday from ten until three. Any questions?"

I shook my head, "No."

Chapter Seventeen

Tuesday, June 25, 1996 9:38 a.m.

I turned over in my bed, my nose hitting nice warm skin. I rubbed my face in Mike's back and he moaned, then stretched and turned over flat on his back so that my face was in his arm pit. He stretched the full length of his body and pulled me close to him.

It was hard to believe that he had only been back from Georgia for two days. And how lucky I was to have him stationed right at the nearby base. But right now he was on leave for a month, so I wouldn't have to worry about him moving into the barracks until our thirty days was up. I didn't know what I was going to do without being able to turn over and feel him next to me, or being able to make love to him throughout the night whenever I got the urge. We hadn't been out of the bed very much in the past few days.

My phone rang just as I remembered the night before. I climbed over the love of my life, straddled him, and picked the phone up off of my nightstand. As I put the receiver up to my ear, I gently guided him into my already waiting body and began to move up and down on him ever so slowly.

"Hello," I said trying to stifle the moan that was building in my throat.

"Karla?"

I could have instantly gone dry right there at the sound of Chiloe's voice. But one look down at Mike, the crooked smile on his lips and the look of total ecstasy in his eyes as he looked back at me, it just was not possible. So I worked it just a little bit harder to keep myself where I wanted to be.

"What's up?"

"Are you busy?"

"Yeah. Mike is back."

There was complete silence on the other end. But I feigned a conversation by continuing to nod my head. Mike was starting to moan louder.

"You with him right now ain't you?"

"Yeah."

I was climaxing now. "I gotta go. I'll call you back."

I clicked the receiver before he could say another word and the phone fell down to the floor as I hit my mark on top of Mike with a scream loud enough to wake up my long time next door neighbor. Mike flipped me over so that he was now on top.

"Who was that?" He asked in between sighs and grunts.

"My friend down the street," I lied.

"The girl that's always gettin' beat up?"

"Yeah."

He answered with another moan and sat up on his knees holding my legs up in the air. "Did she know you was fuckin'?"

"I'm sure she heard you."

"That's what she get for callin' so early." He smiled and I smiled back because he didn't know just how true that statement was.

I lifted my pelvis to meet his strokes, supporting myself on my elbows, and was greeted by an incredible thrust that brought me to another climax immediately.

"So when are you going back to see Lonna?" Mike asked as he devoured the big burrito, made exactly the way that he loved it.

It seemed that nothing about this restaurant had changed since our first date. Even the men in the mariachi band looked the same as we sat in the midst of the lunch time crowd. The only difference was this time I was actually hungry. All of our lovemaking had created an insatiable appetite in me.

"I can't see her for another three months. She's going through detox. I can't even talk to her on the phone. Not that she would want to talk to me anyway."

"She can't be mad all like you say she is," Mike responded with a full mouth. The food at boot camp must have been terrible. "She's gotta know this is for her own good."

I shook my head. New-New felt the same way he did. That Lonna had to have figured out that she had a problem and that I was just doing this because I loved her so much. But that was not the case. The look in her eyes when I took her to Eastover would have killed me if at all possible.

"I'm telling you, the girl hates me right now. Every since I told her she was going to rehab, she's hated me. And in the hospital, she wouldn't even speak to me."

Mike shook his head and took a sip of his beer. "Even when you told her that y'all are sisters?"

I shook my head back at him. "No. She still wouldn't say anything. It was like it doesn't even matter. And the funny thing was I didn't even really want to tell her. I didn't know how she would take it. But it just didn't matter."

Mike shook his head and took a swig of his soda. "She had a lot going on Karly. She had just woke up out of a coma, had put somebody else in a coma, was in a hospital bed, getting ready to be shipped off to rehab. She couldn't respond babe."

I knew in my heart of hearts that what he was saying made so much sense. But I still couldn't get past the hurt of her not saying anything at all. Even if she had expressed a little bit of anger, that would have been better than nothing at all.

My pager went off.

I recognized the number as Chiloe's. I cut it completely off and slipped it into my purse.

"Who was that?" Mike asked wiping his hands in his napkin.

"Phoenell," I lied again.

"Damn, that girl is needy ain't she?"

I shook my head. "That's the same thing Lonna says. She can't stand that girl. And I have yet to figure out why, besides the fact that she's fucking her boyfriend."

Mike put his napkin down and looked at me. "What?"

"Lonna's messing around with Ron. She think I don't know, but I am not stupid. The only person that don't know is Phoenell."

"How did you find out?"

"After Greta's funeral, Lonna left the house. I went looking for her after close to an hour when she hadn't come back. I saw her getting into his car by the store. She didn't see me though." I took a deep breath because I could feel the familiar trembling in my stomach whenever I thought about Lonna and the whole situation. "I want to be mad at her, but I can't. I'm just so hurt about how she's desecrated herself. And for what? Why would she do these things?"

Mike grabbed my hand in his own and held it tightly. "I know you two are close and everything. But you're from two different worlds. You can't see what she's seen, no matter how hard you try."

Mike hadn't seen his father since his return three weeks ago. I guessed I was to blame for that, occupying all of his time with our love making sessions that seemed to last for days. But I had to close up shop when my own father's wife called to let me know he had been admitted into the VA hospital.

"You want me to go with you?" Mike asked as we stepped out of the shower to dress.

"No. I want you to go see *your* dad. It's a shame you haven't been over there to see him yet."

I tried not to stare at him slip on his boxers and his nicely pressed jeans. His body had filled out so nicely at basic training. He'd always had wonderful body structure, muscles in places no one would have imagined, but now everything was even more defined and more noticeable.

"Trust me," he was saying, "Pops understand. I don' heard plenty of stories about him and my moms back in the day. He know how it is."

I smiled not letting the fact that he had compared us to his mom and dad slip me by. I grabbed him by one of the back belt loops of his jeans and pulled him close to me in just my bra and panties. He wrapped his arms around my bare waist, damn near lifting me up off of the ground.

"Okay. Keep it up. You not gon' make it to the VA until tonight, girl."

"Hmph, I wish didn't have to go at all."

"I thought you and your dad had squashed everything."

"We did." I eased myself out of his arms to slip my shirt over my head. "But it's still an awkward situation. We don't really know each other. I just found out I have sisters a few months ago. We just don't know each other."

I turned around after fastening my own jeans. Mike was now sitting on the edge of my bed starring up at me. "What?"

"I was just thinking about what it would be like to come home to you . . .permanently."

My heart felt as if it did a hop, skip, and a twist inside of my chest. I had to put my hand over it as if at any second it would jump out and land on the floor.

"Mike, let's slow it down a little. You just got back. Let's do this thing right, day by day."

I couldn't find any other way to tell him that I didn't want to get my hopes up. And with all that was going on in my life, this was the one thing that I wanted to be predictable.

He stood up and shrugged his shoulders. Then he put his arms around my waist again. "I understand ok. You got a lot of shit going on with Lonna and your books, and your dad." He ran the palm of his hand down the length of my face. "I love you Karly."

"I love you too, Mike. I love you so much."

My father's wife of five months met me on the fourth floor of the VA hospital as I got off of the elevator. They had gotten married as a spur of the moment thing. Some of the family assumed it was to make her an American citizen since she was originally from Kimberley, South Africa. Others said it was so she could collect the insurance policy, Social Security, and VA money if my already sick father died. I never put too much thought into it myself. She was nice to me whenever we saw each other, which was rarely.

Johanna hugged me leaving the familiar six inches between us. She smelled faintly of lilac like Lonna sometimes did and I wished desperately that my sister were here with me. I was so used to going through everything with her, it didn't feel right being in this place by myself.

"How is he?" I asked Johanna as we walked down the hall past the nurse's station.

"He is better. His temperature is still up and he is still throwing up a little. The doctors say its pneumonia. You can go see him if you want to."

We stopped in front of room 415. I didn't really want to go in. As I studied Johanna's micro braids that seemed to be the same milky black as her skin, I tried to think of a good defense for me not to go in. There wasn't one though, I realized while I watched her walk back in the direction we just came from. I was alone before my dad's hospital room. A nurse walked by pushing a blood pressure monitor. She looked at me, wondering what I was waiting for, I was sure.

Finally I took a deep breath, and turned the huge silver doorknob that felt terribly cold in the palm of my hand.

My dad lay in the middle of his hospital bed, his eyes glued to the television mounted on the wall across from him.

"Hey Baby girl," he said finally glancing away from the bidding of the Price Is Right.

"Hey." I sat down in the chair closest to the door, not wanting to stare at him for too long. So I focused on the television as I became conscious of the fact the father I remembered from my childhood, the one that dropped me off at Lonna's house the very first time and left me, was gone. Gone was the processed hair that made people wonder if his waves were natural, gone were the chubby cheeks that we both inherited from my grandfather. Illness and a party that never ended had taken a lot of things from this man. The change seemed to have taken place so quickly.

"How you doing Daddy?" I asked.

"I'm alright, just weak. I can't keep nothin' down. Can't taste nothing."

The Price Is Right was going off now and the music of the twelve o'clock afternoon news began to play.

"I haven't talked to you in awhile," my dad said right before he coughed and spit the contents of his lungs into a tissue.

"I know. I've been writing and traveling," I replied with my half truth.

"I know, I know." By the tone of his voice I thought my father would dismiss that as the sorry excuse it was. Until he said, "I read about Lonna in the paper."

I had almost forgotten how Lonna's last night as a free woman had been so explosive that it made the front page of the Local & State section of the city observer. It wasn't very often that our small town had so much action in one night. There were all the elements of a Lifetime made for TV movie. The drug user with the troubled past, the do-gooder sister, the skanky friend, the innocent victim in a coma, and a bad car wreck.

"Yeah, I guess you did," I sighed shaking my head and looking back at the television half expecting to see something about Lonna.

"Why didn't you tell me she was on drugs?"

"What for?" Was my response when I looked back at him.

"I'm her father just like I'm yours."

I looked back at the TV again. "She's been on drugs for a long time. There was nothing you could do."

I wondered if he were blaming himself. I wondered if maybe it was his fault. Maybe Kelly's death had nothing to do with it. Maybe it was having an absentee father that did it.

Daddy was having a coughing fit that didn't seem to be going away. I pushed the button over his head for the nurse.

"Just hand me that cup over there," he said struggling to point to the rolling cart pushed over by the window on the other side of the bed. The cup had a flexible straw so it was easy for him to maneuver it into his mouth while lying down.

The nurse appeared at the door, just as I was putting the cup down. Johanna was behind her.

"Mr. Shaw, are you okay?" She asked checking the flow of his IV.

"Yeah, I'm alright." Daddy cleared his throat.

"Dade, are you sure?"

"I'm fine. Leave me and my daughter alone for a little while longer."

Johanna looked from my dad to me. I nodded to let her know everything was cool and she left, followed by the nurse.

"So where is she at now, Baby girl?" Daddy asked while I seated myself back in the chair.

"She's in rehab. I put her in rehab."

He shook his head. Then I heard a strangled, "I'm sorry Karla. I'm really sorry."

I looked over at him and he was looking dead at me. "I forgive you, Daddy. But, I can't accept apologies for Lonna. I can't."

I felt guilty knowing that the whole time Mike had been home, Bree basically had been on her own. It was bad enough her momma was dead, her sister was in rehab, and I neglected her whenever I had to travel and she was left with Marco and his girlfriend that she couldn't stand. And now this.

"So where's Mike?" she asked as we sat down to eat the meat loaf, string beans, and mashed potatoes that I cooked.

"He went to go see his dad." I glanced unconsciously at the wall clock that hung beside the door. I hadn't heard from him all day since we both left the house that morning. I hoped everything was okay. I knew the Doone wasn't what it used to be.

"Are y'all going to get married?" Bree asked between bites of food.

"Maybe one day. No time soon."

She nodded as if she understood, and I didn't doubt she did. Even though she was seventeen now, I guess I was still tempted to treat her like a baby and ask her what did she know about getting married. At seventeen I had been naïve and innocent. Even though there was still a touch of inexperience in her, I could see it all through her eyes, she had seen more in her lifetime than I would probably ever see. She probably knew more about sex and relationships than I did.

No parental supervision for a teenager could be treacherous. I longed to take her with me to the many book signings and conferences just so I could keep an eye on her, but she needed school. Bree already had plans to attend the local university as soon as she graduated. I was proud of her for that.

Yet and still I knew about the late night phone calls from boys. Every week it seemed like there was a different one. And there was no doubt in my mind that she was having sex. Because I had no parental training at all and besides, we were only three years apart, I could think of no way to even approach the topic of sex with her. Just another reason for me to wish Lonna was home.

"Jay called today while you were gone. He wanted to know if he could spend the weekend. I told him it was okay. Hope you don't mind."

"No. That's cool."

She went back to eating and I could tell there was something on her mind. I was never the type to push for someone to say anything. That was Lonna's job also.

So we finished dinner in silence.

Two hours of typing nonstop had my fingers cramped to the bone and my butt sore from sitting. Being stretched out on the couch, watching television with Bree had given me the fuel that I needed to catch up on my writing. It had gone neglected for nearly a month now and I was full of ideas.

But then I heard my bedroom door open and hit the wall behind it so hard, that it felt like the whole house shook.

The first thing that entered my mind was Bree. Had someone broken in the house on us? Had she let someone in the house that she shouldn't have? Maybe we should have had that talk at the table after all.

But it was neither of those things. Mike stood in the doorway of the bedroom and my office. The look on his face was one I had never seen from him before. It was like rage and pain all mixed up into one combination that covered his face like a ski mask.

"What's wrong, baby?" I asked standing up from my computer quickly. A sharp cramp slashed through my leg like a butcher knife almost making my knees buckle.

I paid it no mind and continued to walk towards Mike.

"I'm just going to ask you one question, Karla. Did you fuck Chiloe?"

"What!?" I screamed forgetting about my legs or the pain in my behind. Red and a ball of confusion flashed before my eyes. "No. Where the hell did you get some shit like that?"

"He told me his self, Karla."

"Well he told you a damn lie. How could you think I would do something like that to you, Mike? I love you."

He ignored my question and my profession of love for him. "How much time did you spend with him while I was gone, Karla?"

"What do you mean, how much time?"

"Don't bullshit me Karla."

"Mike, the boy had death in his family. I guess I spent a lot of time with him."

He didn't even look at me as he headed towards the closet and grabbed his military issued duffel bag.

"What are you doing?" I asked touching his arm. But he snatched it out of my grip so violently that he almost swung himself all the way around.

"Don't touch me Karla. How the fuck you gonna be all up in that man's face. I'm at boot camp working my ass off so me and you can have a life together. And you here . . ."

"But it wasn't even like that, Mike. Me and Chiloe have been friends since I was twelve years old. We share two sisters. I don't understand what it is that you wanted me to do."

"I wanted you to be true to this shit. That's what I wanted you to do. I saw your caller ID, Karla. That nigga done called you twenty times while I been here. Each time you would tell me it was somebody else. Oh, it's your girl down the street, oh it's New-New, oh it's your mom."

He shook his head and started to pack his clothes.

"Mike, there is nothing going on between me and Chiloe. He is married, and I am in love with you. I don't understand why you can't see that."

"If ain't shit goin' on, why did you lie?"

"Because I didn't want to cause any trouble. Yeah, you're right he has been calling me, and I was wrong to keep it from you. But damn, I didn't think . . ."

"Yeah, you right, you didn't think."

He shook his head again. I watched the muscles pulse in his neck like he was chewing his tongue. He was pissed and he had every right to be. But I couldn't believe that he was taking it this far.

"So you're just gonna leave me? Because of some damn phone calls?"

"You made that choice, not me."

"But I didn't even . . ."

"If that was true, you wouldn't have lied."

"But it *is* the truth. You just don't want to see it. Damn, if you wanted to end the relationship you should have just told me."

"End the relationship? I was the one, just this morning, saying how I wanted to make this thing permanent. But it was you talking about no. No wonder."

"No wonder? You said you understood."

"Shit, I thought I did. Until I found out this shit."

He grabbed his bags up and looked at me.

"Mike, please . . ."

But he wasn't listening to me. He had already blocked me out, I could see that clearly as he turned and walked out the door, almost knocking Bree over in the doorway.

I banged on the wooden door so hard it flew open. Not that it was ever locked. Chiloe never locked his doors unless he was busy. It didn't dawn on me to look and see if Misha's car was home and here I was bursting up into her crib like I was the police.

But she wasn't home and Chiloe sat on his couch, smoking a cigarette and drawing in his sketch book. He looked up at me and knew right away I was pissed.

"What's up? He asked. But he knew what was up. He knew exactly what was up.

"What did you tell Mike?"

He put the sketch pad down and put his cigarette out in the ash tray that sat on the glass coffee table in front of him. Then he leaned over putting both elbows on his knees and looked at me. His green eyes were ice cold.

"What are you talking about?"

"You know exactly what the fuck I'm talking about."

I realized that I was still standing in the doorway of the den. The door to Rajul's house was wide open. It was ok though. I wanted Misha to come back from wherever she was and hear this shit. It was time for her to really find out who she had married.

"He asked me . . ."

"He didn't ask you shit. You volunteered." I couldn't believe he opened his mouth to attempt to lie to me. "And you didn't even volunteer the truth. You gave him some fabricated shit about us sexing. How could you do that?"

"Well, didn't you tell him I was lying?" He sat back on the couch and looked at me like I was the crazy one as he lit another cigarette.

"I can't believe you did this."

"I can't believe you come over trippin' over some shit I told that nigga'. If he felt the same way about you, he wouldn't have believed shit I said."

I was so mad I could have ripped a hole through Chiloe's throat. The room became dark to me with visualizations of myself jumping over the coffee table and smothering him in the cushion of the couch. I could even see the EMS coming to retrieve his body just like they had done Rajul's.

"He asked me if it were true. I told him no. But I couldn't deny the fact that we spent time together."

Chiloe threw his hands up as if he had won the battle. "So you blew up your own spot then."

That did it. Before I even had a chance to evaluate the situation (like the fact that Chiloe outweighed me by maybe fifty pounds and had a whole foot and a half over me in height and he could probably bench press me like one of his many weights) I rushed him like a quarter back knocking his head backwards on the couch and catching a firm grip around his neck with both of my hands.

Even though I was nearly squeezing the breath out of him, he was still able to fight me back as we tussled back and forth on the couch. One of us kicked the coffee table and all of its contents over.

"Karla, Karla," Chiloe said trying his best to restrain me. He managed to pry the fingers of my left hand from around his neck, but I was trying my best to get them back to it. "Karla, stop."

I guessed that was my warning because the next thing I knew, I had landed on the floor, butt first. Chiloe was still on the couch massaging his neck. I got up slowly, winded, and still wanting to kill him, but a little bit calmer. What would it solve for me to go to prison for murdering this fool. So instead, I threw the ashtray that lay on the floor from the knocked over coffee table, aiming for his head but he ducked, turned around and headed for the door.

"Close the door on your way out!"

I called Mike's pager twenty times in a period of one hour. Each time just getting his voice mail before I would hang up, and through a cloud of tears, redial the number. Still, no answer. I lay down on the bed clutching my cordless phone in one hand and my pillow in the other. Warm salty tears ran slowly down my face as I could feel my head starting to pound. I closed my eyes to relieve the pressure and block out the bright light shining from my ceiling. I was too weak to even get up and cut it off.

I was awakened by the sound of the phone ringing right beside my head. Without even waking up fully, I picked it up and answered, even while I slept hoping it was Mike.

"Hello."

"Karla."

I felt the blood rush to my head and the fires of hell flashed before my eyes again.

"What?"

"Look," Chiloe whispered. Misha must have been home. I wondered what time it was. "I'm sorry. For real. I didn't know you would be this mad. You tried to kill me over that nigga'."

I stared at the phone in disbelief. Even through my drowsy state, I could not believe what Chiloe was saying. How could he think that I would not care about the relationship between Mike and me? How could he think that I wouldn't try to choke the shit out of him? Didn't he know how much I loved Mike?

But I kept silent.

"Why you love him so much Karla? Why can't you love me like that?"

"Cause Mike wouldn't do something like this. And he's not married. And he's not a liar."

"Karla, I did this cause I love you."

"Why not try loving your wife for once? That's who you married!"

"I can't love her like I love you. I tried Karla. I really did."

"So you figure cause your marriage is all fucked up, you wanna fuck up my relationship? He dumped me Chiloe and you still don't have me! So what now?"

There was complete silence on the phone. I could hear him breathing though. Why couldn't he answer me? He had an answer for everything earlier today. He was just full of answers.

"I just know that I love you, Karla."

"Well, I don't love you Chiloe. And I never will. This shit is not forgivable. I mean I've dealt with your dumb shit in the past, but this right here . . . I can't forgive. Goodbye Chiloe."

I hung up before he could say anything else. I clicked it back on and dialed Mike's pager number. And again, no answer.

Chapter Eighteen

Monday, September 30, 1996 1:30 p.m.

The hallway seemed endless, or maybe it was just my nervousness.

I had not seen Karla in six months and even though I thought about her every single minute on the minute, I refused to call or write her because I was still angry. Or at least I wanted to be angry.

I had a distorted view of her since I had been away. I could imagine her getting out of a big limo right in front of the group home in a heavy fur coat and black stiletto boots made of the shiniest leather. So I guess I was surprised when I saw her, even though I shouldn't have been. She was the same old Karla in some sparkly jeans, a lavender turtle neck and a cute jean jacket to match the jeans. She wore boots with heals, but they were far from stilettos. She held two large discount store bags in her hands.

I sat on the furthest end of the couch and stared straight ahead into the blank screen of the television. I could feel the heat of Karla's eyes on me, burning a hole through the back of my head like a laser, but I refused to look in her direction.

"How have you been?" She asked finally after what seemed to be a thirty minute silence.

"Fine," I said quietly shrugging my shoulders.

"You look a lot better."

I wanted to shoot her a dirty look. But I resisted. That would mean looking at her, and I didn't want to look at her.

"Daddy died," she whispered.

She had my attention then. But only briefly, to see if she was serious. Her eyes carried an emptiness that I had never seen before in all of the years of knowing her. Had our father dying affected her this bad?

"He had pneumonia. He wanted you to know he was sorry for everything."

I looked back down at the floor. "Okay."

"Everybody else is doing good. New-New said she's coming down the week after next. Bree sent you a card. I got your mail."

I just nodded at everything she said. Then she handed me the bags.

"There's some finger nail polish, some body lotions and sprays. You know the lilac kind you like. There's some soap and toothpaste, a toothbrush, hair stuff, and some stationary so you can write me." She quickly added, "Or whoever you want. I got you some CD's too and some books."

I was grateful for the stuff. I really was. But I wasn't going to let her know that. To my surprise she stood up like she was getting ready to go. I couldn't believe she was leaving so soon. Even if I wasn't talking to her.

"I've got to go to Georgia tonight, so I guess I better get back home and finish packing. There's a writer's conference down there and they want me to say a few words because I'm going to be the youngest one there."

I wanted to hug her and tell her to have a safe trip. But I just could not. She stuck me in this horrible place. I suffered for six whole months, my body going through all the miserable affects of withdrawal. How could I ever forgive her for that?

"Well," she said as if she were waiting for something. Her face still looked so distant and troubled. There was something going on with her and I was beginning to realize it was not all about our father. "I'll see you later."

She turned around slowly and walked out of the den.

As she passed the entry way to the sitting room, I noticed Rachel standing by the wall.

"What?" I asked her nosy behind while she shook her head at me. The front door to the house closed and I knew Karla was gone.

"I don't understand how you can treat your sister like that. Especially since you say you two are so close."

"*Were* so close. Until she stuck me in here."

"In here? And what's so wrong with here? At least she didn't stick you in a county facility. Trust and believe, I've been in one of those and it's like a torture chamber. And it doesn't even help you."

She came and sat down on the couch beside me.

"I don't know if you know how much it cost to come here, but it cost a lot. And I don't know if you know how much writers make, but it's not a lot. Instead of spending what little she did make on her, she chose to put you in rehab. I don't think I would still be sitting around mad about that. Now I can see the first few weeks, I'll even give you the first few months. But I wish I had a friend that cared that much about me."

She looked through the bags sitting on the floor beside my feet and shook her head again. "Then on top of all that, she comes to visit you as soon as you get out of detox and brings you stuff. What more do you want, Lonna?"

I shook my head and looked down at the green carpet under us. "I just wanna go home." I said sounding like the biggest baby on earth. I couldn't help it though.

"Are you addicted?"

"What?"

"Are you a drug addict? Are you addicted?"

I didn't know. I had never really thought about it. Wasn't a drug addict like my late mother, in her shorts that were way to short and her hair slicked back uncombed or washed, by gel. I wasn't that. Wasn't a drug addict like Rosie? Jumping from car to car and abandoning her wonderful husband and child whenever she felt the whim just to support her habit. I wasn't that either.

So what was I?

I slowly rose from the couch and walked to the room that I still shared with no one. I took the sky blue stationary with clouds scattered across it, out of the bag, along with the matching pen. Then I sat down at the desk and began to write.

I wrote about the men that I knew I had been with, but I couldn't remember them because I was drunk or high.

I wrote about the fights I had been in but really couldn't remember why because I was drunk or high.

I wrote about the ugly things I said to Karla, the person who had been there for me the most, but I really couldn't remember what I said or why I said them because I was drunk or high.

I wrote about riding home from clubs with God knows who putting every life that I lived with in danger by letting these weirdoes know where my house was, but I couldn't remember them either. Because I was drunk or high.

I wrote about how I needed to get high off of something every day and then force myself to recover as much as possible so that I could go to work the next morning. How I needed to feel the sting of alcohol going down my throat, burning my tonsils in the process. How I needed to find out who had the best drugs so that I could become close friends with them or even sleep with them. How I needed to forget about the messed up shit that had happened in my life beginning with the death of the only man, outside of my brothers, that I ever really loved and who ever really loved me.

I put the pen down and looked out of the big window into the setting of the late afternoon sun. Without even realizing it, I had written away four hours of my life. There were four girls playing with a light green Frisbee on the front lawn. All they needed was a dog and it would've been picturesque. I balled the papers up and threw them into the trash.

New-New was absolutely radiant in her third pregnancy. Her hair was still blond but cut into a shoulder length bob. Her face was cute and round with those dark eyes that seemed to glow. Her whole being just seemed to sparkle, or maybe it was all that gold that she still wore religiously.

"What's up girl?" She asked giving me a tight hug as close as she could possibly get with that big old stomach. She had five more months to go but to look at her it seemed like only two. I didn't understand why she wanted to have babies back to back to back. But if she was happy, I was happy.

"I'm great."

We sat down on the park bench in front of the house that I would be residing in for five more months.

"How's Andrew?"

"He's good."

"How are the babies?"

"They're fine."

She grabbed my hand then. "It hasn't been that long, Lonna. Really. How are you?"

"I'm okay. I'm working on it. But at least now I do realize that I have a problem."

"Well that's good." She shook her head. "Karla's not doing so good."

"What's wrong with Karla?" I could feel my heart jump to the middle of my throat and my mind began to race frantically. She didn't have any life threatening diseases when she came to see me. I was pretty sure if she had been in some kind of accident, Bree would have called me.

"She's not sleeping, not eating."

I felt better knowing nothing drastic was going on with her. I also felt worse at the same time, though. I had treated her so bad when she came to visit me, even though it was clear to see something was going on with her.

"When Bree and Jay first told me, I thought they were exaggerating. But I found out last night that they weren't. The girl was up all night. She said she was writing, but it's been that way for a while. Marco made her favorite ribs on the grill and she would not eat. And you know Karla got enough meat on her bones for days, but she is starting to waste away in the face. No joke. Then she'll just be sitting there and all of a sudden, her eyes will start to water. You know how she is, she don't want anybody to see her cry, so she'll get up and go be by herself somewhere or she'll try to dry her eyes up really quick."

"It's probably because I won't talk to her," I admitted quietly hoping that maybe she didn't hear me.

"You won't talk to her? Why not?"

For a second it was hard to believe that Karla had not broadcasted my cold shoulder to the whole family. But I was dealing with Karla here and knowing her she was probably blaming herself for everything that was going on. Including the situation with our father.

"I was mad because she put me in here in the first place."

"But . . ."

I grabbed New-New's hand and almost got scratched by one of her many rings. "I'm better now. I know why she did what she did. I know I had a problem." I continued to hold her hand and study the bracelets that laced her wrist. "It's funny because my therapist really couldn't stand me before. But he actually was proud of me for admitting I had a problem. I mean if he wanted to commend me 'cause I have a problem, that's fine."

New-New laughed.

"I'm serious. You know addictions run in our family. And I never really thought about that. And then all the stuff we went through, not knowing who our dad was, not having a relationship with Greta. Rajul's death, Kelly's death." I stopped and shook my head. "I guess I was trying to fix me and that was the best way I could think to do it."

"Yeah, I know what you mean." She looked down at my hands still wrapped tightly around hers and I wondered what she meant by that. New-New quickly changed the subject before I could say anything else. "So you didn't talk to her about anything?"

I sighed long and hard. "She told me Dade died."

"Yeah, Dade." New-New shook her head this time.

"She told me before I came here, that he was our father."

New-New looked at me and smiled. "I knew that already."

Had Karla told her even before she told me? I could feel a slight pinch of anger in the crook of my neck. But I was determined to swallow back.

"Girl, Momma may have dressed like a tramp and everything. Stomach hanging all out and shit. But she really wasn't. All my life I could only remember her with two men. I put two and two together and figured out who our Daddy was. Then when I saw Karla, I mean damn we all look just alike. So I knew. I just knew."

"Why didn't you ever tell me?"

"Because telling you something like that is like throwing gasoline on a grill that's already lit. That's why. And I didn't have any proof anyway. So there was no point in getting you riled up for nothing."

A breeze blew by and I could hear voices behind us. Rachel and Joi were headed to the gym. Rachel was on a mission to help Joi shed twenty pounds. Joi had only lost four since I had been here, and Rachel was leaving tomorrow. Rachel was also on a mission to get Traci a hairstyle. She'd failed at that one too because Traci refused to get a relaxer. First she needed to admit that she was Black and the rest could come later.

"So I guess she didn't tell you that her and Mike broke up?" New-New asked.

"What?"

She nodded. "Yeah. She didn't tell me either. Bree did. They had an argument about something and he left. I know it has something to do with Chiloe because he haven't been coming around like he usually do. And with them broke up, you know he would be on

411

it. I just don't know what happened, and I'm scared to ask her. I don't want her to feel worse or anything. But I think that's the reason why she's going through what she's going through."

I couldn't believe that the couple of the century weren't even a couple anymore. How in the world was Karla coping with all of this. Mike was the love of her life, she woke up in the morning just to say his name. That on top of me, on top of our father dying was more than even Superwoman herself could take.

"Damn."

Rachel was taking her sweet time packing. She folded each piece of clothing perfectly and placed it inside of her suitcase gently like the stuff was going to break at any second. I watched her as I sat on her desk, chin in my hand and elbow on my knees.

"So what are you gonna do?" I asked. She had been the closest thing to a friend I had up in this joint. Sort of like a substitute for Karla. Not as good, but she served her purpose well. I didn't know why I let myself get so attached anyway. I knew when I got here that she would be leaving soon. She only had a few months to go when I came in. But I had gotten attached. She helped me to come to some serious realizations about myself and my situation. And now she was leaving.

"Well since I'm clean now, Pop's gonna give me a position in his company. Something small of course, until I prove myself. I'm gonna go back to school and get my degree in business, so I can do a hostile takeover!"

"Hey aim for the sky," I said giving her a thumbs up.

She smiled slightly and shook her head. Her pony tail swung from side to side. "I don't know what it's going to be like out here. Seeing the world through untainted eyes. I mean, I've been high so long, it's gonna feel funny not to be."

"Well, Dr. Black said the first thing you have to do is let all those shitty people you use to hang with go." I used my therapist's exact words.

"Yeah I did that. I wrote every last one of them letters telling them not to call me and not to come by to see me ever again."

"Are you serious?"

She nodded and sat down on the bed beside her suit case. "I got two back unopened and I got a nasty letter back from one. But I guess the others got the message."

"That was really bold of you. I'm proud of you. Now you can go to school and work and get your life straight."

She nodded. "Yeah, I guess that was kind of brave. I'm just scared of failure."

She sounded so familiar to me right then, that tears involuntarily came to my eyes. "You know what? You remind me a lot of Karla. She's braver than she thinks. She's always second guessing herself and shit. That's you."

She smiled at being compared to Karla I was sure. Maybe that was why we had grown so close. She had a ton of Karla's personality traits.

"You'll be just fine."

"Here," she said fishing through her pockets. And then handing me a piece of notebook paper. "I want you to write me all the time."

I unfolded the paper that read:

Rachel Weeks

2939 Dobson Road

Virginia Beach, VA 23453

"I will. Don't worry."

I sat on the window seat of New-New's huge front window. It was raining hard and it was cold. I could feel the chill of the air coming in through the sheer beige curtains, but I continued to sit in my spot holding my mug of homemade hot chocolate. I wondered when New-New had become so domesticated. Through the vent not only could I feel the slight warmness of the heat but I could hear the faint sounds of her children playing with their father in the basement.

"You're gonna catch cold in your behind, sitting by that window like that!" She said and I smiled. I watched as she entered the living room of her row house from the kitchen. She was wrapped in a silk teal kimono, her stomach poking out like an over inflated basketball.

"I'm serious," she said sitting down across from me on the seat. She looked at my blue wife beater and pajama pants and shook her head. "What's wrong?"

I just looked back at her that time, not saying a word.

"Okay, I mean I know what's wrong, but you can't let that get you down. Karla, you are doing the damn thing, for real. I mean, just look at you."

I didn't know if she was talking about the three book signings that put me in the District area two days ago or the conference for young African American Women Writers that I hosted in Baltimore just one day prior to the first signing. Fortunately, the book signings were over for awhile and I should have been on my way back home to Bree. For some reason, though, the thought of that depressed me and I decided to stay one more day with my sister.

"Is it just the thing with Mike, the thing with Lonna, or both?"

"It's all of that."

She nodded her head like she understood everything. Then she said, "I know. But you gotta look at it like this, Lonna will be home soon. As far as you and Mike, if that thing is meant to be, it's gonna be. Regardless of anything that's going on right now."

I knew she was right. But I didn't feel that way at that particular moment. I had not seen or heard from Mike since the night he walked out of my house. He sent his friend and fellow soldier, Link, to collect a few shirts and underwear that he accidentally left behind. My pride had taken a beating, but I still refused to call him anymore. What was the point?

"I know you love him, Karla. But sometimes, you have to part to grow closer. There's probably some things that both of you need to work out to make the relationship stronger."

"There is no relationship New. He won't even talk to me. All because of a lie."

"What lie?"

"Chiloe told him we slept together."

"What?"

I nodded. New-New was the first person that I actually told what happened. I didn't know if it was embarrassment that Mike had actually walked out on me or just pure pain that wouldn't let the words come out of my mouth to anyone else.

"Chiloe called me fifty times when Mike came back. But I would never tell him the truth about who it was on the phone. I just didn't want to cause anymore friction between the two of them. I didn't want to deal with a lot of drama. I didn't realize that it would just make me look even guiltier."

"I can't believe Chiloe would do some shit like that." New-New shook her head. Then she said, "Yes I can. Girl, Chiloe is ruthless. And dangerous. I'm surprised that's all he did to Mike, was lie. That boy has loved you since you were twelve years old. I know you being with Mike just completely threw him over the edge. I'm surprised Chiloe didn't try to kill him."

I sighed heavily feeling my cheeks grow hot. "No, but I tried to kill *Chiloe*."

"You what?" New-New leaned in closer to me, her eyes growing wide.

"I don't know New-New. It all happened so fast. I drove all the way out to Rajul's house." I could see the events of that day so clearly in my mind as I spoke. "And when I confronted him, first he tried to lie, then he acted like he did nothing wrong. He even tried to make it seem like it was my own fault." I shook my head and looked out of the window, scared of what I would see in New-New's face. "The next thing I knew, I had jumped over the coffee table and was trying to choke the living shit out of him. He had to throw me on the floor to get me off of him."

There was silence from the both of us. The only sounds were the heat, the children, and a car driving down the rain covered street outside.

Then I heard a giggle. And another one.

I looked over at New-New not really sure if the chuckle was coming from her or not. She covered her mouth with her hands and I was sure it was coming from her because the portion of her face that her hand left exposed was red!

"What?"

"I can just see your behind on top of him trying to choke him. He probably thought you had lost your damn mind. Where was Misha?"

"She won't home."

"Now I would pay money to see that shit for real." She almost toppled off of the seat, her belly moving up and down as she laughed. I couldn't help but smile a little.

"I'm glad I could bring so much laughter to your morning, Leonay."

"Girl, I'm sorry. But that shit is funny to me. So what did he do after he threw you on the floor?"

I shrugged. "I got up and went home and tried to call Mike for the rest of the night, but he wouldn't answer his phone. Then Chiloe come callin' me talking about he loved me and he only lied because he loved me and he couldn't believe I tried to kill him over Mike. Girl I was so mad. I still am."

"So that's why he stayed away from the house when I came down there. He probably thought your crazy behind was going to jump on him again. Was this before or after Dade died?"

"It was the day he went into the hospital." I looked at New-New seeing the perfect opportunity to change the subject. "Speaking of which, did you get that check from the insurance company."

"Yeah. I got it. I'm going to get my Mercedes next week," she said looking out of the window and nodding her head, probably envisioning herself riding down that very avenue. "What you gonna do with yours?"

"Bank it. I banked Lonna's too. I'm sure she'll be happy to see something extra in her account when she comes home."

New-New nodded. "Don't think I didn't notice how you changed the subject on me."

She put her hand on my arm and squeezed gently. "Everything is going to be okay. Believe in that."

PART 5

Chapter Nineteen

Monday, April 7, 1997 2:26 p.m.

I walked slowly over to Chiloe as he stood outside of his huge truck smoking a cigarette, not really knowing what to expect. Even though we had been communicating back and forth through letters and phone calls for six months, all of that had seemed so empty to me. Like there was something he just was not saying and refused to say. Something told me it had everything to do with Karla.

And speaking of which, I had been looking forward to seeing those bright brown eyes and chubby cheeks for a few weeks now. Even though, we had not spoken since she received nothing but the silent treatment from me, I figured she would be the one here to pick me up. Instead, I got a call from Chiloe that morning telling me he would be here to pick me up. I wanted to ask him why, but I didn't want to hurt his feelings. His psyche seemed a little fragile to begin with, so I said okay and left it at that.

"Hey, dog," he said hugging me tighter than I could ever remember. Marco got out of the front passenger seat of Chiloe's Suburban and took my bags in his hand.

"What's up big head," he said hugging me with his free arm. I knew I had only been away for a year, but he seemed to have matured in that short period of time. Being a cop was probably making him older and wiser.

"Just glad to be up out of there," I said pointing to the red house like building that had been my home for a year.

"But you do know it was for your own good, right?" Chiloe said looking at me like I needed to get that clear in my head before we took another step.

I nodded, just wanting to get out of the vicinity before Fidora changed her mind and decided I needed more counseling, or Karla had more fees to pay, or anything.

Marco moved to the back, leaving the front seat to me and Chiloe.

"So, you ok?" He asked leaning over and blasting the air conditioner before we could even pull off.

"Yeah, I'm good. Are *you*?"

He looked at me. The expression on his face said that I knew something that I should not have. Really, I didn't know anything but the things he had not told me in his letters. I was still too apprehensive to ask about Karla.

"Yeah, I'm cool."

"How's Misha?"

He shrugged like she was the last thing on his mind and said, "She alright, I guess."

"What you mean, you guess?" Marco piped in from the back seat. He said what I was thinking and I was glad that family connection between us was still intact. I had expected tons of things to change in my absence, but hopefully they hadn't.

"What you mean, what do I mean? Like I said, she alright, I guess. She do her own thing, I do mine. Ain't that much changed."

I shook my head and looked out the window. He was right about that. "I called New-New last night and nobody answered the phone. Where are they?"

Chiloe shrugged again. "I don't know. Maybe she just won't answering the phone. You know with the new baby and everything, she's probably busy."

"Whatever, New can take care of a baby in her sleep with her eyes closed, in the dark! She got enough of them joka's."

They both laughed and I asked, "How's my baby Bree?"

Chiloe laughed and shook his head. But Marco was the one to answer, "Crazy. She passed her SAT with flying colors. Karla's been keeping her straight."

I could have cut the tension in that truck with a butcher knife at the mention of Karla's name. And I knew it wasn't just my imagination. I sat close to Chiloe so I could feel his body stiffen. Something was going on.

I left it at that though, deciding to change the subject. "And Rosie?"

That seemed to have eased the mood, but only a little. "Kerry's gone. For good. To Charlotte." Chiloe shook his head; his body relaxed a little since our conversation had gone in a different direction. "He took Gerald and dipped. Rosie been staying with us. But I don't know how long that's gon' last. She's not doing good."

I thought about my drug habit and what it had done to Karla and the rest of my family. One addict in the family was more than enough, we surely didn't need two. I sighed deeply and leaned back onto the head rest as Chiloe hit the main highway that lead to home. "And Jay?"

The tension was back again, for reasons I could probably guess. Chiloe's face turned a pinkish color and he gripped the steering wheel like it was someone's neck.

"He's alright," Marco said right after he cleared his throat. I glanced back at him and he was looking out of the window.

"Look, I know he's gay, but what's the damn big deal?"

"Hey," Marco said finally looking at me. "I'm cool with it as long as I never see him kissing a dude or anything like that."

Chiloe just grunted. He *had* seen that.

"What about you?" I asked anyway.

"He know he better not come near me, that's all I got to say."

"What? You know he don't want you, so what's the problem?"

"The problem is I ain't cool with having no faggot ass brother. That's the problem. Have people looking at me like I'm down with that shit."

"Nobody's looking at you like you're down with that shit, Chiloe," Marco said in his soothing voice much like Karla's. It was comical. "Everybody knows you're strictly heterosexual."

"That's not the damn point."

"What's the damn point, Chiloe?" I asked.

"The point is his ass is playing catcher to these mudafuckas I grew up with. How you think that makes me look? Don't try to turn this shit back on me. I told him I don't want nothing to do with him and that's it."

Nope nothing had changed at all.

There were two huge white SUV's in the driveway when Chiloe parked his on the side of the road in front of the house. I knew one belonged to Karla, but I could not place the second one.

Marco carried my large suitcase with the wheels that Karla sent me during my stay at rehab. I treasured that suitcase like it contained gold, even when it just held everything that she sent to me and sat in the closet of my dorm room. Despite the fact that we really weren't speaking, every week there had been something new from her to me. Especially when she traveled to different cities. Sometimes it was just a t-shirt with the name of a place, or a teddy bear with the same; she made it a point to send it to me along with body pampering items, toiletries, stationary, and music CD's. I stored everything in the suitcase so that no one would touch them. And as far as I knew, no one ever had.

I could hear the voices as we entered the shelter from the bright mid day sun that was the carport. I wondered who in the world would be here and if Karla even remembered I was coming home today. Maybe she was with all of her writing buddies and they were having a party. The smell of food tickling my nose and the thought that she would even do something like that made me mad. She was taking this not talking thing too far.

But when I opened the door, I was greeted first by a newborn, the color of an Indian Red Crayola, in the arms of my sister who had not lost much of her baby fat at all. Andrew stood next to her smiling proudly in his jeans and polo shirt.

"Welcome home," New-New said hugging me carefully, making sure not to squish the baby that was as round as she was.

"New-New, you keep poppin' out funny looking kids," I said stroking the small hand of my new niece with my thumb and looking down into her smiling face.

"Man, shut up Lonna. Damn, they didn't fix your smart mouth up in there did they?" She asked punching my arm.

"Nope."

I gave Andrew a quick hug, ready to search the rest of the house. But before I could, Bree was coming around the corner of the living room. I gasped because in one year this girl that I use to be able to beat on the top of her round head was now almost taller than me. At the age of seventeen, I knew she probably wouldn't grow very much more, but I was very impressed. Not only was she tall, but she had a figure that was out of this world; a big butt with wide round hips and perky breast the size of baseballs.

"Hey Lonna," she said grabbing me. I remembered when she could only grab me around my waist. Now she was hugging my shoulders.

"Damn girl, you grew!"

She let me go and looked at me. "So you wanna pick on my height too?"

"No, not at all. But damn, you look great."

She blushed then. "Thank you. You look good too. For real. You look happier."

"I feel happier." It was the truth, but I would have felt a lot happier if Karla had been waiting for me like everyone else.

"Well, come on," Bree said taking my suitcase from Marco and grabbing my hand. "Let's go put your stuff up."

I let her lead me down the hall with New-New right behind me. She had given the baby to Andrew who was now in the living room with Marco and Chiloe. It didn't make sense because I knew that was her truck in the driveway. With the smell of food so strong in the house, I just knew she would be in the kitchen cooking her heart out. I remembered a time when she refused to cook anything, now she was just a regular Betty Crocker.

The hallway was dark, but I could see that it had been painted. Instead of the kitcheney orange that it had been since Karla was a little girl, it was now a glossy beige. I wondered when she found the time to paint in between all of her book promotions. Then I noticed that the doors to the bedrooms looked as if they had been replaced also. The old ones were rickety and didn't even lock. The wood was peeling from them also. These though, had that brand new sheen to them and the doorknobs sparkled like real diamonds. I wanted to stop and touch one, but I was pulled further down the hall.

Bree knocked on the door at the end of the hallway. The door that used to be mine. I wondered why she was knocking and who was occupying the room now. Had Karla moved someone else into my spot in just the short amount of time that I was gone? And if so, who was it? I guessed it was probably Phoenell. She had been itching to get that punching bag over here since day one.

Then my mind told me to stop. It was what my therapist referred to as 'negative self talk'. I laughed when he first told me that shit. Until I realized that I did it.

Jay opened the door to the bedroom and I was surprised to see him. Like Bree, he had grown so much more. He was already my height when I left, but now he was even taller than me. I was looking up to my baby brother for the first time ever.

"What's up girl?" He said grabbing me and hugging me, almost squeezing the life out of me. I guess I had expected his personality to be feminine now. I had not seen him since the night I found out he was gay. But he wasn't. In fact his whole manner was strong, rough, and masculine. Much like Chiloe. "Welcome home," he said letting me go finally.

"Thanks."

Then he moved so that I could enter my room. And that was when I saw her. I couldn't even enjoy the totally remodeled room because I was so happy to see her. She walked towards me cautiously, I guess not knowing what to expect from me. But I couldn't hold back any longer and I grabbed her, like I was a dude, and hugged her so tight I could feel her loose her breath.

"I'm so happy to see you," I said into the mass of curls on her head. Her hair had grown back now to the middle of her neck.

Karla's arms went around my neck and she hugged me back just as tightly. "I'm so happy to see you too girl. But look." She pulled away from me and held her arms out so that I could admire the room.

The walls that were once a flat cream color were now white and shiny to bring out the baby blue curtains and baby blue shades at the window. The old furniture that she bought used after she gave away her grandmother's bedroom set was gone and in its place sat brand new oak furniture including a four post bed. I always wanted a four post bed and I could feel the tears coming to my eyes as I ran my hands along the baby blue bed spread adorned with decorative pillows of all shapes and sizes. Under my feet was an extra plush rug of the same exact color.

"Do you like it?" She asked me eagerly. Her eyes wide with anticipation and I flashed back to the first time I ever spoke to her. She had that same look now.

"I can't believe you did all this for me."

"Well, I had help. I couldn't move the furniture and lay the carpet by myself."

"Trust me," Bree said putting a hand on my shoulder, "she did most of it by herself."

"Yep," Jay added.

"I'm sorry, I was busy giving birth!" New-New said as she sat her ass on my new bed.

I shook my head and looked around at my family, especially Karla. Even though I never told her, I was pleased to know that we were blood related and not just the close friends we had always been. I knew at times she had grown tired of putting up with my drug-infested ass. She never failed to amaze me though.

"Thank you. I mean, I really mean that. 'Cause I know, I haven't been that great of a person in a while. I wanna make it up to all of y'all and I mean that."

"There's nothing for you to make up," Karla said grabbing my hand. "I'm just glad you're back and you got some help. Now I know you're not cured or anything and I know it's going to be rough. But we're gonna stick together in this thing. Okay?"

I nodded. That's when I noticed the old closet door that in the past slid back and forth, or at least tried to slide back and forth, had been replaced by new glass doors that made the room look amazingly larger. She hadn't missed a thing when she took on the redecorating task. I wanted to hug her again, but instead I was pulled back down the hall.

"Since you weren't here, I canceled Thanksgiving and Christmas and rescheduled it for today."

Marco, Andrew, and Chiloe were still seated in the living room watching television. I sat down on the couch beside Andrew and took my month old niece from him. Her name was Lea. She was the splitting image of Andrew right up to the blast of red hair.

"Hey Lonna," Marco said leaning forward in the gold chair. "I forgot to tell you, I'm opening up my computer shop next month and I need somebody to run it."

"You're not going to be a cop anymore?" Andrew asked before I could reply.

"Of course I'mma still be a cop. But I figured, shoot, why not make some money off of one of my hobbies. The thing is though, I won't have time to run it and be in there like I want to be."

"I don't know anything about computers Marc." Everything I did know, like the typing, I learned in high school. That was about it.

"I'll teach you everything you need to know. You'll have other people working for you so it won't be a problem. All I really want you to do is handle the books. Stuff like that."

I shrugged. "Okay, if you're going to train me."

I was extremely grateful even though I knew I wasn't showing it. I lost my job at the community college when I caught a case. I was also grateful that no one was mentioning that and any other incidents related to that time of my life. There were no uncomfortable silences like no one knew what to say or do around me anymore. My family chatted and poked fun at each other just like always.

Nothing had changed.

The door bell rang and I heard footsteps scramble to it. Soon I could hear a male voice in the kitchen and what seemed to be Bree's voice, only a few octaves higher.

"Everybody, this is Link," she said walking into the living room followed by a nice looking guy wearing military fatigues. He was tall, with dark wavy hair, very fair skin, and a very muscular body.

"Hey," I said looking him up and down. It was obvious he was older than she was. Never mind the fact that her eighteenth birthday was only a few weeks away.

"This is my sister Lonna that I told you about. Lonna this is Link. He's one of Mike's friends."

At the mention of Mike, every male in the living room suddenly had to clear his throat or cough. Karla was safely in the kitchen finishing up dinner with New-New and I hoped she hadn't heard his name. She still had not mentioned the situation with him to me.

"How you doing?" He asked holding his hand out for me to shake. I took it with the hand that was not occupied by New-New's large baby, my eyes never leaving his huge dark ones. "I've heard a lot about you."

"I ain't heard nothin' about you," I said with a smile. He was exceptionally cute. "Have a seat."

He looked around for a second for a spare place to sit. But everyone was taken, even the arm of the couch where I sat was being used by Jay. He grabbed a chair from the kitchen table and placed it beside the couch.

"How old are you Link?" Was the first question out of my mouth and I watched my sister's face turn pink. She reminded me of Karla, never able to hide her emotions.

"I'm twenty-two."

"Where you from? You have an accent."

"Brooklyn, New York. Born and raised."

"Uh huh. Does Karla know you?"

"Yeah, Karla's my girl. She's real cool. I'm hoping her and Mike get back together soon."

I glanced at Chiloe and saw him looking out of the window just to avoid eye contact with everyone else. I wasn't the only one looking; Jay and Marco were too.

"Yeah, I do too."

Chiloe looked up at me then and I stared back at him.

"So you like my sister?" I asked turning back to Link who was oblivious to the culprit sitting by the window.

He nodded. "Yeah. I do."

"Well, I like her too. So if you hurt her, I'll break your arms. Both of them. Okay?"

I smiled brightly at him and he smiled back at me showing deep dimples. "I understand."

"Good. Staying for dinner?"

I didn't know why we were here. In my whole life, I had never spoken more than ten words to Rosie. We were so distant from each other, she was more like a far-off relative than a sister. A cousin maybe. From far down the line. But for some reason Marco felt it necessary that I talk to her. Just coming from rehab myself maybe I could help her with whatever she was going through. Never mind the fact that I had only been in rehab once and Rosie ventured there three times. And never mind the fact that she had been on drugs since I was in elementary school. I knew this whole thing was a waste of time.

Karla and Bree stood close behind me as Marco knocked on the door of the huge house. The music from the stereo against the wall was low and the house was well lit. The smell of food and scented candles was strong. It was obvious Misha was home.

Rosie sat on the couch. She looked surprised to see all of us trail into the den, one at a time. She had to know something was up. Karla and I together was no big thing, but to have Marco with us too was totally new. Misha came from the kitchen around the corner and greeted us all. She was friendly and loving as usual, but there was something in her eyes. Something was missing as she tried her best to seem overjoyed at seeing us, offering us all drinks and something to eat. She seemed to speak more to Karla than anyone else and I wondered what had gone on between them while I was gone.

I took a seat in the leather armchair beside the couch while Karla, Bree, and Marco remained standing. Chiloe made his way back into the kitchen, leaving Misha behind. Marco followed him.

"What's up?" I asked my older sister and oldest sibling since Rajul passed. She looked awful. Her hair, which had never been long, but was always a nice shoulder length very fine and very straight, was now mostly gone around the edges. Eaten away by drugs. Eyes that use to be bright were now dull, surrounded by pools of yellow. And the weight that she lost was ridiculous. Her clothes just hung on her.

"Nothin' much," she said showing a toothless grin and sifting through a magazine that she held in her hand. She wasn't reading it though.

I didn't know what else to say to her. She didn't seem to upset about her situation. Instead she looked high right then. I wondered if I looked like that during my blue period. I shook my head because I didn't even like to think of that anymore.

"You know, I just got out of rehab," I said hoping that would get the conversation going and off to a good start.

"Yeah, I know," she shrugged.

"Have you thought about going back?"

She put the magazine down and looked at me as if I were from another planet. I knew she had to be wondering who I thought I was, coming in here asking her if she was thinking about going back to rehab.

"Is that why you over here talkin' to me? You think cause you done been in some high saddity rehab, you can come in here preachin' to me?"

Well, that was exactly what I thought, apparently. She had me figured out, it was time to go. "I don't mean to tell you what to do or get all in your business. I just know your kid and your husband probably need you right about now . . ."

"Look," she said sliding to the edge of the seat, "you don't know nothing about my kid and my man. I been in county rehab before, it ain't shit. I ain't got no rich friends to throw me up in no big ol' fancy rehab."

She was looking at Karla then, and with much hatred. Karla wasn't too much worried about it. She didn't know like I knew that crack heads were amazingly strong.

"You treat that bitch over there like she family. Everybody runnin' around here like she all that. She ain't nobody."

Then she stopped and shook her head. Karla just stood there quietly watching her. I guess she dealt with me long enough not to even think twice about what Rosie was saying. I was finished. There was nothing more I could say. So I sat back in the chair and stared off into space.

Rosie was still shaking her head though. She wasn't done. "Y'all some dumb bitches. For real."

That's when I saw Karla swell up. "We're dumb?" She asked, hands on her full hips. "You're the one who can't leave the crack alone, but we're dumb? You the one that gave up your child and your fine husband, but we're dumb?"

Rosie's bottom lip started to tremble. She looked down at her clothes and then off to the side. I knew the feeling. I felt the same way the day Karla told me my butt was going to rehab.

"Look at you Rosie, what do you have?"

"Who the hell are you to judge me?" Rosie asked but she wasn't standing up. She just sat there, wringing her hands hard and trying to avoid Karla's harsh stare. Was she going to cry? I hoped not. There was nothing worse than a crying crack head.

"Nobody's judging you," I said in a much quieter tone. "But don't sit there and act like you don't have a problem and it's everybody else with the problem. When you know good and well, it's you with the problem."

Rosie was still shaking nervously and I feared that we had caused her to desperately need a fix. I shook my head, positive that was the case. I got up from my seat and walked into the kitchen.

"We're leaving," I said to either Chiloe or Marco. Whichever one cared the most. I think it was Marco because he was the only one that turned around and looked at me.

"How did it go?"

I shrugged my shoulders. I knew it had not gone good at all. But I didn't know how to tell him that. He and Karla would have made such a good team, going around saving the world. They both had Capt. Save a Hoe syndrome.

But Chiloe read right through my little shoulder shrug. "You can't help somebody that don't wanna be helped." He paused to light a cigarette. "That's not Lonna sitting in there, man. That ain't even Rosie. That's somebody totally different. She tried to steal my TV last night and I had to beat her ass. Rosie would never have done that shit."

Marco looked from me to Chiloe and then down at the tiles of the kitchen floor in total defeat. I felt sorry for him because I knew how much he wanted everything to be all good with everyone. And he had everyone's best interest at heart.

The front door slammed and Misha rushed into the kitchen. "She's gone. Rosie's gone."

Chiloe looked up from his cigarette. "What'cha mean she's gone?"

"I mean she got up and walked out the door," Misha said defensively. I couldn't blame her, he did sound rather accusatory.

Chiloe looked down at the floor for a second, then put his cigarette out. "She'll be back."

"What's up with Misha?" I asked Karla as we sat watching television in the living room. Karla cooked rice and chicken and we each had a colorful bowl almost the size of our heads.

I hadn't seen Misha since my return from rehab, three months ago. I knew she was busy with school, trying to become a teacher. And the fact that she lived way out in Erwin didn't help much either. She called Karla a lot though.

Karla knew what I was talking about immediately. "She's miserable." She chewed her food before she tried to say anything else. Then she spoke again. "Chiloe treats her like shit all the time. He messes around with other women, and he don't even try to hide it. He calls her dumb and stupid all the time. I think he probably hit her a few times, but when I asked her, she just said, 'What do you think?'"

Why was I not surprised this was going on? He never really wanted that girl anyway. It hurt though, because she was so sweet. She would have been the best person for him. But he could never see past himself to see that.

"The only time she's really happy is when she's in school so I started feeling sorry for her. We started going out to eat and shopping. Stuff like that. And he's mad about that."

"That's not the only thing he's mad at."

Karla looked at me over her bowl of rice. I just rolled my eyes and looked at the television knowing she would blurt out whatever had gone down. She always did.

"I tried to kill him."

Okay, I was not expecting that one. "You what!"

"I tried to choke him to death. He broke me and Mike up. So I tried to kill him."

"Let me get this straight," I said sitting my bowl down on the end table. "You, Karla, tried to kill Chiloe by choking him to death?"

She nodded.

I couldn't hold it any longer. The laughter hit me so hard I fell on the floor holding my stomach. "I wish I could have seen that shit."

"Why are you laughing? I don't see a damn thing funny. You and New-New act like it's the funniest thing."

"Karla, oh my God . . ." I couldn't even spit out what I wanted to say. All I could see was her and him wrestling back and forth and Chiloe's face turning blue. "Are you crazy?"

She shrugged and continued to watch television.

"Okay. I'm sorry." I eased myself back into the chair. "How did he break y'all up?"

"He lied and told Mike that we fucked. When Mike confronted me, it was like he already had his mind made up about what happened. Chiloe called me a lot while Mike was here when he got back from boot camp and every time he called I would lie about who it was, then I couldn't even lie about all the time we spent together."

"You looked guilty."

"Basically." She put her bowl down on the coffee table. "Girl, I got in my truck and drove all the way to Erwin. He wasn't even apologetic about the shit. And that made me even madder. I couldn't help it."

I shook my head, glad for the most part that I had never ever experienced anything like that. I wondered what it would be like to love someone so much that if you lost them, you would be ready to kill somebody. Seemed kind of scary to me.

"How's Phoenell?" I asked. Talking about Karla's attempt to murder Chiloe and his abuse of Misha brought her to my mind.

The questions seemed to catch Karla off guard. She looked at me, mouth open wide and asked, "Why?"

Typical Karla response.

"I was just wondering. I don't have nothin' against that girl, Karla. I mean I'm jealous that you two are so close. And I think she's stupid for letting Ron treat her like shit. But other than that, I'm sure she's a sweet person. I mean she has to be wonderful for you to like her as much as you do." It took a damn lot for me to say that. A year ago I knew that would never have come out of my mouth.

Karla nodded and looked down at the floor. Then she shook her head. "I don't know. I worry about her all the time that one day that nigga' is gonna kill her. And she thinks he must really love her to get so mad at her that he hits her. Can you believe that?"

I nodded my head just as the back door opened. The clatter of much too high heels hitting the linoleum of the kitchen floor filled the house that was so peaceful less than a minute ago.

"What's up?" Bree asked flopping down on the couch beside me. She smelled heavily of a man's cologne and her long dark hair was all over her head. Whatever she had been doing, she didn't take much effort to hide it.

"What's up with *you*?" I asked. Karla just shook her head and went back to eating.

"I have an announcement . . ."

"You pregnant?" Karla and I asked in unison. We wouldn't have been surprised. Upset, but not surprised. Every since her eighteenth birthday, Bree had been running around like a chicken without a head. And we both knew it wasn't all with Link. He was a fool if he thought he was the only one she was seeing. And he was so nice too, I felt sorry for him just like I felt sorry for Misha.

"No, I am not pregnant," Bree hit my arm with her huge Gucci purse. I was just happy that at least she had been smart about that one thing.

"What then?"

"Me and Link are getting married."

Karla and I looked at each other, both feeling like we had missed a big chunk of something. First of all she had just turned eighteen. Second of all she just met Link less than a year ago. And third, fourth, and fifth, she couldn't keep her hands off other men long enough to get through a wedding ceremony.

"You've got to be kidding," I said before I even thought about the words coming out of my mouth.

"Why?" Bree asked totally confused. She saw no reason at all why this was the most ridiculous thing she had ever said.

"Bree, y'all just met not too long ago," Karla said.

"And you're too young," I said.

She seemed to accept Karla's reason. But mine? She turned to look at me like I was crazy.

"I know you not talking about too young. How many doggon' times have I heard the story of how you got engaged when you were fourteen?"

I shook my head knowing the difference between Kelly and me and Bree and Link was like night and day. "It wasn't fourteen it was twelve! Kelly and I had been together for a long time. And would've been together even longer by the time we got married. And besides, I'm not as crazy about men as you are. You know you can't hardly be faithful to that boy."

Karla nodded her head in agreement.

"I can't believe y'all are not happy for me."

"We're happy if you're happy," Karla said before I could even open my mouth to respond. "But please think about this long and hard and make sure it's what you really wanna do."

She gave me a look that said, 'Let it go'. But all I could do was shake my head again.

The doorbell ringing ended the conversation for me anyway.

"Who in the world is that, it's one o'clock in the morning," Karla complained as she stood up. I stood up with her and looked back at Bree as I headed to the front door.

"Tell your men to stop coming over here at all hours of the morning."

"How you know it's for me?"

"Whatever," I mumbled looking out of the curtains that covered the four panels of glass on the door.

But it wasn't for her. "Misha." I said surprised.

"Misha?" Karla sounded like an echo. "I hope nothing is wrong."

But it was one o'clock in the morning. This girl went to bed at nine thirty. So we both knew something was wrong.

She stepped into the house and it was obvious she had been crying for a long time. Her eyes were practically swollen shut.

"Misha," I said taking her over to a chair at the kitchen table and sitting her down. Karla took a seat beside her and Bree got Misha some water for lack of anything better to do.

"What's wrong?" I asked. I knew nothing had happened to Chiloe. She wouldn't have come over if it had. She would've called and we would've gone to her house. There was something else going on.

"I caught him . . ." she sobbed.

For some reason I felt that at least Karla and I realized exactly what she was talking about. I didn't know if Bree did or not.

"He was with that bitch in my house!" She screamed, still sobbing.

Ok, so she had finished the job that Karla started. Where was his body, I wondered. Instead I asked, "What happened, Misha?" as I sat down in a chair on the other side of her.

"I went out to shop, I just needed some air. I came home from the store," she paused to take a drink of water. "And there they were. In my bed!"

I looked over at Karla, behind Misha's head, and I knew her heart was broke for the girl. It was written all over her face.

"We fought all damn night until he finally left and I packed my stuff."

"Where is your stuff?" Bree asked. Her eyes were wide like she was watching a movie on HBO.

"In the car. I'm going back to Goldsboro." She dried her eyes with a napkin and looked at us. "I'm sorry y'all. I couldn't drive all the way back tonight. And I didn't know where else to go."

"It's okay, Misha," Karla said rubbing Misha's arm. "You can stay here and get as much rest as you need, girl."

"Chiloe's gonna be mad when he find out she's gone. You don't think he'll come over here do you?" Bree obviously didn't know what I knew. Chiloe would probably think twice before stepping up into Karla's house, I was sure of it. I shook my head.

"He'll probably think she went home."

Misha wasn't making any moves to get her stuff from her car and prepare for bed. She just sat in the chair, shaking her head. "I feel so damn stupid. I knew he was doing this. I should have left him a long time ago. I should have left him. I should have never married him!"

Then she broke out into uncontrollable sobs. Karla, Bree and I looked back and forth at one another. None of us knew what to say or do for her.

"You're gonna make yourself sick Misha, you gotta stop crying like that." Karla said finally as she got up to get her nighttime Tylenol from the kitchen cabinet. "You can sleep in my room and I'll sleep in the living room. Everything will be ok in the morning."

"Did you call your family?" I asked. I knew they pretty much disowned Misha after she married Chiloe. She had given up way too much for him.

"I talked to my sister. That was it. I'm pretty sure she told our parents."

"I'll go get your stuff from the car," Bree said. She was the only one that still had her shoes on.

"It's the black bag in the front seat." Misha handed the keys to her Honda Accord to Bree and she disappeared into the night.

"Come on," Karla said taking Misha by the arm and helping her to her room. I followed close behind. Soon Bree's footsteps were coming down the hallway too.

"I just don't want you guys to be mad at me," Misha continued to sob.

"Why in the world would we be mad at you?" I asked as I began to unpack the duffel bag that Bree handed me.

"I know when me and Chiloe first got married; y'all didn't really approve all that much."

"But it wasn't you we didn't approve of," Bree answered. "It was the way Chiloe did it. We always liked you. You've always been cool with all of us."

The phone rang; we knew before we even answered who it was. We just knew.

"Hello," Bree answered, picking up the phone next to Karla's bed. A minute passed before she said, "No. I haven't seen her."

There was another pause. Karla and I looked at each other.

"Yeah she's here. You wanna talk to her?"

Bree rolled her eyes in her head and I had a feeling he wasn't asking about Misha anymore. I hoped Misha didn't catch on.

"Alright then. Bye."

She hung up and looked at me first, then Misha. "He asked if we'd seen you. Then he asked about Karla."

We didn't mean to all look at Karla, but we did. Her face turned pink. Misha just shook her head.

"He's such an asshole."

She was just telling us something that we already knew. I wished one of us had told her sooner.

Chapter Twenty

Wednesday, October 15, 1997 10:11 a.m.

I watched Marco from my office as he entered the shop, papers in one hand looking distressed. It was too early in the morning to have that look. I hated when he looked like that, it was never anything good when he did.

He sat down in one of the chairs across from my desk right after he placed the paperwork in front of me. It was a price list he'd constructed for a music studio somewhere that was interested in a new computer system.

"What's up?" I asked after glancing over the price list.

He shook his head. "Rosie hasn't been home in three days."

I stared at him dumbfounded. I mean of course I cared, but she was a crack head. He continued anyway. "Fayetteville police don't want to waste tax payer dollars or man hours looking for a drug addict. So me and Jay went out looking for her last night. We didn't have any luck."

"What about Chiloe?"

He shrugged. "He said he would look around out there, but you know how that goes."

I wanted to tell him that Rosie was a grown woman. If she wanted to come back home, she would. Obviously Chiloe understood that concept. But sitting there in his police uniform looking so discouraged, I couldn't find it in me to say that.

"I'll post some signs up," I said instead. "Maybe that will help."

He nodded, still not looking very positive. "First, I want you to take this price list out to that studio for me. The owner's name is Jonathon."

"But Marc, I thought you were dealing with these people."

"I am, but I gotta get back to work. All you gotta do is drop it off. They just want to look over it."

"They don't have no fax machine?"

He looked at me, exasperation written all over his face. I didn't want to stress him out more than he already was, but a long drive to the country where this studio was located had not been in my plans for the day. "No, Lonna. They don't even have a good computer system, that's why they need us. Now, if you want more money, you better take this price list out there."

He reached in his pocket, pulled out a twenty and flung it on the desk. "This is for gas. Now get out there."

My toe ring broke. That on top of the news about Rosie was a good indication that the day was going to be wack. Just as I was getting into my car, the thing just snapped in half. Leaving my nicely polished toes that peaked out of my sandals, looking naked. I tried to tell myself this was a small thing, not to worry. What did a bunch of 'bama music producers care about a toe ring anyway?

I parked in the newly paved parking lot and walked up to the white cinderblock building. It kind of reminded me of a warehouse. Or maybe even a prison. Yeah, that was it, a prison.

Cold air from the window unit air conditioner hit me in my face. It sat across from the front door in the only window in this area. I felt my hair blow back, all out of place and it made me even madder because I just had it done on Saturday. I wondered what was next for me as I walked to the receptionist desk that sat across the room. Then I realized they didn't have a receptionist. The desk was just for decoration I guessed.

"Can I help you?" I heard behind me as I stood there reading the 'sign in' sheet. Ten wanna be rappers and a girl group all before eleven o'clock. I wondered why these people didn't have jobs to go to on a Wednesday morning. Instead of asking that when I turned around, like I planned to do, I couldn't ask anything at all.

457

He was chocolate brown, with dimples in each one of his cheeks. He wore my favorite color on his six foot frame like he invented it himself. I wanted to run but I couldn't. Marco would kill me. I didn't want to lose my life, even if my stomach muscles were doing flips and I felt the urge to throw up.

"Hello," I extended my hand. The one that should have had a wedding band on it by now, but it didn't. I hoped he noticed as he took it firmly in his own. Then I chided myself for even hoping such a thing. I didn't need a man, what the hell was I thinking! Before I could withdraw my hand though, I realized I probably needed to tell him my name. "I'm Lonna Garcia, I'm with . . ."

"Oh, you're Lonna?" He asked with the brightest smile. I wondered how much Marc had told these people about me and why. "Come in, we've been expecting you."

I followed him down the hallway, pass the waiting room of rappers and singers. There were three doors with occupied signs above them. Only one was brightly lit. He knocked loudly on the door across the hall from it.

"Come in!" A male voice yelled from the other side. The man with me opened the door and I was surprised when he let me in first.

But not before he smiled down at me. I frowned because it wasn't cool the way his smile was making me feel.

"You must be Lonna," the man behind the desk said as he stood up and came around to the other side to greet me. I looked around the office after acknowledging that yes, I was Lonna and shook his hand. His office was smaller than mine with one tattered sofa, not including the two chairs that sat on the opposite side of his desk. There were posters of different music acts and replica gold records hanging on his wall. I knew for sure none of those gold records were made in this studio.

"Have a seat," he said gesturing towards the two chairs. I took the one closest to me and the man with me took the other.

"I'm Jonathon. This is my business partner, Dallas."

Again, he smiled at me. I took a deep breath and wondered who would name their child Dallas? Was he born there or something?

I pulled the paper out of my leather briefcase with my initials embroidered into the leather, my coming home/getting a job gift from Karla, and handed Jonathon Marco's price list.

"So if I decide to go with y'all, when is the soonest he can get it done?"

"As soon as you need it. Let us know what you're going to do, and I can get the contracts drawn up."

He nodded. "Cool. Me and Dallas will look this over and give you a call."

I looked over at Dallas and he was smiling at me. He was so cute. It was time for me to go. I stood up, preparing to make my exit. Jonathon extended his hand and told me how nice it was to meet me. I said the same and headed for the door, followed by Dallas. He followed me down the hall and to my car, without saying a word until we were outside.

"So how do you like your boss? I mean is he cool?"

I nodded jingling my keys in my hand. "Yeah he's real cool. He's my brother."

"Really? Family business, huh?"

"Yeah, we're trying to make it that."

I nodded really feeling like I should go, but not wanting to. "I noticed you're not married. Do you have a boyfriend?"

I cleared my throat, switching back to professional mode, not expecting him to be so forward. My stomach was beginning to twitch again. "No, I don't have a boyfriend," I said pretending to be busy all of a sudden. "You know what? I really should be getting back to work now."

He looked disappointed for a second. I caught a sweet whiff of his cologne as a warm breeze swept by us. It was definitely time for me to go.

"Alright," he said after what seemed like forever. Then he opened my car door for me. I looked back into his eyes to see if he was serious. He must have recognized that look because his gaze relaxed. He didn't look disappointed anymore, but hopeful. He smiled and said, "It was nice meeting you, Lonna. I'm sure we'll see each other real soon."

Bree came into my office and sat down in the chair opposite my desk. She smiled and I smiled back as I tried to hurry my phone conversation with a customer up. This computer stuff was harder than I thought it was. Or maybe it was the customer service I was having to do a lot of. Obviously between me and my sisters, Karla got the people skills. I got the aggressiveness, something that Karla didn't seem to have very much of and something that really wasn't helping in my new job.

"What's up girly?" I asked as I hung up the phone.

"Nothing much."

"You sure?"

"Yeah."

"Ok."

"I missed you while you were gone."

I smiled, dismissing the fact that she had waited so many months to tell me that. "I missed you too. I missed everybody."

"What was it like?"

I had to think for a second because no one had asked me that question. There had been many, 'How are you doings?' and I had even had an, 'Are you better now?' But no one asked how it was.

"Well," I said finally, "it wasn't like prison or anything. It was more like college I think. They had dorms and classes and we even went on field trips."

"Field trips?"

"Yep, we went to a museum. Can you believe that! We had baseball games, cookouts, church, and a library. I did so much yoga I can probably shape myself like an O. I mean it really wasn't that bad. The only thing was going through withdrawal. It hurt, really bad and I was sick all of the time. Some days, I couldn't even get out of the bed."

"Damn, really?"

I nodded wondering how I could describe the way I felt to her without sounding corny. "It was like a cleansing. A rebirth. I mean, it felt bad but afterwards, I felt good. You know? I was angry for a long time at Karla, at everybody. But even that went away."

"I'm glad you're better, Lonna. I mean Karla took good care of me, but she's not you. You know?"

I was speechless. That was the first and only time I had ever heard that.

I pulled the top of the copier in my office down over the contract Marc did up for the studio. I wasn't too thrilled about it at all. I would be spending too much time at the most countrified ghetto place I had ever seen all because of the extensive work that was to be done. It was obvious these guys were true to life thugs and not to mention that it sat out in the middle of nowhere. But I was Marc's head honcho and if I valued my life and my job, I had to do it.

And then Dallas. I had gotten such a good dose of his cologne that I smelled it even when he was nowhere around.

"Hey, you busy?" Karla said entering my office. Apparently, this was the new hang out spot for my family.

"I'm getting ready to take these contracts to the 'bamas. Would you like to come?"

"Lonna, why would you call your customers 'bama?"

I shrugged and went back to copying.

"What's wrong, Lonna?"

I had already told her about the studio and Jonathon. For some reason, I conveniently left out Dallas.

"Nothing," I said shaking my head and flashing a fake smile. I was so used to doing that since I started working that it didn't dawn on me this girl knew if the smiles were forged or not. We'd known each other for too long.

"What's wrong, Lonna?" She asked again. "Did somebody out there say something to you or do something to you?"

"Girl, no. You know better than that. I wish somebody would put their hands on me."

"Well then, what's wrong?"

I turned around and looked at her. "There's this dude that works out there, named Dallas. He's Jonathon's cousin. I think he likes me."

She shrugged as if it was just nothing at all. "And, what's wrong with that? Is he cute?"

"He's alright."

"Well . . . ?"

"Well what?"

"Well, what's the problem?"

I was standing there copying the same paper over and over again without even realizing it. "You know what the problem is."

"What, Kelly?"

I just looked at her and pushed the 'start' button again.

"Lonna, a promise to be faithful only last a lifetime. Not both of your life times, just one. Kelly's been dead for six years. Don't you think it's time for you to have a serious relationship?"

"Look, I just got out of rehab, do you really think I need that extra stress right now?"

"Girl, a man was not what put you in rehab!"

"I know that. But still. I have things that I need to work out right now."

"Oh yeah? Like what? What could possibly prevent you from getting with this man?"

"I'm not just going to go after the first man that decides he wants to look at me, ok Karla?"

"This is not the first man, big head! There've been plenty of other men, and you always make up some lame ass excuse of why you can't talk to them. So now, you've moved to it's because you just got out of rehab even though you been out for half a year!"

"Look, are you going with me or not?"

We both looked down at the copier where I had now printed thirty copies of the same damn contract when I only needed three.

She thought I had been kidding when I told her the studio was in the middle of the country. But when we got out of her truck and looked around, she knew I hadn't been playing. For miles there was nothing but fields. What was in the fields, we didn't know. Across the street from the studio, about a mile down the two lane road, we could see a very small convenience store. But besides that, there was nothing around here.

Despite the desolate land in the middle of nowhere, the studio got pretty good business. How people even found out about this place, I couldn't figure out for the life of me. But they did and they came from miles around trying to be the next big rap star or singer. My computer techs were really excited about doing business with this place; most of them heard this was the best studio in this state.

Karla followed me through the glass door and there sat the empty receptionist desk. It wasn't like they couldn't afford a receptionist. I knew for a fact they had a waiting list a year long.

"Come on," I said taking Karla by the arm and pulling her past the waiting area and down the hallway. The window unit was blowing in my face again and I heard one of the doors in the back of the building open and shut again. I felt my heart leap and I hoped that it wasn't Dallas, but I hoped that it was. It wasn't. Part of me breathed easy as Troy walked towards us.

He was tall (but not as tall as Dallas), dark, and handsome, with a closely shaved haircut and a bright smile. He didn't work in the studio instead he went to college and proudly proclaimed himself to be a career student. He was close friends with Jonathon and had been for years. The first time I met him, while doing a run through with one of my computer techs, I thought about setting him up with Karla. And now as they smiled at each other, I figured it would probably be a good idea to try.

"Hey Lonna, what's up?" He said only acknowledging me for a second until he asked, "Who's your friend?"

"This is my *sister* Karla."

Karla held out her pale, nicely manicured and well lotioned hand. She showed all of her teeth at him as he took it and shook it.

"What's up Karla? I'm Troy."

"Nice to meet you, Troy. Do you work here?"

"Naw, Jonathon is my boy and I hang out here a lot."

"Oh."

I hated to interrupt this wonderful moment but I wanted to get in and out of here as soon as possible. "I have the contracts for Jonathon to sign. Where is he?"

"Come on, I'll take you back there," Troy said still admiring Karla. I didn't know how he made it down the hallway with his eyes on her. I figured he would probably run into a wall or something, but obviously he knew his way around here well.

Music shot from all directions as we traveled down the dark hall. I couldn't help but wonder which door Dallas was behind and who he was with. I could just imagine what these music types were like. He probably had a hoochie on his lap at that exact moment.

Troy turned the knob of a door with a lit 'OCCUPIED' sign and we walked in behind him. Jonathon sat at the soundboard listening intently to a guy who was obviously rapping behind the glass. His hands moved quickly and intensely and his head bobbed back and forth as he spoke into the microphone like it was a true to life person and they were involved in a heated argument with each other. The urge to laugh caught somewhere in my throat because anyone could see, to Jonathon this was serious.

"Hey, Jon," Troy said apparently not affected by the deep look of concentration on Jonathon's face. "Lonna's here."

Jonathon turned around quickly and looked at Karla and me standing by the door. Well really just at Karla. I heard her breath catch in her throat and turned to look at her to make sure she was okay. There was no doubt she was taken by his caramel, 5'9 and stocky muscular frame. I never would have guessed it. It was clear to see that he truly felt the same way about her.

He turned back around and spoke into the microphone. "Yo man, let's take five. I got some business to take care of."

He released the talk button on the mic before the boy could even respond. Then he stood up and walked over to Karla who was too speechless to even hold her hand out for a shake, much less say hello.

"Hey," he said as blown away by her as she was by him.

"Hey."

I think all thoughts of Troy were forgotten right about then and Troy knew it. He was hurt, but I could tell he was not going to let it bother him. There were a lot more females coming in and out of this place.

"I'm Jonathon," he said holding his hand out to Karla as we followed him across the hall to his office. She took it and I heard her say, "My name is Karla. I'm Lonna's sister."

He turned to look at me. "I didn't know you had a sister. I can see the resemblance though."

I flashed another fake smile as he sat down behind his cluttered desk. Karla sank into the tattered couch and I handed him the contract. He couldn't seem to take his eyes away from her long enough to even read it so I cleared my throat loudly.

He glanced at me and then back down at the contract. After reading it thoroughly he said, "Yeah, this looks good to me." He flipped it over and signed it. Then he looked back up at Karla. "Karla, Karla. You look so familiar. Have I seen you somewhere before?"

"I don't think so," Karla replied, her face red as a beet.

"Yes I have. I mean, I know that sounds like a line, but I'm serious. You look so familiar. You sing?"

I laughed. Karla looked over at me like she would knock me out of my chair. It was not my fault the girl had a voice like a squeaky wheel.

"No. I don't sing."

"Where do you work?"

"I don't. I'm a writer."

"A writer," Jonathon said like he was reflecting on the true meaning of the word. Then he said almost jumping out of his seat, "I know where I saw you. You did a book signing at the mall. For your book that just came out."

"Yeah. Back in May."

"Yeah. You signed my book. I had heard so much about your writing that I just had to meet you."

"So have you read the book?"

"No. When can we get together and talk about it?"

If Karla was falling for this crap, she was the only one. I never would have figured him for her type though. Maybe since her break up with Mike, she decided to explore new avenues.

"When ever's a good time for you."

Her face was still a deep crimson as he studied her over the desk. Just as I was about to ask him to sign the other copies of the contract so I could get my sister up out of here, the door opened and in walked Dallas. He was like a candy bar wearing a baby blue jersey and jeans for a wrapper. His gold jewelry that consisted of a watch, a bracelet, and a gold necklace shone like sun light on a newly painted car. I was entranced at first. The room seemed to stand still and I could feel my chest becoming heavy with anxiety.

"What's up?" He asked the whole room, but he was looking at me.

I shrugged my shoulders, or at least I thought I did. I meant to. But I didn't know if I had or not. I probably sat there looking stupid at him with my mouth open.

"Meet Karla," Jonathon said standing up and coming around his desk towards her. "She's Lonna's sister. She's a writer."

"Hey what's up?" Dallas asked extending his hand.

"It's nice to meet you."

"I can see the resemblance." He looked back at me, still sitting there watching him and how he reacted to Karla. Then he winked his eye at me and I felt goose bumps go up and down my arms.

"Lonna's told me a lot about you," Karla replied and winked her eye at me too. I realized, just by the way I was looking that she figured out this was Dallas. No one had even spoken his name yet.

Ok, it was time to go. I got up out of the chair. "I need for you to sign these two also," I said handing the other papers to Jonathon. "I'll call you next week about your website." He bent quickly over the desk and signed each one while I gave Karla a look that I was going to slap her if she didn't head for the door now.

"So what time would you like to get together tonight?" Jonathon asked as the four of us walked to the front door of the building. Dallas stood close to me with his left arm slightly touching mine. I tried my best to keep from looking at him, but damn, I could smell the sweetness that seemed to flow off of him.

"Tonight?" Karla asked.

"Yeah. You said whenever I wanted to."

I couldn't hear the rest of the conversation as Dallas and I stood beside the passenger side of Karla's truck. He put his hand on the door as if he were getting ready to open it for me. But then he stopped.

"Can I get your number?" He asked plain and simply.

"For what?" My voice was trembling and I could feel my bottom lip going in and out like it was breathing on its own. My stomach muscles were even contracting on their own. What the hell?

"So I can call you about six so we can go out tonight at about eight."

I smiled. I didn't want to, but I did anyway. I tried to tell myself that he probably had at least two baby mommas, a police record, and issues with his father. That wasn't even enough to make me not scribble my cell phone number down on a piece of paper inside of my purse and hand it to him. He took it, letting his fingers brush over my hand slightly.

"I'll call you as soon as I finish up here."

"Ok," I shrugged like I could care less whether he called or not.

He opened the door and I stepped into the truck. Then he closed it again for me. "I gotta hook this client up. I'll talk to you, ok?"

I said ok again and watched him disappear back into the cinder block building. Jonathon still had Karla hemmed up on the side of the truck. Anymore closer and they would have been giving Eskimo kisses. My fingers itched to press the horn of the truck. I'd gotten what I knew I came for in the first place and I was ready to go. Fortunately the truck door opened and she stepped in before I could lean over to the wheel. Her face was flushed like she had been running.

"You okay?" I asked as she started the truck up.

She looked at me and smiled. Then she rolled her eyes. "I think I should be asking you the same thing."

I felt my cheeks grow hot. I knew there was no way possible that her blushing thing had rubbed off on me.

"It's ok, Lonna. I won't tell anybody."

I had a flash back of us being twelve and she swore not to tell anyone about Kelly and me. She never did as far as I knew.

"Please don't."

I looked around the restaurant wondering if Karla was having as good of a time as I was. I was pretty sure she couldn't have been. Dallas had a sense of humor like a Def Comedy Jam comedian and I could not remember ever laughing so hard and so genuinely as I was tonight.

"So why are you so mean?" He asked with a mouth full of lobster flesh.

I smirked pretending to be irritated with him. "I don't know," I shrugged. "Maybe I've been hurt by a man and I'm bitter."

He laughed and I laughed too. Then he took a sip of his soda, making me instantly thirsty. "For some reason, I don't believe that." He wiped his full lips with a napkin.

"Why not?"

"You're too mean for somebody to hurt you. And they would be too scared to leave you unless they had to."

Dallas just thought he had me all figured out. I knew I wasn't complicated, but I wasn't such an open book like he made me out to be neither.

"So what happened?" Dallas asked.

I wasn't prepared for this. Not to talk about Kelly tonight. I watched the waitress refill both of our Cokes and then move on to the next table. I debated whether to even tell him or not. I hadn't talked about that night in years. But Dallas stared quietly at me, waiting and making no apologies for wanting an answer to his question.

So I took a deep breath. "He died."

"He died?"

I nodded.

"Did you kill him?"

If I had not found him so appealing, and if I had not liked him so much, I probably would have reached across the table and slapped the shit out of him. But he said it so honestly that the only thing I could do was smile.

"No, I didn't kill him."

He sat back in his chair preparing himself for a long story. "So what happened?"

I cleared my throat and sank back into the soft leather of the booth. I could see that night under the streetlight so clearly in my mind's eye. I could even remember the touch of the cold November air hitting my cheeks and drying up the sweat that accumulated right at my hair line from the sprint to Kelly that started at my front door. It was odd how the forty degree weather was the last thing on my mind that night, but now I could almost feel the air like it was just last night and not almost a million years ago.

"Kelly used to sell drugs for my brother. And the night of my fourteenth birthday party, he got shot up the street from my house."

Dallas wiped his mouth again with the white napkin sporting a red embroidered lobster at the bottom. Then he put it down and looked at me.

"Did the police find out who did it?"

I shook my head remembering my conversation with Chiloe close to two weeks after Kelly's death. Looking back, I wondered if it was grief over Kelly's death or the pain he felt in his heart over Karla that actually caused him to seek retribution. "No, but my brother did. He took care of it."

He nodded, clearly understanding where I was coming from. "Y'all were serious, huh?"

I nodded, fiddling with my fork even though I finished my shrimp at least thirty minutes ago. "We were young though," I said trying to explain away my feelings for Kelly Gordon.

"Young or not, you loved him. People say puppy love don't count, but I think it does. It can hurt just as bad when you're young."

"You ever been in puppy love?" I asked smiling.

He nodded. "Yeah but I was a late bloomer. I ain't have a real girlfriend until I was about seventeen. Girls didn't really like me all that much cause I was too short, too skinny, and too dark."

He certainly out grew all of that very nicely. His tall body was chiseled to perfection and decorated in artful, beautiful tattoos. Yes, he was still dark, but a creamy flawless dark. And when he smiled he showed gleaming white teeth that had probably never seen the likes of a cigarette. He was perfection.

I looked away quickly, trying to hide what he was doing to me.

"So, what'cha wanna do now?" Dallas asked as he stacked the plates on top of each other to make it easier for the lanky waitress who was serving us.

I shrugged my shoulders, knowing for sure I did not want to go home. I wanted to squeeze as much time out of this date as possible.

"A movie?" He asked.

I shrugged again like it made absolutely no difference to me. But my stomach was tied so badly into knots, I felt as if I would throw up. I was getting pretty tired of feeling like this.

It was one in the morning by the time Dallas walked me up to the back porch. Karla's big ass truck sat in the driveway, taking up most of it and all of the lights were on. I wondered how long she had been home from her date. I wondered again if she had as much fun as I did.

"So, when can I see you again, outside of work?"

"When do you wanna see me?" I was shivering a little from the cool morning air and a little from how he was making me feel. I was pretty sure if he tried to kiss me I was going to faint dead away.

"I'll call you," he said taking both of my hands in his own. "I had a very nice time."

I nodded unable to speak for a second. Then I said, "I did too."

He leaned closer to me, almost in slow motion, until I felt his warm lips on my cheek. Then he whispered, "Good night, Lonna," into my ear. Once again his lips brushed my cheek in a sweet departure.

My head was spinning when I opened the kitchen door. The house was so bright, it almost hurt my eyes. I could hear the voices form the television coming from the living room.

Karla lay on the couch, her head propped up by two pillows, watching TV. She was already dressed for bed in her pajama pants and tank top.

"Why are you here?" I asked sitting down in the favorite gold chair.

"Waiting on you," she replied as she looked over at me and smiled. She had that look on her face that said she knew something that I didn't.

"What?"

"How was your date?"

"Fine. How was yours?"

"It was alright."

"How long you been home?"

"Since eleven."

At eleven, Dallas and I were buying tickets for our second movie. I wondered why she was home so early. She read my mind and said, "Jonathon and Troy went to the club. So I came home."

Maybe it was because we had known each other so long and so well that I could see the disappointment on her face, even though she was doing her best to hide it from me. I searched my mind for an easy way to tell her that if she was looking for another Mike, She wasn't going to find him in Jonathon. But I couldn't think of a way to say it. So, I used one of the tricks I learned in rehab, and just kept my mouth shut.

I hated working on Saturdays. That was one of the only things I missed about working at the community college. I never worked Saturdays. But, in Marc's computer store, here I was.

"What's up, Lonna?" Veronica asked me as I passed her standing behind the counter. She was basically new here, hired on Wednesday by me since she was attending the same community college where I had been fired from and majoring in Computer Technology. Of course she came highly recommended by Karla too.

"Nothing much. Don't wanna be here, tired. That's about it."

Veronica just laughed and shook her head as I opened the door to my office located behind the huge service desk and register. The flowers were sitting there on my desk as big as day, stored in a slim crystal vase with a red ribbon tied around it. There were twelve baby blue roses in full bloom. I had never seen or received anything so beautiful in my whole life. I was about to read the card when my office phone rang.

"Hello?"

"I heard you got flowers this morning," Karla announced.

"Who told you that?"

"Veronica. Do you like them?"

"They're okay if flowers are your thing."

I could almost see her shaking her head that was probably still tied up in a silk scarf. What time had Dallas ordered these flowers anyway?

Then I stopped.

How did I even know they were from Dallas. I picked up the card that was stuck between two of the roses and opened it.

"Lonna," I read out loud into the phone, "Thank you for the wonderful night, I look forward to many more. Call me when you get these. Dallas."

"Oooohhhh, Lonna, that is so beautiful."

"Shut up Karla. I have to go."

She sighed loudly in my ear. And I felt a tug at my heart. She probably had received no flowers or even a phone call from the sorry person she had gone out with the night before. I wondered why she was settling for him, because that was exactly what she was doing. I hardly knew the boy, but I knew there was nothing much to him.

"What are you doing for lunch?" I asked hoping to brighten her mood. Maybe I would even take her a flower out of my dozen.

"Jonathon is supposed to be taking me out."

She stressed 'supposed' and I wondered if she believed it or not. "Okay," was all that I could say.

By twelve I was exasperated, just getting off of a phone call with a customer who didn't know Windows from a hole in a wall. After assigning one of my techs to go out and take a look at the idiot's computer, I sat back in my chair and flipped on my CD player.

As soon as I picked the phone up to speed dial the pizza place down the street, it buzzed.

"Yes?"

"Lonna," Veronica's voice rang out. I wondered why she didn't just knock on my closed office door and open it. "Did you order a pizza?"

"No."

"Well there's some guy here with a pizza."

I stood up from my desk to look out of my office window. I had forgotten to open my office blinds that faced the front of the store and I couldn't see anything.

"I'll be out in a second."

I placed the receiver down slowly and opened my office door. There was Dallas standing on the other side of the counter. Pizza box in one hand, motorcycle helmet in the other.

I stopped dead in my tracks so surprised my heart could have leaped into my open mouth. "Dallas!" I said not able to repress the smile that was forming on my lips.

"What's up? I hope you not busy. But I didn't have any clients this afternoon so I figured we could have lunch."

My cheeks were growing hot and my mouth was becoming dry. I could hardly contain myself. Then I noticed Veronica still standing behind the desk watching the two of us.

"Veronica," I said walking over to him. "This is Dallas. Dallas, this is Veronica, Karla's cousin."

He was about to put his hand out to shake hers but they were full. I took his helmet for him so that he could do the gentlemanly thing. Then we stepped into my office.

"This is nice," he said looking around at the comfy quarters I created for myself. My desk was made from metal and glass oddly shaped almost in the form a 'C'. A black leather couch sat against the white wall, beside the window that gave a clear view of the residential side of the downtown area. The office was decorated with black art purchased by Karla on the internet, vases, and synthetic flowers. All except for the ones Dallas sent me just that morning.

I tried to clear my desk as much as possible so that he could sit the pizza down. Then I sat down in the chair beside his. He unzipped his windbreaker and pulled out two cans of Coke. I laughed at the thought of him riding down the boulevard with a pizza strapped to his motorcycle and two cans of Coke in his jacket.

He sat down in the chair and spotted the roses on my desk. "I see you got them."

I nodded, taking a bite of my pizza.

"You didn't call me."

I finished chewing the tiny bite. "I know. I'm sorry. I've been very busy all day."

"It's ok. I understand."

He relaxed a little and we sat there eating our pizza in silence just listening to the music from my radio. Until he noticed the picture of New-New, Karla and I that Mike took on my graduation day. I had it blown up to an 8x10 and put in a gold frame with 'SISTERS' engraved on the bottom.

"So this is your twin?" He asked leaning over my desk to get a closer look.

I nodded. "Yeah that's her. Her name is Leonay. We call her New-New."

"You and Karla look more alike than you and her. But all of you favor in a way."

"Yeah I know."

"What did you do after you graduated?"

I smirked remembering the night I graduated and the consequences that followed shortly after. "I went to rehab."

"Rehab?"

I nodded expecting for him to get up and run out of my office. I had a feeling that this was the last time I would hear from ol' Dallas.

"How long were you there?"

"A year."

He nodded and I hoped the subject was dropped. If he was going to leave then he needed to go ahead a do it. What was the point in dragging this thing out? One heart break per life time was enough for me.

"So what'cha wanna do tonight?"

I put my pizza down and looked at him. "Who said I wanted to do anything tonight, Dallas?"

"Come on," he said smiling even more. "Even if it's nothing but chilling at the crib watching a movie."

I would never let him catch on to how happy I was that he wanted to see me again. It wasn't like me to be feeling this way, it was more of a Karla thing. But I was with it, none the less.

"Ok. You can come over."

"Cool. I'll bring the movies. You just have the food ready."

"I'm getting married, y'all!" New-New screamed at us through the speaker phone.

"What?" Karla said just as happy as New-New was.

"It's about time!" I went back to poking at the homemade macaroni and cheese in the oven to make sure it was done. It was Karla's recipe.

"Shut up, Lonna," New-New yelled back, but the happiness was still all over her voice. She couldn't maintain it.

"Me and Lonna will plan your wedding. You know you gotta get married down here, right?"

I turned around and looked at Karla. She was always volunteering me for shit. Neither she nor I knew a damn thing about planning a wedding. I had never even been to one, much less had one.

"Well, me and Andrew haven't really talked about it yet. But I'm sure he won't mind."

"Don't worry about a thing. You just let us know a date and be here. We got everything else . . ."

"Wouldn't it be nice if she could get married in the back yard of y'all house?" Karla asked once she and New-New hung up. I was checking my two filet mignons in the George Forman Grill and preparing to wash the dishes.

"In the Doone? You gotta be kidding. Who gets married in the projects, outside?"

"Oh come on, as big as that backyard is. We could make it look wonderful and nobody would even remember they're in the projects. I mean we could really do it up. Just make it a weekend extravaganza."

"Ok Miss Extravaganza."

She pinched me on the underside of my arm where she knew I was ticklish and studied the food I was preparing.

"Uuhmm, all this for a man you don't even like huh?"

I turned around ready to smack her but the door bell rang.

"Make yourself scarce!" I said to her as I dried my hands, wet from the dish water, and headed for the door.

"Okay. I'm going to Marc's. His chick is at work, so we're going to Dapper Dan's."

She grabbed her jacket and purse off of the kitchen table where she stopped it in the first place and headed towards the door. I tried not to think of all the fun her and Marc, and Jay were going to have tonight, especially with Marc's girlfriend gone. Nobody really cared for her all that much.

We both stood there looking at Dallas when he stepped through the door.

"Hey Dallas, byc Dallas," Karla said when I nudged her out the screen door.

He laughed and shook his head as he bent over to kiss me on my cheek. "What's up?" He asked in my ear, making me all tingly up and down my spine.

"Nothing much."

"Something sure smells good."

"Thank you."

He laughed again and sat down at the table. I tried to calm my heart down long enough to walk over to the kitchen counter and flip the steak over in the grill. I could feel his eyes on me with every step I took.

"This is a nice house."

"Thank you," I said again. "It's Karla's. She was raised here."

"Really?"

I nodded. He already knew that I was raised in the middle of the one of the most undesirable neighborhoods in the city. I told him over dinner some of the adventures that my nine siblings (Karla also) and I shared. Dallas himself was born and raised in Georgia. I smiled to myself as I could hear Karla calling him a *Georgia Peach* in my head. I just knew one day I was going to slip up and say it to his face.

"Do you have any children, Dallas?" I asked as I fixed his plate. My back was still to him. For some reason, I couldn't bear to look at him right now, alone in the house like we were.

"No. My music is my child right now. My child, my wife, all that. When I told you I was a late bloomer, I meant that."

That was one check mark for him. I was going in for another one. "You ever been arrested."

He laughed and I looked over at him finally. "It's funny you would ask that 'cause me and Troy were just talking about that last night. We were at this club down in Atlanta. It was last year, Thanksgiving weekend and all of us went home, Jon, Jeff, me and Troy. Well, we were at this club and Jon was drunk as hell. So some other cats walked by and Jon said something smart, the next thing we know, we were all fightin'. We spent the night in jail and my brother had to come get us. Troy was bawlin' like a baby. None of us had ever been to jail. So yeah I got a record now. We all had to pay some fines and we were banned from that club for life."

I laughed as I sat his food down in front of him along with some steak sauce. "So you do clubs often?"

He shook his head and stood up to pull my chair out for me like it was second nature. I was amazed. "Not anymore. That was the last time I stepped foot in a club. And I don't even miss it. Now Troy and Jon, they live in the club. But I can't do it. I'd much rather be up in the studio. Or chillin' with a beautiful woman like I'm doing right now."

He had to stop saying stuff like that. I felt my cheeks getting hot again and I was on the verge of being angry about it. How dare he make me feel this way!

"Okay, Ms. I Wanna Know Everything About You, what about you? Obviously you don't have any kids, well I ain't seen any yet. You got a record?"

There I was contending with the urge to tell a lie. But we already talked about rehab, so what was the point in me lying about my record? Might as well tell him everything.

"Yes, I do."

"For real. I was just playing, I didn't know you really had one."

I cut a piece of my steak and popped it into my mouth. "That's why I went to rehab. I mean Karla had already told me I was going, but I was sure I could talk her out of that or something. But that night, I went out and I got high. I beat this girl that I had known for years into a coma. I was charged with assault and drug possession. So yeah, I have a record."

"You beat somebody into a coma huh?"

I nodded. Taking a drink of the sweet lemonade Karla made before she got the phone call from New-New. These confession sessions between the two of us were really starting to get to me. I wondered what it would really take to run him away.

"I can see that." Then he asked, "What happened to the girl?"

"She's alright as far as I know. I haven't really seen her since I've been out of rehab. I don't go back in my old neighborhood that much anymore. I doubt she's still there, I think she went off to college."

"Why is that?"

I sighed deeply. Why did he have to know every little thing about me? "Bad memories I guess."

He nodded like he understood. I doubted that he did. "You still got family over there?"

I shook my head. "Everybody moved out of that house. My brothers. Me, my sisters. Everybody. The house is still there until my youngest brother turns old enough to live by himself. That will be in a few months. But that's it."

"And your mom?"

I looked at him then. Forgetting that I had never spoken about my mother. I told him about Rajul's death on our first date, but I never did mention Greta. "She died right after my brother. She killed herself."

"Damn," Dallas said grabbing my hand from where he sat cattycorner to me. "I'm sorry to hear that, baby. I really am."

"It's ok," I shrugged. "We weren't all that close. She was on medication and alcohol too bad for us to be close. Don't get me wrong I loved my mother and everything, but we just weren't close. That's all."

But he was still shaking his head. I didn't want his pity that was for damn sure. I got enough of that from other people. When he opened his mouth though he said, "You went through all that, and came out like gold, huh. That's amazing."

Chapter Twenty-One

Friday, July 10, 1998 11:53 p.m.

Bree was bumping and grinding her well proportioned hour glass body up against a cutie with a baseball hat that almost covered his eyes. It reminded me of the way Dallas wore his hats. I watched them, wondering where my sister learned to do such bad things and wishing I had the nerve to do them to the light skin, hazel eyed sweetie I was dancing with. He was at least five inches taller than me and had something that was a cross between dreadlocks and an afro. It was ok, he smelled good and he was cute in his baggy jeans and white t-shirt, even though I had to politely remove his hands from my behind more than once. And I was beginning to think I had a red target on my breast, because he could not seem to take his eyes away from them.

New-New sat at the bar talking to a man that looked considerably older. She was nursing some kind of drink. Maybe nursing was too nice of a word because that girl had been steadily kicking them back for two hours now. Then I saw her flash her engagement ring at the dude and I knew their conversation was just about over.

Karla was the most surprising of all to me though. She had never been much of a club person, her last time in one being the night I graduated, but the years had obviously turned her into a dancing fool. Now I knew where Bree learned to be so provocative. The way she slithered her thick body up down and around on this guy, that was the same skin tone, height, and body build as Mike, was enough to get her arrested for something. Her body was glistening with sweat in her black skin tight top and black jeans. I wasn't sure if it was her sweat or his as he grabbed her around her waist and pulled her even closer, grinding into her with all his might but keeping to the beat of the music. It was like reliving graduation night all over again.

The music changed and the DJ slowly eased another record on that was just as fast. I was about to give in to another dance with baby boy, until I spotted Jonathon and his twin brother Jeff across the club by the entrance. The chocolate Philly Karla was with was not letting her go and I didn't know why it was so important for him to let her go, but I knew he needed to.

I said goodnight to my honey quickly and told him how much fun I had but that I needed to go check on my sister. He said ok and let me know that I should come find him once I was done. I doubted that I would and headed in the direction of Karla. Luckily Bree intercepted Jonathon, whom she had met before, and Jeff, who she didn't know from Adam, at the bar by throwing herself at Jeff like a slut in heat. New-New had joined her, but she wasn't throwing herself at anybody, just showing her engagement ring once again.

When I got close to Karla and the dancing man, I could feel the body heat and I felt drawn into their little circle. It was sickening. We might as well all joined hands and danced together.

"Jonathon's here," I said to her not really wanting her to stop dancing with the guy. He was cute. But they needed to move somewhere else, like a very dark corner.

Instead, she instantly pulled herself away from the boy. The ring of body heat, sex, and lust was broken. I felt bad for the boy and I wished she would at least tell him she would be right back. But she didn't. Instead she just walked away like he had meant nothing. All to go find Jonathon.

Bree's breasts were in Jeff 's face but he didn't seem interested. Especially after he saw Karla all disheveled and sweaty. Something told me that was probably a major turn on for him. Jonathon noticed the way his twin brother ogled Karla like she was a hot piece of chicken and by the looks on his face, he wasn't happy about it.

"Hey Jonathon," Karla said and put her arms around his neck. He gave her a half hearted one arm hug with a bottle of Heineken in the other hand. He drank to damn much. Maybe that was what I didn't like about him.

"So this is New-New," he said pointing at my blond haired sister who had turned her attention to someone else. She was showing them her ring too.

"Yeah, that's New-New," Karla said her arms still around him. "And Jeff, this is Bree."

"Nice to meet you," Bree said eyeing Jeff like she wanted to jump on him right then and there. She had forgotten who Link even was.

"I'm glad you're here, "Karla was saying to Jonathon. "Maybe after we leave, we can go to your house and chill for awhile."

Jonathon shook his baseball hat covered head and took his arm from around Karla's waist. "Naw, I got something I gotta do."

At that moment I knew I hated him more than I had ever hated anyone in my entire life because I knew he was lying to her. And he knew I knew he was lying when he glanced at me and I shot him a look that would have made ice combust. I wanted badly to say, "What you gotta do, Nigga? And if it was so important why are you up in here in the first place?" But I didn't. This was New-New's night and I wasn't going to cause a scene, even though she was much too drunk to notice anyway.

I watched Karla as she straightened out each one of the folding chairs and put them affectionately in place. One by one. If I wasn't mistaken, she was even humming something.

"Is she ok?" Marco asked me while down on all fours polishing the old wood on our deck. Karla asked him to do it, and of course he could not turn her down. Everything had to be perfect for this wedding.

My job was tying the peach ribbons and bells to the banister and other things in the yard. Like the gazebo Karla rented along with the chairs that were going into place now. Not to mention the runner that was purchased white, but after three tries, Karla finally got it the perfect peach color that matched New-New's wedding gown. Then there were the peach and white roses that she ordered that had to go in the perfect spots!

"No. She's dating a jerk, missing Mike and running herself ragged with this wedding."

I stepped down onto the next step and began to tie a bell. They were decorated with glitter and simulated diamonds. The ribbons were too. Karla paid Veronica fifty dollars to sit up on her lunch break and Thursday night to decorate them all.

"Why is he a jerk, Lonna?"

I sighed. I didn't know why really. He just was. "He drinks too much, "I said because it was the first thing that came to my mind. "He didn't even wanna spend time with her last night. He's one of those Hollywood types. Too much drinking, too much partying. I don't think he's ready for what Karla's ready for. You know how she is."

"Is it that you think nobody is good enough for her?"

I looked at him like he was stupid. "Mike was."

He shrugged because he was now at a loss for words. He knew I was right. So I continued. "She's looking for another Mike, and he's not it. And this wedding, "I shook my head and moved down to the next step. "She done spent over a thousand on decorations alone, Marc. I'm not exaggerating either. Our phone bill is about three hundred dollars because she been on it with her momma just about every day asking what to do."

"Well, she wanted to do it. And you never know, this could be therapy for her."

"Therapy?"

"Yeah. To get her mind off of Mike and everything else that's going on."

He was probably right he usually was. But I didn't see how. How could a wedding help you get your mind off of your failed relationship?

"So is your boyfriend coming to the wedding?"

I stopped and whipped my head around so fast, I smacked myself in the face with my ponytail. "I don't have a boyfriend!"

"Whatever, Lonna." He shook his head and continued sanding like I was the crazy one.

"I don't. I have friends."

"Whatever, Lonna."

"And I don't know if he's coming or not. I didn't invite him. I mean I mentioned it, but I didn't invite him."

"Why didn't you invite him?"

"What for? Do I really need to take sand to the beach?"

He laughed then, so hard he almost fell face first into the wood. "You're a damn nut."

"I'm serious."

"So you telling me you don't like this cat? Not even the slightest?"

I was at the bottom of the banister now. This is where I took the left over ribbon and wrapped it around the poll and tied it into a pretty bow. "I don't know."

"You sure spend a lot of time with him not to. Veronica told me how he be bringing you lunch and dinner every day."

I shrugged with a 'whatever' on my lips, but I didn't say it. Instead, I turned to look at Karla who was amazingly done with the chairs and was now placing the runner. I wondered what was going through her mind as she did all of this without even looking up once. Her hair, that was due to be done in about two hours, was covered in a baseball cap and she wore biker shorts with a t-shirt long enough to cover her behind.

"You ok?" I yelled over to her simply because I wanted her to look up.

"Yeah," she said standing up from the runner and putting her hand on her hips. "You done?"

"Yeah, I guess I'll start on that gizebu thing!"

"Gazebo, Lonna!"

I laughed and she laughed with me. "While you do that, I'll do the chairs."

We divided up the ribbon and the bells, making jokes at Marco about being able to see the crack of his ass while he was down on all fours. He told us he didn't have time for us because he also needed to replace the sliding glass door that had been broken and fogged up for years. He purchased a new one from Lowe's the night before and now he had five hours to install it.

Bree was telling everyone in the shop how much New-New drank the night before her wedding. She was even throwing in some impressions of her flashing her ring around. She was so silly. I remembered when she was only nine trying to hang with Karla, New-New and I with her big round head. The beautician was working on that same big head now, almost lovingly corn rolling various strands of her long black hair and adding small white beads to the ends. The rest hung full and curled around her shoulders.

New-New sat under the dryer, ignoring us with her head buried in an Essence magazine. She over slept until ten, by then the rest of us were already at the salon. She didn't make it in until eleven and she was supposed to be getting married in two hours.

There was a tap on my shoulder and I tried to look up while my stylist chopped away at my dead ends. Karla was already done and her ear length hair hung in tight Shirley Temple curls that cradled her round face. She dyed her hair so many times and so many different colors that I didn't even remember what her natural color was. The copper in it now worked for her though.

"Have you heard from GG?" She said with her hands digging in her big black purse for something. That girl was forever looking for something.

"No. I told you not to put her in this wedding 'cause she would find a way to fuck it up." My stylist pushed my head back down so that she could finish snipping.

"Oh, hush," she said pulling her cell phone out finally. "What's her number?"

I rattled the number off to her while she punched it into her phone. I wished I could watch her facial expression as she waited for someone to pick up. But then I heard her say, "Where are you? You were supposed to be here an hour ago!"

There was silence. It seemed like everybody in the salon got quiet. The beautician lifted my head up, rubbed something in my hair and began to separate my tresses so that she could curl it.

"What do you mean, you didn't want your hair done here. I tell you what, Giozothis, if you don't have your ass at that house by twelve, with your hair looking decent, your ass will not see the likes of a wedding today! Understand?"

I was sure she didn't give the girl a chance to answer; she closed up that flip phone so quick. Karla's cheeks were red and it was easy to see that she was flustered. She quickly tried to regain her composure as she put the cell phone back into her purse and looked at me. There was no way that redness was going away, though.

"We can be one less bitch," Bree pitched in from her chair. She was being sprayed down now. "Especially that one."

"No, we can't. We have just enough guys for the girls. If we get rid of one girl, we have to get rid of one guy and that will look funny."

"Karla," New-New said from over at the dryer. Her beautician was just taking her out. "Don't worry about it girl. Push come to shove, we'll dress Jay up as a girl. I'm sure he'll be cool with that."

The whole damn salon cracked up on that one. Even Karla couldn't help but crack a smile. But the lady on my head just had to ask, "Well, what did she say?"

Karla turned pinker and I knew it had something, anything to do with this being a black salon in a black neighborhood. "She said she wanted to go to a national chain instead." That was a great way for her to put it. I was proud.

"Hmph, she wanna go to a white place, huh?" The beautician mumbled. She was right though. Being an officer's wife had turned GG into a bourgeois queen and she had been working Karla's last nerve every since she got in for the wedding from Maryland where Damon was stationed now. I was pretty sure it was nothing but jealousy that caused her to complain about everything from the dresses and shoes to the miniature bouquets for the wedding party to carry. No one ever made this much of a fuss over her and it was very likely that no one ever would. She had turned it personal though, taking cheap shots at New-New even wanting to get married after three children.

"I don't know why everybody's making such a big deal anyway, "she said standing in the kitchen doorway while New-New, Karla and I sat at my momma's dining room table constructing a seating chart for the reception. "I mean damn, you almost got a whole classroom. I'm sure a trip to the courthouse and a chicken dinner afterwards will suffice."

New probably just thought her ears were playing tricks on her, so she ignored her and continued checking the peach and white place cards, that Karla had specially made, to make sure everyone's name was there. Me, I just stopped and propped my head up on my fist, glaring at her as she continued to eat the microwave popcorn that sat in the middle of the table in a plastic container like she hadn't said anything at all. But Karla blew up like one of those puffed up fish and her eyes glazed over in an anger I had never seen from her.

"You know what, it's better for her to get married now to somebody that she loves and who loves her, than to marry somebody that cheats on her all the time. Right GG?"

Damon's repeated infidelity was about as much of a secret as his notable absence from the wedding. Every since her move to the area, GG had been confiding in New-New about her husband's indiscretions. New-New could hardly wait to get off of the phone with her whenever she called, so that she could call Karla and me. We thought it would stay between us that we knew more than we were supposed to, but in her anger, Karla had let it go. I wasn't mad at her. I knew by the way the weekend had been going that *someone* was bound to let it slip sooner or later.

The words sounded so calm coming from her mouth, but the look on Karla's face was enough to kill someone. I expected GG to just give in and walk away. But instead she said, "I can see you think you know a little too much of my business."

Karla still didn't flinch. I was preparing to stand up incase GG suddenly lost her mind. "Giozothis, everybody knows your business. It's no secret. So there's no need for you to come in here acting like you have a perfect life. We all know the truth. You're not fooling anyone . . ." Then she added, "But yourself."

"Look, GG," I said, "nobody's gonna be listening to your mouth. If you don't wanna be in this wedding, then say you don't wanna be in the wedding. We'll throw somebody else in your place. No big deal."

GG looked from New-New to me, purposely avoiding Karla's heavy stare. "So you taking up for her?"

"Why shouldn't I? She's my sister too. She's been more of a sister than you have. Do you remember Rajul's funeral GG?"

I heard everyone that sat in the room at that moment's breath catch in their throats. Tension filled the air so thick I could feel it through my t-shirt and jeans. No one ever called her on her absence from Rajul's funeral. Now it was just one of those things that we tried to brush under the carpet and forget about. Until now.

GG was unsurprisingly speechless. She even stopped eating the popcorn on the table. I wasn't done. "You here with so much to say about the wedding, but where were you when that happened?"

She just stood there with her mouth open. I could see water welling up in her eyes. I wasn't moved but New-New grabbed my hand and shook her head to tell me not to say anything else. I didn't, just for New-New's sake.

"Are you going to be in the wedding, GG?" New-New asked still holding onto my hand.

She paused to wipe her eyes because she was a drama queen. Then she nodded, right before she walked away.

The bedroom door swung open so hard it hit the wall. I turned around from trying to fit New-New's tiara down properly on her bleached blond, Shirley Temple curled and swept up on top her head, hair. She was stunning as she sat in front of the mirror in Momma's old bedroom. It hardly looked like Greta's room though, with new furniture, paint, and carpet. Marco and Jay were slowly working on restoring the house and this room had been their first task.

None of us said anything as GG walked in, hair looking mediocre. She hardly glanced at us as she took her dress that was hanging up behind the door, protected in a plastic dress bag, down and went into the bathroom. I glanced over at Karla who sat on the end of the bed beside Bree and shook my head. She shook her head too and looked down at her white shoes with the very small sequence. They matched our white dresses that made us look and feel angel like. They were one piece, sleeveless numbers that hooked with one strap behind our necks. When Karla picked them out, she didn't count on the two us having trouble with them because of our double number, double letter breast. After hours of trying to hide and tuck away things that hadn't moved in over ten years, I suggested pinning the top of the dress to our strapless bras. So far everything was good, nothing had popped out yet. I envied GG and Bree for not having these issues.

"Okay y'all," New-New said looking at the clock of the radio sitting on the deep cherry wood nightstand that matched the rest of the bedroom furniture. "I got fifteen minutes to get this dress on." She stood up from the dresser and took off the pink robe that belonged to Karla. She was all girdled up and tucked in everywhere. Once the bean pole of the family, she was now the plumpest. But it fit her so well, that I figured no one even cared. Especially not Andrew.

It took two of us to get the frilly mess over her head without messing up her hair. Then Karla reached inside of the dress to pull everything, all of those layers of mess down and straightened them out around New-New's feet.

At that moment GG emerged from the bathroom wearing her dress. She stuck a white flower in her hair to make it more presentable. And amazingly it worked.

"You look nice, New-New," she said quietly, not even able to look my twin in her eyes.

If this was her version of an apology, I wasn't accepting. But obviously New-New was because she smiled and opened her arms wide. GG walked slowly over to her and they hugged tightly. I looked at Bree who rolled her eyes. Karla stood up from straightening New-New's dress with a smirk on her face. She took her hand and pretended to punch the back of GG's head. GG didn't see her of course because her face was smothered in New-New's curls, but New-New took one of her arms from around GG and pinched Karla hard on the arm. She let GG go finally and I could see tear marks on GG's face. I had to swallow back an explicative and let it die in my throat.

Being the maid of honor, I walked down the aisle alone. Bree was grouped with Jay because of their height. After them was GG with one of Andrew's cousins. She smiled only slightly as the early afternoon sun reflected off of her light bronze skin. Finally Karla smoothly and deliberately walked down the runner. One arm was linked into Marco's while the other held a miniature bouquet. Anyone would have thought she was the bride as she held her head up so high and confidently like she was born to do this sort of thing. Ray already stood at the end of the peach runner, on the gazebo with Andrew. I watched him closely watching Karla walking down the runner. It was hard to believe twelve years ago, they met in the grocery store right up the street. I figured it was just for her benefit that he brought a female with him to this event. But he could have chosen a better looking one. The one he picked had to be a good six feet and so skinny she was almost transparent. Her weave hung down her back to the point where she was probably sitting on it right then in the decorated folding chair. Her chocolate skin seemed to be caked with makeup that made her look incredibly darker. She didn't talk much, instead she just watched and that unnerved me all by itself. From what I could see, Ray had not spent much time with the girl at all, opting to ogle Karla whenever he could.

After Karla came New-New's Lenora who was now five. I watched as she sprinkled peach rose pedals on the runner, walking quickly so as to not be the center of attention for longer than she had to but smiling wide looking just like her mother. Andrew's family held their two other daughters in the audience with them. Ray's three year old son Melvin was next holding a peach pillow with both hands. On the pillow sat two gold bands with New-New's and Andrew's names and the date engraved on the inside.

The traditional wedding march stopped almost abruptly and a song by Shai that I remembered from the tenth grade began to play over the loud speaker. The judge, a friend of Marc's, asked for everyone to stand with just a hand gesture and everyone turned around to watch as Chiloe and New-New descended the steps of the deck. Some guest that weren't use to such formal events actually had the nerve to *ooohhh* and *aaawww* as they walked down the runner. I was proud because this was my twin and just maybe I would look half as beautiful as her whenever I got married.

I looked out towards the last row. Dallas sat in between two seats, one an empty seat that had been occupied by Jonathon before he got a call on his cell phone, and the other occupied by Link. He seemed to be staring straight at me, but I thought maybe I was mistaken. Until he waived at me. I smiled and I'm sure I blushed and looked away quickly.

New-New was just a whirling tornado of peaches and cream as her new groom spun her around the dance floor more than a couple of times. They laughed and smiled, and gazed into each other's eyes lovingly as they danced their tenth song together.

As the song ended and a new one began, I felt Dallas' hand on my bare shoulder. "You wanna dance?" He asked me in my ear.

The first answer that entered my mind was no despite the chill bumps on my arms. I turned around to look him squarely in his face, about to bring up the fact that I had not even invited him in the first place. But I couldn't do it when I saw those beautiful brown eyes staring expectantly back at me.

"Sure."

He took my hand as we stood up from the table we were seated at and lead me to the dance floor. My skin began to crawl from the heat of the heavy stares that I was sure were on us. I could almost imagine what they were saying.

"Remember her boyfriend got shot."

"Yeah, she was only fourteen going with that grown man."

"She just got out of rehab not too long ago."

"Didn't she almost kill a girl in a club?"

"Uh huh, that was her."

I did my best to shake all of that from my mind, knowing good and well it was just my imagination. Dallas took me into his arms, giving me a reassuring smile and we began to dance. I wished I wasn't wearing this heavy ass gown so I could really feel him next to me, but for now I had to settle. He held me tightly pushing me further into him and the sweet scent of him wafted into my nose. It couldn't have been man-made cologne that made him smell so good. Most of it was just him alone, natural.

I looked over his shoulder and could see Karla and Jonathon dancing slowly and smoothly. Her chin rested on his shoulder and his face was buried in the soft curls of her hair. I scanned the room taking a quick inventory of who was watching them. My eyes landed on Chiloe of course who was seated at the table behind Dallas and mine with some beautiful hood rat looking bored to death. For a brief second, I wondered why he didn't ask her to dance, but I remembered who I was talking about here. Ray stood by the buffet also watching Karla while his trophy next to him piled a plate to the ceiling. I laughed.

"What's so funny?" Dallas asked looking deeply into my eyes like he was trying to read my mind.

"Nothing."

I looked away quickly not able to bare the warmth of his gaze on me. His eyes were doing something to me that I could not explain. Part of me just wanted to run off of this dance floor and hide somewhere while the other half wanted to stay this way, in the safety of his arms forever.

"Are you nervous?" He asked me.

"No, why?" I didn't even realize I was still looking down at the floor.

"You just seem tense. Look, Lonna," he took one arm from around my waste and put his hand on my chin, forcing me to look at him. "You don't have to be nervous or scared or anything. I'm not gonna hurt you."

He smiled then and his dark smooth skin seemed to glow against the disco ball hanging above us. I felt my legs go weak and I could have fell down to my knees right there in the middle of the dance floor in a praying position.

I didn't even realize we were still dancing until the music changed to a Hip Hop song. Jay grabbed Veronica up and they were leading the pack of rump shakers and bootie bouncers. Link and Bree weren't far behind.

"Hey you wanna get some air?" Dallas whispered in my ear so that I could hear him above the music.

I nodded because I couldn't speak and followed him out of the hotel ballroom. We made our way through the back of the lobby and onto the deck of the hotel.

"Damn, this is beautiful," Dallas said admiring the view of the downtown area from here. We were three floors up. The sun was just beginning to set.

"Yeah it is. Karla picked this place. She had a book signing here once."

He nodded with his attention fully focused on me now.

"Dallas, we talk about me all the time, what about you? I really don't know all that much about you. Except that you like music."

He smiled, surprised I could tell, that I had asked. But it was the truth. I felt as if he knew everything about me except bra and panty size and I was sure he could look at me and guess that.

"Well, you already know I'm from Atlanta and I've got two sisters and a younger brother." He shrugged then. "What else you wanna know?"

"What's your family like? I mean you know mine is dysfunctional." In the course of one weekend he witnessed GG have a temper tantrum, Chiloe moping over Karla whenever she was around, Bree flirting with every man she came in contact with, and Jay flirting with every person he came in contact with (male or female).

We both laughed. Then he shook his head. "Every family is dysfunctional in one way or the other. Yours is no worse than anyone else's, in fact I think everybody's pretty cool."

I smiled. "Thank you."

"It can't be that bad, you come from it."

I blushed unwillingly. "So what about yours?" I asked quickly before he could give me another compliment.

He shrugged again and looked back out over the city. "Same ol' story. My grandma raised us until she died when I was fifteen. I didn't know my father. My mom was working all the time. When Jon moved up here with our aunt, I would always come visit him in the summer and holidays, stuff like that. Then when she died, we decided to open up the studio."

"You keep in touch with your family?"

"Oh, yeah. All the time. I go down there a lot. My sisters, they're a lot older, so I don't talk to them too much. But my mom and my brother, we stay close. My brother's in college down there, he's trying to be a lawyer. My mom, she stays with one of my sisters and her husband, so she don't work anymore."

Damn, his life just seemed so normal compared to mine.

"I know what you thinking," he said smiling again. "Trust me, we done had our drama and shit too. Like Jonathon and his momma not getting along, that's how he ended up here with our aunt, me and my dad's family and that drama. But everything works out for good in the end."

Dallas took my left hand in his and held it there, caressing my skin. I was in heaven.

"Maybe one weekend when you're not busy, we can go down there."

I looked at him knowing good and well, I didn't just hear what he said. I must have been hearing shit, day dreaming, anything.

"Huh?"

He laughed, but not loudly. Just enough to make his chest shake. "Maybe if you're not busy, we can go down there one weekend."

I heard him correctly. I knew I had better answer soon before my time ran completely out and he changed his mind.

"Sure. That's cool. "I shrugged it off. It was no big deal for a man to invite me to another state to meet his mother. Right?

Chapter Twenty-Two

Saturday, May 15, 1999 5:18 p.m.

I thought I would have to drag my sister out of this place. Had she forgotten she had a man at home who thought, for some outlandish and silly reason that the two of them were going to get married sometime in the near future? Both Karla and I knew that was a crock of something. If Bree wanted to marry Link, she would have set a date a long time ago. She was stalling. I regretted even bringing her to this little gathering.

We sat on the deck of Jonathon's six bedroom, six bathroom home. It was hard to believe this beautiful country mansion was older than any of us, but it was. His aunt basically built it from the floor up here out in the middle of nowhere when she first moved to North Carolina to build her business. Her business from what I understood from Dallas, was prostitution. The best Black madam in the Bible belt, the money and the house she left behind when she died of the flu at the age of sixty-five, went to the closest thing she would ever have to a child of her own. Jonathon. He invested half of the money into his music studio which was only a country mile away from the house. I had no idea what he did with the other half, but as business and money savvy as he was, I was sure it was safe.

My baby sister, of course, was awed by it all. From the wall in the living room behind the huge beige sectional that was made entirely of glass, the marble fire place, the plush beige wall to wall carpeting, the huge china cabinet that stretched from one corner of the dining room to the other, to the crystal chandeliers that adorned every room. I couldn't blame her for being impressed with the house, even though I preferred Dallas' small one bedroom apartment any day. It was the way she seemed so in wonder over Jeff that was bothering me.

I watched her, watching him play spades with Troy and Dallas all the while sipping on my bottle of soda. I should have been enjoying the shade of the deck table's huge umbrella. But I wasn't. Jeff unnerved me to no end. I looked behind me, across the huge swimming pool to the white gazebo where Jonathon and Karla sat. His arm was wrapped carelessly around her shoulder and with his other hand he held hers. I guessed this was supposed to be a damn Kodak moment. I was not impressed by that either.

"You okay?" Dallas asked looking at me, cards still in his hands.

"Yeah," I lied, wishing that we could go back to his place and watch movies like we had done for the past two nights. "I'm cool."

The funny thing about Dallas and I was that in all of the time we had spent together, nothing sexual ever happened between the two of us, except maybe a lingering kiss here and there. He was always a perfect gentleman and never tried to sneak a feel or say anything even half way explicit to me. There were no underlying motives when he held me close to him on his couch or when he held my hand whenever we went out. The innocence in our relationship was so new and addictive to me that I hardly ever wanted to be apart from him. And that was a novel feeling all by itself.

When I looked back towards the gazebo, after Dallas playfully pinched my cheek making me blush, Karla was descending the steps of it. Jonathon followed close behind her and they were making their way across the three acres of backyard to us. My eyes darted over to Jeff and I observed the way he tried desperately to pay attention to the game and not Karla. By the time she started up the stairs to deck, he had lost the battle and sat his cards down on the table so that he could get the full magnificence of her.

She didn't seem to be paying him even a quarter of the attention that he was giving her. But it was a domino effect because he wasn't paying Bree a quarter of the attention that she was lavishing on him neither. Her chair was awfully close to his for her not to even know his last name and every now and then she would *accidentally* bump her arm into his. I was expecting her to remove his PANTHERS baseball cap and run her fingers through his short corn rolls at any moment. She laughed at the slightest thing he said, even if it wasn't anywhere near funny and slung her black hair over her shoulders so many times I had to start checking my soda for stray hairs.

Karla came over to my chair and crouched down. "I'm about to go," she said scratching her chin with her thumb and resting one arm on the arm rest of my seat.

"Where you going?" Jeff asked and I was surprised that he heard her. He was all the way across the table. I glanced at Jon who stood at the far side of the deck babbling on his cell phone. I was beginning to think it was super glued to his ear.

"New Orleans to see my mom."

"When are you coming back?" He asked and I exhaled loudly and impatiently. I looked over at Bree hoping she was getting all of this. If I had taught her anything at all, I prayed to God it was not to be stupid. She looked slightly uncomfortable.

"Wednesday, I think."

"You leaving tonight?"

She nodded her head and stood up. "Yeah my plane leaves from Raleigh at about eight. She bent over and kissed my cheek while hugging me.

"Is Jonathon going to drive you?" I asked prepared to drive her myself if his sorry ass didn't take her. There was no way I was going to let her make that drive alone.

But she nodded and asked me, "You gonna be ok while I'm gone?"

I looked at Dallas who was looking at me. He smiled. "Yeah I'll be okay."

Karla pinched me as she headed to the other side of the table where Bree was. She gave her the same hug and kiss she had given to me.

"You ready?" Jonathon asked finally closing up his flip phone.

"Yeah."

"Hurry up and come back," Jeff said and I looked at Bree again praying that she was getting all of this because I wasn't missing a beat.

It was dark and raining by the time I closed up Marco's shop for the night. I was more than happy to get up out of there being that I had let everyone go home two hours before me. It was a Saturday night and I knew people had dates and things like that to get to, but being alone in the store surrounded by spare computer parts always freaked me out.

Just as I set the alarm and locked the door up from the outside, I turned around ready to run to my car sitting at the farthest corner of the small parking lot. But it was blocked in by a familiar truck parked horizontally behind it. My heart skipped a beat, glad to see my brother who had been keeping a very low profile since New-New's wedding over a year ago. I was suspicious as to what he wanted, though, on this rainy night.

"Get in," he said rolling the window down on the passenger side. I did as I was told and slid into the truck next to him. His music was down low and barely audible over the wind shield wipers which had a beat of their own. He threw his cigarette out of the window where the rain would quickly kill the hot embers.

"What's up Chiloe?" I asked wondering how and what he was doing. I studied him hard, not able to see any drastic physical changes in him. He was hunched over a slight bit, and that was something I wasn't used to seeing.

"Look," he said producing a white envelope that sat beside him in the seat. He handed it to me.

"What's this?" I was scared to open it.

"Open it."

I looked at him, again hesitating. When I finally attempted to open it, I realized it was open upside down and a bundle of papers, stapled together fell onto my lap. I picked them up slowly and unfolded them. By the grace of the nearby street light I was able to read what it said.

"Misha divorced you?" I asked knowing I hadn't read wrong. Chiloe knew it too so he didn't bother to answer.

"Did you know she was going to do it?"

He shook his head.

"You can't divorce somebody without them knowing, can you?"

He shrugged his shoulders then. "I asked Marc, man. He said she could go to a lawyer and say she didn't know where I was. They would put something in the paper and try to contact me and shit. But if I don't respond after a little while she can go on ahead with it. He said it cost a lot of money to do it that way. Her parents must have gave it to her. You know her daddy is a dentist, her mom's is a professor and shit." He shook his head. "Then I get this shit from *her* in the mail. She knew where the fuck I was all along."

It was damn clever how Misha divorced Chiloe; no legal battles, no fights, no contested and non contested mess. I wondered if she had thought of it herself, because if so, I gave her major props. I felt sorry for my brother, he looked so dejected right then, but I couldn't say that I was surprised. He had it coming and I knew sooner or later the girl would want to move on with her life. And that's exactly what she had done.

"Where's Karla?" Chiloe asked as I slipped the paper back into the envelope. "I went by the house. I saw her truck but she didn't come to the door."

I should have known he was not going to waste too much time grieving over Misha. He probably thought these divorce papers were a free pass to Karla. I just shook my head. If he only knew the real trouble that he had caused for that girl.

"She went to New Orleans to see her mom."

"When is she coming back?"

"Wednesday."

He took a deep breath and I looked over at him. "I wanted to tell her . . ." He paused then and I continued to watch him. "I wanted to tell her I saw Mike the other day. You know he went over to Korea for a few months. He got hurt jumping from a plane."

I turned all the way around in my seat. "Is he okay? What do you mean he got hurt?"

"He hurt his leg really bad. Gashed it open on whatever he fell on. He walks with a limp and uses a cane. But he's doing okay. He's retiring from the Air force because of it though."

I sat back again glad to hear that Mike was doing okay. The thought of him being hurt made me instantly think of Kelly and I never would have wanted Karla to go through that mess. I was just beginning to heal from that myself.

"So that's what you wanted to tell her?" I asked grabbing my brother's hand gently that sat on the seat between us. He didn't pull away, instead he rested his in mine.

"No. Not really." Chiloe stared straight ahead and down the street where cars were traveling at steady speeds even in the rain. I knew most of them were probably headed to the new club that opened up a month ago in the heart of the downtown area. Just a block away from Marco's store. Dallas had been telling me for weeks that we all needed to go their one night for dinner. He loved get-togethers.

I smiled at the thought of him and hoped he was okay in this rain. My cell phone battery died on me right after our last conversation at lunch. I made a mental note to make sure the first thing I did when I got into the house tonight was call him.

Chiloe cleared his throat, breaking me from my thoughts. "I told him about all that stuff I said about me and Karla . . . I told him all that stuff was a lie."

I looked over at him, thinking maybe my ears were playing tricks on me once again. "You what?"

"I told him I lied. I know Karla told you what happened. Didn't she?"

I nodded remembering our conversation and how I ended up on the living room floor from laughing so hard. That was the same night that Misha left and Bree announced she was getting married. I shook my head. "Yeah she told me."

Chiloe didn't say anything. We both just sat there listening to the low hum of his truck motor, the windshield wipers and the music that was still so low I couldn't tell what was playing.

"So what did he say?" I asked after what seemed to be a whole thirty minutes.

"He asked me why I did it." Chiloe let go of my hand and rubbed his forehead so hard I wondered if the skin would come off onto his fingers. "Lonna, I can't explain how I feel about Karla. Nobody understands the shit. I don't even understand it. Why do I think that me and her are supposed to be together but I keep fuckin' it up? I would give anything for her to love me again. 'Cause I know she did. At one time in her life, I know she loved me."

"Chiloe," I said searching for the stuff that I wanted to say to him. Things that would let him know the real deal, but wouldn't hurt him. I could imagine how much it had taken for him to go to Mike and confess what he did. It was almost like me going to Phoenell and telling her that I slept with Ron more than once or twice. But the big difference was he and Mike had been friends. "Chiloe, sometimes the person we love the most, is the person we hurt the most. If you love her, then you'll want her to be happy. Just let her be happy."

"But I . . ."

"You got married to someone else. Then you broke up her relationship with someone who truly, truly loved and cared about her. You done threw her life into spin cycle. She's with somebody now that

531

don't love her half as much as Mike did. Chiloe, let her go." I knew this was a crucial moment for him, so I refused to raise my voice over the hum of the windshield wipers. I wanted him to know I had compassion for him and what he was going through. I didn't completely comprehend why he had done the things he did, but I understood the pain he felt.

"Well, they probably gon' get back together anyway."

He turned his body away from me and looked out of the driver side window. I wondered if that was the case being that Karla was with Jonathon now. I knew she didn't have the same feelings for him like she did for Mike, but I questioned her willingness to forgive Mike for even walking out of the door. I knew there was still some anger in her heart for both him and Chiloe.

I touched my brother's arm. "You hungry? You wanna get something to eat?"

"Marc said he was gonna cook some ribs tonight and I could come over there."

"Sounds good to me," I said opening the passenger side door. "I'll follow you."

But Chiloe grabbed my arm as I was halfway out of the truck. I could feel the rain quickly soaking through my tennis shoes and socks.

"You always there for me, you know? To listen to my bullshit."

That was the closest I was going to get to a 'thank you' and it was cool. I hadn't even expected that much. "It's ok. You're still my brother Chiloe. We *is* family no matter what!"

He smiled that half crooked smile that use to drive females around our way crazy as I closed the door and ran to my car.

Dallas was excited I could tell. He was so joyous, full of life and laughter. It was always like this with him, though. That was one of the reasons why I loved being around him so much. He squeezed my bare knee, that peeked from beneath the only sexy dress that I owned, under the table as he talked. I couldn't help but smile in spite of myself.

There were three main floors in here, one for dancing and two for eating. We sat on the second floor. If Dallas had not made the reservations two weeks in advance, I doubted that we would have been able to get the wonderful seat that we had, right beside a huge window over-looking the dance floor.

Dallas held the attention of everyone at the large round table. Except of course Troy, who was trying to help him tell the story. He was just as full of it as Dallas was, and I wondered if they had been separated at birth somehow. The girl that Troy was with was quiet and appeared to be one of his biggest fans as she gripped his shoulder, it seemed, to keep him from jumping up at any moment.

Jonathon was holding Karla like he thought someone would come along at any moment and grab her away from him. She didn't mind, of course. She liked stuff like that. A knee under the table was enough for me, but her, she loved the hugging and kissing. Images of her and Mike popped into my mind followed by the conversation between Chiloe and I just three weeks ago.

On the other side of her was Jeff. He sat staring with that look of his like he just didn't care about anything that was going on, sitting beside Veronica. She was sweet and everything, but I knew Karla just threw her in the mix to keep Jeff off of herself. She knew the boy was crazy about her; calling her all the time, dropping by when he knew Jonathon was not around. Obviously the set up was not working though. I noticed the way he leaned more towards Karla than to Veronica. I hoped Veronica wasn't getting her hopes up for anything.

"Man, that cat is crazy . . ." Dallas said squeezing my knee again. He was heavy handed and squeezed with awesome pressure. I wanted to squeal, but I caught myself just in the nick of time.

"And he had on this outfit man," Troy said stopping to shake his head.

"Man, I don't know where he got that shit from. It looked like something off of StarTrek."

"Talkin' 'bout he wanna do a slow song," Dallas cut in. It was amazing the way they traded off like that. I couldn't resist the urge to laugh any longer. He looked at me surprised that I found him amusing enough to laugh out loud and rubbed my leg appreciatively.

"Hey there's Bree," Karla said looking towards the spiral stairs that stopped on our floor and continued on to the third. I turned all the way around in my seat to see my sister and her fiancé. I shook my head knowing something was up. Had I mentioned to her that we would be here? I racked my brain trying to remember if I had or not as she made her way to our table walking close to five feet in front of Link. She wore a little black dress that resembled a short sheet and black stilettos. I knew this was a club, but good grief. She looked like she had either just got off the run way, or just got off the pole!

"Hey y'all, what's up?" She asked all of us but she was only looking at Jeff. I looked at Karla and shook my head again. Karla just smiled and tried to talk instead of laughing.

"What's up Bree? How you doing, Link?"

"Why don't y'all have a seat? The more the merrier."

Leave it to my boyfriend. So there we were all trying to scoot closer and closer to the person on our right until there was room enough for two more chairs. Jonathon grabbed two from the table behind us where a couple sat looking quite angry with each other.

"Have y'all ordered yet?" Link asked trying to share a menu with Bree. She wasn't too much interested in what was on that menu, though.

"We just ordered some drinks," Karla said still holding in a laugh or two. I knew if her feet were long enough to reach mine, she would have been kicking the mess out of me. How dumb was Link that he couldn't see his girl making eyes at one of the twins across the table?

It didn't slip by one person though, and that was Veronica. Her slanted eyes were rolled so far up in her head; I thought they were going to get stuck. I knew she wanted to kick Karla in the back of her throat.

"Just order me something," Bree said dismissing the menu in front of her face because it was blocking her view of Jeff. She, on the other hand, was invisible to Jeff. She could have been a speck on the wall paper for all he cared. His eyes were wandering across the room, but they always seemed to land back on Karla.

"But now that you mention it," Troy said nodding his head and looking at his own menu, "I think it is time to eat."

Jonathon summoned the red haired waitress by waving his hand in the air and she almost broke her neck trying to make it over.

It didn't take long for Link to pick something for Bree. I doubted she would eat it anyway, especially if she couldn't look like a pin up while doing it.

"You want me to order for you too?" Dallas said smiling that goofy smile at me that I loved so much.

"Hell no." I wasn't able to hold back a smile for him.

"Awww, that's so sweet," Troy crooned from the other side of me and his girl broke into a million shrill giggles that reminded me of broken glass.

"So, how've you been, Link?" Karla asked. I knew she was trying to dig out of either him or Bree as to how they ended up here.

"I've been good. Working hard. You know they're getting ready to send me to Germany in a couple of months."

"Damn, that is right," Dallas said. "You are in the army."

"Air force. Five years."

"Damn," my man shook his head in disbelief. "How long you been stationed here?"

"I been here for about three years."

"How did you meet Karla?" Jonathon asked and I cleared my throat. Everybody looked over at me and that was a good thing because no one saw Karla's face turn red.

"She used to date my friend Mike. He used to be in my unit."

At the mere mention of his name I saw a cloud pass over Karla's face that told me everything I wanted to know. She still loved Mike.

But then Link did the highly noble thing and said, "That was a long time ago though. Back when I first got in the military."

Everybody seemed to breathe again now, including Jonathon who had shot Karla a look that could have shattered any one of the wine glasses or the glasses of soda that she, Veronica, and I ordered.

"So when's the big day?" Dallas asked after he cleared his throat. Sensing the tension at the table, he had changed the subject and I wanted to hug him for it.

Link opened his mouth to speak, but Bree hurriedly cut him off, "We haven't set a date yet."

Link closed his mouth back up and looked dejectedly towards the dance floor beneath us. I wondered if anyone else could see the hurt in his eyes. Maybe it was just me. I had been hanging around Karla and her damn books to long.

Troy was determined to push the issue, though. "Let me see that ring."

Bree took a deep breath, rolled her eyes back in her head, and held her left hand out for everyone to see the half carat rock on her ring finger. Troy and Dallas oohed and awed like a damn comedy team. I thought I would fall out of my chair as Karla and I exchanged glances across the table.

"That is nice," the girl with Troy said. Those were the first actual words she had spoken to anyone all night, except for cheering Troy on. She had a Jamaican accent to go along with her smooth caramel skin and long wavy hair. I was impressed.

"Thank you," My sister said as she sat back down in her chair. She was trying to tuck her hand out of sight like everyone would just automatically forget it was there if they didn't see it anymore tonight. Her face was visibly pink and I wondered who could blush the deepest, her or Karla.

"Hey Karla, come to the bathroom with me," Veronica said. Her chair was already pushed back and she was preparing to stand up.

"Ok." Karla stood up also and gave me a look that said I needed to come to. So I did.

The bathroom in this place was beautiful. In my blue period, as I liked to call it, I frequented a lot of bathrooms, but this one had every one of them beat with its red velvet circular couch right outside of the stalls and what seemed to be a hundred individual sinks that stretched from one wall to another right under a long oval mirror.

"What's up?" Karla asked as I seated myself on the couch.

Veronica just shook her head with her mouth open. Dumb struck to say the least. "What's up with that boy?" She asked finally.

"What you mean?" Karla asked back playing dumb. I knew exactly what Veronica meant though.

"First of all, he's acting like you the only one at the table. He haven't said two words to me all night. Then Bree comes in and she acting like she just wanna jump on him and givin' me dirty looks."

I smirked and both Karla and Veronica turned to look at me.

"Well, she's right," I said defensively. "You know that boy wants you."

Karla turned a deep red.

"If you knew he liked you, why did you tell me to go out with him?" Veronica asked accusingly.

"Because he can't have me and I didn't want him sitting there staring at me all night."

"But he's doing it regardless of if I'm here or not."

"I thought maybe you two would take to each other better than you did. I was wrong."

"Yeah, you were wrong. 'Cause I can't stand him."

At least I wasn't the only one.

"He's really not that bad once you get to know him," Karla tried to explain away his weirdness.

"Karla he haven't said a *word* to me since we been here."

"He haven't said a word to *anybody* since we been here."

Veronica gestured towards me and nodded, obviously agreeing but at a loss for words again.

"Okay. I'm sorry. I didn't mean for it to go like this."

"It's okay," Veronica said shrugging her shoulders. "I just wanted you to know, this is not what I consider a good time."

"I'm sorry Roni. Really I am. I owe you one girl, for real."

Veronica just nodded, arms crossed and eyes still rolled to the back her head. But when the door of the bathroom shook from the pounding it was receiving on the other side, she jumped. We all did, instinctively grabbing one another.

"Who is it?" I yelled because I was the bravest.

"Baby, it's me," Dallas said quietly from the other side of the door, "I think you better come out. Your sister and her fiancé are having some issues."

I looked at Karla who looked at me and shook her head. I was certain this girl was going to send me back to rehab sooner or later. Instead of going out there, I opened the door to let Dallas in. He looked around first like we may not be alone.

"It's ok," I said grabbing his hand and pulling him into the restroom.

"Damn, y'all got it made, for real. All we got is some stalls."

"What's going on out there Dallas?" Karla asked interrupting him from admiring the bathroom.

He shook his head like whatever was going on was a damn shame. But I knew he wanted to laugh. "Well, that dude, Link, got mad 'cause your sister's eyes were stuck on Jeff. He whispered something to her. She got mad and whispered something back. That's when he got a little louder and told her she was being disrespectful. Of course she came back with the standard, 'You not my Daddy'."

Veronica laughed at the way he put his hands on his hips and rolled his neck in a bad imitation of a female. I was trying my best to keep a straight face, but I was losing. Karla was also holding in her laugh.

"So then ol' boy, he tried to keep calm and I heard him ask her if she wanted to leave. She was like no. But he was more than welcomed to go. Then he asked her if they could discuss this outside, she was like no and told him if he was gonna leave then he needed to go ahead and leave."

"Oh my God," Karla said holding her forehead in her hands.

I shook my head speechless and embarrassed that once again, Dallas had witnessed the craziness of my family. At least Bree anyway. And the bad part about it was, she wasn't even invited to this gathering.

"What are we gonna do?" Karla asked.

I shrugged, selfishly not wanting to leave my date to take Bree's behind home. "Is she still here?"

"Well, when I came in here they were going back and forth and people were starting to stare. That's why I came in here to get you."

"You know we gotta go handle this." Karla looked at me like she just knew I was going to comply. But it took me a second to agree. If Bree wanted to dress the part of a grownup, I figured she better damn well start to handle her own messes like one.

But Karla, Dallas, and Veronica were looking at me. And my sister was outside of the restroom acting like a pure fool.

Dallas had not been exaggerating at all. It seemed everyone on this floor had turned around to see the argument that had escalated from whispers to full blown yelling. People stopped eating and were almost sitting backwards in their chairs to see this circus. I was surprised management had not asked my sister to leave.

"What's going on here?" Karla asked putting her hands on her hips like somebody's mother. She had a look like she was going to whip out a switch at any moment and beat everyone at the table.

544

Bree saw this look just like I did and calmly turned around in her seat, mouth closed so tight her lips were turning white. Link just shook his head. Then he got up from his seat and looked at Karla.

"Can I talk to you for a second?" He asked her.

She nodded. I watched Bree watch the two of them walk down the stairs to the first floor.

"Can I talk to *you* for a second?" I asked Bree once they were gone, disappearing into the crowd of bodies on the dance floor. She didn't say a word, instead she just stood up and headed for the bathroom. All eyes were on us as we walked around tables and chairs, her arms crossed in front of her like a pouting two year old. I wanted to put my three inch heels right up her butt.

"What is your problem?" I asked letting the bathroom door swing closed behind us. There were other people occupying the bathroom now, but I could have cared less. If they were at their tables in the past five minutes, they knew what was going on anyway.

"I didn't do anything. He started it."

"No, Bree. You started it, chasing after that dumb ass Jeff. When you know good and well you have a man already who thinks you two are going to get married. See, this is exactly what I was talking about when I told you you're too young to get married. You're not ready!"

She couldn't respond. It was cool though, because I was not finished.

"And can't you see Jeff is only interested in Karla. He don't even know you're there."

"Karla's got a man."

"So. It's his own brother, but he obviously don't care. He's not paying *you* any attention either way. You're gonna mess around and lose Link, and he's a good man."

She just rolled her eyes at me this time. She was lucky Link didn't knock her round head completely on the floor.

"I mean you were just downright disrespectful," I continued, using the same word Dallas told me Link used just to drive my point home. She looked at me, bewildered for a second, but she soon recovered.

"He caused the scene, not me."

"What was he supposed to do? Sit there and say nothing?"

She shrugged her bare shoulders.

"You need to go home. If Link is not gone, you need to get him to drive you home."

She was about to protest but I gave her a look far worse than the one Karla had given. She was shook as I left her standing in the bathroom. I walked back to the table just as Karla was coming up the stairs. She shook her head at me giving me a look of total exasperation. I knew then that Link had gone.

"We can take her home?" Dallas said standing up. "We can take her home, and go back to my crib. You can eat your food there."

I wanted to protest. But there was no way I could sit down and enjoy my dinner now with every one staring at me like I was going to pull a solution out of my ass. All I could say, though, was, "I'm sorry y'all. Maybe we can do this again some other time."

"Where you going?" Bree asked behind me. I turned around coming dangerously close to smacking her. But when Karla cleared her throat, I put my hand back down.

"Dallas and I are taking you home," I said forcing myself to be composed.

"Where's Link?"

"Gone," Karla said and she offered nothing else. Instead she turned around to her plate and began to pick through it.

Bree looked confused for a second and I wondered how anyone could be so stupid. She had made it all the way to college. Didn't that require some degree of common sense?

Dallas scraped my food into a Styrofoam plate and closed it up. "You ready?" He asked looking at me. His face showed no sign of being disappointed and I was more than grateful.

The ride to my house was long and silent. Dallas played a Tupac CD, so loud it rattled the speakers in the trunk of his two door sports car, to ease the strain, but it wasn't working. In fact, it was making me want to beat her head in even more. He held on to my knee tightly because it was shaking without me even realizing it.

After ten minutes of listening to Tupac rap and clenching and releasing my fist, Dallas pulled into the driveway. A part of me really wanted to see Link's car waiting for Bree, maybe without all the extra people around he could talk some reality into her. But he was not there. I stepped out of the car and lifted my seat back so that she could get out. Bree just looked at me, like she wanted to apologize for ruining my night, but something would not let her. So she went on in the house.

"You ok, Baby?" Dallas asked me as I strapped my seat belt up again.

"No."

"I know, I know." He stroked my leg, still shaking, tenderly. "She's young though. She'll be ok."

I nodded not really wanting to talk about her silly ass anymore. Instead I turned and faced him. "Did you enjoy your food?"

"What part I did eat, yeah."

"I'm so sorry, Dallas."

"Baby, it's ok. For real. We can get with them anytime. And this gives us a chance to spend some time together."

"I just don't know what got into her."

"I told you, she's young. Everything will be cool."

He pulled the car into the parking lot of his apartment complex. As I gathered my things, ready to get out of the car, he ran around to the passenger side to open the door. I was awed every time I came here at how peaceful and clean his neighborhood was. His apartment building sat at the end of a cul-de-sac near a playground. From his second floor balcony I could see a lake in the back of the building. There were ducks sleeping by the lake tonight, all rolled into feathery white balls.

"You not gonna eat?" Dallas said stepping onto the balcony with me. He had quickly changed his black dress slacks and grey shirt to rayon navy blue sweat pants and a brighter than bright wife beater. His tattoos just seemed to shine against his mahogany skin, even with just the light coming from the kitchen inside of the apartment and the street lights outside.

"No," I said shaking my head and tearing my eyes away from him to look back at the ducks. There was a gentle breeze blowing through the trees that seemed almost hypnotic. I almost wanted to close my eyes. "I don't like warmed up food."

"Well, you hungry? It's only eleven, I can order you some take out. Or we can go get something."

I shook my head again and looked over at him standing beside me. He was so damn sweet. I didn't deserve this at all. "No. I think my sister took away my appetite."

He smiled and leaned over the balcony a little. "What'cha think about Troy's new girl?"

"She's pretty." But he probably already knew that.

Dallas grimaced, though. "She's ok. A little too fake for me."

"What do you mean, 'fake'?"

"Her hair, it's not real. You knew that right?"

I could usually spot some fake hair a mile away. Having a full head of beautiful natural hair myself, made it easy to recognize imposters. "No, I couldn't tell."

"Yeah, it's one of those expensive jobs where they fuse the hair into your head or some shit. She's part of this group that I was working with, three girls, including her. When they first came in, her hair was like this short." He held up his pinky finger. I laughed and shook my head. "I'm serious. Then when they started getting gigs, that's when she decided to do the hair thing and the contacts. She always had the fake nails though."

"What about her accent?"

"Yeah, she's really from over there in the islands somewhere."

I shook my head. Boy, you just never knew about people these days.

"I don't know though. Troy said he thinks she's the one. But he change girls like underwear. He's been trying to get with her for the longest time."

"She wouldn't go out with him?"

"I think she thought he was broke 'cause all he did was hang around the studio and go to school. But when she found out he got money . . . well, his parents have money, she was on it then."

"No, not a Gold digger."

He nodded. "In the worse way. I try to tell him. Every day I try to tell him, but he won't listen."

I shook my head. Troy was a nice guy. I hated to see him with someone that didn't have his best interest at heart. Maybe he was the one Karla should have sent Veronica out with tonight.

"So… what about our trip this weekend?"

I spun my head around and looked at him. I knew what trip he was talking about, even though it had been months since we discussed it. He had never spoken of it again, and I figured it was just pillow talk, heat of the moment kind of stuff.

"What trip?" I asked. I just wanted to hear him say it.

"Atlanta. My mom's house."

I shook my head, totally speechless. That didn't happen to me very often. "Why do you want me to go down there and meet your momma?"

He smiled and looked back out at the ducks, not even bothering to dignify that question with an answer, so it seemed.

"I mean," I said trying to brush up the broken glass I heard fall when I said that, "we don't even know each other all that well. I mean, we just met don't you think it's a little soon to be meeting your mother?"

"We been together for almost two years. What's the problem?" He asked blankly.

"There's no problem Dallas."

"You sure?"

"I'm positive. I just don't wanna be hurt. I just don't want anything to happen to this, what we have. I guess."

My heart ached as if tied in a knot right then and I felt vulnerable. He knew way too much.

"Lonna," he said turning around to face me. Another breeze blew through, ruffling the feathers of some of the ducks by the pond. They didn't even stir and I wondered how they could be such heavy sleepers. "You gotta stop thinking that Kelly just up and left you. He died. I'm not going to up and leave you neither. Ain't nothing gonna happen to this what we have. I can promise you, I'm not going anywhere unless I leave this earth completely. You can trust that."

He put his arm around my waste and pulled me close to him. My hands went to his shoulders and I looked into his eyes. "Now, to answer your question, I want to take you to Atlanta so my mom can meet my new wife."

Something hadn't registered quite right in my brain I guess. Maybe I wasn't feeling too good neither. Probably hungry. And the fact that my sister had cut up so badly. All that put together made me imagine that he had called me his wife. But I was pretty sure that had not been the case.

"What did you say?"

"I said, I want her to meet my pretty new wife."

I still stared at him; I know I looked like a deer caught in head lights.

"Well," he said, "I didn't say the pretty part the first time, but I was thinking it."

"Dallas, what are you saying?"

He smiled at me and reached down into just one of the many pockets of his pants. He came back up with a box and my heart flew into my throat. My hands began to shake uncontrollably and I knew I looked like one of those chicks in those romantic movies that I hated so much. The ones where the men propose and the women act like they are going into convulsions. But I could not help it as he opened the box and took out the ring. My hands were just flailing in the air as he tried to catch my left hand to slip the ring on my finger. But instead, my right hand hit his and sent the ring flying off of the balcony. Dallas and I watched in amazement as the ring trickled over the rail of the balcony and floated down to the ground.

"Damn," we said in unison as we both made a b-line to the front door and down the steps. The ducks still weren't moving as we rustled through the grass on our hands and knees trying to retrieve the ring. A light went on in one of the apartments below his and I was pretty sure they were wondering what the hell was going on. The light was helping us out a great deal though.

"I got it," Dallas said finally. We sat up on our knees and I placed my hands in my lap to keep them still. But my heart was still fluttering painfully as I watched him wipe the ring off in his wife beater.

"You ready now?" He asked laughing.

I laughed too. Much too happy for my own good. "Yeah, I'm ready."

"Will you marry me?"

"Yes, Dallas, I will marry me . . . I mean you."

We laughed together again, harder this time. Then he slipped the carat diamond on my ring finger. I gazed down at it in total amazement. It was much bigger than the one Kelly had placed on that very same finger so long ago. And it fit perfectly.

"I love you, girl," Dallas said pulling me up off of the ground and into his arms.

"I love you too."

We hugged as the ducks continued to sleep.

Karla's bedroom door was wide open and her music filled the hallway. I could see her as soon as I entered, sitting in the small room she had built on to her bed room to do her writing. She called it an office, I called it a closet.

"What's up girly?" I asked standing in the narrow doorway. This girl had a ton of books that covered the walls on make-shift shelves that she painted white. You could hardly see the walls because it seemed she had a book for every day of the year.

"What's up, you?" She asked turning around to face me. Her hair was concealed under a pink scarf and she still wore her pink pajamas decorated by sheep, at two o'clock in the afternoon. She must have been working against a dead line.

"Can you come out of here? I'm getting claustrophobic."

She smiled and stood up from her huge office chair that seemed to take up most of the small space. I followed her back into the bedroom and over to her bed where we sat down. Karla cut the television on.

"What's up?" She asked.

"Is Bree here?" I asked remembering I had another sister. I was over the performance she put on the night before. Dallas made up for all of that and I was too happy to be mad.

"I don't know. When I made my breakfast this morning, her door was closed. I left her some pancakes and I been back here every since. I was getting ready to go ask her if she wanted some pizza when you came in. I think she's too embarrassed to face us."

Well, she had every reason to be, but I still wanted to share my good news with her. "Come on, let's go get her."

I started to raise up off of the bed and she grabbed my arm. "Why? What's going on?"

"Come on, let's go get her," I said again. I was determined to break the news to both of them at the same time.

"Come in," a weak voice said behind the closed door when I knocked. So I opened it slowly. Sure enough, Bree was rolled into a ball under the bright fuchsia covers of her bed watching the television that sat across the room on her chest of drawers.

"Hey, Bree," Karla said first as she sat down on the edge of the bed.

"Hey."

"Did you eat any pancakes?"

"Yeah."

"Hey Bree," I said sitting down on Karla's old chaise lounge.

"Hey," she mumbled and she couldn't look me in my eyes. I wasn't surprised.

"I think Lonna has something she wants to tell us," Karla said looking at me expectantly.

"Don't you wanna order pizza first?" I asked.

"No, I want you to tell us what you have to tell us first."

I sighed deeply. "Okay." I took another deep breath. "Okay, last night . . . last night, Dallas asked me to marry him."

I could hear the faint sound of air catching in throats.

"What?" Karla said, no more than a whisper.

"Dallas asked me to marry him. I said yes. We're getting married Friday."

"Wait a minute, wait a minute," she said and Bree sat up in the bed. "You got engaged last night, and you're getting married on Friday? What's the damn rush?"

"There's no rush. We just wanna do this easy and inexpensively. If we're going to the court house, there's no reason to wait for months and months."

Karla and Bree looked at each other and then back at me "Congratulations," Bree said finally raising her voice to an audible pitch.

"Thank you."

"Yeah, congratulations. I was hoping I could plan your wedding too though."

I shook my head. "No, but you can go to the court house with me."

"Court house, huh?" Karla shook her head. "That seems so informal."

I slowly stood up from the chaise and walked over to Bree's phone that sat on her nightstand, giving Karla a dirty look all the while. She was not going to guilt trip me into having a *wedding extravaganza* like New-New's. New-New was still paying for some of the mess she had. Instead, I picked up the phone and dialed our favorite pizza parlor. As soon as I started placing the order, the doorbell rang.

"Damn," Karla groaned. "I wonder who that is. I look a mess."

"I'm not here," Bree said, changing the channel with the remote that she was gripping tightly as she slid back down in the bed. I wondered if she thought there was a chance that Link would come over today. If there was I knew she better take it, but I busied myself giving our address which the pizza guy already knew by heart.

By the time I finished placing the order; Karla was standing in the kitchen with her arms wrapped tightly around Phoenell. I felt a little pain in my heart and I contemplated the concept of it being guilt or not. I had only seen Phoenell two or three times since I left rehab. Most of the time I was working during the day, so I was never home when she visited. She worked at the skating rink in the evenings; therefore we managed to escape each other on a constant basis.

"What's wrong, Karla?" I asked, not really wanting to interrupt but still wanting to make my presence known. For the moment I still lived here.

When she let go of Phoenell and looked at me, the first thing that caught my attention was the black eye. It was the same eye that was darkened the night of her little gathering, the first time I met Ron. It almost seemed as if it had never gone away. I was surprised she still had an eye. She was trying her best to hide her face from my view, but I had already seen enough. I knew what was up.

"Phoenell is going to chill here for awhile. Is that okay with you?"

Not that long ago my answer would have surely been "*Hell no!*" But I wasn't the same person. I was soon going to be someone's wife, I had a great job, and I wasn't on drugs anymore. So therefore my answer was, "Sure. She can have my room. I gotta start packing up anyway."

I of course said all of this with the brightest smile. I could feel it from ear to ear. But Karla's face darkened a little. We hadn't discussed the fact that I planned to be out soon. I realized I should have mentioned it right after I told her about the proposal. I just figured she would already realize it.

"You're leaving?" Phoenell asked, finally looking at me.

"Yeah. I'm getting married." I couldn't imagine a more inappropriate time to tell her that I was getting married. But she asked. "You want something to eat, we just ordered a pizza?"

Both she and Karla looked at me in surprise. And Karla smiled slightly probably grateful that I was treating her friend with some compassion. It wasn't even as hard as I thought it would be.

But Phoenell shook her head. "No. I'm not really hungry. I just want to get some sleep. I been up all night long."

"Okay. Well like I said, you can have my room."

"I really appreciate it. Thanks."

"Let me change the sheets, right quick."

She nodded and I turned around and headed to my room, not realizing that Karla was following close behind me until I tried to close the bedroom door behind me and she blocked it.

"Thank you," Karla said while she helped me remove the sheets from my bed.

"For?" But I already knew.

"For being so nice to Phoeny. He started in on her last night when she came home from work. I know she's tired."

I just shrugged, taking clean sheets out of my dresser drawer. "It's cool. Maybe she should just move up here permanently. To get away from his crazy behind."

But Karla shook her head. "She not gonna leave. She was supposed to have left when Dakota went to college. She's been in South Carolina for two years now and Phoenell still hasn't gone anywhere. Dakota and her husband got their own apartment and everything, and she wants Phoenell to come down there. But she won't leave Ron. I don't know what else to do for the girl."

"Doesn't sound like there's anything you can do, really."

She stood up straight while I placed the new pillow cases on the pillows. "So you're leaving huh?"

I put the pillow down on the bed. "Yes, Karla. You know me and Dallas can't stay here with you and Bree." I smiled. "Don't worry. I'm not going to leave you high and dry."

"You know money is not the issue. It's just that we've always been together."

"And we'll still always be together. Just not under the same roof."

She shook her head and smiled a very faint smile. "You know it's like everybody around me is getting married."

"Huh, not Bree."

Karla rolled her eyes to the back of her head. "I know right."

"And you never know," I hesitated because what I was getting ready to say seemed to be burning a hole in my throat like vomit even before it left my mind. Maybe I was taking this being a better person way too far. "Maybe you and Jonathon will be walking down the aisle soon."

The look on her face was priceless. It was a mixture of shock, horror, and physical illness too. I knew Jonathon wasn't the one for her and I was relieved to know that she knew it too.

"Naw, I'm happy for *you,* Lonna."

PART 6

Chapter Twenty-Three

Friday, June 18th 1999 4:27 p.m.

Lonna pinched me under the table for the millionth time. My leg was getting sore and I was sure I would have a bruise. I looked across the table to see Bree toss her long black hair back off of her shoulders as Jeff leaned over to say something to her. Just as he leaned over, Lonna pinched me again.

"I wanna propose a toast," Troy said standing up and we all put our forks and knives down. He raised his wine glass, filled to the brim, in the air. "To my brother, best friend . . . Dallas man, I knew this day would happen I just didn't think it would happen so soon. I just wanna wish you and Lonna the best in life. You both good peoples, you both deserve all the happiness in the world. Y'all deserve each other."

I could feel the tears come to my eyes when Troy sat back down. Marc, Chiloe, Bree, Jay, Jeff, Troy, Jonathon, Dallas, and Lonna turned to look at me. Being the maid of honor, I guessed it was part of my duty. So I stood up with my wine glass in my hand.

"I'm not use to doing this, y'all," I said wishing that I had written something down.

"It's alright, Baby," Jonathon's half drunk ass yelled behind me and something in me squirmed making me try my best to block out the sound of his voice.

I turned to look at Lonna in her beautiful white dress that it had been like pulling teeth to get her to wear. Even though she had refused the lavish wedding that I wanted to give her, that wasn't going to stop me from making sure she looked absolutely perfect. So I bought the dress that reminded me of June Cleaver, and paid for a beautician to come to the house. Her hair was swept up into a pile of soft black curls, some gathered around her face while some stayed put.

"I just wanna say, Lonna, that no one deserves to be happy more than you do. And I'm very proud and thankful that you're my sister." She smiled and I had to focus my attention elsewhere to keep myself from spilling tears on my own cream colored dress. "And Dallas, I love you like a brother already. But if you hurt her, I'm gonna get you."

The table laughed like I was joking, but I knew in my heart that I wasn't. I also wanted to comment on breaking Jeff 's limbs if he did something to hurt Bree, like Lonna and I knew he would. But this wasn't the appropriate time. So I sat back down catching a strong whiff of liquor from Jonathon. He was a walking, talking, sponge.

Marc stood up next and cleared his throat. "I just want to say, Lonna, you've come a long way. I didn't think I would ever see this day." He stopped and shook his head, probably remembering Lonna's Blue Period. I tried my best not to think of any of that stuff anymore. And I knew Lonna did too.

"I just want to tell you though," Marco continued, pushing his glasses up off of the bridge of his nose. "I'm very proud of you. I mean you're like a caterpillar that turned into a beautiful butterfly."

That was it for me. I could feel the tears spilling down my cheeks.

"Awww," Bree said holding her head to the side and looking at me. That caused Lonna to look over at me and put her arm around me when she saw the tears. I felt my face burning because I had not meant to draw this attention to myself.

Jonathon put his arms around me and I had to fight my natural reflexes not to squirm away.

It would have been nice to just be able to say something was wrong with Jonathon and me. But it was something much more than that. And it had been this way from the beginning of this thing we were loosely calling a relationship, I was just too blind or too stupid to see it. Either way, it didn't matter. I saw it now, that was all that counted. The late nights that he said he was "working", all the phone calls on his cell that he always had to leave the room to take, the partying and clubbing, and the drinking. The time he could not spend with me. I was wasting my time. And I knew this better than anyone. There was no future with Jonathon and me. There was barely even a present. The problem was, letting go.

I had only been alone for a little over a year when Jonathon and I started seeing each other. I wasn't really over Mike, even though there was enough anger in me to replace any feelings of love that I ever had for him, they didn't. And they probably never would. I knew it was on the tip of Lonna's tongue to let me know that Jonathon was no Mike whenever she saw us together. I guessed I put on quite the show that I was actually feeling Jonathon. But I wasn't. He'd single handedly alleviated any possibilities of me ever caring two cents for him a few months into the relationship. The face I made when Lonna mentioned me marrying him probably gave all of my true feelings away. At least to her anyway. I could never hide anything from her.

That's why I often wondered if she knew I was still in love with Mike.

To my dismay, it didn't take Lonna long to clear her stuff out of the house. It was almost like she had never been there at all. I looked around her empty room as I held the mail from today in my hand. The house seemed so quiet now, it was unreal. Bree was God only knew where, but I was guessing she was with Jeff. And Lonna was gone with her new husband to meet his mother in Atlanta. Whenever she did come back she wouldn't be coming to this house anyway. I had never in my life lived by myself before and I wondered, as I wiped the small amount of tears from my eyes, if I could get used to this.

I decided to suck up the tears and stop being a baby about the situation. If push came to shove, I would ask Veronica if she wanted to stay. I figured out a long time ago that there was no chance of Phoenell ever coming to stay. I wondered how much longer Bree would be staying here while I made my way to my room right next door to Lonna's. I was more than ready to get out of these wedding clothes as I kicked my shoes off of my feet and they went flying across the floor.

Bree and Jeff had grown pretty hot and heavy in a very short amount of time. Less than a week. The giggles and looks they were giving each other at Lonna's wedding dinner were nothing less than sickening. I didn't want to be a party pooper, or rain on anybody's parade, but I wondered just how sincere he was when just last week he wasn't paying her a lick of attention. From my pinched up leg, I knew Lonna felt the same way.

I slipped the dress off over my head, stuck it on a hanger and pushed it back into my closet. I didn't know when or if I would ever wear that dress again. Maybe if Veronica or Bree got married. Marco had finally dumped his witch of a girlfriend and as of yet he had no prospects. That only left Jay and that was a joke right there.

I sat down on my bed in my underwear and began sifting through my Friday mail until I came to a small pink envelope with my name written in cursive along with my address across the front of it. Eager to see what was inside, I ripped it open paying no mind to the gold seal embossed with the letter M that held the back flap of the envelope in place.

I scanned the single postcard sized engraved note quickly. It was a wedding invitation to a ceremony scheduled for the following Saturday for a girl named Simone Jackson and Link Montague. I almost dropped the invitation on the floor. Was I in the damn twilight zone or what? Did he and Bree not just break up less than a week ago?

Just as my fingers started to itch to call Lonna, my phone rang. I prayed it was her as I picked it up and read the caller ID. It was Link; his timing couldn't have been more precise if it were planned. I wondered if the invitation had indeed come in the mail or if he had slipped it into my mailbox. I picked the envelope up off the floor as I answered the phone to find out.

"I got your invitation," I said plain and simply. There was no postmark on the envelope. He *had* put it in my mail by hand.

"I know what you're thinking," Link said. I didn't confirm or deny a thing as I let him wonder for a moment if he really knew what I was thinking. But then he said, "I wasn't creeping on Bree. I swear I wasn't. Simone is my ex-girlfriend from way back in the day. We enlisted at the same time and we both ended up stationed here. She just happened to be there for me the other night when everything went down with Bree."

"She just happened?"

He sighed deeply. "Okay, I went over to her place after I left the restaurant. I mean, we've been friends. Always have been. So I

571

didn't know where else to go. I knew Mike was probably still feeling bad with his leg messed up and everything . . ."

"Wait a minute, what about Mike's leg?"

"Nobody told you? You mean Bree didn't tell you?"

"Tell me what?" I felt my heart pounding through my bra like it was going to escape from my chest at any moment.

"Mike was over in Korea for about a month when he hurt his leg jumping out of a plane. I mean, he's alright and everything. He's going to be getting out though."

"Wow," was all I could say. I had not even known that he had gone to Korea. What if something had happened to him over there? What if I was never able to see him again? Those questions ran through my mind for all of five seconds because it finally hit me, if he wanted to see me he would call me. He obviously didn't care about never seeing me again, so why should I?

"Okay," I said for Link to continue. I had a moment, and now it was gone. At least I hoped it was.

"Well, I was really upset Karla. So I had to talk to somebody. The only other people I knew here besides you, Mike, and Bree was Simone. So she ended up being there for me that night and we rekindled what we had."

That was fair enough. It wasn't like Bree was ever faithful to Link. She obviously didn't care about the relationship and hadn't for a long time. Mainly after she met Jeff. I couldn't blame him for moving on, but marriage. That was a little extreme.

He seemed to read my mind and said, "I'm going back overseas in a few months and Simone is too. I just don't want anything to happen to either one of us without us being married to each other. At least if something happens to me she's set. And vise versa. We do love each other, we've loved each other for a long time."

I couldn't say anything to dispute that. Link was a grown man and Bree had messed up the relationship anyway. What else could I say but, "As long as you're happy, congratulations."

"You think you'll make it to the wedding?" He asked.

"Yeah. I'll be there." At least now I had somewhere else to wear that dress too.

I hung up the phone and looked down at the rest of my mail. The small pink envelope was not the only piece of interesting mail I had that day, because the next thing to catch my eye was a long plain white envelope with my name and address written in shaky print across the middle. There was no return address.

The first thought that entered my mind, that I was willing to entertain, was maybe this was from Mike. Maybe he'd written me to tell me the things he could not say over the phone or in person. The thought made my heart beat faster, but the feeling quickly went away when I opened up the plain white paper, folded over three times. This was not Mike's handwriting at all. Just like the writing on the front of the envelope, this writing was shaky barely decipherable. I had to hold the paper close to my face to even understand it. For a second I even figured it was Chiloe. We hadn't had a conversation with each other in literally years. Maybe he was writing me to apologize for what he had done.

What I read made me wish I hadn't even gone to the mailbox that day. I didn't know whether to laugh or cry. One thing I did know was that I needed to call my sister.

I picked up the phone and dialed New-New's cell phone number. I was greeted by the sound of what seemed to be a million female voices. Then my sister's voice said, "What's up?"

"Hey girl. How are you?"

She paused loudly. "Working hard. I can't believe I had to miss my own sister's wedding, man. I have so many daggon' clients today it's crazy. Everybody's trying to get fresh for the weekend . . . you know how we women do."

"Yeah, I know."

"And this wedding man, it was so spur of the moment. I wish she could have given me at least a week's notice. You don't spring nothing like that on a hairdresser!"

I laughed.

"So how was it?"

"It was very nice. I had to make her dress up and get her hair done though. She thought she was just gonna walk up in there looking like anything. Marco took pictures, he's gonna send you some."

I paused for a second preparing myself for what I was about to tell her. I didn't even know how to start. Finally I said, "You know Bree's been kicking it with my boyfriend's twin brother. Right?"

"Girl, Lonna told me about that little episode. So what, they kicking it full throttle now?"

"Supposed to be. But listen to this shit." I opened the letter up and began to read to her, "Karla, I know you're so-called seeing my brother and Bree is trying to get with me. But I know that you know there's something going on between me and you. I know you can feel the attraction between us just like I can. I felt it the first day I saw you and I know you felt it too. It's strange the directions that we are taking, especially when we both know that we should be together. It kills me to see you with my brother. The situation is so messed up." I stopped and shook my head still not believing what I was reading. "New he goes on like this for two pages man."

I could pretty much see my sister putting down whatever utensils she was using in some poor client's hair, standing there with her cell phone in one hand and her other hand on her hip. "Wait a minute," she said. "That's Bree's boyfriend writing that letter?"

"Yep."

"Your boyfriend's brother?"

"Yep."

She sighed heavily into the phone again. "Damn. I can't believe that. And what did he mean 'so-called relationship'?"

"Knowing Jonathon, it could mean a number of things. Or Jeff could just be hating. Who knows girl. This stuff has thrown me for a loop for real."

"Are you going to tell Bree-Bree?"

"How?"

She laughed. "When did he send the letter off?"

There I was again looking at the postmark. "Wednesday."

"So why is he trying to kick it with Bree then?"

"New-New, your guess is as good as mine."

"That no good son of a bitch."

I nodded in agreement, but of course she couldn't see me. "I'm just going to throw this mess away. I don't know how to tell her. The way she is about that boy, she'll think I want him too and then she'll be mad at me. Especially the way he's talking in this letter. She's gonna think I was flirting with him too or something and that's not the case."

"Yeah you're probably right," New-New said quietly. I could tell something was on her mind. Before I could ask her what, she said, "She should have stayed her behind with that other dude."

"Well, he's getting married this weekend."

"What the hell?"

"I know girl. I know."

"Does Bree know that?"

"Nope. I just got the invitation today."

"She's probably gonna trip about that."

"I'm sure she is. Just because she can. When she's the one that caused this mess. Lonna was right when she told her she was too young to be getting married."

"If she knew what I knew, she wouldn't even be thinking about marriage at all."

I wasn't sure what that meant. And she wasn't going to elaborate on it because in the next breath she said, "I gotta finish this lady up girl. And I got somebody still under the dryer."

"Alright then. I'll call you this weekend."

"Ok girl. Take care."

Chapter Twenty-Four

Saturday, Jun 26th, 1999 2:57 p.m.

I looked down at my watch, mad at myself for having the bad habit of always being early, knowing full well this wedding wasn't going to start on time. Veronica cleared her throat beside me.

"What?" I asked, not looking at her instead at the fair amount of people who had shown up. Simone and Link hadn't done to bad for this to be such a short notice event. The small military chapel was almost full.

"Stop looking at your watch, where else you gotta be?"

I shook my head. I could think of a number of places I *wanted* to be besides here. I had to admit the wedding thing was starting to bug me out. If I had to look at one more bride, I was going to scream.

"Nowhere," I said quietly. That was the most depressing thought I'd had in a long time.

Of course my 'so-called' boyfriend had been too busy to attend this event with me. It was always like that with him. We never went anywhere together anymore because he was always busy. It had gotten to the point that I didn't even ask anymore. It was just a waste of time and energy.

"Don't look back ok?" Veronica said leaning her head close to mine.

Her telling me that was also a waste of time and energy because as soon as she said it, I did it anyway.

The sun was so bright streaming through the chapel doors that I could not see the face of the tall muscular figure standing in the doorway. But I knew instantly who it was. Even as he walked with a slight arch in his back to gather the full support of the cane in his right hand, I knew. My stomach clenched painfully making me feel for a moment that I had to go to the restroom. The urge quickly left me but the fast pace my heart had taken up did not.

I watched from my fourth row seat as Mike slowly walked down the aisle, looking as good as he always had, except a little more mature, and seated himself on the left side of the church in the sixth row. I couldn't take my eyes off of him and I could feel my lips begin to quiver as I watched him adjust his cream colored slacks to sit down comfortably. If I had tried to speak at that moment, I knew no sound would ever have escaped my mouth.

I could not put a name to the emotion that ran through me when our eyes finally met. I had never felt my heart split in so many different ways, feeling so many different things at one time. As he stretched his sweet lips in that crooked smile that I knew I still loved

so much, I arched my right eyebrow, shot him the dirtiest look I could

muster and turned back around in my seat. But I longed more than

anything else in the world to walk back to him and fall into his arms,

but not before I punched him in the eye for walking out the door that

night. I looked down at my hands that were shaking so bad I couldn't

even place them in my lap.

"Damn, girl," Veronica said also watching my hands. "He still

has that affect on you? Why don't you go talk to him?"

"Are you crazy?" I asked shooting her the same dirty look I had

given Mike.

Her squinted eyes went as wide as they could for a second.

Then she burst into laughter. At my expense.

Suddenly the sound of the organ on the pew of the church

filled the chapel, Link entered through a door at the front of the church

with another man directly behind him they wore military fatigues. One

by one three women wearing taffeta military green bride's maid

gowns walked down the aisle. They were followed by three more

males in fatigues.

"You put together a better looking wedding than this," Veronica whispered in my ear and I slapped her hand knowing full well I agreed.

The music switched and we were directed to stand. Everyone turned around in anticipation to watch first the little girl with her long black hair done in pigtails adorned with beige ribbons to match her dress. She dropped taupe rose pedals on the white runner of the chapel as she walked slowly down the aisle, smiling all the way like a professional.

As she passed Veronica and me, my eyes wandered over to Mike. At the same time his eyes wandered over to me. I played it off as if I were looking around at everybody and hadn't even seen him. I knew I was being foolish, but I couldn't help it. There were parts of me that still wanted to be mad, and maybe they were. But there was so much more of me that was still very much in love. I didn't want him to know that.

The wedding ended uneventfully with every guest bestowing hugs and kisses on the bride and groom as they stood at the back of the church. Veronica and I did ours quickly. I didn't even know the bride and I wondered if she knew I was Link's ex-girlfriend's surrogate sister. Of course I wondered this as I rushed out of the church and through the gravel parking lot to my truck.

"Why you walking so fast," Veronica complained but she kept up with me all the same.

"I'm just ready to go home," I lied. I didn't want to go through seeing Mike again. She read right through me.

"Yeah ok."

I was overjoyed to see the black Camaro parked in my driveway after I dropped Veronica off at her house. I knew what that meant, and I almost tripped on my high heels getting out of my truck to get into my own house.

When I opened the door though, something wasn't right. I could feel the thickness of tension in the air like someone had set a forest fire right by the back door. It weighed on me making me feel twenty pounds heavier at the least. I reached down to take my heels off, hoping that would ease some of the pressure and made my way into the living room.

Sure enough Lonna sat on the couch and Bree stood right in front of her. They looked suspended in animation as if they were posing for a picture. But that soon ended and they both turned to look at me. I smiled, knowing the smile probably wouldn't be returned. Whatever was going on was about me, I couldn't for the life of me remember anything I had done wrong though.

"What's up?" I asked wondering who would be the first to speak.

"What's up?" Bree asked coming towards me with a look in her eyes like I had never ever seen before. It was a look of madness and pure craziness mixed up, cooked, boiling over and getting stuck in the bottom of the pan. "This is what's up. What the fuck is that?"

She threw a pink envelope and a white envelope at me. I watched them float down to the floor where they landed in front of my feet before I even bothered to touch them. Lonna stood up from the couch the minute the papers hit the floor and grabbed Bree's arm. "Bree," she was saying, but that was all she said.

"What the fuck is that?" She asked me again like she hadn't heard Lonna call her name. At the same time I bent to retrieve what she threw like I didn't already know what it was.

"Why were you in my trash?" I asked her not caring to answer her question. She could plainly see what it was.

"Why was I in your trash? Why you got my man writing you letters? Why you at my ex-boyfriend wedding? Did you think I wouldn't find out about it?"

"Number one didn't nobody tell your crazy ass boyfriend to write any letter. He did that on his own. So you need to ask him that shit. Second, I'm grown, therefore I can go wherever the hell I want to. Including your ex-boyfriend's wedding. Y'all not getting married don't have nothing to do with me, that's your fault."

Her hand rose up so quickly I almost didn't see it. Luckily my sister still stood behind her and she grabbed Bree's arm quickly and smoothly in mid air as if she had been trained to do just that. I had not even flinched though.

"Why are you mad at me?" I asked thoroughly confused. Didn't she know the great pains I had taken to get Jeff off of my back? I had never encouraged him.

"You got my fucking man writing you damn letters, and you gon' ask me why am I mad? My damn ex-fiancé marries somebody else, you go to the wedding like it ain't nothing and you gon' ask me why am I mad?"

Bree put her arm down and turned around to look at Lonna, almost as if she didn't know where she was. It took her a minute to regain her bearings and she snatched her arm away from Lonna, almost violently. I could see my sister raise up a little like she was going to slap Bree into the middle of next week. She thought better of it though.

"Man, fuck you Karla. For real!"

We watched Bree walk out of the living room, shaking the house as she slammed the back door shut behind her.

Lonna looked at me and I could feel my insides cave in. Maybe I had done something wrong but for the life of me I didn't know what it was.

"You look nice. I'm having a serious case of déjà vu though, but you look nice."

She smiled brightly at me and I had no other choice but to laugh. Then I shook my head. "Lonna, I didn't do anything for that boy to write me this letter. And Link . . .I mean he invited me. I couldn't just tell him no because him and Bree broke up. We were friends before they started dating. I'm the one that hooked them up."

"I know all that Karla. Jeff was feeling you a long time ago and wouldn't pay that girl no attention. The only reason he with her now is because she wouldn't leave him alone. She stupid if she think he don't still want you."

I sat down in my favorite gold chair and my sister took her place on the couch across from me. "So how was the wedding?"

"Ugly."

I thought she would tumble off of the couch laughing, like she had so many times before, as I described the military green dresses and the bride's drab beige one that looked almost antique. The only pretty moment was the little flower girl that just so happened to be the daughter of the bride. Her father was not Link.

"Mike was there," I said when Lonna was done getting her jollies.

"Really? Did you talk to him?"

I shook my head.

"You know I didn't get around to telling you, I talked to Chiloe before Dallas and I got married."

"Really?"

"Yep."

"And?"

"Well, Misha divorced him. She made it seem llke she didn't know where he was, and then sent him the divorce papers in the mail."

"Wow."

"Yeah, I didn't think that girl had it in her, but she did him up style. That was just smart."

"Pretty much."

She hesitated and I knew there was more to this story. I sat back in my chair and waited.

"But," she said finally, "Chiloe told me he talked to Mike."

I sat right back up then. What more could he possibly say? He had done so much damage already. Why and how would he want to do even more? I felt my body tense up and my temples began to throb.

"Calm down, girl," Lonna said noticing every inch of rage that was about to explode from my pours. "He told Mike the truth."

"What?" I asked knowing good and well I didn't hear her correctly.

"He told Mike the truth. That y'all didn't do anything."

I sat back in the chair somewhat speechless. At least my head wasn't throbbing anymore though.

"You okay now?"

I nodded and Lonna smiled. "Good. Let's go get something to eat."

I stood up ready to go. But then I remembered something. "Let me go change clothes right quick. I think I'm gonna burn this dress."

After a wonderful meal at a Chinese food buffet with Dallas, Jay, and Marco, Lonna drove me home. I had almost frozen to death in the small restaurant so she quickly turned on the heat.

"You okay?" She asked me as we drove silently down the street.

"Yeah. I'm alright." I knew she realized I had a ton of matters on my mind. I turned to look at her. She was looking straight at the road intently and the sun was just beginning to set. "You talk to New-New lately?"

"Yeah I called her while I was in Atlanta."

"How did she sound to you?"

"Like her and Andrew are having problems."

I didn't know why I was stunned that I wasn't the only person who had gotten that. My sister had so much more insight than I gave her credit for. "What made you think that?"

She shook her head as she gripped the steering wheel, still looking straight ahead. "They been having problems since before I got out of rehab. You can hear it in her voice and sometimes she'll say little things. But then she'll change the subject really quick like she didn't say it. She probably thought getting married would fix the situation, fix herself, but it isn't working."

"It's funny the things we do to fix ourselves, isn't it."

Lonna looked at me then and smiled. "Yeah, it's a hoot."

Bree's car wasn't in the driveway. Lonna and I looked at each other again. We both had the same sinking feeling that something was not right. It wasn't as serious as death, but something was definitely wrong.

The silence in the house was deafening as I stood in the kitchen. Something even smelled different to me. Lonna made her way to the living room to cut the television on. It helped but only for a moment. I watched as she moved on down the dark hallway then. It was eerie the way we always seemed to think alike. I took a second to contemplate that before heading down the hall with her.

The bed was made. The fuchsia comforter with perfect lip shaped designs was pulled up and tucked in under the matching pillows just as pretty as a picture. But there were no clothes thrown around the room in various places like there usually was. The small stereo that sat on top of the dresser was no longer there. The telephone, shaped like a pair of lips to match the comforter that sat on the nightstand, was still there though.

I watched as Lonna opened and closed some drawers just to confirm what we both already knew. Bree was gone. Packed up and moved like a thief in the night, but taking nothing but her own belongings.

Lonna hurriedly slipped her purse off of her left shoulder and dug through it until she found her cell phone.

"Hey Jay," she said after hastily punching in a number and waiting no more than five seconds. "Is Bree there?"

I heard 'hmmm's' and 'uh huh's'. Then she said, "Yeah. Alright then. Bye."

She wasn't there. I knew she wouldn't be there and I knew that Lonna did too. She was trying to have hope. I had already given up. It took a moment for me to decide if I wanted to cry or shake my head and call the girl stupid. Instead I shrugged just hoping that when she got hurt, it wouldn't be so bad.

Lonna on the other hand had come to a different conclusion. She opened her flip phone right back up and typed in another number. I watched as her peach colored skin grew pink with rage.

"Hey my ass!" she yelled into the phone. "What do you think you're doing?" There was a pause. I could hear the voice on the other end of the phone yelling also, but I could not make out what it was yelling. "No, Karla didn't tell me to call you. And don't tell me about starting shit, not after the shit you pulled earlier." Another pause, this time shorter. Again I could hear the voice on the other end of the phone. "That *'bitch'* took care of you when there was no one to take care of you. You seem to have forgotten that Orphan Annie! And now you there with that boy, and he don't bit more want you there than I would want him here." There was another break. I watched Lonna shake her head, her long pony tail swinging back and forth, and squint her eyes up like she was confused. She looked like our father right then. "Bree, stop being so naïve. Grow a damn brain! Karla didn't make him write all that shit. He wrote it on his own. Karla is still in love with Mike, what in the world would she want Jeff for? You know just like I know that she would not try to talk to your man or anybody that you wanted. Your boy is trifling. That's all there is to it."

I got stuck on, 'Karla is still in love with Mike . . .' Was it that damn obvious?

"You right," Lonna continued, "I don't know what's going on in your empty ass head. But I know that Karla didn't do anything wrong.

Don't think you're gonna come back in this house when he fucks up. And he will fuck up." I looked at her then like she was crazy. How could she ban Bree from the house?

"How you gonna ban her from the house?" I asked as she flipped her cell phone closed without saying goodbye.

"Easy. She's an adult. She better start acting like one."

Jay and I watched Troy flirt hard with Veronica from the balcony of Lonna and Dallas' apartment. As they searched through Dallas' vast array of music together on the living room floor, I took note of how my younger cousin threw her head back and laughed, making her long dark hair go even further down her back, as Troy spooled forth one amusing line after the other. The fifteen minute love between him and the Caribbean princess with the hair weave had ended less than a week after my sister got married. Nobody knew why. Not even Dallas, and he and Troy were tight as sardines.

"Heard from Bree?" Jay asked me.

I turned around to look over the balcony where Lonna and Dallas were barbequing on the complex provided grills. I watched as he removed the cooked food from the heat of the grill and gently placed it into the pan that Lonna held with oven mitt covered hands. I looked closer because those were my oven mitts.

"No," I said finally.

"She's foul."

"She's young."

Jay shook his head and took a sip of the beer he was too young to be drinking. Fortunately for him, Marco was working. He never would have gotten away with it if Marco had been here like he was supposed to be.

"Hey Karla, where's your man at?" Veronica called from the living room where she still sat with Troy. They sat closely together with his arm semi around her, but his hands on the floor so no one could really say his arm was around her. He'd stepped up his mack game and Veronica was eating it up.

I turned back around and shrugged. "Who knows," I said watching Troy's facial expression the whole time. I knew he knew.

Jonathon and I hadn't even seen each other in two weeks. There was the occasional rushed phone call. As if checking in to make sure I still considered myself his girlfriend. Unbeknownst to him, apparently, I didn't. I was a free agent and had been for some time. Just like him.

The apartment door opened. Chiloe walked in carrying two grocery bags that appeared to be full.

"Let me help you with that," Troy said welcoming the opportunity to change the subject of Jonathon.

"What's up?" Chiloe said greeting Jay and I with a nod of his head as he handed two bags to Troy. I turned back around without even acknowledging him as Jay said what's up back.

Time put those two on semi-decent terms again. Especially since Chiloe found himself with no one except the family he had left. His mother and older brother were dead; his wife was gone, divorced from him now. Most of his boys had grown up and finished playing the hood games years ago, the ones that weren't taken by the streets anyway. And I detested him. That didn't leave him with much of a choice.

"Hey!" Lonna yelled from the grass below us. "One of y'all grab a pan and bring it down here."

"I'll be right there," Jay yelled back before I could volunteer and made a b-line for the kitchen.

"Y'all need to hurry up with that food!" I yelled down to my sister.

"You should've ate before your ass got here!" she yelled back at me laughing.

"It'll be ready in a minute," Dallas said shaking his head at his wife. They were so cute together it was mind blowing.

It didn't take long for Jay to meet them downstairs. He handed the pan to Lonna and instead of coming back up, he sat down on a tree stump a few feet from the grill and lit a cigarette.

"What's up?" I heard behind me, over Veronica's laughter.

"Nothing." I said without even turning around. It didn't take a rocket scientist to figure out Chiloe was standing only a few inches away from me. I could smell the marijuana on him and he wasn't even smoking at the moment.

In a second he was beside me, leaning over the banister with me. I wanted to go inside, but there I was again, not wanting to be rude either. So I stood there wondering if he noticed Lonna's discreet looks up at us. She did it so smoothly.

"How've you been?" He asked.

"Alright."

"I read your last book, it was good."

"Thanks."

"You working on another one?"

"Yeah."

"What is it five now?"

"Six."

I looked at him out of the corner of my eye. He was nodding his head. I hadn't seen him since Lonna's wedding and even then, I hadn't paid him much attention. But here with nothing else to do, no one else to hog my attention, I noticed some things about him that I had not seen before. He was getting older. It was evident from the slight weight he put on and the very faint lines around his eyes and mouth. His green eyes seemed a little dull to me, maybe from too many years of smoking and drinking or too many years period.

"When did you start reading books?" I asked looking back at the grill that was currently empty. Lonna, Jay, and Dallas were now headed up the stairs to the apartment.

"When you started writing them."

We stood in silence looking out at the partial forest behind the apartment building. The three o'clock in the afternoon sun was bright, but the temperature was comfortably mild. The day would have been perfect if not for the absence of Bree.

"Talk to Mike?" Chiloe asked still looking out at the trees.

"No. You?"

I knew the answer to that before he even nodded; recalling the conversation Lonna said she had with him. He knew I knew also and said, "Lonna told you, didn't she?"

I nodded my own head this time not bothering to look at him. He continued to talk anyway. "He's going to school for Criminal Justice, trying to get full disability. He don't know how that's going to work out though. But he gets to go to school for free. To be a probation officer."

I didn't know how I felt about hearing all of this from Chiloe. I should have known firsthand what was going on in Mike's life. He was supposed to be my man; we were supposed to be together right then. And it was Chiloe's fault that we weren't. I felt anger somewhere inside of me again.

"I know you're still mad at me," Chiloe said as if he could feel the resentment materializing. "What I did was real stupid and wrong. Trust me; I pay for it every day when I can't talk to you like we use to talk." He stopped and I looked at him to see why. Chiloe just stood there, back bent leaning on the rail, looking out at the trees. His hands were clasped together tightly in front of him.

"I just wanted you so much," he continued softly and I had to strain my ears to hear him over the steady chatter going on inside of the apartment. "I guess I really didn't care about what *you* wanted."

He stood up straight. "I didn't care about what anybody wanted. Not you, not Misha, not Mike. I'm selfish as hell, I know. This shit was just new to me. You were new to me. I never felt this way about anybody."

"What would you have done if you had me, Chiloe? You telling me that after a while you wouldn't have treated me just like you treated Misha? Or at least tried to, because I wouldn't have let you. You would have tired of me just as easily as you fell into whatever it was you were feeling for me."

He shook his head. "I don't think I would have. I haven't yet."

I racked my brain for something to say. Anything to discourage him from thinking that for thirteen years he had been in love with me. Not that it wasn't a strong possibility. People did stupid shit everyday in the name of love.

"I know you don't love me, Karla. I know you love Mike. It's cool. I just want you to be happy. That's why I told him the truth."

If he expected a 'thank you', it wasn't coming. When he saw that I wasn't going to respond, he said, "I want you back in my life."

Something in me knew that this was coming. Here he was, wanting to play like he hadn't messed up my life in the worse way. A way that I knew I couldn't repair on my own and I had no idea if it would ever be repaired at all.

"I can't trust you."

He slumped back down over the rail and shook his head. "I lost. I know that."

"It wasn't a game. This is my life and . . ."

"You better come eat, especially after complaining about how hungry you were," my sister said appearing in the doorway of the balcony. She had shown up in the nick of time because I didn't want to talk to Chiloe anymore. I could probably forgive. If I tried hard enough. But forget and act like nothing ever happened? That was something totally different.

Lonna gave a knowing look as I passed her in the doorway. She realized she came at the perfect time. "I'm going to wash my hands."

I left her standing there with Chiloe and closed the bathroom door behind me. I took a deep breath because for some reason the conversation with Chiloe had left me shaking.

But then there was a knock at the door.

"Who is it?" I asked thinking Chiloe had followed me into the bathroom. Didn't he know, at least for now, our conversation was quite over?

"It's Troy."

"Troy?" I asked wondering why he was knocking. I walked right by him on my way to the bathroom, so I knew he knew I was in here. What was going on today?

I opened the door slowly. But he pushed his way on in and closed the door. I was too confused to even ask what he was doing, much less block him from entering.

He held up both his hands in defense and said, "I just wanted to talk to you alone for a second."

"About what?" I asked still unsure of his presence and hoping he could hear all of that in my voice.

He put his hands down and leaned against the bathroom sink. I watched as he shook his head, face more serious than I had ever seen it. Then he spoke. "Look, Karla. I don't want you to be mad at me or nothing." He paused and took a deep breath. "You're a wonderful girl and I like you a lot. That's why I'm telling you this. I should've told you sooner, but you know Jon is my boy . . ."

I should have known this had something to do with Jon. I had a feeling deep in the pit of my stomach of what he was about to say. Suddenly, I needed to throw up.

"Look, Jonathon's been messing around with other girls."

And there it was. I didn't hear any bombs drop, no dramatic music because hadn't I already known? But still I asked, "How do you know?"

Troy shook his head and a painful look slowly came over his face, "What you think happened to me and Candace?"

"Candace, the Caribbean chick?"

"Yeah. He slept with her. He's still fucking her."

I didn't know if I felt sorrier for him than me, if I was mad because I was played, or because someone that was supposed to be his friend had done something so dirty to him.

"He slept with your girl and you didn't say anything to anybody else?"

Troy shrugged. "That's still my boy. We never let a chick come in between especially one like that."

"Well, thank you for telling me," I said quietly wanting him to leave the bathroom and leave me alone.

"I'm sorry Karla. It's just that Jon, sometimes man, he feel like he gotta pull rank or something. And this shit right here is how he do it."

I opened the door. "Thanks Troy."

Separation had always been a hard thing for me to handle. Even if there was no love between the other person and me, separation was still a detrimental thing to deal with. Maybe I had been scarred as a child somewhere down the line.

This is why I found it so hard to break up with Jonathon for good. I realized that we should have been done and over with a long time ago. This was the reason why I couldn't bring myself to have a sexual relationship with him. He stopped questioning me about it after six months though. I supposed he was getting so much on the side that he just didn't need whatever I had to offer. That was fine.

I wasn't surprised that his BMW sat outside of the studio at ten o'clock in the evening. I let my Navigator idle in the parking lot for a few minutes, debating on whether I was going in or not. What would I do if he wasn't alone? What would I do if he was alone? I had no goodbye speech prepared. My mind traveled back to being 12 years old and breaking up with Ray McCarthy. I had given him the 'it's not you, it's me' spill that came from watching soap operas religiously with my grandmother. Life had been so much simpler than.

Guilt made Troy offer his key to the studio to me before I left Lonna and Dallas' home. He knew I was probably headed to do what I had come here to do. Lonna offered to come with me once I told her about Jonathon's sorted escapades, at least the watered down version that Troy had given me. I was sure there were a lot more details floating around somewhere, but they were all irrelevant now.

I used Troy's key.

Jonathon was alone. He sat at a soundboard in a dark and unoccupied sound booth. The instrumental was loud and his head bobbed up and down with it while his right leg followed along. Of course he didn't hear me when I came in.

I cleared my throat. If I opened my mouth to speak, what would come out? Impromptu was not exactly my thing.

He jumped at the sound of my throat and swiveled around quickly in his chair.

I stood, he sat and we stared at each other for what seemed eternity. Until finally he said, "Hey. What's up?" as if the fact that I was there had just registered with him.

I shook my head, still scared to open my mouth.

"How did you get in? I know I locked the door."

"I borrowed somebody's key."

He looked confused and I hated to drag this out. My mind raced with things I could say. I didn't want to be mean no matter how wrong he was. I couldn't take being that way. I just wanted to get my point across as quickly and thoroughly as possible. I also wanted to let him know what I knew. "I think we need to talk."

Jonathon shrugged. I could still see the confusion in the wrinkling of the brown sugar colored skin that was his brow and in his eyes that were a darker hue. He motioned to a chair beside him. "You wanna sit down?"

But I shook my head, adding more to his confusion. "No. I think I'm gonna stand. This won't take long."

He leaned forward in his chair towards me and locked his hands together in front of him. His eyes were strongly focused on me, and I could not remember ever having his attention like this before.

I took a deep breath; put my arms behind my back placing my palms flat on the door behind me just to steady myself. This was just as hard as I thought it would be. I found my voice somewhere and managed to choke up, "Jonathon, I know that you're messing around with other women . . ."

He was about to say something as he jumped up from his chair. But I held my right hand up to stop him from even bothering. I wasn't going to let him deter me from what I knew I had to do and we weren't going to have a long complicated conversation about it neither. He shut up but his arms were still outstretched as if he were trying to figure out what I was talking about.

"I just came here to let you know that I know, and that I'm going to walk away from this now before it goes any further."

"Any further?" He looked at me like I had lost my mind. "We been kicking it for about two years!"

I wondered what difference he really thought that made. Had that not occurred to him when he was sleeping with someone else, that we had been kicking it for two years? Either way the relationship started declining after three months. Why we were even still together was beyond me.

"I don't want to argue with you Jonathon. And I'm not going to make it seem like it's not what it is. I'm done. It's over. You can continue to do you, and I'll do me."

Before I could blink, his face was within inches of mine and I was practically pinned to the door behind me. The thought that maybe I should have brought Lonna entered my mind and flittered back out.

Whatever was going to happen was going to happen. It didn't matter, I did what I came to do and I was done. I stood my ground. I had been around and dealt with much scarier nigga's than Jonathon Carey and he was not going to shake me.

Every inch of his alcohol soaked breath hit me in the face as he spoke. "Who you been talkin' to?"

"That don't even matter Jonathon. It's over."

I attempted to prove my point by gently nudging him out of the way so that I could open the door. But he wasn't having that and grabbed my wrist.

"It's over when I say it's over."

I quickly touched the cell phone in my pocket with my free hand, ready to dial Marco's number on speed dial, just in case things got out of control. The look on his face though, said that he really didn't want trouble. He just wanted things his way. I stared him deep in his eyes, that were surprisingly clear despite all the liquor I was sure he had been drinking.

"What can I do to make you change your mind?" He asked. He licked his lips and looked as if he wanted to kiss me, gently pressing his thick body into mine. I held my head back until my neck began to cramp and pressed myself further into the wall with no desire in me at all to kiss him. That left a long time ago.

"Nothing. Let me go."

Jonathon looked at me for a second. Then he let me go and backed away. A look of sobriety instantly came over his face.

"So you breaking up with me over what somebody else said? Who was it?" He asked.

I shook my head and opened the door. "It's not important Jonathon. And you can't tell me it's not true. Can you?"

He stood there for a moment looking down at the carpeted floor. There was nothing he could say. Not concerning that anyway. "You can't give me another chance?"

I shook my head not wanting to explain that the relationship was dead anyway. Him cheating was a mute point with me. "Take care, Jon."

I really meant that as I closed the door behind me.

Chapter Twenty-Five

Tuesday, August 10, 1999 12:00 p.m.

My house was crazy silent. I cut my stereo up to fill the void, but it really didn't work.

After three weeks of traveling under the guise of writer conferences and visiting my mom, I had no other excuse. I had to face the loneliness of the house once and for all. There was no where left for me to go.

I took my last outfit out of my biggest suitcase and threw the suitcase into the back of my closet. Just as I was about to hang the outfit up, my phone rang. I debated for a second whether to answer it. I had some much needed writing to do, not to mention the fact that I was sad. I really didn't feel like talking to anyone.

By the time I made up in my mind to not answer the phone and finish unpacking instead, whoever it was went to my voicemail. A minute later, however, it was ringing again. The caller ID said PRIVATE NUMBER.

"This is Karla," I said not to polite.

There was no answer.

"Hello?" I asked getting more impatient by the moment. Today was not the day for this. In fact, this month was not the month for this.

"Hey Karla, its Bree."

"Bree-Bree?" I asked like there could be more than one. It was more of a shock than anything else though. I hadn't heard this voice in a month and a half.

"Are you busy?"

"No," I lied looking at the suitcases that still lay on my bed. Then there was the half written novel that I needed to push out of my head, and my voice mail was probably full. My cell phone had been powered off for most of my trip.

"Canyoucomeoverandhelpmemove?" She asked jumbling her sentence so much that it all came out like one word. I hardly understood what she was saying.

"Move? I didn't know you and Jeff were moving."

"We're not, but I am."

I held the phone in disbelief. I knew it would happen, but not this soon. At a loss for words, I finally managed to say, "Okay."

The trunk of her car was already almost full. No wonder she needed me and my SUV, the girl had acquired much junk in the short time she had been staying in the two bedroom condo with the man of her dreams. His nice income probably helped to support her shopping habit, a full scholarship and Pell grant money still wouldn't pay for all of this.

I climbed the stairs to the second floor where the door was wide open and yelled her name.

"I'm back here," she answered.

I walked slowly down the long hallway of the sunlight lit home. I had to admit Jeff had good taste. Everything in here was pure white, from the curtains to the plush leather couches to the carpet. Anything that wasn't white was glass, for example the humongous glass entertainment system and the glass coffee table. Just like his twin brother, Jeff's wall behind his couch was made of a huge mirror that covered the entire space, making the condo look even larger than it really was. I was very impressed.

Bree was standing in the middle of her and Jeff's bedroom, the largest bed room in the huge house, with her hands on her full hips trying to decide what else she wanted to take and what she wanted to leave behind. There were already four packed boxes stacked up against the wall. I looked at the large pile of female clothes that lay halfheartedly on the platform bed, some on hangers the others just were.

The walk in closet was completely empty on one side.

"What's going on?" I asked looking around the rest of the room. It wasn't as neat as the rest of the home maybe because Bree was in the process of moving, but it was all white also with sparse furniture. A bed, a nightstand, and a chest.

"I'm leaving him Karla. I can't take it anymore."

"What happened?"

"He went to Georgia this weekend without even telling me. You know how I found out Karla?"

"How?"

"His damn momma left a message on the phone for him to make sure he brought her some kind of damn cornmeal that she can't find down there. Corn meal, Karla! That was Friday right, the message was on the phone when I got home from school. So I called down there to see if he was there and guess what."

"What?"

"His dumb ass answers the phone! So I asked him when he planned to tell me his ass was going to Georgia. You know what he said?"

"What?"

"I wasn't home when he left so he couldn't tell me, and anyways I'm not his wife. What kind of shit is that? Then he comes home last night mad at me because I ruined his weekend with his family. So you know what I did?"

"What?"

"As soon as his ass left for the studio this morning, I called Jay and told him I was coming to live in the house with him. Then I started packing my shit." She stopped for only a second and shook her head. "It's not just that though, Karly. I was so wrong about him. Lonna was right."

"So you did all this in two hours?" It was only twelve in the afternoon. I knew the studio opened at ten. She was fast.

She nodded catching her breath from all the screaming she had just finished doing. Then she said, "Actually one hour, I had to ride around and get some stupid boxes. That took about an hour."

I picked up a box and carefully carried it down to my truck. She followed suit with some of the clothes from the bed. She had already managed to fit three boxes into the trunk of her silver older model Eclipse. Stuffed animals were strewn on top of them and the front seats. She was able to push the big pile of clothes into the trunk, but that would probably be it. Her space was very limited. Everything else went comfortably into the back of my truck.

"I called Lonna," Bree said as she locked the door of the apartment with her key. "But Veronica said she's out of the shop at a work site. She's probably still not talking to me anyway. I don't blame her."

We started down the stairs, until she grabbed my arm. I turned to look at her.

"I'm sorry, Karla. I'm sorry for everything. I was so stupid. Please forgive me."

I had already forgiven her when she called me. So I just gave her a hug and we walked to our cars arm in arm.

"Look, can you follow me to the studio? I wanna give Jeff back his key and," she stopped and looked at me, "you know I need somebody there to have my back."

"I understand. It's cool."

The studio was unusually crowded for a Tuesday afternoon. I briefly recalled the last time I had been here, a month ago. Bree didn't give me time to dwell on it though, as I watched her quickly swing her car door open as soon as it stopped and jumped out. I had to run to keep up with her as she swung open the front door so hard it almost knocked both of us over. I wasn't mad at her though. I understood she wanted to get this over with. There were probably a lot of emotions going through her that she didn't mention. I wondered what else had gone on between her and Jeff. Was he a cheater and a liar like his brother?

Somehow she knew exactly which room Jeff was in at the end of the hall. The occupied sign above the door shone brightly in the dark walk way, but Bree wasn't about to wait for a convenient moment. She opened the door just as hard as she had done the front door and walked right on in with me behind her. Jeff sat opposite the thick glass of three boys crooning into a mike. They each had on white sweatshirts, baseball caps, and jeans.

He turned around when he heard the door whip open, just as Bree slammed the door shut. The door opened again shortly after she closed it and Troy and Jonathon walked in. No doubt if they weren't in recording sessions, they couldn't have missed the noise that she made starting at the front door.

Jeff, seeing his boys in the room with him, got up and came towards Bree and me.

"What the fuck you doin' here?" He asked holding his hands out and shaking his head in disbelief. The gesture was very familiar to me. "I'm working!"

"I came to give you your fuckin' key back nigga'."

She didn't actually *give* it back though. She threw it back. It bounced off of the solid glass separating us from the three boys still standing in front of the mike, with a hard thud. Everybody watched it as it landed on the floor.

"What the fuck you doin'?" He asked, apparently still not getting it.

"I'm leaving Jeff. You can have whoever the fuck you want." Then she looked at me. "Just make sure she wants you too."

She turned to head for the door, but Jeff caught her by the arm. "Can you please wait until I get off of work to talk about this?" He yelled.

"Hell no! Fuck you."

She snatched her arm away and headed for the door again. I followed close behind.

"You better had not taken nothing from my house, bitch!" He yelled as we passed Troy and Jonathon at the door. I looked at him, just to see his facial expression. He opened his mouth as if he wanted to say something, but quickly closed it when I turned my face away from him and kept walking. Troy watched me nervously as if I was going to blow his cover. Of course I wasn't, but at that moment I decided Veronica needed someone with a backbone.

After stopping for fast food for dinner, by the time I got home it was six o'clock. I had no personal accomplishments to mention for the day. But it was okay. At least Bree and I were back on speaking terms. That was good enough.

My computer was waiting for me like a faithful pet. I cut my desk lamp on and sat down in my chair to eat while I waited for it to boot up. I had no idea what I was going to type, or if I was even going to type at all. I pulled my four hundred and sixty five page novel up and looked at it.

This had been happening to me for over a month now. I tried to remember if it started the day that my sister got married or the day that Bree left. All I knew was that when it came to my writing lately, my mind was numb. My mother said I needed a vacation from the writing. That seemed insane to me. It wasn't that I couldn't afford a year off. I could physically survive easily for a year without working, maybe even more. But would I survive mentally? What would I do if I wasn't writing?

That's when I realized how empty my life really was and I felt a cold tear slide down my cheek. The reason why I had been able to spit out six novels in a total of seven years hit me in the middle of my face. There was nothing else to my life. This was it. This was not the way I had envisioned my adulthood as a teenager. But then again, it was just how I envisioned it.

My phone rang. I quickly wiped away my tears and answered it.

"Hey, Karla," New-New said on the other end. She sounded as bleak and troubled as I felt just by the way she said my name. She didn't have to say another word for me to know something was not right.

"What's wrong?" I asked quickly, not giving her a chance to conceal what I just heard. My problems were quickly forgotten.

She sniffled, not hiding the fact that she was crying. Or she had been crying. "I'm on my way down there," she said finally.

"Why? What happened?"

"I can't take it anymore, Karla. I just can't do it anymore."

"Do what, sweetie? What's wrong?"

She was crying again. "I can't be married to him anymore, Karla."

"Okay, just calm down. Where are you?"

"On 95."

"Where on 95, have you hit North Carolina yet?"

"Yeah."

"Ok, you shouldn't have that much longer to go. Just calm down, drive carefully. Where are you going when you get here?"

"I guess to the house. I don't know."

Jay was going to love this, I was sure. Having Bree there was fine. They were both college students, single, and young. But having New-New and three extra kids was something totally different.

"Call me as soon as you get there."

At ten o'clock I called myself trying to sleep. At least I wasn't staring at the computer screen like I was crazy anymore. Now it was the ceiling. My phone rang, though, and that plan became a dud also. Before I even picked up the phone I knew it was about New-New and I also knew I would not be going back to sleep anytime soon.

"New-New's here," Lonna said to me. Her voice was wide awake, a far contrast to my mind.

"At your house?"

"No, she's at *the* house. I'm on my way now."

"I'll be there in a little bit."

I hung up the phone with her and sat straight up in the bed, ready to get redressed. Maybe this was the fulfillment I needed. I knew New-New would need plenty of help with her three girls. The three of them had never lived in North Carolina and had never been away from their father for a long period of time. This was going to be a big culture shock for them and they would need all of the love a family could give them. It couldn't have been easy driving down the interstate with a crying mother at the wheel. Then there was New-New. Who knew what she had been through that made her even consider leaving her three story brownstone and comfortably profitable hair salon to come back here. Not to mention leaving the man she had loved since she was twelve years old.

I was pretty much satisfied again with my life as I pulled up in front of the old familiar house in the Doone. Marco was in the process of doing minor repairs like replacing the gutters and painting, but it was a work in progress. At least with Jay living here the yard was taken care of on a regular basis.

I didn't even have to ring the doorbell. Lonna opened the door as soon as I stepped onto the well lit porch. Bree sat in the living room along with New-New who was holding a glass of ice water, her hair micro-braided and pulled back into a pony tail. She wore none of her signature gold. I was reminded of the fight she, Lonna and I got into at the basketball court years ago on a chilly fall morning. But as I neared the couch where she sat, I soon realized there was a huge difference between that day and now.

New-New was, if not already, close to nine months pregnant. Again.

"Why didn't you tell somebody you were pregnant again?" I blurted out before I had a chance to think about it. I sounded like Lonna and I wanted to kick myself for it. This was a delicate situation, to be handled with care. I feared I had blown it already though.

New-New shook her head and shrugged. "I don't know. I guess I was hoping it would just go away."

I flopped down on the old brown couch, the only thing Marco had not replaced in the house yet, beside her. She had never said anything like that about any of her children. Even her first pregnancy at the age of sixteen made her ecstatic. New-New had taken on her motherhood role with such ease I figured she was born to do it. But looking at her now with salty tear stains running down her cheeks and blood shot red eyes, maybe I had been wrong.

"Where are the girls?" I asked.

"Up stairs with Jay. He's reading them a story. I guess I scared the shit out of them."

"What happened, New-New?" Lonna asked sitting down on the other side of her on the arm of the couch. Bree remained seated on the ottoman in front of the couch. Her right hand held up her chin while her elbow sat comfortably on her knee. She looked as if she were hearing a bedtime story herself.

"It's nothing that happened, I just can't take anymore."

"Anymore of what?"

New-New shook her head. Then she sighed deeply. "Don't get me wrong. Andrew takes care of us and everything. We don't want for nothing. And now that I have my own shop, everything is gravy. The money is." She paused again. "But me and Andrew . . . I don't know. He changed when his uncle put him over the DC dealership. And I know he's messing around. Sometimes he don't even come home for days at a time."

"So how did you manage to get pregnant again if he don't come home?"

New-New stared straight ahead at the carpeted floor. Lonna, Bree, and I looked from one to the other. I knew somebody better say something before Lonna did.

"That ain't Andrew's baby, is it?"

It was too late.

I heard some glass fall, and some crickets.

"That's why you didn't tell us. 'Cause it's not his. Whose is it?"

"Lonna!" I said wanting her to stop her interrogation. But that was my sister. There were no secrets in the land of Lonna.

"Whose baby is it, Leonay?" Lonna asked again, ignoring me.

New-New shook her head, put her free hand to her face, and started crying again. She said something, but I couldn't understand it. I knew Lonna would fix that problem though.

"Who?" She asked holding her head to New-New's mouth.

New-New raised her head quickly, obviously angry, and said, "Ray's ok."

"Oh my God," I heard come from the back of my throat somewhere, covered in disgust.

Lonna just sat back up and shook her head while Bree continued to stare at us as if she were hearing the best fairy tale yet.

Hours seemed to pass before any of us even moved. We could hear movement above us, instinct made us all look towards the ceiling.

"Everything's gonna be ok," I said finally stroking New-New's ponytail.

But Lonna continued on her rampage, "Does Andrew know."

New-New shook her head.

"Does Ray know?"

New-New nodded. "I told him."

"What did he say?"

"He just asked me what I was gonna do 'cause he don't wanna mess up his relationship with his baby momma. They just got back together right after I got pregnant."

Lonna shook her head. "This is fucked up."

I felt the same thing, but I just couldn't say it. What was done was done. There was no point in making New-New feel worse. I slid closer to her on the couch and continued to stroke her hair until she put her head on my shoulder.

"I was just trying to feel better," she said shaking her head. "I've been so lonely and so hurt for the longest time."

"But, New-New," I said barely audible to even myself, "you and Andrew couldn't work it out? You two have been together for so long."

She raised her head slightly. "He haven't wanted me for a long time. I mean we still have sex. But as far as him loving me . . ." She shook her head and her voice trailed off. Then she laid her head back on my shoulder.

"So you figured if you slept with Ray one night, everything else would get better?"

I gave Lonna the evil eye over New-New's head and she shrugged. But New-New still answered the question. "No, it was more than once."

"More than once?" I asked absolutely shocked. Number one I had never taken my sister for the type to cheat on Andrew, especially not with his brother. Ray was the last person in the world I would've imagined her with, if I was going to imagine her with someone else at all. Second, to let it be an ongoing thing, and again with Ray of all people! I was shocked.

New-New was nodding her head. "Yeah."

"How long has this been going on?" Lonna asked.

New-New looked up and shook her head. "Since before I got married."

None of us knew what to say. Bree stretched and changed positions, I continued to run my fingers through New-New's braids, and Lonna sat on the arm of the couch gnawing away at her lip.

"So what are you going to do?" Lonna asked finally adding a little sympathy to her voice. I wondered how long it was going to take her to soften up. This was our sister we were talking about, not some whore off the street. And even though what she did was wrong, that was really neither here nor there now. Our job was to be there for her no matter what.

"I don't know. I know I gotta go back eventually. I mean I've got my shop and the girls have school. It's just we got in this big argument and I couldn't take it anymore. I just started packing. I had to go somewhere. Then he was like well, if I leave and the baby is a boy, he's gonna take him."

I thought Lonna would fall off of the couch laughing. "Not if it look like his brother, he won't."

I had to fight to hold back a laugh. Bree was also trying to control herself.

"This shit ain't funny," New-New moaned, her head in the crook of my arm now. At least she wasn't crying anymore.

"Girl, you might as well laugh about the shit now. That baby gonna be here in one more month. Ain't nothing else you can do but laugh . . ."

"It beats crying," I said, still rubbing New-New's hair.

"I know that's right," Bree said stretching. This was the first words she had spoken in an hour.

Chapter Twenty-Six

Thursday, September 23, 1999 6:12 p.m.

"I gotta get out of that house," Jay said scaring me half to death as he stood at my office door. So many people had keys to my house that sometimes I forgot.

"Boy!" I yelled throwing a crumbled piece of paper that held a wad of gum at him. "You scared me!"

"I'm sorry. I rang the doorbell I guess you didn't hear me." He sat down on the edge of the bed right outside of my door where we could still see each other.

"What's up?" I asked him returning my eyes to the blank sheet of paper that was my computer screen. I had been there most of the day, only leaving the house to go to the mailbox right outside my window.

"What's up is I'm running a damn daycare in the Doone."

I smiled. "I don't think New-New will be there for long "

"She went looking for houses today."

"I figured she would."

"But still. And Bree running around like she got playmates. I can't tell who's grown and who's not. It's crazy."

He shook his head. "I saw Mike the other day while I was cutting the grass."

I tried not to be phased by what he just said even though I felt my heart leap at the mention of his name.

"Oh yeah."

"Yeah. He asked me about you."

"What did you say?"

"If you didn't care, you wouldn't even have asked me that. You know that right?"

"Jay. Please. Don't try to use your psychology on me. I'm not one of your case studies."

"You close enough. I think you're depressed."

I dropped my head into my hands.

"I'm serious Karla. I've been watching you."

I looked at him then. "Jay, I'm fine. For real."

"You're sitting in front of a blank screen." He sat forward with his elbows on his knees.

We both looked at the computer screen. Then Jay said, "To answer your question, he wants to talk to you, but he's scared. He thinks you're mad at him."

"He's right."

Jay shook his head in that little shaking his head kind of way, like I was being stupid again.

"Come on, let's go get something to eat," he said looking at his watch which from a short distance resembled a Cartier. I wondered which one of his loved ones had given him that. With two girlfriends and one boyfriend, it was no telling.

"Where?"

"Dapper Dan's."

"Dapper Dan's is a bar."

"We can play some pool, eat some food. It's better than you sitting here in front of that blank computer all night."

He was right.

He was pulling more men than I was. I shook my head and took another swig of the expensive imported beer that Jay ordered for me, against my will. I had never been much of a drinker and Jay wasn't old enough to order beer. But as he put it so eloquently as we stood at the bar, where Jay knew the bartender so he didn't bother to card him, one time was not going to hurt me.

I held my pool cue in one hand as I watched him pimp his way back to resume our game. He was all smiles and I didn't know if I was amazed at all the gay men in our small town or just the fact that he had collected yet another phone number. This would make his running tally ten, both men and women. I smiled back at him and shook my head once again. I shouldn't have been surprised though. Even though slim, Jay still had a very nice slightly muscular frame. His olive skin and green eyes were nothing short of brilliant, just like all of his older brothers except for Marc. Marc had the darkest eyes I had ever seen.

"They're biting tonight," he said as he took his stance, ready to try his luck at getting his #3 ball into the corner right pocket. He made it, like I knew he would and strutted around the table like a true thug.

"Tell me I'm the bomb, Karla."

"You the bomb, Jay," I laughed. The beer was kicking in.

Just as he bent down to do damage to the ball sporting the #4, I could feel my cell phone vibrating hard against my right leg. I never would have heard it over the music, the boxing match playing on all four televisions around the bar, and the drunken crowd.

I thought nothing of seeing Phoenell's number on my caller ID. That was a usual thing. We hadn't spoken very much due to my traveling and her work schedule though. Ron was probably out doing his dirt and she was bored. I figured Jay and I could pick her up and come back. The night was somewhat young, and unfortunately I was single.

Instead of her voice asking what was up, all I could hear was sniffling. And not, the 'my head is stuffy' sniffling. But hard crying sniffling as if someone was sad or hurt.

"Phoenell," I said before she could even say anything. There was a gulp and more sobbing.

"Karla," she sounded strangled like she was choking on something.

"Phoenell, what's wrong?" I asked putting my cue down. Jay had given up on the 4 ball and was now standing beside me.

"Come get me please," she said, every word a struggle. But she didn't need to say anything else. I grabbed Jay's hand and we made a dash to the exit. He didn't bother to ask me what was wrong as he darted Marc's old Civic in and out of traffic to get to my neighborhood. He understood the girl was in trouble as I continued to hold the phone to my ear listening to her moans and groans of pain. She wasn't saying anything and I wasn't asking, just telling her to told hold on and that I would be there soon. It was too much of an effort for her to speak.

We passed my house and Jay took the corner wildly trying his best to follow my garbled directions. "Pull in right here," I said finally pointing to the brightly lit little shack of a house.

Clothes were thrown from one end of the house and met me right at my feet in front of what used to be the front door. It looked like a burglary, the way the door was taken right off of the hinges. I wondered why in the world someone would choose this house out of all the nice houses in the neighborhood.

"Where are you?" I asked trying my best to step over things. The moans and groans from Phoenell had ceased. It was okay because Jay and I were already headed down the cluttered hallway.

"Damn," I heard behind me as I dropped my cell phone and my knees hit the hard crusty carpet of Phoenell's bedroom. That one word shook me and I realized this wasn't a burglary at all. I crawled quickly over to her, but I didn't seem to be moving fast enough. She was in and out of consciousness. Her head lolled slightly from side to side while she labored to breathe. The front of her work uniform was blood stained along with her battered and bruised face.

"Come on," Jay said pulling me away from her and scooping her up into his arms like a newborn. We left the house just as we found it, door off the hinges and all.

I felt coldness run through me as I sat in the waiting room of the hospital waiting for someone to tell me something. It had been an hour and a half already and after two Cokes and one bag of chips, my stomach hurt and I was restless. I got up from my hard plastic seat and walked over to the one big window of the waiting room for the fiftieth time. I watched the ambulances as they pulled in and out, people limping up to the front door of the emergency room, and others who had already been seen as they waited for rides.

I sent Jay home thirty minutes ago. I didn't want the situation to get more embarrassing for Phoenell. She didn't know Jay very well and I wanted to keep her situation just between us, unless she said otherwise. However, I did call Dakota to let her know what was happening, she had a right to know. She made me promise to call her the minute I heard anything.

A woman straggled through the door, alone, carrying most of her belongings in three plastic bags. Her middle finger length hair was all over her head, her t-shirt was ripped from front to back exposing bruised skin and a torn bra. She did her best to hide her damaged tear streaked face, but I saw it if no one else did. I couldn't take anymore then. I rushed the nurse's window almost knocking two patients over as I did. I had never been much of a drama queen, but I was going to try my hardest to tap into it tonight. I conjured up the most depressing thoughts I could relive, the night Mike and I broke up and the death of my grandmother, to get tears to come to my eyes. It worked as I stood in front of the nurse's station staring into the face of a stout nurse in a baby blue sweater. Her dark brown hair, peppered with gray was piled on top of her hair in what my mother would call a bouffant. Her grey eyes were poised to tell me 'no' until I opened my mouth.

"I've been waiting out here for an hour for my friend. I bought her in, she was beaten badly. Please let me go back and see her."

I felt a single tear trickle down my cheek and I knew it worked when she said, "Oh lord, come on honey. We'll find her."

And she escorted me through the automatic double doors into the emergency room.

"What's her name, Sweetie?" She asked; her Southern drawl was heavy.

"Phoenell. Phoenell Beale."

We stood in front of the dry erase board where all of the emergency room residents were written in red, green, or blue. Each color meant something different. Phoenell's name was in blue.

"Come on, Sweetie. She's over here in bed 8."

When she pulled the curtain back, Phoenell lay on her side facing away from me. I thanked the nurse profusely and sat down on the stool beside the bed.

"Phoeny," I whispered.

She didn't respond and it bothered me. So I repeated her name louder. I didn't dare shake her to wake her up if she was sleeping. Finally she turned to look at me. Her eyes were red and puffy and her lips looked swollen. She had been cleaned up and I could see the bruises on her forehead, cheeks, chin and neck very clearly now.

"Are you ok?" I asked the dumbest question in the world when I already knew the answer.

"I lost the baby," she managed from deep down in her throat.

I made no mention that I didn't even know she was pregnant. These people and their secret pregnancies were killing me. Instead, I leaned over on the stool and put my arm around her. Her arm facing me was ice cold and I did my best to warm it up. She began to cry. I lay my head on the pillow beside her head and felt her pain. I wanted so bad to ask her if she was going to press charges, if she was going to leave him alone, if she was going to move on with her life and forget about him. But as her body wrenched and heaved with uncontainable hurt, I didn't. I knew she didn't want to talk about any of that right now.

"They want me to stay overnight in observation, to make sure everything's ok."

I nodded my head to assure that I wasn't going anywhere.

"I really wanted this one Karla," she said so softly that if I had not been right beside her, I probably would not have heard her.

I focused on *'this one'*. There had been other babies at some point and time. My mind would not let me entertain the question of what had happened to those babies.

She shook her head and continued to cry softly. I dug into my purse for a soft tissue to give to her because I knew hospitals only gave the hard kind that could scratch your skin off.

"How far along were you, Phoenell?" I asked as she wiped her nose and face.

"Four months," she mumbled.

Damn, four months and I didn't even know. She wasn't even showing. I felt real tears come to my eyes, unlike the ones I created at the nurse's station. I couldn't believe anyone could be so cruel.

I sat by the window in Phoenell's double room on the second floor in the observation department. She didn't want the blinds opened so I was trying to get as much sun light as I possibly could. She lay on her side again, facing the pulled curtain that separated her bed from the other patient's. But the bed on the other side was empty right now.

I wished for a notebook or a good book. I was bored and flipped through the limited cable channels on the small television suspended from the wall, over and over.

"You know I was pregnant before," a tiny voice said in the darkness of the room.

"When?" I asked Phoenell's back.

"Back when I first met you. But he made me get an abortion."

"He made you?"

"He told me if I didn't, he would leave me."

I shook my head, glad that she couldn't see my facial expression. I was never the type to judge anybody, but she was making me cringe. There was an inner conflict going on within myself because she was one of my very best friends.

"He thought it was somebody else's," she continued trying to explain away Ron's maliciousness. "If he had known it was his, he would never have told me to get rid of it."

"Why did he not know the baby was his?"

I watched her back move as she shrugged, still not facing me. "I guess he's just scared I'm going to cheat on him."

I rolled my eyes, once again glad she could not see my face. I was exasperated. "Didn't he know this one was his?"

I heard her take a deep breath like someone had punched her and her back began to tremble. "This was an accident."

I wanted to scream. But I knew that I couldn't. Instead I got up and headed for the door. Hating to leave her alone, I knew I had no other choice right then, the pain in my chest from my imprisoned scream was more than I could handle. "I'm going to get something to eat Phoeny. You need anything."

She didn't say anything; instead she just shook her head. Her face was still turned away from me. I realized it had been a long time since she looked me in my eyes.

I opened the door and crept out.

I stubbed my toe crossing the threshold into the house. Lonna snickered like something was funny behind me.

"Okay, y'all, this is the living room," New-New said waving her hands around. I was impressed. It was a spacious area with a huge bay window, nice beige wall to wall carpeting and cream colored walls. The smell of new house was strong as I passed New-New on the right and entered her kitchen with the arched shaped doorway. It was small and straight to the point with all new white appliances. Through the kitchen was the hallway where the three bedrooms sat.

"I mean, it's smaller than what we had, but you know, I had to do what I can do."

"It's nice, New-New," I said coming back up the hall after investigating the two bathrooms and three bedrooms. I walked past her again into what I presumed was the dining room area, a small space off from the living room. Lonna was squatting down scrutinizing the fireplace in the living room when I came out of there.

"You sure this is what you wanna do, New-New?" She asked. I knew she didn't mean the house. The house was nice with a huge backyard for the girls to play. It was located in a quiet neighborhood not to far from me and far enough away from the Doone.

New-New leaned back against the wall behind her to support her big belly. "Girl, yeah. I'm good."

New-New went to a lawyer the week after she arrived in North Carolina to file for a separation from Andrew. Lonna and I watched in amazement as she went through the stages of renting to own a house, appointing someone over her DC shop, and planning to open another one right here in our town, all the while nine months pregnant with a baby she really truly didn't know what to do with. She hadn't even mentioned the baby the whole time she had been here. I had no idea if it was a boy or a girl and I hadn't seen her with any baby items at all. I knew Lonna was thinking the same things I was, but she opted to keep her mouth shut this time.

"It's nice," I said again for lack of anything better to say.

"Yeah," Lonna said. She had finally removed herself from in front of the fire place and was traveling around the house in the same manner I had.

"Why are y'all being so phony with me?" New-New asked suddenly. I looked down the hall at Lonna who had turned around abruptly. "Y'all think I can't tell?"

I turned back to the fireplace, preferring to let Lonna handle this. She was so much better at speaking her mind than I was at times like these. I knew this situation caused for her unique way of voicing concerns.

She slowly walked back into the living room. "Okay, New-New," she said sitting her purse down on the floor and putting her hands on her hips. "What are you doing?"

"What do you mean?" New-New eyes turned to narrow slits on Lonna and I remembered that distinctly as part of her fighting stance. Her temper had cooled considerably from our preteen and teen years, but still.

"New-New, we're just concerned about you girl," I said quickly. "You're doing all this stuff, you're getting ready to have a baby any day now, and you haven't even mentioned if it's a girl or a boy. We are very concerned."

New-New slid down to the floor, landed on her butt, and stretched her long legs out in front of her, crossing them at the ankles. She made sure her short peach maternity dress was pulled down far enough over her thick thighs and then she put her left hand on her forehead.

"I don't know y'all. I'm so scared. I don't know what to do," she cried.

Lonna and I were both beside her in a second, hugging and caressing her arms and hair.

"Girl, you know we're gonna be right here with you. You don't ever have to go through anything alone," Lonna said and I knew she meant it. I meant her words also even though they did not come from my mouth.

"It's a boy," New-New continued to whine. She shook her head and her long blond braids, that she wore loose today with a white head band, swung stiffly from side to side. "I still love Andrew. But I know he's not going to want me, when this baby comes out looking like his brother and all the rest of our kids look like me and him." She raised her hand into the air and plopped it back down. "And Ray, he don't really care one way or the other. I fucked up for real."

"You need to tell Andrew the truth," Lonna said. She caught both New-New and I off guard with that one.

"Are you crazy?" New-New hollered and the sound echoed through the empty house like a song.

"No," Lonna replied calmly and out of character. "He needs to know the real reason or *reasons* why you left. You not even giving him a chance to decide what he wants to do."

New-New stared straight ahead with a dazed look in her dark eyes. We sat in silence like this for what seemed to be hours as the sun beams dipped and swayed through the windows of the den, kitchen, and living room and onto the bare carpet and walls around us. Even with no furniture the house was comfortable and roomy. It made me consider moving, but only briefly. Maybe my house could use a good remodeling.

Just as I was in the midst of planning the remodeling in my head, New-New spoke. "I'll tell him, but I'm not telling him who the baby belongs to. I can't do it."

"What if Ray pops up wanting his baby?" Lonna sounded as if she were struggling to make this girl understand.

But New-New just shook her head again. "He don't care about this baby. It was all just fun and games to him. I was just trying to feel better about me." With that she started to cry again, covering her eyes with her hand. "He already said it's up to me what I want to do. And this is what I want to do."

Lonna and I looked at each other. Neither one of us would have ever thought in our wildest dreams that we would be having this conversation with New-New.

Veronica was sitting on my living room couch, her work clothes from Marc's computer store still intact, yapping away on her cell phone. I tried to motion for her to get off so that I could talk to her but she held her pointer finger with the brightly colored acrylic nail up to tell me to wait. There was no question in my mind that she was talking to Troy.

I sat down in my favorite gold chair by the window, again thinking about how to remodel my home, and Lonna sat down on the other end of the couch with Veronica. New-New had gone to pick her children up from the private school she stuck them in two days after she ended up back here.

"What's up?" Veronica asked finally, breaking me from my thoughts.

"What's up with *you*?"

She blushed and hung her phone up. Then she shook her head, "Nothing."

"Yeah, ok nothing," Lonna said laughing.

"Where's Phoenell?"

Veronica pointed to the hallway. "She haven't been out since I been here. I heard her yelling at somebody on the phone. But I haven't seen her."

I wasn't surprised. Phoenell had been out of the hospital for three days and the only thing she did was sleep. I couldn't even remember seeing her eat. I was worried out of my mind for her, which was the main reason why I asked Veronica to come over after work.

"Probably Dakota," I said looking out the window. "I hope it wasn't Ron's ass."

"Why would she be yelling at Dakota?" Veronica asked.

"Dakota told her she was coming down there and that was all there was to it. No questions, no nothing. Her behind is going. But you know Phoenell is not trying to hear that."

"Why did he beat her up this time?" Lonna whispered leaning closer to me. Her eyes were wide in anticipation of my answer.

"Basically, he's got a new girl and Phoenell popped up talking about she was pregnant. So I guess the best way to get rid of both her and the baby was beating her half to death. What I can't believe is she told the police she didn't know who did it."

Lonna shook her head. "His ass would be dead right now, for real."

"I know, right," I said shaking my head and knowing my sister was not exaggerating. If she didn't get to him first, she had a brother that would.

"So when is Dakota coming?" She asked slipping her shoes off and making herself comfortable.

"Friday."

I stood up from my chair and stretched, kicking my shoes off also. "I'm going back here to check on her," I said.

I knew that Lonna would probably grill Veronica in my absence concerning her and Troy. I would catch up later I was sure. Phoenell was my focus right now as I knocked on the door to Lonna's old room. There was no answer on the other side so I opened it slowly and looked through the small crack.

She was in the bed. The baby blue blinds were closed and the heavy covers were over her head. The lights were off and anyone would have figured it was close to nine o'clock instead of four o'clock in the afternoon.

"Phoeny?" I said softly but loud enough for her to hear.

"What?"

"Are you ok, you need anything?"

"I don't *need* a babysitter, Karla."

I didn't know if she meant me or Veronica, so I said, "Sorry," either way. I stood in front of the dresser. "Are you hungry?"

"No."

"Have you eaten?"

"No."

She sounded exasperated with me. I didn't mean to smoother her at all. I was concerned for her. Not only was she not eating, but she had not spoken more than five words to me since she had gotten out of the hospital. I searched my mind from top to bottom for anything I had done or said wrong, but I couldn't find anything.

"Well, I'll be in the living room if you need me."

She didn't respond. I guess I really didn't expect for her to as I closed the door softly behind me.

Something woke me up at 2:30 in the morning and for the life of me, I could not figure out what it was. I strained to hear the silence over my stereo that sat on my night stand. I could detect no sound and no movement from anywhere else in the house when I finally cut the stereo completely off.

The hall way was still, just like it should have been. As soon as my feet touched the cold hardwood I regretted it. I should have worn socks, sometimes I forgot how cold this house could get. I definitely needed to look into getting carpet. No, just having the whole house redone was a better idea. I made a mental note to look into that first thing in the morning.

I glanced briefly into the dark living room, just to make sure everything was in one piece. There was nothing out of place and all three locks were still intact on the front door. The same was true for the back door in the kitchen. Nothing had changed from when I retired to my room at ten thirty after listening to Lonna complain about her twin over the phone. She and Veronica both left at nine after convincing me to cook them a quick meal of cheese steak subs, baked potatoes and salad. The food that I saved for Phoenell still sat on the stove. I slid it into the refrigerator hoping that maybe she would eat it later on that day while I was out helping New-New pick out furniture. She would have the house to herself because I refused to let myself find someone to 'baby-sit' her again. The feeling of having done harm to what little dignity she had left ate at me. Of course that had not been my intention, but people died every day from good intentions.

I started back down the cold hall, switching on the heat on the way. I knew it was really early in the year to have heat on. When my Grandmother was alive, the heat went off at the end of March. It didn't come back on until the end of October. My Grandmother was probably turning over in her grave this September morning. And speaking of her, I decided to stop in front of her old door. It was still closed. I didn't want to wake Phoenell up, but I wanted to make sure she was alright. The thought of her thinking I was checking up on her ran through my head. But tonight, the way I had woken up, I needed to make sure.

I knocked, but there was no answer. She was ignoring me again, I guessed. So I opened the door.

The covers were turned back on the bed in a way that meant she was headed somewhere when she got up. I could still see the imprint of her body in the fitted sheet. There was a wet spot on the pillow and I didn't know if she had been crying or slobbering. Then I saw the light on underneath the bathroom door.

So I sat down on the bed to wait.

I glanced over at her suitcases to the left of me, closed and neatly stacked on top of each other in front of the closet where my grandmother kept all of her Sunday dresses, appointment clothes, hats and shoes. Everything else she had kept neatly folded in her drawers. I remembered every Saturday night my mother and I would search the hat boxes that sat in no particular order on the top shelf and the shoe boxes in the bottom of the closet to coordinate with whichever of the trillion outfits my Grandmother had chosen to wear to church the following Sunday.

A thought occurred to me that I had never even dared to ask my mom or my grandmother. Had never even thought about it before. *'How many pairs of shoes did one woman need?'* I only owned six. My grandmother had at least fifty. All different colors for all different occasions and each seemed to have an outfit and hat to match. Cleaning out her closet had taken a good two weeks and four people. Most of the shoes had been thrown away or given to good will due to them being stretched to oblivion by my grandmother's wide and flat feet. I smiled. Lonna was a shoe person too.

"Hey Phoenell," I said becoming impatient. Had I not noticed that there had been no movement from the bathroom in awhile? Had I been so caught up going down Memory Lane that I hadn't even realized I had been waiting for someone to come out the bathroom, who obviously was not even in there? Sometimes my mind would wonder that way, and before I knew it, I had daydreamed a whole hour or more away. That was why my mother called me a *born writer*, that and my imagination of course.

I knocked first. There was no answer and I had not really expected one. No one could sit in complete silence this long. I turned the knob only to find the door locked. I wasn't sure what to do from there. Was I supposed to pick the lock with a kitchen knife like my mom use to do when either Veronica or I locked ourselves in the bathroom by accident? Or was I supposed to wait patiently.

Before I realized it, I was heading back towards the dark kitchen, this time cutting lights on each step of the way. First the ceiling light where Phoenell slept, then the hall light, and finally both kitchen lights that supplied sufficient light to the living room as well. I walked over to the dish rack to retrieve a kitchen knife. There was one right in my view, easy access, in the front of all the silver ware. Once it was in my hand, though, I stopped, not really sure of what my next move should be. I found myself at the phone, sitting on the kitchen table.

"Hello," Dallas answered, his voice thick with sleep that he probably wouldn't be able to get back tonight. I regretted waking him.

"Hey Dall. I'm sorry to bother you. But is Lonna there?"

"Yeah, Karla, is everything ok?"

"I don't know," I said truthfully.

"Hold on."

I could hear the rustling of the sheets the two of them shared. And then Lonna's deep voice, "Hello."

"Lonna, can you guys come over here?" I know I sounded just like a twelve year old. I felt twelve years old again and I desperately wanted my mother right about then. Lonna was the closest thing to her right now.

"Karla, what's wrong?"

"I don't know."

"It's Phoenell ain't it?" she asked knowingly. I could hear an *'I told you so.'* somewhere in her question but I couldn't pick it out. I just knew I needed the both of them right then.

"I don't know," was all I seemed able to say for the moment.

"Ok. Don't do anything until I get there."

'Don't do anything until I get there.' The words played over and over in my mind as I sat at the kitchen table, not even bothering to go back to my grandmother's room. The room that Lonna slept in for five years. The room that Phoenell was supposed to be sleeping safely in until Friday when her younger sister would come to get her and whisk her off to South Carolina. There she would be safely away from Ron and his fist. There she could go back to school and experience a real life.

'Don't do anything until I get there.'

I sat at the table in my brightly lit house having this conversation with myself to keep my sanity. Lonna didn't have to worry about me doing anything. I knew that if I opened that bathroom door that would be the end of my sanity. Something in that bathroom would set me off and I would probably end up in someone's padded room before the day was done. I grabbed my forehead and put my face down on the table, wondering what I was going to do.

Hours seemed to pass before I heard the hustle and bustle at my front door. The sound of keys in the lock seemed deafening. Then it swung open hard hitting the antique television stand that sat behind it.

Lonna ran to me and grabbed my shoulders as if I had already spoken something totally ridiculous and she needed to shake some since into me. I couldn't remember opening my mouth so I stared back at her wide eyed.

"What's wrong?" she asked.

I finally shook my head and held my right palm out. "I don't know. The bathroom door is locked, but she ain't in there."

Lonna looked at the knife, still in my hand. Why hadn't I sat it down? "You open the door?"

I shook my head and she looked up at Dallas who was standing right behind her. He stared back at her for a second and then said, "I'll go."

I gave over the knife and watched him disappear down the hall that was well heated by now and into the bedroom. Lonna got down on her knees beside my chair and wrapped her arms around my shoulders. She was dressed in gray sweat pants and an extra long orange t-shirt. She wore a red and white bandana around her long hair. Neither one of us said a word as we waited patiently for Dallas to come back from tearing the old bathroom door down. I knew the whole thing would probably need to be replaced after he got through with it. It took a woman to open that door.

I finally pulled another chair over for Lonna to sit in. She slid into it and took my hand into her own. We just looked at each other. She reached up to stroke my hair. We still didn't say a word.

More hours seemed to pass again as we sat like this. It could not have taken this long to open that damn door. It was falling apart to begin with, the only thing I had not replaced for Lonna when she came out of rehab. For some reason it had slipped my mind almost like it didn't even exist. I did some more ear straining and could hear voices. Mainly Dallas. It was hushed but I could still hear. I wondered if Phoenell had been in the bathroom after all. Maybe she just wanted to be alone for awhile. Maybe I had caused this big scene for nothing. She was going to be extra pissed at me for sure now.

Before I could even make myself get up out of the chair and head to the back bedroom to face the music of her anger, there were heavy masculine footsteps in my hallway.

Dallas stood right in front of Lonna and me. The knife was no longer in his hand and I wondered where and why he had left it. I watched him intensely as he pulled another of my kitchen table chairs around to sit directly in front of me. Then he leaned closer to me and rested his elbows on the knee portion of his gray sweatpants. He interlocked his long dark fingers of each hand.

I was amazed that Lonna wasn't jumping down his throat for him to spit out whatever it was he needed to say. Did she read something in his face that I couldn't see? Did being his wife make her privy to what every movement of his mouth, eyes and hands meant?

"Karla," he said exhaling deeply. The smell of Colgate was heavy on his breath. "Phoenell is dead."

"No," I said. Not because it wasn't so. It could very well have been so. But I wasn't going to admit it to them. So I said, "No," again.

"Yes. I already called 911."

He looked at me sternly as if to tell me that was final. I hung my head, mostly in shame from sitting here telling him no when I knew the correct answer was yes. I knew it when something that I could not explain woke me up that morning. I knew it when I felt the coldness of the kitchen knife's metal in my own hands after plucking it from the dish rack. Wasn't that why I called my sister and her husband over? So that I wouldn't have to find her myself?

Lonna was hugging me tightly. "I'll call her sister, ok."

I just nodded. Then, even though I knew the answer, I asked, "How did she die?"

Dallas looked at Lonna as if asking permission to tell me. Then he looked at me. "Looks to me like she took an overdose of pain medication. There's a prescription bottle on the sink, its empty. Then she got into the bathtub to lie down. I didn't touch anything though."

We sat there motionless for what seemed forever. I had been doing this a lot tonight, it appeared. It even took the three of us a few moments to move when there was a knock at the back door. For a second I allowed myself to entertain the thought that maybe Phoenell wasn't dead after all. Maybe Dall's eyes had just played a cruel and ugly trick on him and he hadn't seen Phoenell after all. Here she was at the door. That thought lasted for a hot second, and then it was gone. I snapped back into reality as Dallas' chair scraped against the linoleum of the kitchen floor and he went to answer the door. Lonna stayed by my side not saying a word, just stroking my hair.

My home was invaded by paramedics and policemen. Dallas talked to them, his mouth moving quickly but I could not understand a word that they were saying. Lonna's grip on me became tighter as one of the police women sat down in the chair Dallas had been warming. She was heavyset with red hair that was taken back in a loose pony tail. Her face was specked with freckles and as I attempted to count them, I wondered why they had not sent Marco.

She began her interrogation of me with no sympathy at all. At least it felt like an interrogation. It started with Phoenell's full name, age, and address. I told her about the situation that landed Phoenell in the hospital to begin with and how long she had been at my house. I also told her that Dakota would be coming the next day to get her sister. I left out how mad Phoenell had been at me and how I was hovering over her like some damn guard monkey. I left out how I failed my friend miserably.

"We're going to call her sister," Lonna said as if dismissing the officer. She stood up and I read her badge for the first time. It said, Warren. Officer Warren.

"Come on," Lonna said taking my hand. "You can go back to bed and I'll call Dakota."

The paramedics came through just as I slid my chair back under my kitchen table. Phoenell's body lay covered on the stretcher that they were not trying to be too careful with at all. That's when it hit me and I began to cry. But not some loud obnoxious cry, just some tears that streamed quickly and steadily down my cheeks and onto my peach nightshirt.

I heard Dallas ask the officer if he could clean up. I didn't hear her reply as Lonna lead me away from the kitchen. There were still a few people in my Grandmother's room taking pictures and collecting evidence. I wanted to yell out that I didn't mean for her to die. Instead, I just let Lonna drag me into my room.

"Are you okay?" She asked as she pulled the covers up over me all the way to my chin and folded them back.

I just nodded my head and sunk down even lower in between the sheets. Lonna walked over to my dresser where I kept my address book. I watched through hazy eyes as she searched the book for Dakota's name. I meant to tell her that Dakota and Phoenell had different last names, but I could not seem to get my mouth open.

By the time I sat up in my bed again, the sun was all the way up. Fearing that I had slept all the way to the next afternoon, I reached for my alarm clock on the nightstand and knocked over the phone. Lonna was in the room in two seconds.

"What's wrong? Are you ok?" She asked rushing to my bedside.

"I'm fine. What time is it?"

"Eleven."

She picked the phone up, placing it back where it belonged and sat down on the edge of my bed.

"Dallas cleaned up and stuff. Dakota is here. It only took that girl two hours to get here. I know she was flying down that road."

"Where is she?" I asked dreading the worse. What would she think of me? Would she be mad at me? Would she blame me?

"She's at the funeral home, making arrangements. She took it okay. Better than I would have if one of my sisters died. But not G.G." She smiled brightly and I smiled a little back. Then she said, "She called some of Phoenell's close friends and stuff so I'm pretty sure they'll be over. Dallas went to the store to get some food. Girl, I can tell you live alone. There's no damn food in this joint."

"There's food here."

"Karla, Ritz crackers and peanut butter and jelly do not constitute as food."

I smiled again. She was purposely trying to make me laugh, I guess to prepare me for what was really on her mind. She looked me deeply in my eyes as she rubbed my leg over the sheet and said, "I called Mike."

I didn't know whether to be angry or thankful at her. She recognized the look on my face and squeezed my leg; there was no being mad at Lonna. "Really?" I asked not bothering to change my facial expression.

"Yeah. I told him what happened. He asked me if you were ok. I told him no. He said he would be over later on this afternoon."

I sat back in the bed. "I know you didn't call him acting like I was a damsel in distress did you."

She looked me square in my eyes, making no apologies what so ever for what she had done. "Yes I did. If this is the only way I can get you two back together, then so be it."

I wanted to be pissed. But my insides were jumping with anticipation. Then I thought about Phoenell and my mood dampened a little. My good friend had just died and I was thinking about a man. What kind of person was I really?

"Come on," Lonna said patting my leg. "Get dressed 'cause you know the house is going to be full of people in a little while."

I thought about it for a second. The house being full of people. "She didn't have anybody but the few people Dakota probably called, Lonna."

"Don't you remember when Rajul and Greta died? People come out of the woodwork when you die. So get up."

I did as I was told and headed to the bathroom.

Lonna was right. When I hung up the phone with my mother and ventured to the other part of the house, I felt like I was entering someone else's. My living room and kitchen were full of people that Phoenell and I had gone to school with.

There were even some that I didn't know. I greeted people politely, but not exactly sure of what they were thinking of me. My heart was heavy with shame as one by one I was asked if I were ok. I had no real answer for them, but I nodded anyway, refusing to speak more than I had to. I wanted no one to think I wanted the spotlight on me. This wasn't about me.

My sister found it necessary to cook tons of food. Fried chicken, potato salad, corn bread, collard greens, string beans and biscuits. I didn't even know she knew how to cook like this as I walked around my kitchen table where she sat the food up nicely, watching people pile their plates to the sky. The few people that obtained chairs sat in them protectively. The not so lucky ones sat on the floor with Styrofoam plates in their laps. Some even stood against the wall holding their plates in their hands while others withstood the chilly air on the steps of the front and back porches.

"Karla," someone said behind me as I lifted foil from over a long glass casserole dish of baked chicken one of the visitors brought with them. I wasn't going to eat it. I had no appetite. I turned around to see Dakota. It had been five years since I had seen her. Her once sandy hair was now dark brown and she was taller. Not as tall as her sister, but taller. Other than that she had not changed much at all.

"Hey Dakota," I said.

"Hey girl." She grabbed my hands as we stood facing each other. I was so nervous I could feel my fingers shaking against her skin.

"I wanna thank you," she said finally.

"For?" Was she being sarcastic? I remembered her little smart mouth as a kid, and how she irked Phoenell to no end. But now was not the time for it.

"For taking care of her."

Her was implied. Neither one of us wanted to come out and say *her* name to the other. What effect would it have if we did, I wondered.

"You were always there for her," Dakota continued. "And I don't know what to do to thank you."

"But it's my fault, Dakota," I said breaking down more vocally than I had intended. The last thing I wanted to do was draw attention to me. But I could not repair the dam that had broken in me. "If I had just . . ."

"If you had just what?" Dakota asked still holding on tightly to my hands. "There was nothing you could do. It didn't have anything to do with you. You did what you could, more than you should have probably. I appreciate that. For real."

I was grateful for her words. At least I knew where I stood with her. But my standing with myself was way off. There was still a gnawing at my heart that I could not shake. And a helpless feeling that made me feel less than.

"I'm gonna bury her in South Carolina. So she can be close to me," Dakota said as if she were explaining her decision. She didn't have to explain to me. Phoenell didn't belong to me, never had.

"I understand."

She nodded her head almost with relief. "I went to the funeral home today. We're just gonna have the funeral over there on Saturday and then take her body down to Conway. I didn't want a wake or anything, but people can go see her at the funeral home if they want."

I looked down at all of the food on the table, which had increased tremendously as more and more people came to pay their respects. I could hear my front door opening and closing every ten seconds. Lonna was in and out of the kitchen, making sure everyone was taken care of and all of the food was displayed properly. I knew she was tired. I wished I had the state of mind to take over for her, but there was just no way.

When I looked back up at Dakota, Mike was standing between the doorway of the kitchen and the living room. He looked unsure if he should come in or not. I was unsure if I should invite him or not.

"Where are you staying?" I asked Dakota as I tried to pull my attention away from him and focus back on her. She walked over to the kitchen door and looked out at the yard where five male classmates of Phoenell and I stood in a circle.

"My husband and I are at my father's."

I nodded my okay. I was prepared to offer her a place to stay if she needed it. Obviously she didn't.

"I'm going to go back there now. Where it's quiet."

I nodded again. I knew how she felt. I wanted to retreat to my room also.

"Where's your mom?" I asked quietly not wanting to cause Dakota any unnecessary pain.

She shrugged her shoulders and a cloud of indifference swept over her slightly pudgy face. I knew their mom had up and left in her eleventh grade year. Dakota had gone to live with her father, leaving Phoenell alone with Ron. From what Phoenell told me, Dakota never forgave her mother and I could see that nothing had changed.

Not surprisingly she offered no further explanation and instead said, "I got you a limo. I decided it would make sense if we left from here, is that ok?"

"That's fine. Let me know about any cost . . ."

Dakota shook her head. "No, Karla. I can't do that."

She wanted me to let it go, I didn't know if I could. "Are you gonna take some of this food?"

She smiled at me and shook her head. "No, I can't eat."

I knew the feeling as she stepped out of the kitchen door onto the porch, made her way past the men in the circle and everyone else without a word, and got into her car.

A few seconds after the door closed behind her there was the warmth of a large hand on each of my shoulders. The fingers stretched to my jawbone and caressed the skin on each side. I closed my eyes.

"You okay?" Mike asked me.

I nodded not wanting to lose the best feeling I'd had in years. I knew that if I turned around something would happen and I would lose him again. He squeezed my shoulders and slipped his arms easily around my waist as he put his face in my hair and pulled me closer to him in a tight perfect fit.

"I wanted to talk to you this morning when Lonna called me but she didn't want to wake you up."

"I know. She told me."

"When's the funeral?"

"Saturday."

We were silent for a long time, watching the birds flying, hearing people come in and out of the kitchen. The people outside were beginning to disburse and I wondered why they had come in the first place. Did they think there was still something to see in the house Phoenell died in?

I shook my head as I watched car after car pull away. "I don't even know why they came," I heard myself say quietly.

"Pay their respects." Mike said his hands now massaged me deeply from my waist to my shoulder.

"They all knew what was going on, but they did nothing. Nobody did anything."

I was angry at myself again. This time for even feeling a single ounce of guilt in front of these people. None of them said anything when she came to school with black eyes. None of them said anything when she dropped out in the eleventh grade. None of them, except for me.

My body shook involuntarily.

"It's ok Karly," Mike said kissing the back of my neck and hugging me even tighter to him. "It's ok."

I fought with Dakota until she just gave up on picking out and paying for Phoenell's dress. The one that she would be buried in. It was something that I had to do, there was no other way.

Lonna stood close behind me as I searched the rack for a white dress that would suit my friend. Phoenell loved white. But not just any white dress would due. It had to say her name when I saw it. It had to be something I could imagine her in.

I was thankful for Lonna not letting any, '*I told you so's*' come out of her mouth. I knew she always felt that Phoenell was mentally unhealthy and needy. I also knew that she knew I couldn't save everybody and she was just waiting for me to figure that out. She stood quietly by me, feeding the masses (with a little help from Bree and Veronica) for the past day and half, making small talk with them while I mourned; all the while trying to lift my spirits.

"New-New had that talk with Andrew," she said taking up the search for Phoenell's dress also.

"You're kidding?" I stopped looking for a dress and looked at her. I wondered when this had taken place. I could hardly believe that she had really done it. "So what happened?"

"He's mad as hell. He told her he never wanted to see her again and she wasn't getting a penny of his money. Can you believe that thirteen freakin' years and all he can say is '*you not getting a penny of my money'.*" Lonna stopped to shake her head. "You know what though; New-New had much more to do with that marriage not working than she lets on. I mean really Karla, I don't care what happens between Dallas and me, ain't no way I would even think about having sex with his friends, much less his damn brother. I mean for real, what brought that on? And you know as well as I do that she's been obsessed with Andrew since the time he moved in our neighborhood. All those fights she got in over him. If his ass won't coming home, you know she wouldn't have let it ride. Not like that. Now I'm all for change and shit, but you can't tell me being a mother has changed her that much. I'm sorry, she's my sister and I love her more than anything else in this world, except my husband and the rest of y'all. But New-New's shit is not smelling like roses right now to me."

I laughed and the white lady standing near us, who had been eavesdropping on the whole conversation turned a deep purple.

"Well Lonna," I said when I recovered and the lady moved on about her business, "there's nothing we can do but be there for her."

Lonna shook her head and continued looking. "I'mma be there for her, but she need to come clean about what was really going on."

"I know for me, personally, I know too damn much right about now. I don't need to know anymore."

She poked me in my side. "You jealous about her and Ray?"

"Girl, you gonna make me throw up," I said laughing even louder this time. I finally found the dress I was looking for. It was short and plain. The material was white satin with little flowers embroidered into it. It screamed Phoenell. "You like this?"

I held the dress up for her to see. She glanced over it involuntarily half-heartedly. I was sure it didn't matter to her one way or the other what Phoenell was buried in. But at least she was trying to act like she cared. That was all that I could ask for.

"Yeah, it's pretty. How much is it?"

I hadn't even checked the price tag; I had been so excited to find it. I probably would have never checked if it weren't for the skeptical look on Lonna's face. She knew it could have been a thousand dollars and I still would have bought it, and shoes to match! But as acting Voice of Reason for me, she wanted to know how much it was and I had no other choice but to tell her.

"Sixty," I said bracing myself for the lecture I was going to get.

"You're gonna put a sixty dollar dress on a dead person?"

I knew she didn't mean to be so insensitive, but that was Lonna.

"Yes," I answered back.

Instead of her saying anything else, she just shrugged. I was surprised but I wasn't taking any chances so I quickly headed to the register.

"Is Mike going with you to the funeral?" She asked as I took the dress that was left on the hanger in a dress bag to keep it clean and wrinkle free and headed to the shoe department.

I nodded feeling happier than I looked, I was sure. He hadn't left my side since the day at my back door. We had even consummated our relationship three or four times in the last day and a half. It was eerie the way we slipped back together as if we had never been apart for two years.

"I'm really glad you two are back together," Lonna said and I remembered that I never thanked her for the phone call she made.

"Thank you Lonna," I said like a preschooler.

"For?"

"For calling Mike."

She laughed this time and I did too. Again we drew the attention of the people around us.

There were people parked on the grass, in my driveway, on the street in front of my house, in front of my neighbor's house and in the back of my house. They would all be moving once the funeral procession formed.

I sat at the kitchen table with Dakota and Mike. She wore a black wide brim hat to match her black dress. I could hardly see her face due to the veil that covered it and she looked like a little girl playing dress up. I smiled remembering her younger days and I knew Phoenell would be proud of her now.

There was no food laid out today and Lonna had finally gone home. She had some much needed rest to get and I was sure she wanted to spend time with Dallas. I knew she felt bad for the way she felt about Phoenell and the liberties she had taken with the only man Phoenell had loved. The man who was the reason why she was gone. That was the main reason for her doing everything she could for me, except going to the funeral. But Bree and Veronica were there. Both sat across from me at the kitchen table dressed in black and carrying on a quiet conversation between themselves. I didn't know when I would ever stop owing Veronica for her favors, but Bree owed me this one and a million more.

Dakota's husband of one year stood leaning against my refrigerator. He was tall, but not as handsome as I pictured him. He was brown skin, with a small nose that seemed too small for his face.

His hair was cut short, which was a plus and he could pull a suit off very well. I chided myself for judging the man that way. He was probably the sweetest person and I knew he meant the world to Dakota.

I looked over at Mike who was staring back at me. He smiled when our eyes met and I smiled back as he grabbed my hand tightly in his own. Just as he brought it to his lips to kiss my fingers, my unlocked door opened and the funeral home director walked in.

I had been to enough funerals to know what to do and where to go. As a matter of fact, I was sick of funerals, even though the last one had been Greta's five years ago. All the same, we followed the funeral director's instructions. There were two black limousines parked among all the other cars. The first one was for Dakota and some other family members of her and Phoenell. The second one was for Mike, Bree, Veronica, and me.

Mike put his arm around me tightly and pulled me closer to him in the seat. He sat near the window while Bree and Veronica sat across from us. Somewhere under my grief was peace from being with him. The smell of him comforted me along with the strength of his embrace. I couldn't imagine a better feeling in this world.

"Let's just go somewhere for a couple of days," he whispered quietly in my ear.

"Where?"

"You'll see. I don't have school on Monday and I can miss Tuesday. One day won't hurt."

If he had said we were going up into space on a spacecraft for NASA when the funeral was over, I was sure I would have agreed eventually. Excitement bubbled up inside of me in spite of our surroundings.

"I can't believe how many people were at your house," Bree said shaking her head and looking out of the window behind my head. I was sure there were at least twenty cars following us closely.

"Everybody in Fayetteville must have known her," Veronica responded. She too was looking over my head.

"I didn't know she knew so many people. They weren't around until after she died."

"That's how it is most of the time," Mike agreed rubbing my arms.

"You were always there though," Bree said. "That's enough."

Something about that made me feel worse. Maybe if I had not have tried to be there so hard, just maybe she would still be alive. I shook my head, trying to shake that thought out. I figured I was through with the *If I's*. I guess I had been wrong.

The parking lot of the funeral home was already crowded with cars and people. A lot of them had to park in the empty lot across the street. As we exited the limo I was busy watching all of the people around us when I felt someone grab my hand.

I turned to see Dakota and followed her into the funeral home.

I didn't know when or if I would ever get the images of Phoenell as she lay in the casket right in front of my face out of my head. Her hair was pulled back into her signature ponytail, but the make up the undertaker packed on her face was way out of character. Phoenell never wore make up. It was obviously put on to cover up her many bruises.

I watched through swollen tear blinded eyes as, after the service, people came up one by one to view her body. A few people touched her hands that lay on top of each other across her stomach; some even touched her shiny black hair.

I embraced Dakota as we stood outside the funeral home. I wanted to do so much more, but everything was over now. There were so many things I wanted to express to her, like how sorry I was for everything, but there was no point now.

A strong wind swept by almost blowing Dakota's hat to the side. At the same time it blew in Ron and a younger version of Phoenell on his arm.

"I'm sorry about your loss," he said casually as if he had been a mere family friend. An older lady stood slightly behind him to his left. She looked down at the ground when I looked at her. The girl beside him seemed to stiffen as my eyes traveled her face. Instinct made Ron put an arm around her waist.

Dakota was dumb struck and absolutely speechless. Standing as close to her as I was, I could hear her breathing becoming labored. One glace at her and I could see her struggle in the erratic rise and fall of her chest under her black dress. At the comprehension of her distress, something came over me and I couldn't stand there and let her go through this. I would never feel okay again if I did.

I looked at the young girl, with nothing but pity I hoped and said, "Do you know he use to beat her?" More than just the girl heard me. Over her shoulder, people were watching us and everyone seemed to be frozen in time. Veronica, Bree and Mike were more than likely praying that I didn't act a fool at this funeral.

The young girl didn't say a word. She just looked at me like everyone else, mouth open and eyes wide. Even Ron was flabbergasted for a moment. He soon recovered though and acted as if he were going to approach me. I could feel Mike's hands on my back, however, and I knew he wouldn't.

"What the hell you talkin' about?" He asked but his voice cracked.

I paid him no mind, shaky voice and all, and continued to stare the little girl down. "Did you know she lost two babies because of him? He made her have an abortion and then he killed the second one!"

I heard a gasp from somewhere, but I couldn't stop. If Ron's skin had been the color of mine, he would have undoubtedly been red. He stood clenching and unclenching his fist like a madman.

"Then he left her and that's why we're here today."

I turned around, unsure if I wanted to keep the other stuff inside. I realized I just couldn't so I turned back around to see the girl still standing there, not knowing what to say or do.

"Oh yeah, and he was fucking my sister behind Phoenell's back."

I heard a few, *'Oh hell's.'* Some of them may have come from Veronica and Bree. "He gave her drugs in exchange for pussy and she had to go to rehab."

"You know none of that shit is true, don't you baby," Ron said holding the girl by both shoulders, but she was still facing me in a trance like state.

"Oh come on Ron. Let's see how many people here know about you versus who don't. And we'll see what's true and what's not."

Even the older lady with him, who I assumed was his own mother, stared at him in disbelief. But my focus remained on the little girl that looked to be no more than eighteen years old.

"I just want you to think about what kind of man you want to associate yourself with. Because this one here really ain't shit."

Ron lunged at me then, but he looked over my head at Mike and stopped midway.

"What you gonna do, hit me Ron?" I asked. My grief had somehow turned to anger in a matter of seconds. I wanted to hurt Ron so bad I could feel it in the tips of my fingers. "Like you use to do Phoenell all the damn time? All the time. Go ahead and hit me, Ron. I'll be the last damn person you ever touch. That's a promise."

Mike was pulling me closer and I knew I was really done now. All I could do was look at the girl and hope that she made the right decision. Hopefully her friends and family would never have to do what we had just done for Phoenell because of Ron.

I felt Mike's strong hand on my thigh even before I was fully awake. He shook it lightly and I opened my eyes. Looking at him for just a second and past him out of his window, I saw sand and darkness. I could hear the gentle swishing of water, tons of water.

"Come on," Mike said. By now he had gotten out of the truck and was on my side, opening the door for me. He gave me his hand because his truck was a good two feet off of the ground, and I stepped down.

We were parked in front, almost underneath a beach house. The house sat overlooking the water on wooden pillars that looked to be about fifteen feet high. There was a staircase that met us at the sand and lead to the front door of the house. I followed Mike as we climbed slowly due to his leg. I took some of the grocery bags that he held in both hands to make it easier for him to maneuver with his cane. He fumbled for the correct keys, my duffel bag and his on his left shoulder.

I looked down at the bags in my hand and wondered when and where we stopped to buy groceries. I had to have slept all the way from Fayetteville.

When Mike was finally able to unlock the door, I stepped in with him close behind me. He quickly found a lamp and I looked around. This place was beautiful even by the dim light of the lamp that sat on one of two end tables; I was captured by the peacefulness of the space. Decorated in softer than soft blue, everything in the living room seemed to blend in together. The couch, a plush sectional with blue pillows thrown here and there, merged with the glossy bare walls that were void of any type of paintings or pictures. Vases, painted of the same blue and full of white flowers, sat here and there around the room. I could feel my toes, even through my shoes, sinking into the extra rich carpet that stretched down a small hallway and ended at the doorway of the extremely white kitchen.

"Baby, where are we?" I asked again.

"Wilmington," Mike said as he put our bags down and took the grocery bags from me. He walked past me and into the kitchen.

"Is this your place?" I asked following him. The smell of pine cleaners hit me in the nose hard once I stood beside him at the refrigerator.

"Well, it was my mom and dad's. But after Mom passed, I don't even know if Dad came up here that much anymore. I came up here when I got back from overseas and cleaned out a lot of stuff."

I looked around, feeling like a kid wanting to touch and see everything. Instead I walked back into the living room and over to the sliding glass door that stood on the other side of the couch. I pulled back the sheer white curtain and looked out the window at the ocean that stretched for miles and miles.

"I stopped at the store and got us some food; I didn't wanna wake you up. I think I remembered all the stuff you like. I got us a microwave dinner for tonight, something quick to eat. Is that ok?"

I nodded still looking out of the window. I couldn't remember ever seeing anything so beautiful. In all of my travels; book signings, conferences, even vacations as a little girl, I had never been to the beach. I imagined it so many times but even in my wildest imagination it was nothing like this. The way the water rose and fell down crashing into the sand on the shore, then drifted back as if to change its mind about coming any further was breath taking.

"Go take a shower baby," Mike said as he banged around in the kitchen. "I'll have dinner ready when you come out."

I reluctantly grabbed my duffel bag from the living room floor and made my way to the back of the house. Behind one closed door was a small bedroom that contained a bed and a chest. It faced the other side of the house away from the water. The bed looked like a twin with plain sheets and no pillows. Beside that was another room identical to the first. Across the hall from that was a bathroom. At the end of the hall, behind another door, was a much larger bedroom. The bed in here was king sized with crisp white sheets, comforter, and three overstuffed pillows. Diagonal from the bed was a huge window facing the ocean and a dresser with a television on the end of it. Beside the bed sat a nightstand with a single white lamp.

I sighed heavily and sat my duffel bag on the bed to collect my things for my trip to the bathroom located in the room. I wondered what I was doing in such a beautiful place.

Mike had the radio on when I opened the bathroom door. His shirt and cane were propped up against the sectional. I watched him for a moment as he sat our places at the small white lacquer table, in just a sleeveless undershirt and jeans. He still had the same beautiful muscles that he always had. He was still nothing less than extraordinary. I sighed heavily again and he looked up from the table.

"You hungry?" He asked coming towards me and placing his arms around my waist. I placed my hands on the smooth dark skin of his chest and arms and leaned in closer to him. He moaned and kissed my neck.

"Not really, but I'll eat." I would much rather have skipped the food and started in on him. But for some reason I couldn't remember eating that day.

"Come on," he said leading me over to the table with a long stem candle in the middle. I noticed he had dimmed the lights a little as he sat the microwave dinner of Salisbury steak, macaroni and cheese and green beans in front of me.

I smiled and he smiled back as he poured slightly chilled sparkling apple cider into two wine glasses. "These glasses are old," he said explaining the foggy tint to them. I didn't mind at all.

He pulled my chair out for me and watched as I sat down. My eyes followed him to his side of the table where he sat down also.

"My Dad," he said right after we said grace and began to eat, "bought this house right after we bought the house in the Doone. We had just moved to Fayetteville, I think I was about nine."

"Yeah, I forget you weren't born there like I was."

He shook his head and smiled, "Nope. Kansas City baby." He laughed. "Well not exactly Kansas City, but close. So anyway, we use to come up here before my mom got real sick. I hadn't been here since she died, though, until Dad mentioned it when I came back from Korea. I went to go see him, you know he's in the rest home now."

"No, why? You're dad was healthy."

"Yeah, that's what he thought. That's what we all thought until he had a stroke. He's paralyzed on the right side of his body. And I couldn't take care of him because of my leg. You know, some of the stuff that he needs done. Hopefully he'll regain some strength and he can go to one of those assisted living places."

I shook my head. "I'm sorry."

Mike just shrugged. "It's ok. But anyway, he said take care of the house. I thought he meant our house-house. But then it dawned on me, he meant this house. So after Link's wedding I came up here and spent the rest of the weekend just cleaning up and shit."

I took a sip of the apple cider and watched him from across the table. Looking at him eat reminded me of all the enchiladas we consumed at our favorite Mexican restaurant.

"It had been closed up for awhile," he continued, "so I had to go and get some cleaner and some new sheets. Everything. I ain't ever cleaned like I did that night. For real."

"Well, you did a wonderful job," I said chewing my own rubbery steak. The flavor was good though, so I couldn't complain.

"I'm glad you like it."

"I love it here. It's beautiful Mike. Thank you for bringing me."

He blushed and looked deeply at me, "Anything for you Karly." I watched as he stopped chewing and picked at his food with his fork. "You know, I been wanting to talk about what happened. I guess it just hasn't been the right time."

"Mike . . ." I said not wanting to discuss Chiloe or anything else that had to do with him.

"Wait a minute, baby. I need to say some things to you."

He put his fork down and I lost my appetite, putting my fork down also. Mike cleared his throat. Then he spoke, "Karly, I know I was wrong. Very wrong. But when he told me you two had . . . well you know, I just couldn't think straight. I mean, Chiloe was my boy, he was the last person I expected to lie to me. Then the fact that he called you all those many times," he stopped to shake his head. "I mean it just looked bad to me."

687

He grabbed my hand that was placed on the table. "While I was overseas all I could think about was you. I wanted to write you, but I had no idea what to say. I kept thinking what if I die and you never know how much I still loved you. And then I get back and Chiloe shows up talking about he lied." He shook his head again. "You can imagine how stupid I felt. Then I see you at Link's wedding and you looked so beautiful that day. I was looking at you and thinking that could have been us getting married that day instead. Then Jay told me you were seeing some dude with a music studio, and the way you looked at me at the wedding and you didn't waste no time gettin' up out of there." He shrugged. "I knew you hated me."

"I never hated you. I was angry with you, but I never ever hated you Mike." I slipped my hand out of his and placed it on the soft skin of his cheek. I could feel small hair bumps and stray coarse hairs against my finger. I kissed him, tasting Salisbury steak juice and apple cider on his lips.

By the time Mike got out of the shower, I was stretched across the king sized bed flipping channels on the old television set. The only things available were fuzzy local channels. I automatically assumed, like a hotel that as soon as I cut the television on I would get crystal clear cable networks. I was wrong.

"What's on," Mike asked as he approached the bed, with a slight limp, in the nude.

"Not a thing," I said hitting the power button on the remote without taking my eyes off of him. Limp or not he was still gorgeous.

"You wanna see where I got hurt?" He asked standing over me now at the bed.

"Sure." I sat up on my knees in front of him and he placed his right leg on the bed, extending it. Even in the darkness I could see the darker skin above his knee. There was at least a six inch long, six inch wide gash in his leg. I touched it gently.

"I'm sorry Mike," was all that I could think to say.

"It's okay Karly." He removed his leg and sat down beside me. "I messed up some nerves in it when I fell. I hit this big ass boulder or something. When they took me to the hospital, it looked like my leg wasn't even connected to the rest of my body." He smiled and shook his head like it was one of the funniest memories he ever had. Then he said, "But everything's better now. My leg, my life, everything."

"Why is that, Mike?" I asked already knowing the answer.

"'Cause I have you. You know that." He placed his hand on my pajama pants. "Lay down."

I did as I was told and watched him as he lay down beside me. He held me close to his damp skin, while he slid the hand that wasn't around me into my pajama shirt and pulled it over my head. I shivered from the cool air, but the heat from his body warmed me quickly. My nipples instantly perked, though, due to the coolness. I watched Mike's eyes study them as his teeth bit into his bottom lip. He caught me looking and smiled, deciding to move on. His hands traveled slowly from my stomach and into my pajama pants. He pulled them down, one leg at a time with one hand. I watched his smile widen as he discovered that I wore no panties and hadn't since before dinner. I heard his moan and felt it start in his chest as he caressed my legs, stomach and cleanly shaved pubic area.

I snuggled in closer to him, unable to get enough of his heartbeat, his breathing, and the feel of him. I felt pure felinity as I stretched and purred under his warm skillful hands.

"You like that?" He asked as he squeezed my ample breast.

"Yes," I moaned. Not having been touched this way in years, I had forgotten how good it felt. I wrapped my arms around his neck and pulled him even closer to me to cover his face in soft sweet kisses.

"I love you, Karly," he whispered the name he'd given me so long ago.

"I love you too, Baby."

"Show me how much you love me."

I pushed him over so that he could lie flat on his back, my mind bubbling over with ideas. First with my tongue, I drew a somewhat squiggly line slowly across his neck, stopping to suck and kiss gently. Then down to his nipples, bringing each one to a round hard ball with my lips and teeth. He moaned and buried his fingers in my hair as I moved on to his belly button. The line was deliberate and sweet as I tasted the soap on his body. At his belly button, I slobbered it completely and blew into it, creating goose bumps all over his chest and arms.

Mike arched his back. "Mmmm," He moaned stroking my hair like a well loved pet. In turn I gave his belly button more tongue play, dipping in and out sucking gently. His moans became louder, but I had to move on.

From his belly button I traveled down to his pubic area. I felt his being tense up and I smiled as I ran my lips through his vast curly hair. He squirmed as I gently tugged the hairs with my teeth, in anticipation of what was to come.

"Karla."

"Hmm?"

He laughed at my audacity to actually answer him. He had to know what was coming next as I laughed with him and moved down further. Mike was his full and erect nine inches, curved to the right. The sight of him made my mouth water and I wasted no time slipping my lips around him and taking him in as deeply as I could.

Briefly I remembered that I had never done this before and I could easily slip up and hurt him. I made sure to keep my teeth a safe distance from his sensitive skin as I sucked him with much enthusiasm. My spit dribbled from his manhood onto his balls that I cradled safely in my hands.

The fact that I was an amateur did not seem to bother Mike as his body arched and flopped around me. I could feel the surprise and yearning in him as he squirmed and groaned louder, pulling my short hair. I loved the sounds that he made as I stretched out between his legs, settling comfortably into my task.

Until he grabbed my hair furiously and said, "Baby raise up, I'm cumin'."

I eased his grips on my hair with my own hand loosening his fingers, gave him a '*so what*' look and continued on. He was going to get the full service tonight.

"Baby . . ." he moaned, unable to finish the whole sentence. I was getting quite creamy between my legs listening to him. I gave myself a mental high five.

"Baby . . ." he moaned again. Then, "Karla, Karla, Karla."

He was screaming a soft agonizing scream now and I was loving every minute of it. I continued sucking slowly, my head resting on the inside of his right thigh.

Nobody was stopping!

"Karla, I'm cumin'."

And cum he did. As he did so, I pushed his semen, with my tongue, back out of my mouth, letting it dribble down his rod and onto the bed sheets. He held my hair in a death grip once more as his body tensed so hard I thought he was going to hurt his leg all over again. His back lifted a good foot off of the bed and bounced back down. He slowly let my hair go and I breathed again.

I sat up on my knees and watched his body give way to tiny convulsions. Watching him go through the aftershocks of passion aroused me in ways I had never ever known. Then again, I had never known a lot of things except with him. There was a good reason why he was my one and only. No one made me feel the way he did.

"Damn, baby," was all he could say as a broad smile formed on his face. He reached for me and held me close to him again. "Let me do you," he whispered.

I wasn't about to protest. Not one single bit. I lay flat on the bed, legs opened wide. But he wasn't going straight for that. Instead he started with my lips. Tasting each one down to the corners of my mouth. I moaned in pleasure as he sucked and licked. He treated my neck front and both sides the same way. Careful not to bruise me, he drew my skin into his mouth tenderly. This man knew where all of my spots were hidden. He knew what made me do what and he used that to his advantage when he moved down to my breast, one of the most sensitive parts of my body.

My moans became louder in pure delight as he nursed, licked, and squeezed. One at a time, and then two at a time and then back to one again. He took his sweet time making sure that no area on my breast went untouched by his lips and tongue until finally he was done and moved on. What his mouth did not cover, his hands took up the slack caressing and squeezing my body leaving behind erotic hand prints that seemed to burn and melt into my skin.

When I felt his warm breath between my legs finally I sat up on my elbows. I remembered when we were young how I loved to watch him as he feasted on me. The moonlight bathed his muscular back as if he were a male statue made of black onyx while his head worked methodically between my legs. I was in pure ecstasy when he put one finger slowly inside of me and eased it back out again, over and over. My breath caught in my throat and I thought for sure I was going to die of elation.

"Mike," I moaned and he chuckled, using both thumbs to massage my clitoris while his other eight fingers cupped and kneaded my behind in the palm of his hands like dough. His tongue followed his thumbs or vise versa. I didn't know as I put *my* hands on his head full of closely cut wavy black hair, and pushed his face further into me. My legs were wrapped tightly around his shoulders and crossed at the ankles so that he could breath.

It started in my toes, as usual, but this time it moved up quickly catching me off guard, making me arch my back so hard it hurt. I tried to squeeze my legs shut, but Mike held them apart with both hands, watching closely as I came. When I was done and exhausted I reached for him, just like he had done me. But *he* wasn't done. Instead of feeling my arms with himself, I felt him spread me apart from the top to bottom. Then his wet tongue licked up everything along the path. His work was in vain, I was cuming again.

With this one he let my legs go as I trembled on the cold bed sheets, my legs shut tightly with my arms in between them. Mike grabbed my ankles roughly and stretched me out, turning me from my side and back onto my behind. The way he manhandled me made me shudder even harder and I screamed in agony, cuming for the third time.

I watched as he licked his lips, then his fingers. He smiled, proud of his work, as he lay back on top of me. I opened my legs submissively and neither one of us said a word as he easily slipped inside of me.

"Karla, Karla."

I turned over in the bed. Mike's whole body was facing me with his head supported by his hand and shaking my side.

"What's wrong baby?" I asked sitting up.

"You up?" He asked then grinned mischievously at me. I couldn't help but smile.

"I am now. What you want?"

"Nothing."

"Nothing? What time is it?"

"Three."

The room was freezing. Mike noticed me shivering and the chill bumps on my body despite the heavy comforter. He got out of bed and stepped into the hallway, I assumed to cut the heat on. I heard the vents rattle not to long after.

"Why are you up?" I asked.

"I been up. You were snoring over there."

"Whatever!"

I smiled at him as he took me into his arms and held me close to his chest. His body was still warm and smelled faintly of sex. I loved it.

"I have something I need to ask you, Karly."

"I'm listening."

He let me go and reached into the nightstand drawer beside the bed. I wondered why we only slept on one side of the bed instead of in the middle since it was so huge. We may have started out in the middle, I didn't remember. I knew wherever he went during the night, be it the edge of the bed or the bottom of the bed, I followed.

I watched as Mike got down on the floor putting his weight on his good leg and keeping his bad leg bent at the knee. He took my left hand, that lay in the spot he just occupied, into his own.

"Karla, will you marry me?"

He said it so easily. Like he had been rehearsing and thinking about this for a while.

"But we just got back together," was my 'automatic Lonna response'. As soon as the words left my mouth I thought about the first time he mentioned making our relationship permanent. I remembered the excuses I gave him and that very night we broke up. I regretted that day and probably always would. I refused to let that happen again. I prayed that he would ask me again.

Mike didn't seem fazed too much by what I said. "I know that. But I know that I love you. I know that we've wasted too much time already. You're the woman I want to be with for the rest of my life. I love you."

"I love you too Mike. Are you sure this is what you want?"

He just smiled and slipped the ring onto my left ring finger. It was a perfect fit. He knew I wouldn't say no again.

"I've been waiting for this Karla. For a long time."

I nodded because I had too. "Yes, I'll marry you, baby."

He smiled and slowly rose up from the floor. Then he kissed me deeply.

PART 7

Chapter Twenty-Seven

Saturday June 9, 2001 2:23 pm

Life is funny.

Those words had been echoing through my brain all day,

haunting me like a bad dream or an even worse song.

Life is funny.

Even as I slid the lilac Matron of Honor gown down over my

seven months pregnant belly, that line almost slipped out of my

mouth.

Life is funny.

I turned to look at New-New who was obviously oblivious to

what was going on in my head. She sat in a silver folding chair, busy

trying to fasten the thin straps of the mauve pumps that matched her

Bride's Maid gown around her fat calves. I prayed for the millionth

time that I would not get any bigger after I gave birth to this little girl

whose name was already Dalany Kay Autry.

"Are you all almost ready?" Karla's mom asked bursting

through the door of the wedding chapels dressing room, like there was a fire somewhere in the building, making the pink flowered wreath on the door shake feverishly. She was breathing heavy from nervousness and I knew at any moment she would start wringing her hands.

Karla seemed to be the only calm one in the room. She stood in front of a large cheval mirror trimmed in gold, just admiring herself in her bright white wedding gown. It was plain and sleeveless with wide straps that supported her breast a whole lot better than the halter top gowns we wore for New-New's wedding.

"Yeah ma, we're almost done," she said quietly and I could feel a million spiders crawl up both of my arms. I brushed my skin as if knocking the imaginary insects to the beige carpet then I glanced around quickly. Neither Karla, New-New, Bree, Veronica or Karla's mom were paying me any attention. Karla was still in the mirror but her mother stood behind her now, adjusting her straps that did not need fixing. Veronica and Bree played with their hair in the mirror while New-New wrestled with her other shoe.

I walked over to my low heel shoes that sat beside the door of the bathroom, connected to the dressing room. They slid easily on my slightly swollen feet without any straps. Pregnancy had its advantages.

Maybe Karla was watching me the whole time in the mirror, because she turned around quickly and said, "Lonna, you okay?"

She startled me. Even though I had heard that question from her nonstop all weekend, there was something in her voice this time. Something that gave me the strong urge to yell, 'Hell no I'm not ok.' There was something wrong with this whole scene, I just didn't know what.

So I didn't say any of that. Instead I shrugged and said, "I'm fine. Stop asking me that."

"If you get tired of standing up there, you sit down," Karla's mom said.

"I'll be okay." I shook my head because we had been over this a million times. Karla even wanted to change her wedding date until after Dalany was born. I was dead set against it. I was beginning to think maybe she should have postponed it.

That was crazy though. I just had butterflies, that was all. The closest person in the world to me was marrying the love of her life, what could be better than that.

The wedding chapel director knocked once on the open door and walked on in. "Okay ladies. We're ready. Matron of Honor, Maid of Honor, then Bride's Maids please.

I was first in the line, followed by Veronica. Her dress was also lilac and her shoes boasted the straps that came up her calves like New-New and Bree's. Our dresses were very snazzy and came right above our knees with low necklines and bell sleeves. They were really cute, but I was determined to never ever be this size again, so I would never be able to wear mine again.

Karla walked to the front of the line holding her gown up so that it would not brush the floor. She stood in front of me and adjusted my dress so that my bra would not show.

"Life is funny, isn't it?" She asked and I felt air catch in my throat causing me to cough hard.

Karla's manner remained the same, even as I choked and she rubbed my back to relieve me. I almost did not want her to touch me.

"What did you say?" I asked after I had recovered. My head and throat burned.

"I said, life is funny isn't it? It's almost like we've come full circle, huh?

There was a look in her eyes that I could not place, but it looked so familiar. The piano music began to play and I wanted to scream for everything to stop. Karla's mom disappeared around the corner so that she could be escorted down the aisle by her husband.

The director had her hand on my elbow. I knew I should have been moving but I couldn't take my eyes off of Karla.

"I love you, Lonna," Karla said once again in that eerie composed voice that caused my stomach to clench with nervousness. Then she looked at New-New, Bree, and Veronica. "I love all of y'all."

My husband held my arm tightly and whispered, "You okay, baby?" as we walked down the aisle, me with the biggest fakest smile I could muster.

"No," I whispered back not breaking my smile.

"What's wrong? You feel okay?"

I didn't have time to explain as we parted ways. Him to the right and me to the left. Veronica and one of Mike's cousins were next, followed by New-New and Andrew. Even though they were in the process of reconciling, they both looked uncomfortable. I wondered if I was the only one who thought about how much reconciling they were really doing still living in separate states. New-New had never spoken about how the idea to reconcile came up. Maybe naming the son, who looked enough like Andrew to actually be his, after him was enough to put a broken marriage back together. If you could call it back together. I didn't know and I knew I would never know.

Life is funny.

Bobby walked down the aisle with Bree. It had never occurred to me that he and Mike had kept close contact over the years until Karla announced that he would be in the wedding. But there was no reason why they wouldn't have, Bobby and Mike were tight when we were younger. I remembered them playing dominoes in our back yard and craps on our deck with Chiloe and the rest of the neighborhood boys. But when Mike had stopped hanging around Chiloe so much, Bobby had to. Just as everyone expected he and LaShae had gotten married. They even had a son to show for their efforts. But after losing his job along with countless others at the local tire plant, Bobby found it easier to love alcohol more than LaShae and they divorced. He was on the road to recovery, but the alcohol and everything else in life had aged him well beyond his years.

The piano stopped and the whole chapel was filled with the sound of an orchestra along with the highest soprano voice I had ever heard. It was beautiful in a Halloweenish sort of way. I had no earthly idea why my sister chose this music.

She walked down the aisle alone. In rehearsal the night before, it looked so perfect. But today, it wasn't right. I looked to the front row at her mother. She wore my feelings on her make-up covered face as her brow wrinkled and her lips pressed tightly into each other.

I looked over at Mike who stood no more than four feet away from me at the front of the chapel, waiting on his bride. His tux was white, a sharp contrast to his dark chocolate skin. I had never seen him smile so hard as he watched Karla. Her eyes lit up under the veil just a little. But there was something else there. Just like in the dressing room.

"Family, friends, guests," the official began, "we are gathered here today to join Michael and Karla in Holy matrimony . . ."

He went on to boast about Karla and her smile when she first came into the chapel to inquire about wedding services, how she talked about Mike like he was the best thing since peanut butter and jelly, and how a couple with so much love between them was a blessing from God.

"If anyone have any reason why this man and woman should not be joined together, speak now or forever hold your peace . . ."

I looked down at Karla's mom again, who had specifically requested that part be left out of the ceremony. We didn't need any unexpected drama from either side, but especially Karla's. Karla's mom gave a furious half shake of her head, stunned I was sure. From her seat she glanced around the church to make sure no one planned to start anything. Every behind sat still and silent. The official nodded his agreement to their silence. Just as he opened his mouth to continue, a sharp pain flashed across my stomach like a bolt of lightning, almost knocking me over. Veronica caught me by my elbow.

"Girl, you okay?" she whispered. "You need to go sit down."

"No, I'm good," I said struggling to stand up straight. I just wanted to hurry and get all of this over with.

The urgency hit me even more when the door to the chapel opened and Chiloe walked in. I watched him take a seat quietly in the back of the chapel. Then I looked at my two other brothers, Marco and Jay, who stood firmly in their positions as ushers as if they were both on police duty. Marco shook his head and squinted his eyes gesturing his head towards Chiloe. Jay shrugged his shoulders, both just as confused and uneasy as I was at Chiloe's uninvited presence.

Since Karla was in fact a local celebrity, Mike and her mother did not want to take any unnecessary chances with her safety. So they hired Marc to do security and double as an usher equipped with his personal gun and handcuffs. Jay insisted on being his unarmed side kick. I was thankful for both of them, for reasons I wasn't even sure of as I watched my oldest brother in the back of the church. He wasn't even dressed for the occasion in an army brown jacket, jeans and a t-shirt.

Mike and Karla had not turned around. They were too busy crying, staring at each other and exchanging white gold wedding bands. Mike's hand shook terribly as he held Karla's pale hand with fresh French manicure nails in his hand and slid the ring onto her finger. I looked closely at her, through her veil, and could see tears sliding down her chubby cheeks. My eyes began to water at more than just the sweetness of that moment. Just like the rest of the day, there was something else here in this wedding chapel that was making me cry.

The official was saying something now. But I wasn't paying attention. My eyes drifted along with my mind around the chapel. From Marc and Jay, to Chiloe, to Karla's mom, to Mike's dad in his wheel chair parked in front of the front row behind Mike, and back to Karla and Mike. Some girl began to sing something. I didn't know her, but she was a friend of Karla's. Her song was slow and sad, much like a funeral. I began to scream inside for her to shut up. But she couldn't hear me.

I noticed Veronica's hand on my elbow then, to hold me up. I wondered how long it had been there as another pain shot through my stomach. This time, I didn't let it show. I stood still as a statue as my insides felt like the baby in my womb was making a salad out of them. My eyes watered even more. Karla's head whipped around to look at me as if she knew exactly what was going on with me. I stared back at her.

The girl finished up her song and sat down. By now it didn't matter to me one way or the other. I just wanted this whole thing to be over with. Karla and Mike lit their white unity candle trimmed in lace, and knelt to pray. Everyone in the chapel bowed their heads, except for me. I took this as a chance to double over from the pain, but not before I noticed my older brother again sitting amongst the prayers. His head wasn't bowed either. There was something in his green eyes that sent chills up and down my arms and legs and it made my pains worsen. This time Veronica noticed and grabbed me again. Both of my elbows ended up in her hands as she dropped her bouquet to catch me.

My own husband rushed towards me as soon as the prayer was over and he lifted his head and opened his eyes. I couldn't hold back the tears from the pain and I felt my body collapse against him. His arms wrapped tightly around me. The official looked at me and decided to rush through the rest of the ceremony.

"I now pronounce you husband and wife, you may kiss your bride."

Karla kissed her new husband passionately and I stood up straight, still holding on tight to Dallas. He wiped the tears from my eyes and asked me, "You ok, baby?" Karla looked at me, full and complete comprehension in her eyes and smiled.

I smiled back for the first time that day, because finally I knew.

She turned around and headed down the aisle. Her new husband holding tightly to her waist. The wedding guests stood in their seats and clapped making a beautiful joyous sound that filled the flower covered chapel walls from ceiling to floor.

"Can you make it baby?" Dallas asked me. It was our turn to follow the bride and groom down the aisle. I nodded slowly, not taking my eyes off of Karla.

The guests were crowding in now, taking pictures on their disposable cameras, admiring the bride's hair and dress, shaking hands with the groom and patting him on the back. Marco and Jay moved in closer, but not to close. Neither wanted to alarm the happy crowd.

Karla's mom stood in her seat and brushed the back of her cream suit down. She wasn't as happy as the rest of the crowd. Her brow was creased and I could see the worry lines around her mouth and eyes, even through the makeup. She watched Karla as hard as I did, her eyes never leaving the back of the girl's dress.

"Come on baby," Dallas whispered to me again, but neither one of us were making a move. This was not the way we rehearsed it the night before. We were supposed to skip gaily out of the church, being showered by sunflower seeds. Why had Karla stopped? Why weren't we moving?

I was determined to get down the aisle to Karla. Something in me said that I needed to. With my first step, though, I felt the wetness run down my legs like water.

"Oh my God girl," Veronica said behind me. "You going into labor?"

I hardly heard her and no one else did at all. Everyone was watching Chiloe who was now standing in front of Karla. His eyes were ice cold and I hadn't seen that look from him in awhile, but never when he looked at Karla. It was almost as if he didn't recognize her at all.

Another sharp pain shot through me and I fell to my knees. No one realized I was on my knees except for Dallas and Veronica who were both busy attending to me. I paid no attention to the water that had just escaped my womb and the pains shooting through me consistently. I tried to scream for Karla but my voice seemed to be caught in my throat. I couldn't get a sound from me.

Everything and everyone in the chapel went deadly silent. Dallas and Veronica were still and the only thing that could be heard was Chiloe's movement.

The next sound was deafening and ripped through my mind and body like an ax. Finally the scream tore through my throat and hurt my tonsils on the way out. My head felt as if someone had bashed it open with a beer bottle.

I saw Karla look down at her stomach. I saw the blood on her dress and hands as she stared in disbelief at Chiloe for what seemed like forever. He stared back at her, probably unaware of the tears streaming down his own face. Finally she crumpled like a leaf to the floor. Her body hit the red runner with a thump that opened the flood gates of the chapel.

Karla's mother screamed and rushed to her child. Mike screamed and fell to the floor beside his wife. Marco grabbed Chiloe hard and rushed him to the ground near Karla's body where he handcuffed him without hesitation. Veronica left my side and rushed to Karla. But none of this happened before I was on my knees crawling through the misery my body was in to get to my sister who I could hardly even see through my tears and pain.

I never made it to her. Dallas grabbed me from behind and pulled me close to him, trying his best to shelter me from the scene, but I had already seen it. Karla lay cradled in Mike's arms, blood covering his white tuxedo as well as the front of her dress.

"Baby no," he cried and rocked her back and forth, holding her tightly to him. He shook his head furiously over and over again, tears pouring from his eyes like a built in water hose. Her mother stood close by, also being shielded from the moment by her husband. While both her and Veronica's screams of, "Oh my God," filled the world right then.

I crumpled again to the floor. I didn't know if the screams coming from me were from pain or for my sister. I knew I was in labor, had known from the first shot of pain. I tried to ignore it though because I knew Dalany was still breech and she was only seven months. Weak with aches and grief, I couldn't even sit up anymore. The last thing I remembered were Mike's sobs and unadulterated moans as he held his dead wife, my sister, I collapsed behind the two of them.

I woke up in the hospital, oxygen mask over my face being wheeled down the hall in a hurry on a stretcher. The bottom half of my body hurt so bad, it almost didn't feel like mine. I opened my mouth to scream into the mask but once again I couldn't. It caught in my throat and choked me. I coughed hard, and the pain deepened.

Dallas held my hand tightly, running along the stretcher. His touch was suffocating to me and I wanted him to let go so that I could rip my own hair out due to the pain. I felt the need to thrash my body against the cushion of the stretcher until it went numb, I wanted everything to just go numb. I got my wish in a matter of seconds.

I woke up again staring at the bright hot light bulb of an operating room. I heard voices all around me, but none were familiar to me. I was still being overpowered by the oxygen mask but at least now there was no pain. Just weakness.

My mind floated back to a hot day in 1989.

Three girls walking to the store. Ponytails, shorts and Keds and Nike's. Their smiles were as bright as the sunshine that bathed their clear youthful skin and hair. Clouds seemed to envelope them like chariots for princesses and the world belonged to them. They just didn't know it yet.

And at the end of 1989, I saw my daughter for a fleeting moment. She wailed like a dying monkey, the dying monkey I swore that I would never ever give birth too. She wriggled her arms and legs as if trying to escape the doctor's hands. Delany was big for seven months just like I knew she would be, but she still needed oxygen just to be sure. I knew she would survive. I knew Dallas would take care of her, just as he had taken care of me.

I heard one of the unfamiliar voices say something about blood. I shrugged my shoulders in a silent *so what*, at least I tried to. No one around me knew that I had given up. No one around me realized that despite my husband and my baby who had just entered the world, I could never go on. The only thing I fought now was the urge to close my eyes because I didn't want to miss anything. I wanted to see everything.

I saw my street on a cold October night. I felt my knees on the cold damp gravel. I felt Kelly dying in my arms. I felt his heartbeat stop against my hands as the blood trickled from his mouth.

The doctors and nurses were shuffling around me quickly and I could faintly hear the clinking of metal instruments.

I saw Rajul's house. The paramedics rushed quickly by me as Rajul's body was wheeled out and into the wet night air so that he could be loaded into the back of an ambulance. I saw my old house in the Doone. I could hear Bree and Jay's wails and Marco held them tightly to keep them from going upstairs, to their dead mother.

I was in the country, a little place called rehab. Writhing in pain on a hospital bed as my body went through withdrawal of so much junk that I willfully put into my system, day after day. Writing down the ills of my life in front of a window as some girls played Frisbee.

My eyelids felt like they weighed fifty pounds each by now. I gave up my struggle to keep them open and closed them. I only wanted to keep them closed for a moment. But then I saw Dallas and the way he looked the first day I saw him. The smile he gave me at New-New's wedding reception. We were in the grass searching for my engagement ring soon after, and after that we were making love on our wedding night.

My heart monitor began to flat line. I felt the hard coldness of a defibrillator pressing against my bare chest. Someone yelled, "Clear," and a shock wave ripped through my body.

Then I saw Karla. She moved before me like a movie, from the time we were twelve until today. Of course all of the scenes contained me and they were all hugs. Every hug we had ever given each other, from the hug after Kelly's death, to the hug when her grandmother died, to the hug when I got out of rehab, and all the hugs in between

"Hey girl," I heard behind me as I stood over my body. Boy I looked rough.

I turned around to see Karla. Still in her wedding gown that was now clean from all the blood. She smiled at me.

"Why Karla?" I asked.

"Why not Lonna?"

I shook my head, not able to explain that I wasn't ready to go. We had lived the life, no matter how short. Dallas would raise our daughter and I knew he would do a wonderful job, missing me hard. Mike and Karla's mother would grieve her until the day they died I was sure.

I shook my head as I looked at my best friend who seemed perfectly content with the situation. Her smile was wide and genuine as usual.

She wrapped her arm around mine. "You're going back. Don't worry. Go raise that little girl. She's gonna be wonderful, you know that right?"

"What?"

"Go back, Lonna. I love you."

She leaned over and kissed me on my forehead. My forehead remained wet after she departed. She let go of my arm slowly.

"I love you Karla."

She smiled brightly at me again. Her eyes, shiny with tears that had not fallen yet, watched as I reentered myself. The heart monitor machine slowly began to beep again. A collective sigh of relief was heard throughout the operating room.

My baby was a week old by the time she finally got to come home. I never did mention my very last conversation with Karla to anyone. But I did whisper it to Delaney every now and then as we sat in our white rocking chair located in her nursery. Her daddy put the room together all by himself.

I watched my older brother cop a plea and go to jail for life without parole for my sister's murder. Everyone else in our family turned their backs on Chiloe, even Marco the most neutral one. But I just could not bring myself to do it. Just like the rainy night in his truck, I didn't understand what he did, but I was compassionate towards the way he felt. I could never forget that he took my sister, one of the few loves of my life, and the aunt of my baby away forever, though. Mike never forgot it either.

He had Karla's last book published posthumous and began his work on a movie based on the book. The book was based on our lives, and I was not surprised. Our lives made a damn good book.

www.ingramcontent.com/pod-product-compliance
Lightning Source LLC
Chambersburg PA
CBHW052338020726
47503CB00001B/14